ALSO BY ANNA ELLIOTT

Twilight of Avalon

DARK MOON OF AVALON

AVALON

A NOVEL OF TRYSTAN & ISOLDE

ANNA ELLIOTT

A TOUCHSTONE BOOK

PUBLISHED BY SIMON & SCHUSTER

NEW YORK   LONDON   TORONTO   SYDNEY

Touchstone
A Division of Simon & Schuster, Inc.
1230 Avenue of the Americas
New York, NY 10020

First Touchstone trade paperback edition September 2010

TOUCHSTONE and colophon are registered trademarks of
Simon & Schuster, Inc.

For information about special discounts for bulk purchases,
please contact Simon & Schuster Special Sales at 1-866-506-1949
or business@simonandschuster.com.

The Simon & Schuster Speakers Bureau can bring authors to your live
event. For more information or to book an event contact the Simon &
Schuster Speakers Bureau at 1-866-248-3049 or visit our website at
www.simonspeakers.com.

Manufactured in the United States of America

10   9   8   7   6   5   4   3   2   1

Library of Congress Cataloging-in-Publication Data

Elliott, Anna.
    Dark moon of Avalon : a novel of Trystan and Isolde / by Anna Elliott.
       p.   cm.
    1. Iseult (Legendary character)—Fiction. 2. Tristan (Legendary
character)—Fiction. I. Title.
PS3605.L443D37   2011
813'.6—dc22

                                                            2009049279

ISBN 978-1-4165-8990-7
ISBN 978-1-4391-6456-3 (ebook)

To Nathan

Dramatis Personae

Dead Before the Story Begins

Arthur, High King of Britain, father of Modred, brother of Morgan; killed in the battle of Camlann

Constantine, Arthur's heir as Britain's High King, first husband to Isolde

Gwynefar, Arthur's wife; betrayed Arthur to become Modred's Queen; mother to Isolde

Modred, Arthur's traitor son and Isolde's father; killed in fighting Arthur at Camlann

Morgan, mother to Modred, believed by many to be a sorceress

Myrddin, Arthur's chief druid and bard

Rulers of Britain

Cynlas, King of Rhos

Dywel, King of Logres

Isolde, daughter of Modred and Gwynefar, Constantine's High Queen, Lady of Camelerd

Madoc, King of Gwynned and Britain's High King

Marche, King of Cornwall, now a traitor allied with the Saxon King Octa of Kent

Saxon Rulers

Cerdic, King of Wessex
Octa, King of Kent

Others

Fidach, leader of an outlaw band of mercenaries
Eurig, Piye, and Daka, three of Fidach's men, friends to Trystan
Goram, an Irish king
Hereric, a Saxon and friend to Trystan
Kian, a former outlaw and friend to Trystan, now one of King Madoc's war band
Nest, cousin and former chatelaine to King Marche
Marcia, Nest's serving maid
Mother Berthildis, abbess of the Abbey of Saint Joseph
Taliesin, brother to King Dywel of Logres, a bard
Trystan, a Saxon mercenary and outlaw, son of King Marche

Isolde's Britain

Prologue

I have been a tear in the air,
I have been the dullest of stars.

I have been a course, I have been an eagle.
I have been a coracle in the seas.

LITTLE MORE THAN THE WORDS remain, now, of the wisdom of the Old Ones. A wisdom that once allowed men to read the future in the flight of birds or walk unharmed across a bed of burning coals. All that remains of Avalon, now no place in this world, but only a name in a harper's tale. A faint, mist-shrouded echo of what once was Britain's most sacred ground. Hidden like the Otherworld behind a veil of glass.

Once the gods of Britain ruled this land. Cernunnos, the horned god of the forests, father of all life. And his consort, the great mother goddess, known by many names: Arianhod, mistress of stars, mistress of the silver wheel. Donn, goddess of sea and air. Morrigan, mistress of night. Of battle, of prophesy, of magic and revenge.

Some say it is from her that I take my name. Morgan.

Men have given me many names besides, in my time. Sorceress . . . witch . . . whore.

And now I stand at a cliff's edge, looking across the battle that will soon be fought to my own end.

Camlann, the battle will be called. The last bloody fight between Arthur, High King of Britain, and Modred, his traitor heir. Between Arthur, my brother, and Modred, my son as well as Arthur's own. All because Modred seized the throne of Britain, and with it Arthur's wife Gwynefar.

Or is it because I myself could not let go of a hurt years old? Though I kept my word to Arthur and never named him the father of my child. That was the price I paid to have Modred raised as Arthur's heir: allowing Morgan, as much the daughter of Uther the Pendragon as Arthur is son, to be branded harlot, slut, devil's mistress.

I never spoke aloud the ugly truth of how Arthur's son was forced on me, in drunken violence after a battle fought and won.

Never spoke it aloud to any, at least, except my own son. If I had not—

Too late now for such questions. Too late to alter the course of any of our lives.

But it would be good, as I look down at the raven-dark head of my son's only daughter, to believe that the power of Britain's gods was not broken, when Roman sandals first trampled Britain's soil. When the legions in their silver fish-scale armor defiled the druids' sacred groves, fouled the sacred pools, and built their straight roads and marble temples like scars on the land.

It would be good, on this eve of battle, to believe that the voice of the goddess and her consort the horned one can still be heard, like the silent echo after thunder.

A gift of those same gods, I have always thought the Sight. The power to hear the voice of all living things. To catch glimpses of *may be* or *will be* in scrying waters like those before me now.

Again and again, those waters have shown me the battle to come on the fields of Camlann. And once I cared for nothing else. Nothing but the fight that would witness Arthur's final downfall.

But now I see beyond the battle a shadow of blackness rising across Britain like the dark of the moon.

And my own end will not be slow to follow. I have seen the signs. A vision of a woman, death-pale and clad in white, who crouches at a fast-moving river and washes a bloodied gown I know is mine. A great black hound that stands by my bed at night and watches me with red and glowing eyes.

I do not fear my own death. Indeed, I would welcome it at times. But now, as I look from the scrying waters to the girl at my side, I am afraid. Coldly afraid. No use in denying it now.

My granddaughter. Daughter of Modred and Gwynefar. Isolde, her name is. *Beautiful one* in the old tongue. And she is beautiful. Frighteningly so, even at twelve. White skin with the luminous gleam of the moon. Delicate, finely shaped features. Softly curling black hair and widely spaced gray eyes. A shining girl, beautiful indeed.

Her face is grave, composed as she binds up a cut across the palm of her hand. A cut I made, payment in blood for the power to keep her safe in the midst of rising dark.

But at this moment I would give a hundred times that payment in my own blood to know that the charm of protection would do any good at all.

Isolde. She has been my light in the darkness these last twelve years. But what will be hers when I am gone?

My gaze turns to the scrying bowl, with its chased pattern of serpents. Dragons of eternity, forever swallowing their tails. And slowly, slowly, an image appears on the water's surface. Wavering, swirling, shivering, then growing steadily clear. A boy's face, though already it holds the promise of the man he will be in a short year or two's time. A lean, handsome face, with a determined jaw and steady, intensely blue eyes set under slanted gold-brown brows. A good face. I see no cruelty in him. And that is far rarer than one might suppose.

I had not meant to let Isolde see the vision the scrying waters have granted me this time. But before the image has faded, she looks up from the bandage she has tied across her hand—a neat job, I have taught her well—and catches sight of the boy's face. I can see her gaze take in the shadow at the back of his blue eyes, the grim-set line of his flexible mouth.

She doesn't question why the boy's face should appear, now, where shadows of Arthur and Modred and Gwynefar have gone before, but only nods. "That's very like him. He almost never smiles."

Neither might she, were her father Marche of Cornwall. Neither might I.

Marche of Cornwall, who will soon betray my son and lose for him the battle at Camlann. At least I need not bear the guilt of my son's death and Britain's downfall entirely alone.

I feel sympathy for few in this life, where so many bemoan sorrows wrought entirely by their own hands. But this boy, son of Marche, does stir me to compassion. Sadness, even. Though he would scarcely be glad to know it. He has pride, I think, as well as strength of character and reserve beyond his years.

But I have guessed at the bruises he has carried beneath his clothes—marks of his father's fists—from the time he numbered less than half of his now fifteen summers. I know he tries to protect his mother from Marche's anger, as much as he can. Though his mother is far too much of a broken, empty shell to notice much or to care.

Still, compassion or no, I answer in a voice entirely unlike my own. As though I were suddenly one of the foolish girls who come and beg love potions from me before lying with their young men in the woods at Beltane. Age must be making me soft, indeed.

"It's because he has no one in his life to love him," I hear myself tell the girl at my side.

"I do." Her face is so serious, her gray eyes very grave, though she can scarcely be old enough to understand the meaning of what she says. Not even old enough for the words to make her afraid. "I will."

BOOK I

Chapter One

WHEN SHE'D LET HERSELF BE led to the great carved oaken bed, they left her, though she knew they would wait outside the door. Marche would have made sure of his witnesses.

She dug her nails hard into the palms of her hands. It's only my body, she thought. I won't let him touch the rest of me.

She slipped her hand under the mattress. The cloth-wrapped parcel was where she'd left it the night before, and she drew it out, untying the strings that held it closed then drawing out a woolen ball, smeared with the cedar and mandrake paste. If Marche discovered it, she would be dead, as surely as she lay here now. But if she conceived a child—Marche's child—

She thought, suddenly, of Con. Of what Con would think if he knew she was about to give herself to another man. And not just any man. Marche. The traitor who had caused Con's death.

She thought for a moment she was going to vomit, but she fought the sickness down, whispering the words through clenched teeth.

"You can face this. You have to."

Her hands were unsteady, but she reached down and thrust the paste-smeared ball deep inside her. In the darkness beyond the bed, she heard a door open—

. . .

ISOLDE CAME AWAKE WITH A JOLT and lay a moment, her heart pounding, her breath painful in a throat that felt swollen and dry. She pressed her hands to her temples, drawing a shuddering breath, and gradually the dream retreated, the frantic beating of her heart slowed. Though since it had not been a dream—or rather not only a dream—she had to close her eyes and count one hundred, shivering as the sweat dried on her skin, before she could force herself to move.

Five months. Five months nearly to the day, since she'd given Con's murderer her marriage vow and escaped from him the next day. Three months since the king's council had declared her marriage to Marche of Cornwall void, on the grounds of Marche's treason. And by now, she could almost put it behind her and keep the yawning jaws of memory at bay. Until the dream came again, and she was flung back into that night, feeling its echo in her very bones. Feeling soiled, slimy all over, and as though she could scrub and scrub until her skin was bleeding raw and still never be clean again.

Isolde opened her eyes. It was nearly dawn; a faint, pearly light crept in through the room's single narrow window, showing the clean rushes and herbs scattered on the floor, the heavy carved furniture and tapestried walls. She'd fallen asleep on the wooden settle beside the hearth; her limbs felt cramped, and the muscles of her back and neck were aching and stiff.

Isolde drew another steadying breath, then forced herself to rise, to go to the window, unfasten the shutter, and look out, breathing the damp, earth-scented spring air that came at her in a rush.

The great hill fortress at Dinas Emrys was an eerie place, always, surrounded beyond the outer wooden palisade by mists and silence and gnarled trees growing on rocky mountain ground. Now, though, with the gray dawn breaking over the eastern hills, and with a soft, penetrating spring rain breathing tattered gray patches of fog over the canopied trees, the mountain fort felt apart, outside the world beyond the hills. Outside even of time, a space somewhere between truth and tale.

Beneath this mountain and a man's lifetime ago, so the bards' songs and fire tales ran, Myrddin the Enchanter had unearthed a sacred pool and there been granted a vision of a pair of warring dragons, one white and one red. And on their final desperate battle, Myrddin had prophesied the triumph of the red dragon banner of Britain's armies over the invading Saxon foe.

Though that, Isolde thought, was the kind of story folk clung to in times such as these—like the stories of Arthur, king who was and shall be. Who had not died at Camlann with all the rest of Britain's hope, but instead slept amidst the chimes of silver apples on the Isle of Avalon and would come again in the hour of his country's greatest need.

She had a sudden, piercingly sharp memory of Con, asking Myrddin once if the tale of the warring dragons were true. Con had been—what? Fourteen, she thought. Fourteen, and already Britain's High King for two long years—just days before returned from facing his first battle with a deep sword cut in his side.

Isolde could see him, even now, as he'd lain in the king's tapestried bed, restless, because he hated at all times to be still, his face tight with the pain he wouldn't admit to, and his dark eyes still lost in the memory of all he'd seen and done. Isolde had stitched the wound and sat by him at night, waking him when he relived the blood and killing in nightmares and cried out in his sleep—as all men did after battle, for a time. She'd been fifteen herself then—nearly five years ago, now—and wedded to Con the two years since he'd been crowned.

Myrddin had stood at Con's bedside in the bull's-hide cloak of the druid born, a raven feather braided into his snow-white hair, and Isolde had seen in his eyes a reflection of the pain in Con's. Though his voice, when he spoke to answer Con's question, was dry.

"Dragons? Oh, to be sure. I keep a pair at home for use in the kitchens roasting haunches of game."

And then, when Con moved impatiently and started to speak, Myrddin held up a hand, and said, his face suddenly grave, "You wish to hear what I know of dragons? Very well." His voice held suddenly the lilt of a harper's song—or of prophecy. A faint, musical echo that made his words seem to hang shimmering in the air a moment after he'd done. "Dragons doing battle I have never seen, either in vision or in life. But I did once, many years ago, see a pair of the creatures—a she-dragon and a male—engaged in their mating dance." He shook his head, fingering the strand of serpent bones he wore at his belt. "You'll have heard, I suppose, how it is dragons mate?"

Con was lying back on the pillow, eyes closed against a fresh spasm of pain and a sheen of sweat on his brow, and shook his head without much interest, his jaw clenched tight.

"Very carefully." Myrddin's lilting voice was still tranquil, his sea blue eyes grave. "All those spines and breaths of fire, you understand."

Con had laughed so hard he'd torn out half his stitches, and Isolde had had to put them in again. And he'd slept without dreaming for the first time that night. Though always, after that, the sadness in Myrddin's eyes when he looked at Con was never quite gone.

Now, seeing again Con's laughing face—and Myrddin's high-browed, ugly one, gentle with reflected pain—Isolde felt a hot press of tears in her eyes. Five months, too, that both of them had been gone. But then, she thought, that was the nature of grief. She'd learned that, these last seven years. One moment you thought the pain was finally—finally—beginning to wear smooth at the edges with the passage of time. And then the next you were crying like the loss was still only hours old.

At least, though, the months since Myrddin and Con had died at Marches' hands made it easier to set grief aside in the face of what now had to be done. Isolde blinked the tears back, scanning the spread of hills beyond the palisade walls.

But there was nothing to be seen besides the sweep of trees and rocky hills and mist. No ominous column of greasy black smoke above the tree line. And no sign of alarm, either, in the fortress's outer courtyard beneath Isolde's window.

Though that, she thought, only meant that last night's attack hadn't occurred anywhere nearby.

Slowly, she turned to the washbasin and earthenware jug of water that stood by the hearth, where the heat of the fire would keep it from freezing in the nights that were still frostbitten and bitterly cold. Too great a risk, now, to keep Morgan's scrying bowl, with its ancient chasings and serpents of eternity etched on the age-smoothed bronze sides.

Isolde shook her head. She'd long since ceased to question the ebb and flow of the Sight that ran in her veins—gift by blood from the time when the Old Ones had watered the trees with milk and wine and oil and cast silver into the rivers and streams. Or so Morgan had told her, years ago, now. But she did sometimes think that the Sight was, in fact, neither a blessing nor even a curse, but some huge joke on the part of whatever gods or air demons or powers of the Mother Earth governed such things.

She'd been called Witch Queen for all the seven years she'd been wedded to Con—had been tried on a charge of sorcery five months before. And in all that time, she'd had not a flicker of true Sight, what her grandmother had once called the space inside where one might hear the voice of all living things, echoing like the strings of an unseen harper's lyre.

Only now, when she'd escaped so nearly being burned for a witch, when she walked a knife-edge line amidst the remains of the king's council—on the one side the only one among them to expose Marche's treason, on the other, still the daughter of Modred, King Arthur's traitor son. Still the granddaughter of Morgan, enchantress, sorceress, and devil's mistress—

Only now, she thought, when even a breath of ill rumor will bring a second charge of witchcraft—and a sentence of burning that I could not possibly hope to escape again—does the Sight return.

The strewn floor rushes rustled and sent up a breath of herb-scented air as Isolde knelt, lifted the pottery jug, and carefully poured water into the basin, filling it to the brim, so that the shimmering surface of the water swelled out just above the basin's edge. She set the jug down, then fixed her gaze on the surface of water inside the bowl.

Until a few weeks ago, the water would have been frozen in the mornings, and she would have had to set the pitcher by the fire to melt enough of the ice—for bathing, not for this. Because if the wash water had been frozen, so were the mountain passes and the roads, and Marche and Octa's armies had withdrawn into winter quarters. But now, with spring's thaw, the snows had melted and the streams were running again, and the raids and fighting that had bloodied the autumn had begun again.

Looking down into the basin of water, Isolde saw at first only her own reflection, raven black hair plaited in a heavy braid down her back, with a few curling tendrils loose on her brow, gray eyes set wide in the smooth, pale oval of her face. Isolde kept still, clearing her mind, pushing all thoughts aside, consciously slowing her whole body—the beat of her heart, the pulse of her blood, the rise and fall of her own breath—forcing all to move in the same steady rhythm. *In and out. Out and in.* Reaching inside herself for the place where the quivering harp strings of Sight were tied, the space where she might hear the voice of whatever the water chose to say.

And, gradually, an image took shape on the water's surface, as Myrddin's dragons might have taken form in the pool of the bard's tales. Wavering and indistinct, at first, overlaid still by her reflected face. Then the image cleared, and she saw the smoldering ruin of a hut, the thatch ramparts blackened and fallen in, the walls collapsing in on themselves, a sullen, dirty spire of smoke rising to hang in the air above.

Another shudder twisted through her, but she kept her eyes fixed on the wavering image, forced her breathing to remain deep and slow. She could see, now, small crumpled figures in the muddied earth before the hut, hear the distant frightened bleat of a goat. Smell—

She was standing in the rain, on the narrow goat track running through the village, the smell of smoke and charred flesh acrid in her throat. A man lay in the dirt to her right, his throat cut, blood pooled all about him, mixed with the wet, mucky earth. A raven had found him already. The bird was pecking at his eyes.

Two more lay nearby—a woman and child. A girl, maybe six summers. Maybe eight. Hard to say. The woman's mouth was open. Face stupid and surprised. Skirts torn. Thighs of both the woman and girl were rusty with blood.

A moment's regret. The girl was a pretty child. Should have had her before the rest of the men.

Isolde felt herself turn away, felt herself speak in a rough voice that was her own, and yet not her own. "Nothing more for us here. Come on. We can make Cadar Idris if we ride out—"

And then with an abruptness that was like a thunderclap, the vision was gone, and Isolde was once more kneeling beside the washbasin and looking at her own shivering reflection, her palms slick with sweat, nausea rolling through her in waves. She drew in a ragged breath and pressed her hands tight against her eyes, swallowing bile and wondering whether it would do any good to give up the Sight again, as she had seven years before. Or whether this slithering, clinging awareness would stay inevitably with her the rest of her days.

Though at that, this vision was no worse than the last, when she'd seen Marche's newfound ally Octa, Saxon king of Kent, riding down an old woman who fled from her burning home. She'd seen him clearly: a big man with graying blond hair and a braided beard, who'd laughed as he ran the woman through with his sword.

And this vision was far, far better than when she'd slipped inside Marche's thoughts to feel him dreaming of his father Merchion, dead now these thirty years. In the dream, she'd felt

Marche aching from his father's blows, biting his lips until the blood came in an effort not to cry. Hoping that one of these days his father would love him if he could only be strong enough. Isolde had seen Marche of Cornwall wake crying wet, gulping sobs like a small child before at last that vision had broken.

Now Isolde drew a steadying breath and tried to push all memory of that aside. *The stars will still shine tomorrow, whatever—*

And then she stopped herself. Not Trystan's words. If he wasn't dead like Myrddin and Con, he was gone, all the same. Another to be put away. However much it hurt, still, every day.

A groan from the bed behind Isolde made her start upright, realizing that it was this same sound that must have broken the vision a moment before. She pushed the basin aside and quickly turned.

The girl who lay beneath the fur-lined blankets was Isolde's own age, twenty, or maybe a year or two less or more. Her face, even in health, would have been too thin and sharp featured for beauty, the dark eyes sly and set close together, the skin pasty and scarred with the marks of childhood pox. Now, though, the flesh was almost yellow, drawn tightly over the bones of cheek and jaw, and her eyes were both sunken and hectically bright.

And beneath the fugue of high fever, a reek like putrid flesh hung about the bed—the stench of the discharge from where Marcia had scraped an unborn child out of her body with a dirty knife, leaving her womb a mass of scars turned to poison that spread, in spite of all Isolde tried.

Now, seeing Isolde, she licked dry lips and made a feeble motion towards the wine jar on a table nearby.

Isolde crossed, poured wine into a cup, then helped the girl to drink, supporting Marcia's head and shoulders and guiding the cup to her mouth. When she'd taken several swallows, Marcia pushed the cup away, then shifted restlessly, her lips tightening as the movement jarred her lacerated womb.

"Why are you kind to me? You ought to hate me after what I did. I tried to have you burned for witchcraft. Tried to make you believe this child was King Constantine's."

Isolde set the cup down on the bedside table, wiping a drop of wine from the rim. "So you did."

"Well, then?"

Isolde was silent, for a moment recalling the witchcraft trial so vividly that she could almost smell the smoke from the great central hearth of the council hall. Feel herself, standing before the king's council, her whole body bruised and aching fiercely with the marks of Marche's fists. And Marche's voice, condemning her to be tied to a stake in the ground and burned alive.

Then she looked down at the other girl's fever-flushed face and nervous, restless hands, picking fretfully the edge of the linen sheet. The memory of the smoke and the bruises and the councilmen's watching eyes faded, and she shook her head.

"I don't hate you."

She'd hardly, Isolde thought, have needed the Sight to sense the pain that gnawed at Marcia night and day. But as it was, every time she stood by Marcia's bed she could feel the raw core of anger and grief and loneliness Marcia guarded jealously and with all her strength, like a child clutching a favorite toy—or as the dragons said to sleep beneath the surrounding mountains hoarded their gold.

Isolde had never liked Marcia—and still, if she were honest, couldn't like her now, though she had lain for nearly three weeks in Isolde's care. But she could be achingly sorry for the other girl, who lay here slowly bleeding out the pitiful fragments of the life she carried—and held clenched inside her such a raw, desperate, ravenous need for love that she ended by pushing all hope of it away with fits of temper and sharp, sly looks, and a venomous tongue.

"I'm a healer, and you're suffering. And if I can help you, I will."

Even that, though, made Marcia's brows draw together, and

she shot Isolde another sidelong look, voice petulant and sharp with dislike.

"So I'm a duty to you, then? A pity case?"

Isolde said nothing, only smoothed the down-filled pillows so that Marcia might lie back once more. As her hand came away, though, her fingers touched something beneath the lowermost pillow, something sharp enough to prick her skin.

"No!" Marcia tried to twist, grabbing at Isolde's hand. But then as Isolde drew the object out, she stopped and sat staring, her pockmarked face set and her dark eyes both defiant and somehow frightened as well.

"Well? I suppose you know what it is?"

Isolde looked down at what she held. "So I do."

What lay in her hand was a crudely made doll, little more than a bundle of rags with a face painted in a rusty brown Isolde knew must be dried blood. The body of the doll was pierced through with several bone needles and skewered through the neck by a pair of great bronze-headed pins.

"It's a curse doll." Isolde fingered a ragged scrap of cloth wound about the doll's body. "Made for me?"

Marcia sank back against the pillows, eyeing Isolde with a look that was half frightened, half angry.

"Is that all you can say?"

Isolde had a sudden memory of what her grandmother had once said to her across the beside of an old huntsman—a crabbed, elderly man with a badly broken arm who cursed and threw his own slop jar at them every time either Morgan or Isolde came near. *You'd need the patience of a saint to nurse the sick without losing your temper. And the horned one help us, child, we're neither of us likely to be named holy by the Christ or his God.*

Isolde looked from the blood-painted little figure to Marcia's sullen face and angry eyes. "What should I say? 'Marcia, have you been trying to ensure I die a death of searing agony? And do be honest, please?'"

Marcia said nothing, only set her mouth in a thin, hard line.

Isolde knew, though, that she was both afraid and in pain. She let out her breath and said, more gently, "It's all right. Just because I'm caring for you doesn't mean you have to be grateful—or even like me. Go ahead and hate me if you want. I don't mind."

There was a silence, and then Marcia asked, in a slightly altered voice, "Are you going to stop taking care of me?"

Isolde heard again the mingled defiance and fear in Marcia's tone. "Of course not," she said. "As long as you need me, I'll be here." She rose and poured out a measure of poppy-laced cordial into the wine cup. "Drink this," she said. "It will help with the pain."

Marcia swallowed the dose and was silent, looking down at her hands, picking again at the edge of the sheet. Then abruptly her fingers clenched. She looked up at Isolde and burst out, "I had no choice, you know. It wasn't my fault. They made me testify against you. Marche and Lady Nest." Her face twisted, eyes fever-bright and wide, her voice rising, "I couldn't help it. I couldn't. I—"

An edge of hysteria had crept into her tone, and Isolde put a hand on the girl's shoulder, easing her back onto the pillows again. "Hush, it's all right. Don't think on it anymore. You do what you must, and live with it after. So do we all."

Marcia's eyes were starting to grow heavy with the poppy syrup, but she said, her voice once more sullen, "What would you know?"

The memory of the dream crawled over Isolde's skin once again, and she realized that she was unconsciously rubbing the place on her wrist where purple bruises had showed five months before. Deliberately, she forced her clenched hands to relax, took up a damp cloth, and began to wipe Marcia's face. Her forehead, the flushed, pockmarked cheeks, the thin, sallow neck.

"At least as much as you do."

When she'd finished bathing Marcia's face, she set down the rag and picked up the ill-wish doll again. Drawing out the pins, she crossed the room and laid the now limp figure on the logs of the hearth fire. From behind her, Marcia said, her voice sounding feeble and resentful both, "I paid good coin for that."

Isolde stopped herself before she could say, *Then it will make expensive smoke.* That was the worst, she thought, about losing your temper with someone gravely ill—that you were sorry for it almost at once. She kept silent, and after a moment Marcia asked, "You're not afraid of it?"

Isolde watched as the doll took flame, shriveled, and burned. "I think if my safety depends on pins stuck in a nasty little bundle of rags, it's more or less a lost cause in any case."

"Then why are you burning it?" A hard, malicious edge crept into Marcia's tone. "Are you afraid someone will see it and blame you for it?"

"They probably would, at that," Isolde said. The Witch Queen, she thought, returning to her old ways. She turned back to the bed. "But, no, I wasn't thinking of anyone's thinking it's mine. If Garwen sees this, she'll be frightened—and grieved. And whatever you think of me," Isolde said evenly, her eyes on Marcia's thin face, "Garwen deserves better of you than—"

She broke off as the door behind her opened, and the woman she'd been speaking of came into the room. No one, Isolde thought, as Garwen entered, would believe she'd been mistress to Arthur himself in her youth—and a great beauty, so the stories ran.

She was a small woman, no taller than Isolde herself, with a plump, pillowy body, and a red-cheeked, rounded face that might have been pretty once but now looked crumpled, like a withered apple—though she couldn't be more than forty or forty-five. She had a weak, indeterminate chin and large, misty blue eyes, and she wore a gown of rich purple shot with threads of gold that made her look older still.

Her fingers shone with gold rings, and her sparse gray hair was caught back with a pair of jewel-studded pins. A number of gold and silver chains hung about her neck, one with a heavy cross of the Christ worked in silver and set with chips of some luminous green stone. All likely crafted from the melted-down battle trophies taken off dead Saxon warlords.

But Garwen wore the finery almost carelessly, without a trace of vanity, and if her face was soft and slightly foolish, it was also sweet and very kind. She ought, Isolde thought, watching her, to have a husband and sons to care for her and a bevy of grandchildren clustered about her knees. And instead she had only a life as a ward of the crown at Dinas Emrys, a lifetime of accumulated finery about her neck and wrists, and the hollow memory of her only son—Arthur's son—Amhar. Amhar had joined his half brother Modred in civil war against their father—and had died by his father's own hand.

Isolde could summon up an image, now, of Amhar's face—though it still felt strange to be able to do it. Strange to have memories again where once had been only empty blackness in her mind. Amhar had been a handsome, black-haired boy, seven or eight years older than she herself. She could see him now, kneeling before her father, touching his lips to the blade of a sword, drinking the cup of ale that would make him oath-sworn as Modred's man. She'd been maybe seven at the time and had thought Amhar looked like the hero of a harper's song.

Isolde had never heard Garwen speak of the past, of Arthur, or of her dead son. But she had felt no bitterness from the older woman, either—though as Modred's daughter, Garwen surely had cause to hate her if anyone did. And Garwen's lot, Isolde supposed, might have been far worse. Had she been mistress to anyone but Arthur, she'd almost certainly have been reduced to following the army as a common whore after the great king's death.

Now, as Garwen entered, Marcia looked up, a brief flare of something like hope lighting her fever-bright eyes. Then, seeing Garwen, she sank back against the pillows, turning her face towards the wall.

Isolde, watching a bleak, despairing look fall over the girl's

face, felt a flash of anger. She could guess whom Marcia had
hoped to see.

Marcia was serving woman to Lady Nest, who had been lover
to Marche before he'd abandoned her to turn traitor and swear
allegiance to Saxon allies. Nest was a prisoner at Dinas Emrys—
a prisoner in name, though she had the freedom of the fortress,
like Garwen and Isolde. But Lady Nest kept entirely to her own
rooms and had never once set foot in Marcia's sickroom—nor
even, so far as Isolde knew, sent word to ask after her maid.

Garwen, too, must have seen Marcia's look, for she watched
the fevered girl a moment, her soft pink mouth tightening almost
imperceptibly before she turned to Isolde.

"The king is here, Lady Isolde." She had a prattling, slightly
honking voice and a breathless way of speaking as though the
words tumbled out too quickly for her to keep up. "He rode in
with the men of his honor guard. Before dawn, it was."

Isolde straightened in surprise. "Madoc has come here? Why?"

Garwen shook her head. "That I don't know. But he sends
word to ask an audience with you. He waits in your workroom."

"My workroom?" Isolde had started to tuck the blankets
round Marcia once more, but at that she looked up quickly. "Is
he injured, then?"

Garwen shook her head again. "Not he—one of his men, so
I heard tell. I don't know either which man it is or how grave are
his hurts. Only that Madoc asks you to come so soon as you may."

"Of course." Isolde started to turn, but Garwen caught hold
of her hand. Her fingers were plump, dry, and cool against
Isolde's, but her grip was surprisingly strong.

"Wait. I've something for you." Garwen drew out a small parcel tied up in a knot of cloth from an inner fold of her gown and
pressed it into Isolde's hand. "It's a guard against devils, you see?"

Unwrapped, the parcel contained a poorly made iron ring, set
with a chip of white bone or stone and incised all around with
Latin words.

"That's a sheep's bone," Garwen said, pointing to the chip of white. "And the devils enter in—drawn by the scent of death, so the man that sold it to me said. Then the cold iron and the holy words trap them inside."

Isolde turned the ring so that she could read the crudely carved Latin words. *May the fire of God consume the evil one,* she thought it read, though several of the words were misspelled and almost illegible.

In the months she'd been at Dinas Emrys in Garwen's company, Isolde had accepted gifts of pearl-white stones, sprigs of motherwort and cowslip, and water blessed by wandering saints. Garwen was an easy mark, always, for any traveling seller of charms or spells who might pass Dinas Emrys's gates. That was probably where she'd gotten the cheaply made iron ring. And this was why Isolde had burned the blood-smeared curse doll before Garwen could see.

Isolde had also let Garwen hang a hare's foot from Marcia's bed and lay a dried toad under the mattress, because, as Garwen had said in a low, half-embarrassed voice, it wouldn't hurt and it *might* do good. Isolde had seen far too many warriors die in protracted agony—however many charms they carried or whatever words they scratched on their swords—to believe it herself. But she never argued.

Garwen, for all her breathless prattle and plump, slightly foolish face, had about her a sense of a locked door. A core of pain somewhere deep inside that no one was allowed to see. And besides, Garwen had good reason to be afraid. So did anyone at Dinas Emrys—anyone in Britain, for that matter. Maybe not of devils, exactly, Isolde thought. Though in many ways the term was close enough.

"You will keep it close by, won't you?" Garwen asked.

Isolde slipped the ring onto the fourth finger of her right hand and felt a small bur in the poorly hammered iron scrape her skin. "Of course I will," she said. "Thank you."

· · · · ·

ISOLDE SENSED THE PAIN FIRST OF all. A jolt of fire that shot through her every nerve and made her stomach lurch and her vision blur momentarily. Five months, and still the violence of the awareness caught her off guard, like stepping from a prison cell into a dazzling noonday sun.

She drew in her breath, though, locking the sensation away in a place where it could be borne, and stepped through into her workroom.

The room she used to prepare simples and dry herbs was on the ground floor of the fortress, with a single narrow window that faced out on the walled kitchen garden. The early morning sun slanting in showed a cool, square-built room with a flagged stone floor, a raftered ceiling hung with bunches of drying herbs, and a heavy wooden table, the surface scarred and worn smooth and dark with age.

Now a man stood, one hand resting on the window ledge as he looked outside to where the pale, tender green shoots of carrots and beans and peas were just beginning to poke through the soil. His body was outlined against the light, but even with his face in shadow Isolde recognized the broad, heavily muscled build of Madoc, ruler of Gwynedd and now also Britain's High King. He wore riding gear, still, tall leather boots that reached past the knee and a fur-lined cloak, fastened at the shoulder with a heavy bronze brooch.

A great brown-and-white war hound lay at Madoc's feet, head resting on its outstretched paws, and at Isolde's step in the doorway the big dog sprang up and bounded to greet her, tail furiously beating the air. Isolde put out her hand, and the dog snuffled her palm.

"Good dog, Cabal. Good fellow. Lie down, now."

Garwen had been right, she thought. It was not from Madoc that the fiery jolt of pain had come; he was unhurt, as far as Isolde could tell. Though no one, Isolde thought, who had known Madoc a year ago would recognize him now. The burns that had covered his face five months ago were healed to thick, ropy scars, twisting his skin and pulling his features slightly askew. He had let his beard grow, so that the worst of the damage to his neck and chin was covered, but even still his face looked fearsome, like Marcia's blood-painted doll. Or like an idol of the Old Ones roughly modeled in clay.

She had never, though, seen Madoc himself betray the smallest awareness of the scars, either by look or by word. He was still no more than thirty, and a man of action, his nature shaped by years of war, quick to anger and slow to forgive. Not one to pay the face he showed the world much mind, save that it betray nothing of fear in the face of a battle to be fought and won.

Now, though, the grim line of his mouth relaxed, if only slightly, as he watched Cabal settle himself in response to Isolde's command.

"That dog obeys you a deal faster yet than he does me."

Isolde watched Cabal lie down once more at Madoc's feet, body curved in a neat bow, and shook her head. "He knows I miss having him with me, that's all."

She thought of the weeks after Con's death when Cabal, Con's war dog, had refused to leave her side, lying in one corner of her rooms with a look of almost human grief in his liquid dark eyes. Now Cabal was Madoc's. And she wouldn't, she thought, have wished for the big dog any other place. He was a war hound, trained for hunting and battle. Though she did miss him, more than she would have believed.

Madoc had straightened from his brief bow of greeting, and now said, with the bluntness that always marked his speech, "Then you'll be glad to know that he's come to no harm in what fighting we've had. But I am sorry to tell you, Lady Isolde, that we can still bring you now no word of Camelerd."

Isolde was aware of sickening disappointment, as well as spreading cold fear—though she had not really expected Madoc would succeed in learning how Camelerd, her own country, fared in the war that raged back and forth beyond Dinas Emrys's mountain fastness and high stone walls.

Camelerd was hers, her own domain by right of her birth, however little her place as Con's High Queen had allowed her to attend herself to its rule. And now she could see nothing of the kingdom; Marche himself was not there. She remembered, though, with a feeling like ice-cold needles pricking every part of her skin, the vision she had seen earlier in the basin in her own room. Burned-out huts kicked savagely apart . . . mother and child lying dead in their own blood. If Marche was not in Camelerd, there were still his Saxon allies. And Camelerd was too rich a country to expect or even hope that those allies would not attack, spreading ruin of the same kind to every corner of the land.

Madoc's face, though, looked gray with exhaustion beneath the angry scars—and Isolde was still conscious as well of a dull, relentless pain that radiated like the heat of a fire in the corner of the room to her right.

She nodded and said only, "I thank you, my lord Madoc, for the efforts you have made."

Madoc made a brief, impatient movement, dismissing the thanks, but his reply, if he made any, was lost to Isolde. Her body tight with a kind of dread premonition, she had turned to where a second man sat slumped on the room's corner bench, his features still more shadowed than Madoc's in the dim light. Even so, though, Isolde knew him, too, at once.

Kian.

He wore the green badge and leather armor of Madoc's honor guard, his whole bearing as accustomed to the soldier's gear as if he'd never lived as an outlaw, never hunted and fought for Trystan's band of masterless men. But then, Isolde thought, Kian had been a soldier more than half his life, in the years before Camlann.

He would be nearing fifty, now, a barrel-chested man with a grim, remorseless face under a shock of grizzled hair. His face now was a mass of purpling bruises, his mouth swollen and torn, a cut over one brow trailing a line of dried blood. He held himself as though his ribs ached. And he had, too, Isolde saw, a patch over one eye, held fast by a leather thong.

It was from there—from beneath that leather eye patch—that Isolde could sense the worst of the pain, and a sharp twist of guilt went through her. If not for her, Kian would never have left Trystan, never have sworn his oath to Madoc—never be sitting slumped in her workroom now, one eye lost. For the eye was gone. Even without looking, she was sure of that.

Kian's whole body, though, seemed clenched, and he watched her from the shadows with a set, rigid look she'd seen countless times before in the soldiers who came into her care. Men badly wounded—often with arms or hands or lower limbs gone—who dreaded the debility being noticed for the first time. And more than that, dreaded all signs of pity or sympathy as they would salt rubbed into an open wound.

And so Isolde turned, reaching for her scrip of ointments and salves, before saying, mildly, "Goddess mother. I hope the other man looks worse, at least?"

Kian grunted, his brows climbing into his thatch of grizzled hair. "Don't give me much credit, do you? Think there was only one?"

Isolde smiled, if only briefly. Beneath the bruises, Kian's face was that of an old man, gray and at the last extremity of exhaustion. She could feel how tightly stretched he was, how hard he worked to maintain control and keep from shattering apart. Still, if he could joke, that was at least a hopeful sign.

She studied him, wondering whether she ought to look for the full extent of his injuries now. She glanced at Madoc, though, and decided to wait. Kian was a soldier, and Madoc his lord. And by this time she'd treated enough men like Kian to know he'd hate like bitter poison to have his wounds examined under Madoc's eyes.

Instead, she broke the seal on a jar of ale and handed it to Kian. "Here. Drink this. It's about the best I can offer for the pain."

Kian took a long pull at the jar, then sat back, wiping his mouth with the back of his hand, considering her with the one visible eye. "Well, now. Can't say I was keen on being doctored, but maybe it's none so bad after all."

Isolde saw him grimace, though, as he set the jar beside him on the bench.

Even without looking, she could feel the marks of a heavy boot over his ribs—where he'd been kicked viciously as he lay curled on the ground. But Isolde stopped herself before she could say anything more. Kian wouldn't want the seething anger she felt for whoever had done this to him any more than he would have wanted the burden of sympathy.

She opened a stoppered vial of goldenseal infusion and, taking up a clean linen rag, started to sponge the dirt and dried blood away from the multitude of cuts and abrasions on Kian's hands and forearms. That much, she judged, he wouldn't mind before his king.

Then she glanced up at Madoc, still standing by the window. "What happened?"

"Ambush." Madoc unclasped his hands from behind his back and rubbed one along the length of his jaw. "Well carried out, really." His mouth tightened. "Hit our supply wagons, in the rear of our train. Dirty whoreson—" He checked himself. "Dogs knew we'd have to turn the spearmen and cavalry around and fight, with food rations running as short as they are."

Isolde took a pot of comfrey salve from the uppermost shelf. She had a rule for herself: she never let herself hesitate to mention Marche, never allowed her voice to waver in speaking his name. And so now, smoothing the ointment over Kian's scraped knuckles, she asked, "Marche's men?"

Madoc's head moved in brief confirmation. "They were. Effectively, at any rate. Some wore Marche's colors, I know. Some Saxons. Some with Owain of Powys's badge on their shields. We fought them off—just. But they outnumbered us. Took two of our supply wagons as easily as catching pox from a village whore." A faint tinge of color crept into Madoc's face, and he added, "Your pardon, Lady Isolde."

"Granted."

Madoc gave another short nod of acknowledgment, and then his face tightened. "Took a dozen captives, as well as the wagons. Kian"—Madoc jerked his head in Kian's direction—"was one."

That explains, then, Isolde thought, the ridged marks where tight rope bonds have worn the skin raw about Kian's wrists. She glanced up at Kian's battered face. "But you escaped?"

Kian's look was impassive beneath the bruises, the line of his mouth grim. He jerked one shoulder. "Was that or have my guts turned to fodder for the ravens."

"And the others?"

Kian hunched his shoulders but said briefly, "Oh, aye. Got them free, as well."

But none of those others, Isolde thought, can have been as badly hurt as Kian, otherwise they would be here as well. She knew she couldn't ask, though, why Kian had been the only man to come to serious harm—any more than she could have spoken of the bruises on his ribs.

She'd seen men broken by torture or battle—many of them. Enough to know that Kian was not one of those. But she was aware of the fiery ache of his muscles, the throb from the empty socket of his eye. And she could feel, still, how thin and brittle was the veneer of calm he held over those jagged memory shards.

And Kian was hardly one of those who found talking a relief for memories or fear. Isolde knew him well enough to be sure of that. If Kian chooses to tell me, she thought, I'll know. But to ask would only make him relive the beating he'd taken to no good cause.

Madoc was speaking again, half turned away to stare out across the quiet walled garden once again. A kitchen boy in rough undyed tunic and woolen hose had come to kneel in one of the furrowed beds, pulling weeds from among the rows of plants with quick, efficient jerks.

"We gained one scrap of information, though."

His face, too, was impassive and grim beneath the weariness, but the set of his shoulders and back and the tightness of his mouth spoke of the tautly controlled fury the capture of his men had raised.

"We learned that Marche has offered a bounty in gold for information on the whereabouts of his son."

Isolde had been spreading ointment over Kian's wrists, so that the words caught her unprepared. Though, she thought, she supposed she ought to have expected something of the kind. She knew—if anyone did—the man Marche was.

Still, her hands jerked involuntarily, so that she almost lost her grip on the pot of salve. But Madoc was still turned away, and Kian was slumped back against the wall, the visible eye drooping closed; they neither of them saw. Isolde waited a moment, then said, "His son?"

She'd kept her voice level, but still something made Madoc glance round at her. "You'd have known him, wouldn't you? Marche was oath sworn to your father—that is, before he turned his coat at Camlann."

Isolde nodded slowly, turning back to begin winding a strip of clean linen about the scored rope marks on Kian's arms, reminding herself of her own rule. "Marche has been good, always, at tacking his allegiance to whichever side the winds of victory are blowing from. And yes, I did know his son. Years ago, when we were both children, though." She paused, tied the bandage off in a knot, then asked, "Do you know why Marche should be seeking him now?"

She felt Kian's muscles twitch in her grasp, and he started to speak, but then seemed to check himself. After a moment, Madoc said, "That's why the information is of some value. Rumor is that Octa of Kent is seeking alliance with Cerdic of Wessex. Already he's allied himself with Octa of Kent. Which would give their united forces effective control of the whole goddamn eastern Saxon shore."

Madoc's fist struck once against the stones of the window ledge, and Cabal, still lying at his feet, stiffened, ears lifting at the angry tone. Madoc, though, drew in his breath and went on, more calmly, "Already Marche and Octa have an alliance between them. And Marche and Cerdic were once allies as well—under your father. Marche betrayed that alliance at Camlann. Something Cerdic would be slow to forgive, if he's considering a joint alliance between himself, Octa, and Marche. But on the other hand, Marche was once wedded to Cerdic's daughter. His son would also be Cerdic's grandson. So Marche offering gold to any bringing him word of his son—" Madoc raised a hand and let it fall. "It's enough to make me think the rumors of Octa seeking Cerdic's friendship are true. That Marche is working at finding anything—or in this case, anyone—who might tip the scales of Cerdic's goodwill in his favor."

Isolde was silent, staring at the wall opposite. It was strange, too, to now be able to remember Cerdic's daughter. Marche's wife. To look back across the years to see Aefre, daughter of Cerdic, as Isolde remembered her. Fair-haired and pale, with a slow, sweet voice—cringing reflexively when anyone spoke to her and carrying herself as though her ribs ached.

Isolde could remember, too, earning herself a lashing for slapping a noblewoman's face when she'd been mocking Aefre's painfully stammering speech. And Morgan, her grandmother, putting witch hazel on the lash marks on her hands and telling her to save her temper for those who stood a chance of joining in a fight—because Aefre had none.

Though even Morgan had salved Aefre's bruises with tight-set lips and very gentle hands. And given Aefre a daily posset to take that made sure she never conceived another child.

Another ripple of memory swept through Isolde of her own dizzying relief when her monthly bleeding had come on, five months before. Despite her rule, her lips felt stiff, and it was hard to make herself speak the words. She shook her head, though, drew a slow, steadying breath, and said, "Yes, of course.

I do remember. And the marriage was part of Marche's oath to my father. A way of cementing their allegiance with Cerdic in the war with Arthur and those who remained loyal to him."

Madoc snorted. "Marriage or no, Cerdic would have kissed the a—" He stopped. "Hand of the devil himself if he'd offered to make war on Arthur on Cerdic's behalf. Cerdic had his army crushed by Arthur's forces at Badon Hill. He'd neither forgive nor forget the defeat. But Octa of Kent must be hoping he'll forgive Marche the betrayal at Camlann. Or at least overlook it enough to unite with him against us."

Isolde had a sudden flash of the image of Octa of Kent laughing as he spurred his horse onwards towards the fleeing old woman. Running her through with his sword. And overlaid with the image was memory of Marche's face as he'd spoken of his Saxon ally five months before. His eyes those of a man trapped and at bay, as though he'd set events in motion that now spiraled beyond his control. Octa of Kent would make a bad enemy. And should he decide that alliance with Marche was worth less than alliance with Cerdic of Wessex, Marche had good reason to be afraid.

Isolde blinked away the image of Marche's face, slammed the door on whatever feelings the thought had aroused. Bad enough that he walked into her dreams without his haunting her waking hours as well.

She turned back to Kian, starting to wind a bandage about his other wrist. Marche's son by Cerdic's daughter could, she knew, pose the greatest threat to an alliance with Cerdic. He would likely know exactly how his mother Aefre had died in the days just before Camlann, when Marche planned to turn to Arthur's side. And a marriage tie to a Saxon king might have damaged fatally his chance of acceptance by Arthur and his men.

Which is almost certainly, she thought, why Marche is seeking word of his son now. That and because Marche would spill his last drop of blood—spend his last ring of gold—to hunt down and punish anyone who had beaten him in a fight.

Isolde could feel Madoc's eyes on her, and he asked, after a moment, "You don't know yourself where Marche's son might be?"

Isolde knotted the bandage before asking, without looking up, "Why?"

"Might make a hostage—a bargaining point for dealings with Marche. God knows, we've need of any advantage just now."

"I see." Isolde was silent a moment, then at last rose from her place beside Kian and set the jar of salve back on its shelf. "But I can't help you. I don't know where Marche's son might be now. He could be anywhere." She paused, her eyes still on the ordered row of bottles and jars. "He could even be dead."

There was a brief moment of stillness in the room, and then Isolde turned back to Madoc. "Is that why you came? To ask me about Marche's son?"

Madoc's eyes were dark, deep-set, and very intent in his scarred face, but he shook his head. "Only part." He was silent a moment, brows drawn in thought, then said, "Two more parties will be riding in over the course of the next day or two. I expect Cynlas of Rhos and Dywel of Logres to arrive with their war bands."

Isolde had begun to shred dried comfrey leaves for a poultice to work on Kian's bruised torso and ribs, but at that she looked up, surprised. She had met Cynlas, ruler of the northern kingdom of Rhos, a handful of times. A giant of a man, forty or forty-five, with a brutal, blunt-featured face and flaming red hair.

"Cynlas of Rhos? Isn't he—"

"My oath-sworn enemy?" Madoc finished, mouth tightening briefly beneath the black beard. "He is." He gave a short, harsh laugh. "Isn't that what's always doomed Britain from the time the Romans broke the power of the tribes? That we'd always rather tear at each other's flanks instead of uniting to face a common foe?"

Isolde saw a muscle jump in Madoc's jaw, but then he gave another short laugh.

"And what is it they say? Keep your enemies closer than your friends if you want to live?" He was silent once more, his gaze momentarily abstracted, as though his thoughts again followed some inward path of their own, then shook his head.

"We've need of fresh allies. All the more since Owain of Powys joined his armies to Marche and Octa's united force." He turned from the window to look back at Isolde. "You'll remember what happened. Owain had betrayed us once—allied himself to Marche and repented of it, so he claimed. I'd small choice but to take him at his word. Powys can raise an army two hundred strong—and we'd need of every man, every spear, with Marche and Octa breathing down our spines."

Madoc paused, his scarred face hardening, eyes turning dark as he went on, striking one closed fist against his open palm. "And you know what happened. Three months ago, Owain sent one of his bloody limp-wristed messengers to me and named the price, in gold, of his continued allegiance—without it, he'd take his two hundred spears and join Octa and Marche. And I sent a message back that he could take his spearmen to Marche and on- ward to hell before I'd pay him a single copper. And that I'd tear out the liver of any messenger he sent me after this one."

Cabal whined and started to rise, but Madoc quieted him with a hand on the big dog's head. Isolde could almost feel the anger radiating off him in waves, though in the end he only drew breath, raised a hand, and let it fall. "I believed—I still believe that an allegiance that can be bought isn't worth having at any price. And yet—" He broke off, mouth twisting, and gave an- other of those short, unpleasant laughs. "And yet what am I pro- posing but to try buying the friendship of a man I trust even less than Owain?"

Isolde started to speak, but Madoc held up a hand again. "I'll explain. But let me set out what I intend in order. We've not much time—and there is a favor I would ask of you, Lady Isolde."

Isolde felt her muscles tense themselves, but she turned to set a copper pan of water over the coals of the brazier. "Go on."

"The king's council has been split, these last months. There are those—Cynlas and Dywel among them—who say we should never have retreated from Cornwall. That we should have rebuilt the old fortifications, dug in, and prepared for Octa and Marche's siege."

Kian had been sitting in silence, head tipped back against the wall, arms folded across his chest, and his single eye shut, but at that he snorted. "Rebuilt the forts in Cornwall? Why? So that we could be living warm and snug when Marche's forces slaughtered us all? We might as well dig our own graves, lie down, and shovel the dirt back over our heads."

For a moment Madoc stood with his arms braced against the stone window frame, and Isolde, watching, saw the muscles of his back and shoulders bunch and tighten beneath the fabric of his tunic. Madoc had accepted the High Kingship only because his leadership was the council's best hope in the face of Marche's betrayal and coming attack—accepted, Isolde knew, even though he himself had neither sought nor wanted the High King's crown.

And now, Isolde thought, he shoulders the burden not only of defending against Octa and Marche but also of uniting all the council's warring factions. Keeping the quarrels and animosities among the rest of the country's petty warlords and kings under control—and the rest of the councilmen's ambitions as well. If Madoc held the High Kingship out of duty alone, there were many others who would seize it from him for their own gain. Small wonder if Madoc's face showed gaunt and worried beneath the scars.

Now Madoc seemed to make a deliberate effort to relax his grip on the stones and turned to Kian with a short nod.

"As you say. We might as well dig up the stones here and expect to find Merlin's dragons as think we could hold out against a prolonged siege—any more than we could face Marche and Octa's forces in set battle and not simply water the earth with our blood. Their numbers are simply too great. And so instead—"

He paused, anger and frustration edging into his tone once

again. "Instead, we have drawn off into the Welsh hills, where the terrain is too rough and food and supplies too scarce for Marche and Octa's armies to remain banded together in united assault. We defend hill forts like this one. Meet their raiding parties from time to time. Pick off as many of their men with our archers as we may."

He stopped and drove a fist once more into the palm of his open hand. "And wait and watch while they raid a settlement here—burn a farm there—like wolves taking down the weak and young from a herd of deer."

A vision of the burned settlement she had seen in the water basin seemed to gather and press against Isolde's eyes once again. The water she'd set over the brazier was boiling, though, and she poured it over the bowl of shredded comfrey leaves, watching the fragrant steam rise and trying to block the echo of Marche's thoughts from replaying again and again in her mind. *Do what you must,* she'd told Marcia. *And live with it after.* Except that she sometimes felt as though that one night had marked her, like one of the swirling blue-colored tattoos the Old Ones had pricked with needles into their skin. A poisoned tattoo that was slowly eating its way through to her bones. And I'm lucky, she thought, I could have been born into Aefre's life and been fifteen years wedded to Marche instead of just the one night.

Madoc was speaking again, his hands clasped behind him, feet spread slightly apart, and his voice quieter now. "Which brings me to the reason I've come—and the favor I would ask of you, Lady Isolde. What do you know of King Goram of Ireland?"

Isolde set the empty water pan down and looked up, startled. Whatever she'd expected, it was not this.

"King Goram?" she repeated.

"He was at one time—"

"Another ally of my father's in his war with Arthur," Isolde said. "Yes, I know. My father had three allies. Cerdic of Wessex, as you said before. Goram of Ireland. And Marche. Marche was wedded to Cerdic's daughter. And Goram was wedded to a daughter of Marche. Carys, her name was. A bastard daughter—he had no children by Aefre but his son. But it made for a blood tie, all the same."

Isolde looked up at Madoc. "I never knew her. Marche had sent her to a convent to be raised by the holy women. And I was only seven or eight when she was sent to Ireland to marry King Goram. But I do remember after Camlann—after Marche had betrayed my father and his other allies. Goram joined Arthur and so survived the battle on the winning side—"

Isolde stopped and was silent a moment, working to keep her voice steady and calm, telling herself angrily again that she didn't flinch away from speaking Marche's name. Or from recalling that time, now that her memory of it had returned. "The king's council—or what remained of it, at least—made Marche guardian of my grandmother and myself. So that I was there when the messenger arrived from Goram. This would have been . . . I don't know. A week? Maybe two weeks after the battle at Camlann. Goram's messenger brought Marche a bag—a finely tooled leather saddle bag—with the compliments of his king."

Isolde took up the bowl of comfrey leaves. "And when Marche and his men opened it, they found Carys's head inside. Packed in salt, to preserve it on the road from Ireland. Though the flesh was starting to rot and come away from her skull all the same."

Madoc was silent a moment, his scarred face expressionless, and then he said, "I see. I'd like to say that I don't care a goat-rutting goddamn whether or not Goram—"

And then he stopped himself, with an apologetic look at Isolde. "Your pardon again, Lady Isolde."

"Granted," Isolde said again. *Goat-rutting goddamn.* She sometimes wondered whether men were taught to curse at the same time they learned to ride and hunt and fight with swords. Madoc would have passed the lessons easily, at any rate. He'd as coarse a mouth as any foot soldier or smith. And yet the mere fact that he'd checked himself from swearing in front of her spoke of just how much he'd changed since the council had chosen him High King.

But then, Madoc of Gwynedd was a man of contradictions in many ways. He heard mass sung every morning, even had a priest ride out with his army on campaign. And Isolde remembered Con telling her once of how Madoc had walked barefoot about a chapel seven times in the dead of winter as penance for taking the name of the Christ in vain.

Isolde glanced up at Madoc now before turning her attention back to the bowl in her hands. "You may as well speak freely, Lord Madoc. I've stitched and cauterized wounds for more men than I can count from the time I was thirteen. I can almost guarantee I'll have heard at least the equal of any curses you can find."

Madoc's tight features relaxed, and he gave a short laugh—an easier one, this time. "All right, then," he said. "I'd like to say I don't give a rat's piss whether Goram eats his own young or needs a map and both hands to find his own ass—so long as he's willing to lend his spearmen to fight Octa and Marche. I'd like to say it—but I'd be lying if I did."

Madoc stopped, raising one hand and then letting it fall. "And I'd be lying, as well, Lady Isolde, if I claimed I was happy about the favor I ask of you. All the same, though, I can't see that we've any other choice. Marche and Octa between them have the power to crush Britain entirely. And King Goram has agreed to a meeting on Ynys Mon, in four days' time, to listen to the offer we make as the price of his allegiance."

"Ynys Mon?" Isolde repeated.

Madoc nodded. "A midway point between Gwynedd and Ireland. You've traveled there before?"

Isolde shook her head. "No, never." She had a sudden, piercingly clear memory of her grandmother speaking of the place, though, when Isolde herself had been no more than eight—an image of Morgan twisting up her mouth and spitting before she told the story of Suetonius of Rome and Ynys Mon.

Ynys Mon, the Dark Isle, had been holy ground, once—

the sacred isle of the druids—before the Roman legions had crushed the tribes of Britain under their sandaled feet, scarred the land with their knife-straight roads, cut down the trees, and plowed up the earth to build thick-walled temples of gleaming white stone. And Suetonius, desperate to break the druids' power, had marched his forces to the holy isle, burned the sacred groves, defiled and violated the pools. And, so Morgan had said, with a brief, angry shimmer of tears in her age-dulled eyes, driven a knife blade between Britain and the gods for all time.

Now Madoc had gone on, a weary tinge of bitterness again creeping into his tone. "Goram won't come cheap, of that much I'm sure. But what you tell me . . ." He paused, then looked up at Isolde, his dark eyes hard and a little bleak in his disfigured face. "I might think I'd sooner make my bed in a pigsty and sleep on a bed of sh— filth than ally with Goram. But what you tell me means that he may hate Marche enough still that he'll send his spearmen to our aid."

"He may."

Isolde was silent, a picture forming in her mind's eye of the Irish king, as she remembered from the handful of times she'd seen him as a child. A bandy-legged, bull-chested man with gray eyes and black hair that hung loose to his shoulders, draped in a heavy bear-pelt cloak and wearing a golden torque as thick as her wrist around his heavily muscled neck. Certainly, Goram was a man slow to forgive an insult or wrong.

Madoc passed a hand through his cropped black hair. "And I've seen what's left of the raided villages after Octa and his forces have done with them."

Not only you, Isolde thought. She kept silent, though, and Madoc went on, his face darkening, "Some say he's mad. I don't know. But mad or sane, he's one that fights for the sake of killing. Because he likes the blood and watching men die. I've seen bodies on a battlefield that he carved up with his sword just for pleasure. And there was one place—a settlement in the south—where he'd lost some of his men in the fight. And he rounded up every woman in the place—old and young, even the small girls. Had them buried alive in the grave he'd dug for his warriors—for their pleasure in the afterlife."

"I know. Octa was an enemy of my father, as well—before Camlann. 'Octa of the Bloody Knife,' he was called by my father's men. And with reason." Isolde thought of Emyr—one of her father's fighting men taken prisoner by Octa in battle. He'd lived—had escaped Octa's camp and somehow made his way back to Modred's hall. A miracle, really, because he'd been tortured until his wits were entirely gone. When Isolde had seen him, he'd been a weeping, cringing shadow of a man, gibbering in pain, soiling and wetting himself at any sudden movement or loud noise.

Her grandmother had taken one look at him and then, without hesitation, given him a draft that ensured he went to sleep and never woke again.

Something of the memory must have showed on her face, because Madoc opened his mouth as though about to ask a question. Isolde shook her head, glancing over at Kian.

"No, don't ask. It would tell you nothing but what you already know."

Madoc watched her a moment, but then nodded and said, "At any rate, we are agreed that an alliance with even King Goram may be justified if it will prevent Marche and Octa from wholesale slaughter across the countryside. Cynlas of Rhos and Dywel of Logres have already pledged their attendance at Ynys Mon—that is why they ride in with their war bands today. So that we may make the journey to Ynys Mon as one party. And that, then, is the favor I would ask of you, Lady Isolde. That you accompany us to Ynys Mon—speak to King Goram on Britain's behalf. He may be more inclined to listen to you, for the sake of the oath he swore as your father's ally."

Isolde nodded slowly. "I suppose he may," she said. "Though he wouldn't remember me. I don't think I was more than seven or eight the last time I saw him."

She paused and glanced at Kian, still slumped in the corner. His eyes were closed, but she knew he was not asleep. Only retreated to a space deep within himself where he could ride the pain she could still feel grinding at him like waves pounding the shore.

Her eyes moved briefly to the vial of poppy syrup she kept on an upper shelf. That would grant him sleep. But the poppy would also trap him in dreams from which he couldn't awake—which would almost certainly be crueler, just now, than the pain.

She turned back to Madoc and said, "Tell me, though—the rest of the council has approved my attendance at the talks with King Goram?"

Madoc studied her with something like appraisal at the back of his eyes, then he gave a short nod. "Very well. Several of my councilmen spoke out against the idea of your attending. Cynlas of Rhos said a woman's only use was to warm a man's—" Madoc broke off once more, and Isolde saw a faint tide of color creep up his neck under the beard.

Madoc jerked his head. "But his opinion is irrelevant. I believe it worth the attempt for you to join the negotiations on Ynys Mon. And as your country's High King, I ask that you attend." His eyes, dark and deep-set in his ravaged face, met hers. "Ask, though." He stressed the word. "Not order. Ynys Mon is but a half day's ride from here. But any journey may be dangerous in times such as these."

"I hadn't been expecting a safe season, even in this place. And if you wish it, yes, I will come to Ynys Mon."

Isolde paused. The comfrey leaves were softened, now, to a verdant green, and she took up a pouch of powdered slippery elm to tip into the bowl, as well. She could well imagine what Cynlas of Rhos's words might have been—the ones even Madoc couldn't bring himself to repeat. Or not within her hearing, at least.

She'd expected almost at every moment to have this conversation or one like it these last five months—ever since the council had ruled her marriage to Marche invalid. On the grounds of

Marche's treason, of course. Not because she'd been forced to the marriage against her will.

Isolde had taken up a pestle to mix the comfrey and slippery elm into a paste, and she had to force her hand to relax its grip on the stone handle.

This, though, was why she'd agreed to the council's proposal that she be sent to this remote spot. The reason she'd come without argument to Dinas Emrys, despise herself for the cowardice of it though she had—and did still, come to that.

Now she gave the herbs in the bowl a few smooth, rocking strokes with the pestle before saying, "But there is more, isn't there?"

Madoc hesitated, and Isolde saw doubt or suspicion flicker briefly across his scarred face, saw him draw back with a kind of instinctive aversion, like a horse scenting wolves. She said, with an effort to keep the impatience out of her tone, "I was Constantine's queen for seven years, my lord Madoc. Since I was thirteen. I'd hardly need witchcraft to guess that there is more to my presence on Ynys Mon than simply a hope that he may be softened by the memory of his friendship with my father. Have you offered him a marriage tie to strengthen any proposed alliance? The lady of Camelerd in exchange for whatever spearmen he chooses to send?"

Madoc was silent a long moment before replying, his dark eyes intent on her face. At last he said, "You're young, Lady Isolde, to look like that."

"How do I look?"

"I've seen eyes like yours—looking back at me from an enemy's face across the divide of a shield wall."

Isolde turned her gaze away. "Perhaps. But I'm old enough, my lord Madoc, to have been married twice by the council's will. Old enough, too, to choose my battles—and not to enter a fight unless I've at least a chance of winning."

She glanced at Kian, still sitting with his eye closed, and for his sake—and because it wasn't entirely fair to blame Madoc for the way of the world—made an effort to keep her voice low.

"I could cry," she said, "or I could take this bowl of comfrey leaves and fling it as hard as I can against the wall. Or I could say that I would rather beg by the side of the road than wed Goram of Ireland or any other man. And still I would be left with the same choice. I can either marry the man the council chooses and keep a measure of control at least over Camelerd and how the lands in my trust are ruled. Or I can be locked behind the gates of a Christian house of holy women—as my mother was—and see Camelerd carved up, divided amongst you all. If anything of the land remains, after the burning and slaughter by Octa and Marche's men."

Madoc let out his breath, his shoulders sagging as though with sudden weariness. "I may wish that I could deny the truth of that—but I can't. The proposal to offer Goram marriage to you and so the control of Camelerd has been made. And I do ask, Lady Isolde, that you consider what the gains won by such an alliance might be."

Madoc stopped, his eyes, dark and intent, fixed on Isolde's. "But I swore to the king's council," he said, "as I swear to you, now—that you are under my protection as High King. And that I will ask of you no marriage that is not of your own will."

Before Isolde could answer, Madoc had turned to where Kian still sat unmoving, head tipped back against the wall. "His eye is gone," Madoc said quietly. "But I know you will do for him otherwise all you can. I leave him in your care."

Chapter Two

WITHOUT THE LEATHER PATCH, THE empty socket of Kian's eye was bloody, red, and angry and inflamed. Isolde had treated injuries far worse these last seven years. She felt still, though, a hard lurch of mingled sickness and helpless anger at the sight—as she always did when confronted with a wound that no amount of skill at healing could ever make whole.

But Kian was sitting with his shoulders both hunched and rigid, his jaw set as though anticipating a blow. Madoc was gone, but even still she could feel him hating the necessity of having his weakness and injury laid bare. Though Cabal, remaining behind at Madoc's command, had come to sit at Kian's side, brindled head resting on the wounded man's knee.

Isolde closed her eyes briefly, deliberately put all thoughts of the interview with Madoc—all thoughts of Marche—all thoughts of any world at all beyond her workroom's four stone walls aside. She waited until she existed in a place with Kian alone, suspended in time. Then she opened her eyes. Isolde started to take the measure of his injuries, feeling as gently as she could for broken ribs, checking his hands and arms for other broken bones, and feeling with her mind as well the source of each individual hurt and pain.

That meant that she caught, too, from time to time, brief, broken flashes of memory, jagged as pottery shards in Kian's mind. *A man with a broken nose and a greasy, flea-ridden beard . . . a dull knife, heated in the fire . . . the reek of his own vomit as he lay on the ground and—*

Isolde's hands felt clammy before she was even halfway done, and she paused a moment, pushing a stray lock of hair out of her eyes with the back of her hand. Easier, she thought, in many ways, to tend the wounded when she'd been still without the Sight. But then, too, she was far more skilled a healer when she could sense every cracked bone, every cut, every part of bruised skin, and feel the pain of them almost as her own.

At last she sat back on her heels. Kian's injuries were nasty—all the more so because they'd been inflicted with the calculated intent to cause pain. But none was likely to kill. If the mutilated eye stayed free of poison, and none of the other lesser wounds turned bad, he would live.

"Well?"

Kian had sat silent throughout her examination, his gaze fixed on his own muddied riding boots, one hand clenching and un-clenching on Cabal's thick leather collar. Now his voice was edged with something like anger—though Isolde knew it was more for himself and the men who had done this to him than for her.

"Nothing broken, that I can find," she said. "Though you'll likely feel for weeks as though you've had an entire herd of cattle trample across your back. You've maybe one hand's breadth of skin on you that isn't bruised purple and green or scraped raw."

She made the words deliberately matter-of-fact, willing both anger and pity entirely out of her voice. It seemed to help, for Kian grunted, gave Cabal's head a clumsy pat, and then took up the jar of ale once more, a measure of color ebbing back into his face as he drank.

"A hand's breadth, eh? Can't say I noticed it myself."

Cabal subsided with a heavy sigh onto the ground at Kian's feet, and Isolde forced herself to smile. Though looking at the bloody eye socket, the smile felt more on the edge of crying. She blinked, though, rose, and turned to where she'd set the still warm comfrey poultice she'd made on the table, taking up a horn spoon and starting to spread the mixture between layers of clean linen.

She'd seen wounded men—men with the marks of torture on them—many, many times. Enough to know that though Kian wasn't broken, the worst for him was almost certainly yet to come.

"What do you think of the plan to seek alliance with King Goram?"

Out of the corner of her gaze, she saw Kian's shoulders relax at the question into an attitude of simple consideration. His face was marred on one side by a long scar, won years ago on the fields of Camlann, and he raised a hand, rubbing the mark unconsciously with the back of his thumb.

"Well, there's the old saying. If you meet a rabid wolf and an Irishman, kill the Irishman first."

Isolde laughed in spite of herself, and the corners of Kian's thin mouth lifted slightly as well, though his bruised face turned grim again almost at once.

"But like Lord Madoc says, I can't see that we've any choice but to try for a treaty with Goram. Not that I'd trust a pact with him unless it was written in his own heart's blood. But still, there's another saying among fighting men. That the enemy of your enemy is also your friend. If Goram hates Marche enough to fight him on our behalf, well, then—" He stopped, shrugged, then winced at the movement. "Reckon most of the council feels about the same."

Isolde nodded. She took up the comfrey poultice and pressed the square of herb-saturated linen gently across the empty eye socket, then replaced the leather patch to hold it fast. She felt Kian's breath go out in an explosive rush and his hands clench on a fold of the traveling cloak he still wore. He didn't speak, though, and after a moment she asked, only in part still seeking to divert Kian's mind, "And what about Madoc himself?"

"What do I think about him, you mean?"

Kian was silent, rubbing the old battle scar once more, some of the lines of pain in his face loosening their hold as he appeared to consider his words.

"Well, he's not one for talk. I doubt any of us that fight with him have had more than a dozen words out of him in the time we've served. He doesn't boast, either, the way fighting men like a leader to do. And the gods know we're not winning victories under his command. But still—"

Kian jerked one shoulder again and shook his head. "I doubt there's one among his men wouldn't follow him into a wolves' den waving a haunch of raw meat. Somehow he's that kind. Might even"—Kian's voice turned briefly sour—"stand a chance of winning if he'd anything like a decent amount of men and weapons and food to command."

He stopped and was quiet a moment before looking up and meeting Isolde's gaze, answering the question she had actually, if silently, asked. "Don't worry yourself," he said gruffly. "I've no regrets about kissing his sword blade and swearing him my oath." He touched the eye patch. "Even with this—even if I'd died for it—no regrets."

Kian sat in silence as Isolde bound a second poultice over the ugly bruises on his ribs, bandaged and salved the rest of his raw scrapes and cuts.

"You can stay here awhile," Isolde said, when she'd done. "I'll go, if you like, and you can rest quiet where you are."

Kian's face looked slightly grayish beneath the bruises and scabs, but he shook his head. "Reckon I can make it to my own bed."

He made no move to go, though, only sat staring down at his own hands, resting with blunt-tipped fingers splayed on his knees. Then, abruptly, he looked up. "You knew him, then, this son of Marche's? Knew him well, I mean?"

The question took Isolde by surprise, so that her hands went still on the heap of dirty linens she was bundling together to be washed clean. She could feel, though, an odd intensity to Kian's words. Somehow tied, she thought, to the memories that still hummed like bees beneath the surface of his control.

She said, slowly, "Marche was my father's ally—as I told Lord Madoc. He lived at my father's hall, Marche and his wife and their child."

She paused, staring unseeingly down at the blood-smeared rags as a wash of still unaccustomedly vivid memory pulled at her like the undertow of a wave. Marche's son was part of the time she'd walled off in her mind, locked away in a small hidden space inside her and forgotten until five months before. And after forgetting for so long, remembrance now often caught her like a blow, blotting out the time in between so that what she spoke of might have happened only a day before and not seven years. "So yes," she said at last. "I did know the son."

Isolde hadn't meant to go on, but somehow the quality of Kian's silence and the steady look in his undamaged eye was what in another man might almost have been a plea for more. Isolde wondered for a moment whether he might suspect the truth about the son of Marche and his Saxon bride. But she could sense that this mattered to him, though she was not yet certain—not entirely certain—just how. Besides, she thought, telling him can hardly make a difference now.

She was silent, her gaze traveling over the solid gray stones in the opposite wall, tracing the shadows cast by the strings of hanging herbs. Then she said, "We grew up together—almost from the time I could walk, I can remember playing with . . . him."

She paused and glanced up at Kian. "You'll know the story. It's sung in these times by every bard in every fire hall in the land. How my mother Gwynefar betrayed Arthur and wedded Modred—my father—when he tried to seize Arthur's throne. I don't remember her. She fled to a convent almost as soon as I was born. And my father wasn't one to concern himself over-much with a daughter. So I was raised my Morgan, my grandmother."

Isolde paused, searching for words that would capture the fierce, tender, clear-eyed, iron-willed woman, who, even when Isolde had known her, had still the remnants of the beauty she'd been when young. She could find none, though, and after a moment she went on.

"I'm sure you'll have heard the tales of her as well. She's called sorceress or witch in nearly every one of those bard's songs. And maybe she was—I don't know. She taught me all I know of herb craft and healing and—"

Isolde stopped and drew a breath before going on. "She loved me," she said after a moment. "I never doubted that. But all the same, it was a . . . lonely life for a child. There were other children, of course, at my father's hall—the children of his nobles and servants and fighting men. But they were all afraid of playing with a witch girl."

She looked up at Kian again. "I'm very like my grandmother, so I've been told—or like what she was when she was young. And children can be cruel little beings." She paused, looking back across the years and added, "Though to be fair, it was my own fault as well. I came on a band of the older boys beating on one of the younger ones—just for sport, and because they could. They'd given him two black eyes and knocked out one of his teeth. I was seven, I think, and I lost my temper and made them all beg the younger boy's forgiveness and told them if I ever caught them doing anything of the kind again I'd curse them and turn them all into slugs."

Isolde stopped and gave Kian a brief twist of a smile. "Scarcely surprising that the other children about the hall were too much afraid to even speak to me after that. And I'd no brothers or sisters. Instead, I had—"

She caught herself. "Marche's son. He was—is, I suppose, if he's still alive—two years older than I am."

Kian shifted his weight on the bench, but he didn't speak. Isolde could hear, from the outer court beyond the kitchen garden outside, the thud of horses' hooves and the calls and shouts of men. One or other of the king's war parties—Cynlas's or Dywel's—must have arrived.

She went on, "He was never afraid of me—or of my grand-mother. I don't know why. But I can remember playing together when he was—oh, four, maybe, and I was two or three. Long before he left the women's quarters to train with the men, at any rate, and that would have been when he was seven and I was five."

Isolde paused, watching the dust motes dance in a ray of sunlight that slanted in through the window. From outside, she could hear the faint drunken buzzing of bees and the throaty trill of a mourning dove's call.

"Even then, though, I used to follow him everywhere, every chance I got." She smiled a little again. "I probably drove him to distraction—though he never said so. He used to take me fishing, sometimes, when he'd time off from learning to ride and fight with a sword and all the rest. And he showed me things—how to throw a knife. Catch fish. Build a fire in the woods. That sort of thing."

She stopped as another sudden, knife-sharp memory came back. Herself, nine years old and leaning over the edge of a small fishing skiff, trailing her hand in the water and squealing in sur-prise when a fish's slippery, oddly bone-hard mouth nibbled on her fingertips.

"I knew you couldn't do it," the brown-haired boy beside her had said.

She'd looked up. "Do what?"

"Keep still long enough for me to actually catch anything." He tugged one of her braids and grinned. "Now keep quiet, or I'll throw you over the side and let you swim back to shore."

Isolde shut her eyes a moment. If she wasn't yet accustomed to living with memory again, she wasn't used, either, to the waves of longing for that time each separate remembrance brought. She could dismiss as cowardly the wish that she could go back to safety of the world before the battle at Camlann. What was far harder to dismiss was how much she missed herself, the way she'd been then.

Kian shifted again, as though seeking to ease the strain on his bruised back, and the sound brought her back to the present. "We had our own secret language, too—signs we'd worked out to leave messages for each other with stones or dry branches or leaves, that sort of thing. We even swore a blood oath of friendship. When I was ten and he was twelve. Mostly"—she smiled a bit—"mostly because he said a girl would just be scared sick at the sight of blood, and I wanted to prove I wasn't afraid."

She paused, her eyes on her own clasped hands. "We were friends, though—really friends. He was well liked—popular with the other boys. And the men as well, because he was good with a sword. And completely fearless in battle. He'd won that reputation for himself before he was fifteen." Isolde gave Kian a one-sided smile. "Or completely reckless. Depending on who you ask. I remember once, one battle—he was fighting with my father's men. They were in a hill fort under siege—no chance of escape—and facing Arthur's combined forces. And they were outnumbered by at least two to one. They none of them thought they'd live to see another day. And T— Marche's son, stood up and volunteered to go alone to Arthur's camp, pretending to be an escaped slave with intelligence to offer about my father's side.

"For them to believe it, he had to look as though he'd been mistreated. He battered his face and arms with a rock so he'd be cut and bruised. And then he walked straight out of my father's fort, into the enemy encampment, and into Arthur's war tent. He gave Arthur a story about being one of my father's body slaves who'd managed to get past the guard and over the fort's outer walls. And he offered to show Arthur and his men how he'd managed it. For a price in gold, of course. Only, of course, it was a trap. The party of men—thirty of Arthur's best commanders—were taken captive. Arthur had to draw back and call off the siege if he wanted them ransomed." Isolde shook her head. "I don't know to this day how he—Marche's son—got free. Arthur would have had to have put him under guard, with orders to kill him if he turned out to have lied."

She looked up to find Kian watching her, brows raised. "And he told you all this—Marche's son?"

"Of course not." Isolde shook her head, her mouth curving in another crooked smile. "I heard about it from the rest of my father's men—they talked of nothing else for months. Marche's son would never have told me himself. He'd have known I'd be furious with him for taking the risk. And he'd have said, *It had to be done by someone, and why not me?* And I'd have been angrier at him still for being right—and for not losing his temper and shouting back." She glanced at Kian again. "He almost never did. Lose his temper, I mean. He was . . . " Isolde stopped her smile fading as she searched for a word. From outside came again the soft trill of birdcalls in the garden just beyond the window, and the whickerings of horses and shouts of men in the outer court beyond that.

"Private, I suppose," she said at last. "Guarded. Very self-contained. Because of his mother, I think."

This was drawing near again to everything she dreaded speaking about, and Isolde felt the usual tightening of her stomach. She made herself go on, though, looking up to meet Kian's bruised gaze. "Marche's wife had a miserable, hellish life. I'm not even sure I'd wish her lot on Marche himself. When we were children, growing up, her son used to try to protect her as much as he could from Marche's beatings. And usually wound up whipped or beaten himself for it. It only got worse as he got older. Because then he was old enough to fight. Hit back when his father struck him—which of course made Marche angrier still."

Isolde's hands clenched involuntarily, but she made them relax and went on. "I doubt anyone ever knew anything of that but me. He—Marche's son—never told anyone. And he never, never cried or let anyone know that his back and ribs were more often than not one solid bruise under his shirt. I doubt I'd ever have known, either. But my grandmother was a healer—and by the time I was six or seven, she was teaching me. I knew enough to recognize someone with injuries when I saw him. So I'd make Marche's son let me salve his bruises. Or strap his ribs if Marche went further than usual and cracked a bone. He hated it. Marche's son, I mean. And he never talked about his father to me—or even told me straight out that it was his father who beat him. But still, I think he let me get past his guard more than anyone else."

Isolde stopped. For a moment Kian sat without speaking, the cool, still silence of the workroom drawing in about them. Then Kian said, "You're speaking of Trystan, aren't you? He's Marche's son."

The words were more statement than question, and Isolde realized as he spoke that she felt no surprise—that she'd been expecting this almost from the moment Madoc spoke of the bounty Marche offered for the capture of his son.

She gave Kian another small twist of a smile. "Was it the 'completely reckless' part that gave it away?"

Kian snorted despite the lines of pain that tightened his mouth. "Well, I'll not say that's not got Trystan dead to rights. There's bravery and there's madness, and Trystan walks the line between them like no one else I've ever known. But no. Them that attacked us used his name—Trystan. And besides—"

Kian stopped, his shoulders hunching. Isolde felt him controlling himself with an effort, but he went on, his voice unchanged. "One of them had been Owain of Powys's man. Recognized me from the time at Tintagel, five months ago—knew he'd seen me with Trystan."

Isolde saw again the broken fragments of memory she'd glimpsed in tending Kian's wounds. "So that's why the bearded man took you to torture, and not any of the others who'd been captured?"

Kian's muscles jerked, one hand reflexively touching the patch over his eye, and Isolde felt a quick stab of compunction mingled with anger at herself. She was tired, still, with the effort of blocking out awareness of the pain her treatment of Kian's wounds had inevitably caused. Though that, she thought, was hardly an excuse.

She said, quickly, "I'm so sorry, Kian. You don't have to answer that. Forget I ever asked."

Cabal had risen and now whined softly, butting his head against Kian's arm. Kian rested a hand on the big dog's head, then picked up the jar of ale and brought it to his mouth, downing several long swallows before at last he set it down. Isolde could almost hear him forcing a rush of memory back into its box. She knew, though, that there was nothing at all she might say that would ease the struggle or soften the effect of her words. She watched helplessly for what seemed an endless moment before he looked up at her again and asked abruptly, "Did you know who Trystan was, then, when you saw him five months ago?"

A memory struck Isolde of Trystan as she'd first seen him those months before, dirty and unshaven, eyes red-rimmed with fatigue, slumped against the stone wall of Tintagel's prison cell. Captured by Con's army as a Saxon spy, guarded, interrogated, and beaten by men who'd no more idea than she herself had done that they kept prison watch on Marche's son.

She shook her head. "No—at least, not at first. I'd . . . blotted out nearly all my memories from before Camlann. Because it hurt too much to remember them after. And besides—" She moved one shoulder. "He was barely fifteen the last time I saw him. And—what? Two and twenty, now. He'd changed. So had we both."

She paused, staring at the wall straight ahead. "Though I did remember, in the end."

"When you went back to get him free of Marche's prison?"

Isolde nodded. "Yes. I knew then who he was." She stopped again, recalling that last scene with Trystan—when he would have slipped away without speaking to her, without so much as telling her good-bye, if she'd not happened on him just before. When she'd added Trystan, her childhood companion and only true friend, to the list of all the others who'd gone and would never come back.

She folded her hands shut, opened them again, then looked up at Kian once more. "Why do you ask?"

Kian took another draft of ale, then sat a moment without speaking. Then he raised a hand to touch his eye patch once again, and instead of answering, asked, "How did you know the man who did this had a beard?"

Isolde, too, was silent a long moment before she spoke. Then finally she said, "Let's each of us take a question we don't have to answer, all right?"

She thought there might have been a faint flash of amusement in Kian's gaze, but then he shook his head, looking down into the half-empty jar of ale. He drew in his breath, then said without looking up, "They say that you can . . . see things."

Isolde's eyes moved once more to the workroom's shelves, the ordered rows of pottery jars and the hanging herbs above, the copper brazier with its still glowing coals. "Yes," she said. "I know they do."

Kian's shoulders hunched, and Isolde saw his fingers tighten on Cabal's collar once again. Then his head lifted and his one remaining eye met hers.

"Could you see Trystan, if you tried?"

Let another charge of witchcraft be brought, Isolde thought again, and she'd face a sentence of burning she couldn't hope to escape. And yet—

Isolde met Kian's weary, pain-dark gaze once more. Strange, she thought, that it should be Kian I trust. Not five months before, he'd spat at her feet and called her a she-devil and nearly cut her throat. But she did trust him—more than any. And even if she'd not, she knew she couldn't have ignored the unwilling, half-shamed look of anxiety at the back of his gaze. Not when she could still feel in him the ragged pulse of memory her thought-less question of a moment ago had stirred.

She said, slowly, "I can try."

To all things, Myrddin had once said, there is an ebb and a flow. And that the only constant in this world and the Other alike was change itself.

Isolde filled a shallow copper pan with water and set it on the scarred wooden table, peripherally aware that Kian had sat up a little on his bench and was watching her with an odd blend of uneasiness, disbelief, wonder—and something like simple curiosity as well—on his battered face.

The Sight was altered, since it had drifted like sea mist back into her, bit by bit, those months before. Maybe because she herself was changed. Or maybe, she thought, simply because the Sight ebbed and flowed with all the rest.

She had the dream. And she could feel the pain of those she worked to heal—catch flashes of memory, sometimes, as she had from Kian, if they were bound and knotted together with the pain. She couldn't read other thoughts, though. And thus far she'd seen nothing but the smoldering trail of Marche's destruction in scrying water of any kind.

Kian was watching, though, and so Isolde emptied her mind, focusing her gaze so that she stared both at the water's mirror-smooth surface and past it, to something beyond. She let her breathing slow, her heart steady, reaching inside herself for the place where the strands of the Sight were tied. She let the echoes creep in, first of the Old Ones, the soft lilting voice that spoke from somewhere deep beneath the fortress stones—deep as the caverns where Myrddin's dragons were said to lie. And then—

HE MOVED THROUGH THE FOREST WITH the ease of long practice, pausing now and again to listen for any signs of pursuit and ignoring the steadily mounting pain from the wound in his side. You must be getting soft, he thought. The quarry guards would have gotten another four nights' work, at least, out of a man in your shape.

Still, by this time he could probably have walked backwards and

*in his sleep through a fully pitched army camp without being heard
or seen. Much less along a silent wooded path, with the memory of
Hereric's agonized face in his mind's eye to keep him moving ahead.*

*A rustle sounded up ahead in the damp leaf mold underfoot, and
he froze, molding himself against the trunk of a beech tree, one hand
moving automatically to the hilt of his sword. Probably nothing but a
badger or a deer. But then he didn't want to die swearing at himself
for stupidity, either.*

ISOLDE CAME BACK TO HERSELF TO find that Kian was gripping her
arm, his face blanched beneath the angry bruises and scrapes. She
pressed her hands to her eyes, drawing breath like a swimmer
coming up for air.

"It's all right. I'm all right."

Kian's breath went out in an explosive rush, and he sank back
on the bench, grunting involuntarily at the jarring of his bruises.
"Powers of Satan. You looked like you were seeing a vision of the
damned in hell."

Cabal, too, was beside her, thrusting his nose into her palm, a
high, anxious whine sounding in his throat. Isolde put a hand on
the big dog's neck and drew another slow breath.

"No. Nothing like that. I didn't see anything. Not really. It
was just—"

She shook her head, shivering a little, a prickle of cold sliding
down her spine as she tried to recall the feeling. As if a chill hand
gripped her by the back of the neck, and she saw—

"There was a man. And a feeling that he was in . . . danger, I
suppose. Trouble."

"Trystan?"

She could hear the tension in Kian's voice as he asked the
question, but she could only shake her head again. "I don't know.
Honestly, I don't know. I . . ."

Another of those huge, cruel jokes, she thought. That the

Sight should show her nothing of actual use—just enough for the fear of uncertainty, which was always the most gnawing fear of all. Though Kian wouldn't thank her, she thought, for trying to spare him worry or pain.

She met Kian's look directly and said, "I can't be sure. But if you ask me what I believe, then yes, I think it was Trystan I saw."

"Danger." Kian rubbed the back of his thumb along the long, puckered scar, then grunted. "Wouldn't exactly have needed the Sight to guess that much."

"I'm sorry."

Kian shook his head. "Aye, well. Shouldn't have asked you to try it, maybe."

Isolde could hear the flat weariness in his voice, see the lines of exhaustion and pain deepening about the corners of his mouth. She knelt before the low wooden chest that sat beside Kian's bench, lifted the lid, and drew out a pair of folded blankets.

"Lie back and rest now," she said. "You need to sleep—and it may as well be here as anywhere else."

To her surprise, Kian made no protest—which was itself a mark, she thought, of just how pain-sick and tired he was. He swung his feet, muddied boots and all, up onto the bench, the breath hissing through his teeth at the effort. But he took the blankets from Isolde before she could cover him, tossing one carelessly over his legs and bunching the other behind his head.

"All right. Been out of the nursery long enough to make my own bed."

He lay back, then, his eye drooping closed, arms crossed over his chest. "You needn't stay on my account, you know—you can go."

"I know," Isolde said. "Lie down, Cabal."

The big dog turned in place three times, then settled himself once more on the floor beside Kian's bed, and Isolde drew out a wooden stool. Another mark, she thought, of the depth of Kian's exhaustion that he didn't object. But the first day was always the worst, when men like Kian dreamed themselves back into the blood and killing of battle or the terror of capture. Isolde always sat by them, to wake them if they groaned or cried out in sleep, as she had with Con.

She took up a bunch of dried lavender whose small dusky purple buds were ready to be picked free of their stems and sat down, thinking of Con laughing with Myrddin five years before. And when he'd done, the shadowed, haunted look had ebbed from Con's eyes and somehow into Myrddin's, as though the old man had taken his boy-king's blood-soaked memories for his own.

But Myrddin's magic—if magic it had been—was as beyond her powers now as then. She couldn't blot out Kian's memories or drain them off into her own mind, any more than she could restore his eye. She could only heal his wounds as best she might—and try to keep him from reliving the agony of them in nightmare while he rested here.

For a long while after Isolde had sat down, neither of them spoke, the silence of the workroom broken only by the soft rustle of the dried leaves as she worked, and by Kian's slow, slightly rasping breaths. She knew, though, by the rhythm of those breaths that he wasn't yet asleep.

At last he said, "He'd have gone north, likely, when he left Tintagel."

"Trystan?"

Kian nodded. "Signed on with whoever would pay the most for fighting men. And the chiefs in the Pritani lands are always on the lookout for swords to add to their war bands. That's what I'd have done, in his place."

"Then he'll be far out of reach of Marche or any of his men."

Kian shifted on the bench. "Aye. He'd be well away. Unless he's less sense than I credit him for."

Isolde forced herself not to ask the obvious question, but Kian answered it all the same, his thin mouth hardening in brief satisfaction. "And no. Them that did this"—he gestured to his eye—"know nothing but what they might have before. I didn't give them anything."

"I'm sure that's true." Isolde dropped a handful of the tiny dried lavender buds into a stitched linen bag, sending out a breath of spicy, flower-scented air. Then she looked up and asked, suddenly, "What about Madoc—does he know that Trystan is Marche's son?"

Kian was silent so long before replying that she thought he'd at last fallen asleep after all. But then, slowly, he shook his head and said, "He doesn't. Not so far as I know, at least—and I reckon he'd have said something if he did."

"You didn't tell him, though?"

Kian let out his breath, then shook his head again. "No, he's heard no word of it from me." Kian's eye opened, and he stared up at the ceiling. "I'll tell you, I lived outlaw with Trystan for three years. Fought at his side and at his back more times than I can say. Never swore him an oath, mind. And I left five months ago, to pledge my service to Lord Madoc. Drank his ale and kissed the blade of his sword and made him the death vow and all. So maybe I was wrong not to tell him the whole when he asked what the bastards who captured us wanted to know. But—"

Kian stopped and lay without speaking a time, pain-bleared gaze still fixed on the ceiling above. "Well, Trystan and I were guarding each other's backs before ever I laid eyes on Madoc, that's all."

Isolde watched him shift himself, wince, and then shift again, as though trying to find a position of ease. She said, "I suppose it's no good my asking whether you couldn't get Lord Madoc to grant you a month's leave from fighting duty? No, all right. I know—I might as well try to teach you to embroider in colored wool. It would likely be easier."

Kian's laugh was a harsh breath of mirth, no more, but it was a laugh. Then he turned his head, his battered face softening slightly as he looked at her and gave her hand an awkward pat with his big, calloused one, his voice turning gruff once again. "Don't mind for me, lass," he said. "I've been a sight closer to death than I am now. I'm not that easy to kill."

• • •

'NIGHT HAD FALLEN WHEN ISOLDE AT last stood again outside Marcia's sickroom, her hands and the skirts of her gown still smelling faintly of the lavender blossoms she'd picked from their stems. Kian had slept, woken to take a meal of bread and cheese, and slept again, dreaming only at the last, when he'd muttered in his sleep and come awake with a ragged shout.

Isolde had offered to let him stay on the workroom's bench through the night, but he'd shaken his head and heaved himself to his feet, saying he'd need of outside air. He'd gone, now, to walk the stone ramparts and then take his rest as he could with the other men, on pallets thrown on the floor of the fortress's fire hall. Isolde had watched him make his way along the passage and out of sight with slow, dragging steps and had felt again a clutch of cold fear on his behalf for what he faced.

Though at least Cabal was with him. The dog had wakened with Kian and come to butt his head against Kian's side until Kian said that he'd take Cabal out as well. And Isolde couldn't, she knew, have kept him back without wounding his fiercely hoarded pride. She could only tell him to come to her if the pain grew too great for him to bear and let him go, limping slightly, one hand resting on Cabal's neck as the big dog trotted along at his side.

Marcia was asleep when Isolde entered the sickroom, lying still beneath the blankets in the great carved bed, her fever-flushed face faintly yellowed by the light of the candle on the side table. Garwen, too, had slept, nodding in a chair by the hearth, though she came awake at Isolde's entrance and sat up, starting to rise.

"No, it's all right. Don't get up." Isolde crossed first to the bed to lay a hand on Marcia's brow. Still burning hot and dry, without a trace of relieving sweat. Marcia stirred, slightly, at the touch, a shadow of pain crossing her sleeping face, but didn't wake, and Isolde took a place on the low wooden settle beside Garwen's chair. "Thank you for staying with her."

Garwen waved the thanks away. Despite all the gold rings, her hands moved deftly, rolling up the drop spindle and woolen thread that had fallen from her lap as she slept.

"I'm always happy to be of use for a time."

A tray with the remains of an evening meal lay on the table beside the bed: a bowl of what looked to have been broth and a half-eaten round of bread.

"Did she eat, then?" Isolde asked.

"She did." Garwen tucked the spinning into a basket by her side. "Told me to go away and leave her be first, of course. Said she didn't want any broth or bread or food of any kind." Isolde could hear in Garwen's voice the echo of Marcia's sharp, fretful tones.

Garwen looked up, an unaccustomed gleam of humor appearing in the faded blue eyes. "I told her what she might be wanting and what she was going to have were two different things, and she was going to drink the broth if I had to hold her mouth open and pour it in."

Then she stopped, a shadow crossing her face as she looked back towards the bed. "Poor child," she said again. "Not her fault if she was born with a nature to curdle cream and a face to match. Can she live, do you think?"

Isolde thought of the noxious trickle of brown that had begun to mix with the discharge of pus and blood from Marcia's womb. She shook her head. "No. She punctured the bowl, as well as the walls of the womb when she rid herself of the child. I doubt she'll last longer than a few days more."

Garwen sighed but nodded. "I thought so, from the look of her. Still—"

Her eyes were on Marcia's face, but her look altered, somehow, as though the knot of pain inside her had briefly slipped beyond her control. "Maybe it's for the best. It's not as though, is it, she'll leave anyone behind to be crying for her when she's gone, poor girl." She paused, then added, as though she spoke more to herself than to Isolde, "And it's lucky you are, isn't it, if you lose a child before they're grown enough to break your heart."

Strangely, just for a moment, Isolde could see a faint glimmer in the older woman's face of the beauty she had once been, and she thought of Garwen's lost son. Amhar, dead by his father's hand, because he'd joined Modred, her own father, in his doomed rebellion against the High King.

"I'm sorry," she said. "I remember your son Amhar. He was a brave fighter—and a good man."

Almost at once, the flicker both of bitterness and youth in Garwen's look was gone, leaving her simply a plump, middle-aged woman once more, with a lifetime's wealth in looted Saxon gold about her neck and with a half-embarrassed faith in protective charms.

Garwen's eyes clouded behind a mist of tears, but she shook her head. "Thank you, my dear. But . . . don't be sorry. The gods—God, I mean—knows women have enough to bear without taking the blame for men's warring and killing ways as well. And it's a long time ago now."

She was silent, and then her eyes lifted to meet Isolde's. "It's a hurt that never stops bleeding, though, does it? Lose a child, and it's—"

Isolde saw for a moment a tiny grave outside the church yard in Cornwall where Con, too, now lay buried, remembered standing beside it and feeling as though she'd ripped off a piece of her own heart and buried it under the rocky soil. "A broken place inside you that will never be whole," she said.

Garwen watched her, then nodded as though in confirmation, making the gold pins in her sparse gray hair spark in the firelight. "I thought you'd be another that had lost a babe. You've the look of it in your eyes."

ISOLDE OPENED THE WINDOW SHUTTERS AND stood looking out over the fortress courtyard, just as she had in the hour of dawn. The night now was moonless, the sky foggy and gray with luminous clouds, but the courtyard below was lighted by torches set into the walls above gateways and doors. She could see the sentries on the timbered walk atop the outer palisade, their shields painted with the gold lion of Gwynedd. Dinas Emrys was one of Madoc's own holdings, defended whether he himself was present or no by a force of his men.

Isolde turned away to see that Marcia was awake, her head turning restlessly against the pillow, eyes fever-bright and a hectic flush on her cheeks.

"Do you want something to make you sleep?"

Marcia shook her head, lips pressed tight. "No. Nothing. I won't take it if you try."

"Then I won't try," Isolde said peaceably. Instead, she poured water into a cup and held it to Marcia's lips.

The other girl let out an involuntary sigh as the cool water touched her mouth, and she drained the cup before pushing it away. Then she turned her head, looking across towards the window where Isolde had stood a short while before. She was silent a moment, then, "You've never asked me who the father really was."

Isolde set the cup down on the bedside table. "Would you have told me if I had?"

"No."

"Well, then."

Marcia turned her head restlessly, thin fingers still twisting together. "He doesn't know, either." She was silent, dark gaze focused inward, then burst out, her voice suddenly harsh, "He doesn't deserve to know. I might have told him. I might have been glad to carry the child, if—"

"If?" Isolde repeated.

But Marcia shook her head, pressing her lips tight together once again. "Nothing. And it doesn't matter. The child's dead."

She stopped. Her voice was still bitter, but there was a glistening of tears in the close-set dark eyes, and a raw edge of pain in her tone. She stared straight ahead, gaze suddenly bleak. "The child's dead," she said again.

Isolde watched her a moment, then touched Marcia's shoulder and said, "I'm truly sorry."

Marcia went rigid, but then her shoulders slumped and she started to cry, silently, the tears rolling slowly down her face. She choked them back, though, pulling away from Isolde's touch, and sat staring down at her nervously clasped and twisting hands.

"It . . . wasn't for you," she muttered, her voice so low that Isolde only just caught the words. "The curse doll." Marcia's head lifted and she met Isolde's eyes. "It wasn't for you. It was for—"

She stopped, and though Isolde waited for her to go on, the other girl only shook her head. After a moment, though, Marcia shifted in bed and asked, "Is it true you're to go with Lord Madoc to Ynys Mon?" And then, when Isolde nodded, Marcia was silent once more.

"Don't trust them." Marcia's head lifted abruptly, and her hand came out and gripped Isolde's arm.

Marcia's grasp felt like the clutch of a bird's claws on Isolde's skin, hot and dry and sharply hard.

"Who do you mean?" Isolde asked.

"The men of the council. Don't trust them—any of them." Marcia's throat contracted as she swallowed, and when she went on, her voice was a whisper, thready and light. "There was treason among them before. And there'll be treason again. No," she added, as Isolde started to speak. "Don't ask. Don't ask me any more. Just . . . be careful. That's all."

Marcia let go her grip on Isolde's arm and sank back, turning her face to the wall. Then, just as abruptly, she turned her head and looked up at Isolde once again.

"I'm going to die, aren't I?" Her hands were clenched tight on the edge of the blanket, and she said, before Isolde could reply, "Don't lie—I can see in your face it's true. I'm going to die. And be damned for killing the child."

Isolde started to reach towards the other girl, then stopped herself. Marcia would only view touch as an insult or added gall. "I think," she said instead, "that God or anyone else would think you've suffered enough."

Chapter Three

THE BANQUETING HALL WAS LIT by pine torches set in brackets along the walls, the fragrance of the resin sharp in the air. Madoc's fortress at Caer Gybi on the isle of Ynys Mon was newly built; the timbered walls of the great banqueting hall were still unseasoned by years, though they were hung with tapestries and the trophies of war—Saxon war helms and double-headed axes, feathered spear shafts and polished swords, even a Roman gladius, the blade dulled with time.

Nothing, Isolde thought, to show that this had once been a holy place. Whether crushed by Rome or only by time, the gods of Ynys Mon were gone. Not even their echoes now remained.

She wondered whether it was that empty void where there should have been a lingering shadowy remnant, at least, that had made her certain from the moment she'd stepped into the hall that this meeting was doomed to fail. Or whether it was only the dark, brooding presence of King Goram of Ireland that cast such a pall of futility over every word spoken here thus far.

Isolde took a swallow of sweet honey wine from the cup

before her, her gaze on the man who sat at the far end of the hall's high table. Time, she thought, had been unkind to the Irish king. She would scarcely have recognized King Goram as the man she'd seen more than ten years before.

All those at the high table wore richly formal dress; Isolde herself wore a gown of deep crimson color, the neck and sleeves embroidered with gold thread, and her hair was caught up in a gold net seeded with pearls. King Goram of Ireland wore a tunic heavy with gold braid, the sleeves and collar trimmed with ermine, and a silver wolf-skin cloak was pinned to one shoulder with a ruby brooch as big as a child's fist. Once vigorous and well built, though, his body now looked bloated, heavy, and flabby beneath the costly clothes, and rolls of fat spilled over the thick golden torque at his throat. Streaks of white now showed in his hair, and his face, too, looked ravaged, the skin puffy and shot with broken veins, the dark eyes all but lost in pockets of flesh.

And yet, Isolde thought, anyone in his presence would feel the force of the man, the iron-hard will beneath the ruined frame. Madoc was speaking to him, and though Goram was sprawled with seeming indolence in his place, eating of the platter of roasted boar, his gaze was keen and shrewd, never wavering from Madoc's face.

A black-haired harper sat on a wooden stool beside the high table, his carved-wood instrument resting on his knee, and Isolde, listening, tried to fix her thoughts on the scene around her and to blot out the chill of the dream that had come to her the night before. Tried to block out, too, the memory of what the waters had shown her in the hour before dawn—though she'd needed the knowledge that vision had brought, before setting out with Madoc and the rest of the party on the day's long ride through the forests and the journey across water to Ynys Mon.

The harper's song soared high above the mingled men's voices into the raftered ceiling overhead, and for a moment Isolde did forget all else in a sudden, aching memory of Myrddin. Though this man was almost as unlike the old, white-haired druid she had known as could be imagined.

Taliesin was both brother and bard to King Dywel of Logres, who now sat at the high table on Goram's other side. But where Dywel was a big, darkly handsome, square-jawed man, with streaks of white at the temples of his tightly curling black hair, Taliesin was sleekly plump in his fine cream-colored wool tunic and breeches, with an oiled dark beard and a full-cheeked face. A face, Isolde thought, that ought to have been good-humored but was somehow marred by the twist of his mouth and the look of sullen, smoldering bitterness about his dark eyes.

Strangely, though, his voice was very clear and true, and the plump hands moved over the strings of his instrument like twin birds, with incredible speed and grace.

Who clears the stone-place of the mountain?
What the place in which the setting of the sun lies?
Who has sought peace without fear seven times?
Who names the waterfalls?

The song and the noise from the lower hall were enough to cover the voices of the men, so that Isolde could only guess at what Madoc was saying to the Irish king, but she saw Madoc pause as though waiting for an answer from the other man. Goram was silent, working at a scrap of gristle from between his teeth with the point of his knife. He was still slouched back in his chair, but Isolde, watching his face, thought that the look in his black eyes spoke of a mind behind the seeming indolence of his pose—a mind that was calculating his every move with deliberate effect.

The Irish king raised a hand and barked out an order to one of the slaves behind him, taking a deep draft from the drinking horn the man refilled before sitting back in his chair and fixing his gaze on Madoc once more to make reply.

King Goram had brought with him to Ynys Mon some forty

of his own spearmen, who now took up the benches at the lower end of the hall along with Madoc's own guardsmen and the war bands of the two men who sat, after Dywel of Logres, on King Goram's other side.

Cynlas of Rhos was a big, hatchet-faced man of fifty or thereabout, broadly built and tall, the weathered skin of his face beginning to loosen over the bluntly prominent bones, his ox-blood-colored hair and mustache just threaded with gray. He'd brought with him his son, Bedwyr, and a younger mirror of his father—though Bedwyr's fiery hair was perhaps a shade lighter, and his nose had been broken and inexpertly set.

Both father and son looked angry. Cynlas sat immobile with his arms folded across his chest, while Bedwyr shifted restlessly in his seat, turning his wine cup over and over in his hands, eyes darting this way and that. Bedwyr's chin was thrust out, his face belligerent, making him look somehow younger than his eighteen or nineteen years. Even from the far end of the table, Isolde could feel the tension seeping from both men, though whether the anger was for Goram or for Madoc she couldn't say. Cynlas had lost tracts of land—good land—to Madoc in a series of border skirmishes, had his cattle raided, his men slaughtered, and his settlements burned. As had Madoc, of course, by Cynlas's spearmen.

But then, Isolde thought, watching Cynlas's grimly set face, *Cynlas has been shamed by defeat, and Madoc has won the place of High King. Bitter gall to be forced to sit at table with Madoc, then, drinking his ale and eating his meat*—however great the need for alliance might be.

The tension also seemed to have spilled over into the lower part of the hall, where the guardsmen of the kings at table sat on wooden benches, eating and drinking mead. They were all but silent, with none of the shouting or laughter usual in a banqueting hall, and sharply divided, Madoc's men on one side of the room, Cynlas's on another, with Goram's own war band ranged on benches to the rear of the hall.

Isolde, watching the men eyeing each other across the central hearth, thought that the atmosphere of the great hall felt like hot glass, ready to crack and shatter into violence at any time. Already two of the men—one of Cynlas's and one of Madoc's—had exchanged a series of insults that escalated into a brawl. The two combatants had had to be pulled apart by their fellows from where they'd been locked together and pummeling each other with fists, because the evening had begun with the heaping of all arms in a pile outside the doors, token that this was a meeting of peace.

Now the harper's song came to an end, so that Isolde caught Goram's final words.

"—say of Marche and Octa may be true. But what is it to me? You—you yourself, Lord Madoc—have watered the very earth beneath this hall with the blood of my finest warriors. So I ask you, why should I care whether Marche and Octa together burn your settlements or take your wives for their whores, save that it leaves fewer cattle—and fewer women—for my men to seize by raid?"

Isolde saw Madoc's jaw harden as though he were clamping his teeth down on the reply he might have made. A mark, she thought, of how much Madoc had changed in the time he'd served as High King. Five months ago, he would have fisted the Irishman in the mouth for a speech of that kind.

Cynlas, though, made a quick, convulsive movement, his hand moving to where the hilt of his sword would have been, had he not removed the blade and laid it in the pile of weaponry outside the hall door with the rest of the men. The movement was not lost on Goram. The Irish king turned in place with an almost serpentlike speed that was surprising in one of his bulk. Then he stopped, the veiled black gaze flicking indifferently over Cynlas before he spoke.

"Ah, yes. Cynlas of Rhos," he said. "And his son." The Irish king's gaze moved to Bedwyr at his father's side, and he paused. Then, "You had, though, another son once, I think? I would be careful, my Lord of Rhos, in your place."

For a moment, Cynlas was utterly still, then he half rose from his seat. His face had gone bloodless to the lips, leaving his skin mottled with red and white.

"You—" he began hoarsely.

Dywel of Logres, beside him, laid a warning hand on Cynlas's arm. "No. Not worth it."

Dywel was a tall, strongly built man, with a square, slightly blunt-featured, handsome face, dark eyes, and a ready, if slightly vacant, smile. A big, simple, good-tempered man, slow to anger, who cut his food into tiny pieces and spoke with a slight lisping awkwardness because most of his teeth had been lost to battle or age. And yet Isolde remembered Con telling her stories of how in setting foot on the battlefield, Dywel was transformed, like one of the skin-walker warriors in the ancient tales, who shifted shape to take on animal form.

She herself had set the broken arm of one of Dywel's fighting men after the fighting last year in Gwent. The man had been wounded by Dywel himself, because in the heat of battle, his vision clouded by the red warrior's mist, he scarcely knew friend from foe. But then, she thought, Dywel is a king without a land. The kingdom of Logres had been lost to the Saxons in the years after Camlann, leaving Dywel with nothing to lose in a fight save his own life.

Now Cynlas jerked at Dywel's touch, then turned and stared at the other man as though he'd forgotten Dywel's existence. Then, "You think I—" he began.

The exchange had caught the attention of the lower part of the hall; Isolde saw the men of Cynlas's war band turn to watch their lord and begin to mutter angrily amongst themselves. And for a moment, she felt a now-familiar, almost physical revulsion for everything about the banqueting hall. The acrid smoke of the fire, the scent of sweat and unwashed bodies and roasted meat and ale from the drinking horns.

And for men who, Briton or Irish or Saxon, knew only one thing, so it seemed. How to fight, to kill, to hurt—how to carve one another up into bloody, aching pieces—and then send the fragments home to be either buried or stitched together as best their women could.

"I think you will sit down, my lord Cynlas." Madoc, too, had risen from his place and now broke in before Cynlas could finish, biting off each word. "And unless what you're about to say is an apology to Lord Goram, I think you keep still."

There was a long moment's pause, while the eyes of the two men locked. Then, slowly, Cynlas sank back into his chair, and Madoc turned to King Goram, though he raised his voice enough that it would carry to every corner of the now silent hall.

"You ask, my lord Goram, what the threat from Octa and Marche has to do with you, across the sea. But the sea between Ireland and Britain is not wide." Madoc paused, then added evenly, "You of all men know this well."

Isolde thought a half reluctant flicker of humor appeared in the Irishman's small black gaze at that, but he kept silent, and after a moment Madoc went on.

"If war parties can cross from Ireland to Britain, they can also cross the other way. And—" Madoc stopped. "And as I have likewise already explained, Britain is willing to offer payment for the services of whatever spearmen you send."

Madoc's scarred face was set as he spoke the final words, and Isolde knew what the humiliation of that offering cost him. He went on, though, after only the briefest of pauses. "I and the men of my council agree that a tenth share in the levies collected in each of our lands will be paid you for every hundred count of men."

Goram raked his fingers through his graying beard and grunted. "Send a thousand men, then, and I'll take the whole of what you bring in."

Madoc gave him another level look, then inclined his head. "Just as you say."

Goram was silent for the space of several beats, then he said slowly, "A weighty decision. With your permission, my lord Madoc, I will seek the will of the gods in this."

Madoc seemed to hesitate, but there was little he could do but give his assent. He jerked his head again in brief agreement, and King Goram turned to where Isolde now saw an old man in the robes of a druid had come to stand at his side.

"Hywell. What do your gods say? If I should send my spearmen to fight Octa and Marche, would it be victory or defeat they would meet?"

The druid was a small man, his back stooped and crooked with age, his face like a living skull, yellowed flesh clinging to his bones above a stringy gray beard. He wore a filthy, tattered druid's robe, the white color gone gray with dirt and age, and his grizzled hair was greasy, tied in a multitude of tiny braids. He had been staring at the floor, thin shoulders hunched, lips moving silently as though in meditation or prayer. At Goram's question, though, Hywell started and raised his head, darting what Isolde thought was a nervous, half-cringing look at the Irish king. He was silent, then bowed, first to King Goram, then to the hall at large.

Then Hywell turned to the curtained doorway at the back of banqueting hall, calling out an order. And—Isolde stiffened, registering the sound—from somewhere behind the curtains came the frightened bleating of a sheep or goat.

IT WAS A GOAT. THE ANIMAL was dragged in by a boy as ragged and filthy as Hywell himself. A brown-and-white kid with soft brown eyes and a slender neck. Hauling on the rope about the goat's neck, the boy pulled the animal to where Hywell stood before them in the open space between the high table and the lower hall. But the druid didn't even glance at either the goat or the boy.

Hywell's clawlike hands were upraised, his bearded face turned up, his eyes closed, and his lips moving once more as though in silent prayer. Then, slowly, he began to spin, first in one direction, then the other, slowly, at first, then ever faster, until his matted hair and beard flew out, his tattered robes becoming a single whirling blur. He screamed, once, a high, piercing shriek that ran up Isolde's spine—for all she doubted very much that Hywell could have read the will of the gods if it had boomed in a voice like thunder through the hall.

And then, abruptly, Hywell stopped, staggered, steadied himself, and drew from some inner fold of his robe a bronze-bladed knife.

He gestured again, and the boy dragged on the rope once more, drawing another frightened bleat from the goat as it was forced to its knees. Hywell lifted the knife, and murmured a few words in the old tongue, eyes on the animal before him and a dribble of spittle at the corner of his mouth.

Isolde, watching, realized that she was far more distressed than she would have been if the exchange between King Goram and Cynlas of Rhos had ended in a fight with swords. Likely, she thought, that was a terrible reflection on her as a healer, but true all the same.

She looked down, staring at her own clenched hands, but she couldn't block out the sound. The dull thud as Hywell's knife thrust struck home, the goat's frightened, piteous bleats as it lurched to and fro across the floor in its death throes. Isolde's nails were biting hard into the palms of her hands, her knuckles white, before at last, after a final, bleating moan, silence fell on hall.

When she looked, she saw that the goat had collapsed near the far wall, slender legs splayed, and that already Hywell was crouched beside the body, his hands wet and red to the wrists as he spread the entrails apart.

"The signs are plain." Hywell rose to his feet, wiping his bloodied hands on his robes and turning back to the room at large. "My lords. Marche and his troops are preparing to attack from the north. A mighty force." He turned, rheumy eyes fixed on Goram, cracked, dry voice thinning in the open space of the great hall. "My lord Goram. You must not send troops to

Britain's aid. A fight against Marche will reap only death and defeat."

For a long moment after the druid had finished, no one moved, no one spoke. And then a murmuring buzz went round the hall as the men of either party began to stir, darting uneasy glances this way and that, exchanging angry mutters.

Isolde, sitting with her hands still clenched on a fold of her gown, hadn't intended to speak out. But then she happened to glance at King Goram, his eyes dark with a satisfied, complacent look as he surveyed the hall and the blood-smeared body of the goat.

"Then the gods are wrong," she said.

Isolde saw the heads of the men on the lower benches turn in her direction, saw Hywell himself stiffen, a flicker that might have been either anger or fear crossing his skull-like face. Goram, though, too, had turned and was eyeing her up and down, a look of speculative calculation as his dark gaze.

"I have heard of the Lady Isolde, granddaughter to Morgan, the enchantress of Avalon," he said at last. "You, then, are the Briton Witch?"

Isolde saw the pit his question opened at her feet and asked herself why—after a lifetime of sitting through occasions of this kind—why in the name of all Arthur's companions she couldn't have kept her temper one night more. She was still angry, though. Both for the killing of the goat—and for the memory of Marche's daughter—and because she was supposed to be considering the gain she might win for Britain by marrying this man. She returned Goram's gaze. "Perhaps I am. You, then, are the Irish Tyrant?"

She saw several of Goram's guardsmen stiffen on their lower benches, and for a moment Goram himself was utterly still. Then, abruptly, he threw back his head and gave a great, booming laugh, his whole body shaking beneath the silver wolf's pelt cloak.

"The Irish Tyrant," he repeated. "Perhaps I am." Then he stopped and eyed Isolde again, keen dark gaze fixed on her face as he leaned back once more in his chair. "So, then, Lady Witch, what do you say? Do you promise me a victory if I send my spearmen to battle against Octa and Marche?"

"No. I never promise endings."

Goram stroked his beard. "It seems, then, that your powers of foretelling are of less use than Hywell's."

"Perhaps."

"And yet you tell me that Hywell's gods are wrong?"

Isolde willed the memory of her last night's dream and the morning's water vision away. If it crept over her now, she'd not be able to match King Goram's even tone.

She lifted one shoulder. "Either that or that Hywell was mistaken about the signs. It must be difficult to read the future in a goat's intestines."

Out of the corner of her gaze, she saw the old druid make a quick, spasmodic movement, then stop at a quelling look from King Goram. She thought amusement flickered once more in the Irishman's eyes, though his brows rose, and he lifted his drinking horn to his lips, still watching her face.

"You speak as though you were certain."

"I am."

Goram was silent a beat, his gaze narrowed, then he said abruptly, "You were wedded to Marche, so they say."

"I was."

"And is that, then, why you can guess"—Goram's voice laid slight emphasis on the word—"at his next move?"

Isolde saw again the trap he'd laid at her feet. But if she'd come to this moment by losing her temper, she could at least now refuse to be drawn. She lifted one shoulder again. "Perhaps."

For a long moment, Goram's eyes met hers, and then he shook his head. "You've spirit, at any rate. Enough that I'm almost sorry to refuse what you and your party request. But not enough to change my mind." He shifted again, transferring his gaze from Isolde to where Madoc sat at his side. "My regrets, my lord Madoc. But my answer is no."

. . .

HE'D DISLOCATED THE FIRST AND MIDDLE fingers of his right hand; it was obvious once the swelling started to go down. He'd done it before—though it had been only one finger that time. He'd pulled the bones back into place himself then as well.

He wasn't looking forward to repeating the process, but his options were limited. Either do it himself or—what? Ask Isolde, if he actually managed to talk his way past whatever guard was posted?

Night had closed in around him; the air was chill, pale moonlight slanting through the thick canopy of branches overhead. Trystan tipped his head against the tree trunk at his back and tried to think what the cursed hell he would say if he did get inside the fortress gates. If he actually did see and speak to her again. The thought was part like a swallow of raw spirits, part like a wound torn raw.

Trystan looked down again at his hand and let out his breath. Might as well get it over with.

The pain made bright specks of fire dance before his eyes and sweat break out on his brow, but he got the first bone back into place. He set his teeth, then took hold of the second one.

That was harder, but at last he felt the finger joint slip back into place, and the pain was better after that. A kind of blunt pounding that spread upwards along his arm. He wiped the sweat from his eyes, broke a couple of loose sticks apart for splints, then sliced a strip off the hem of his traveling cloak to use for a bandage. He finished wrapping the injured fingers, then had to hold the end in his teeth so that he could tie it off with his free hand.

He lifted the bandaged hand before his face; there was just moonlight enough to survey his own handiwork. Isolde would have done a far neater job, but it would hold.

Trystan stared out into the deepening shadows as the figure that walked in and out of his dreams night after night rose before him. A girl, small and slight and fine-boned, with raven black hair and milk-pale skin and widely spaced gray eyes.

Christ's blood, he thought. You sound like some bloody harper's song. And one of the less inspired ones, at that.

An outlaw and a Saxon mercenary—to use the least tainted of the words he might have called himself by now—and the Lady Isolde of Camelerd. It was—what was the word he wanted? Laughably futile?

He stretched his legs out and leaned back, closing his eyes. The ground was hard and damp beneath him, but he'd slept in far worse spots. That was his life, the life of a man who lived as mercenary and outlaw both. You fought for whoever would offer the highest pay, kept on the move, never allowed yourself to sleep deeply or long unless you wanted to wake with a knife at your throat—or in your heart.

Tonight, though, even the half-waking doze he trained himself to maintain at will eluded him, and he found himself instead staring up at the scraps of night sky visible through the leaves and thinking of Isolde, seeing her face still in his mind's eye.

Against his will, he imagined the shadow girl's gray eyes widening at the sight of him, saw her running towards him, throwing her arms around his neck, and laughing the way she had when she was a child.

Trystan muttered a disgusted oath. Yes, right. And Arthur might wake from the dead and come charging out of the hills to fight Saxons again. Trystan shook his head. He should have stuck to pulling dislocated finger joints back into place. That had been a walk on a summer's day by comparison to the realization that he was going to have to see her—speak to her—again soon. And not tell her he'd been in love with her all their lives.

An owl's soft, mournful call from somewhere in the trees nearby made him stiffen, then relax, though from long habit he kept his hand on the hilt of the sword at his belt and scanned the surrounding darkness for any sign that he was not alone.

Trystan shifted again, tracing the pattern of moonlight-silvered branches above and trying to remember a time when he hadn't felt this way about her. They'd known each other practically since they could walk, so he supposed there must have been one. But as far back as he could recall, it was just there, like his right hand or arm.

He let out his breath. "And may the gods help you and all fools too stupid enough to know a hopeless cause."

Somewhere off in the darkness to his right, a voice spoke. "May I be of some assistance, friend?"

Trystan jerked upright, wondering whether he was losing his mind. He'd never yet encountered a god who answered a cynically muttered invocation with a polite cough and offer of aid. But he supposed there was always a first time.

"EASY, YOU BLASTED BEAST!"

Kian's horse, a brown, raw-boned gelding, had drawn up sharply at the sound of a bird's call in the trees overhead, snorting and tossing its head and dancing in place. Kian jerked hard on the reins, and the horse subsided with a final shake of its head. Then, wiping the rain from his eyes with the back of his hand, Kian glanced at Isolde, mounted beside him on her own black mare.

"Bloody creature. Suppose that's what comes of being an infantryman. Never feel right on anything with four legs."

They had departed Caer Gybi at dawn, together with Madoc, Dywel, Cynlas, and all the rest of their combined war bands, crossing back from Ynys Mon to the mainland in the shore ferrymen's round curricles. Madoc had left horses under guard on the mainland shore two days before, and riding they had crossed the shifting sand dunes and the shimmering salt flats where small rivers emptied into the sea. Isolde had looked back, just once, across the glittering silver-blue water towards the shore of Ynys Mon. The tide had been on the ebb, the stretch of rocky shingle and sand along the coast a ribbon of yellow beneath the green plain of land that had once been—but was no longer—the site of the druids' oak groves and sacred pools.

Now they were out of sight of the holy isle. They had crossed a wooded valley and come far enough that the deep green-blue expanse of sea could no longer be seen, far enough that the air no longer held a faint mud and salt tang. Ahead of Isolde, a long line of mounted men threaded a way through the winding forest track that led back to Dinas Emrys. The men—soldiers and councilmen alike—were squinting to see through the misting rain that drifted through the dense canopy of spring leaves above.

Kian, Isolde thought, watching him, had recovered far better and more cleanly than she could even have allowed herself to hope. Isolde had seen little of him in the days he had spent at Dinas Emrys before the meeting on Ynys Mon. Kian had kept to himself, appearing only briefly in her workroom when the dressings on his lost eye needed to be changed, his face gaunt and set tight. And if he still relived the loss in nightmare, he never spoke of it to Isolde.

But when Madoc had offered him the choice of remaining at Dinas Emrys, Kian had refused, insisting he was well enough to ride. And now, riding beside Isolde, though he held himself still a little stiffly, the bruises on his face were fading to yellow and green, his single eye alert as he turned his head, scanning the path on either side before urging his horse on.

The gelding, though, refused to move, nervously shifting and stamping in place, ears twitching.

"What—" Kian began. And then, from up ahead, Isolde heard a high-pitched whine and then a solid, meaty thud, saw one of the men before her topple back in his saddle, hands clawing at the shaft of an arrow lodged in his throat. Before she could react, before she had even time to be afraid, a long, drawn-out howl sounded from somewhere in the trees to her right, and men erupted onto the path.

"Down!"

In an instant, Kian had dismounted, dragged Isolde from her

saddle, and handed her both the reins of her own mount and his, even as he drew the sword from his belt.

"Stay back!"

And then he was gone, plunging ahead to where men had charged from the trees, swinging swords and great double-bladed axes in whistling arcs. Saxon foot soldiers, wearing dirty gray wolf pelts over leather war gear, matted flaxen hair loose on their shoulders as they charged.

The path was suddenly filled with the clash of swords, with terrified screams of the horses and shouts and grunts and angry cries as the line of mounted men turned to meet the Saxons' attack. She saw Kian square and settle his shoulders, sword at the ready, before launching himself into the fight, and even in the midst of fear, Isolde felt a burst of astonishment at the breathtaking, self-sacrificing, fearless stupidity of his entering battle in his current condition.

But then, she thought, Kian would almost certainly as soon fall on his sword as stand back from a fight. And nor could she have held him back—not without offering his pride an insult he'd never forgive.

Her heart beating hard, Isolde dragged the horses backwards, away from where the fighting was going on. From around the animals' broad backs, she could catch glimpses of the battle: Madoc, his scarred face set, exchanging ringing sword blows with two of the attacking men. Cynlas and Bedwyr, fighting back to back, swords flashing as three or four of the Saxons circled them and delivered vicious, hacking blows with their own axe blades.

All at once, one of the attackers was before her, sword upraised. Time seemed to hang suspended, as, for an endless, heartstopping moment, the Saxon man's eyes, clear and pale as winter ice, held Isolde's, and his muscles bunched, preparing to strike. And then seemingly from nowhere a great brown-and-white war hound launched itself at the Saxon man, knocking him off balance so that he lurched and took a staggering step to the side.

Cabal stood between Isolde and the attacker, head lowered and front legs spread wide, the fur on his neck bristling and his teeth bared in a growl. The Saxon man shouted and raised his sword again, and Isolde's breath froze as she waited for the whistling blade to come down on Cabal's neck. But the blow never landed. A sword point burst through the Saxon's stomach, parting the leather of his war shirt in a bubbling spurt of crimson, and he toppled to the ground.

Behind him, Kian set a foot on the man's back, bracing himself to pull his blade free. His chest was heaving, his scarred face streaked with blood from a cut above the brow.

He caught hold of Isolde's arm. "Are you all right?"

Isolde stood frozen, staring down at the body before them, her blood drumming in her ears as the waves of shock rippled through her from head to foot. Cabal was beside her, whining, butting his head against her hand, and she put a hand on the big dog's back. Then she shook her head, eyes still on the dead Saxon at their feet. "I'm not hurt." And then to Cabal, "It's all right. Good fellow, Cabal. Good dog."

Kian wiped sweat from his eyes with the back of his hand, then said, "We've three men down. Two dead, but one could do with a healer's care."

Isolde looked up. Her vision seemed dizzyingly bright, each separate detail of the woods around them piercing her gaze like shards of ice. But the fight was over. Three or four more of the attacking Saxons lay dead at the edges of the path. One man—the closest—lay faceup, an arrow in his bloodied throat and his braided blond hair spread out on the ground. One of the horses, too, was down, lying in a pool of blood from its cut throat. Isolde could hear distant crashing in the underbrush, as the rest of the attackers fled—doubtless pursued by whichever of the men Madoc had given the command to hunt them down.

Madoc himself was kneeling in the churned, muddy earth a little distance up ahead, beside the body of another man. Seeing Isolde, he jerked his head, motioning for her to come. She approached, Cabal padding along at her side. Seeing them, Madoc shook his head, some of the grim lines etched into his face momentarily loosening their hold.

"Why I bother giving that hound orders I don't know. He was off towards you like an arrow from a bow the moment the fighting began."

Isolde rested her hand on Cabal's neck, then said to him again, "Good dog, Cabal. Go and lie down now."

Cabal moved to obey, and Isolde turned back to the group about the wounded man. Cynlas of Rhos, too, hung over the prostrate body, his chest still heaving with the recent fight, and only when he moved slightly aside to let her through did she recognize the man on the ground. Bedwyr, Cynlas's son.

"Still alive," Madoc said briefly as Isolde kilted her skirts and dropped to her knees beside him. "And the only one of the wounded to be so."

Isolde nodded. Bedwyr's hair was wet with sweat, his eyes clenched tight and his lips drawn back in a grimace of pain. Isolde's heart was still racing, her whole body turning cold as the sweat on her ribs prickled and dried, but she started to take stock of the wounded man's injuries. Her hands were shaking, though, and she had to close her eyes, force herself to draw two or three deep breaths, then begin again.

He'd taken a wound in his upper arm; Isolde could see the muscle and sinew laid open, nearly to the bone. Someone— Madoc or Cynlas—had tied a roughly torn length of cloth just above the wound, slowing the bleeding. Even still, though, the blood was coming in bright crimson spurts with every beat of Bedwyr's heart.

"Lady." Bedwyr's voice was a whispering gasp, and Isolde looked up to find his eyes, pain-filled and pleading, fixed on hers. Both the restless energy and belligerence were gone, and he looked simply young and terrified. His chest heaved as he fought for breath. "Lady. Don't let me die. Please. Don't let me die."

And then a spasm shook him, making him arch his back and

groan through clenched teeth. "Hurts. Oh, God." The muscles of his neck stood out like cords.

"I know." Isolde scarcely knew Bedwyr. But she had sat this way beside countless men like him, these last seven years. "I know it hurts. Here." She slipped her hand into his on the uninjured side. "Take my hand. Squeeze as hard as the pain grips you."

Bedwyr's eyes closed again, and his fingers, sticky with blood and dirt, closed over hers, hard enough to grind the bones together. Isolde scarcely noticed, though, as she turned back to finish taking stock of the wounded man's hurts. The arm could be cauterized. And if the cut doesn't turn to poison, Isolde thought, he might even survive. Though he would likely never raise a sword again. But the rest—

Her gaze moved to the pair of feathered arrow shafts that protruded from the middle of his tunic. One bolt had caught him in the pit of his belly and penetrated deeply, leaving only perhaps a hand's breadth of wood visible above the surrounding blood-soaked leather tunic. The other had struck him higher, penetrating the cage of his ribs.

Another spasm shook Bedwyr, his heels digging into the muddied ground, his fingers clenching hard on Isolde's once again. His breath came in short, whistling gasps, his lips were faintly tinged with blue, and when Isolde felt for his pulse, it was thready and fast like the frantic beating wings of a bird. Isolde thought, I could cauterize the wound in his arm. I could even pull the arrows free—though I'd need the help of at least one of the other men. And Bedwyr, she thought, would still die.

He might not die today. Nor yet even the next. But she'd seen injuries like these too many times before not to know the inevitable end. Bedwyr would linger in slow, ever-increasing agony as the wounds festered and bled inside him and his breath grew shorter and ever harder to draw.

"Can you do anything for him?" It was Madoc who spoke.

Isolde took her hand away from the hectic pulse in the wounded man's neck. For the space of several of Bedwyr's harsh, whistling breaths, she watched the rise and fall of his chest. Then, without speaking, she drew her own knife from the girdle of her gown, slid the blade under the length of cloth above the arm wound, and with a rending tear, cut the strip of fabric free. Cynlas made a quick, jerky movement, then stopped. He was a soldier, Isolde thought, as well as a king. He'd have seen arrow wounds like this one before, would know the inevitable end as well as she.

Isolde sheathed the knife, then reached to take Bedwyr's hand again, smoothing the russet hair back from his brow. "Squeeze my hand as hard when it hurts. It will be better soon. I promise."

Chapter Four

"Oᴜʀ ғᴀᴛʜᴇʀ, ᴛʜᴀᴛ ᴀʀᴛ ɪɴ heaven, hallowed be Thy name."
Madoc's voice sounded harsh with weariness, cutting across
the damp forest stillness and the soft trills of birdsong from the
trees overhead.

Madoc had ordered them wait for the return of the guardsmen he had sent in pursuit of the fleeing Saxons before moving
on, though he had posted his men in a defensive ring, on guard
for fresh attack. And now, surrounded by Cynlas and a handful
of his men, his face still spattered with blood from the recent
fight, Madoc was praying over Bedwyr's lifeless body.

Isolde sat on a fallen log a little distance away down the
path, trying to focus on Madoc's words, though she kept hearing
Bedwyr's voice instead. *Lady, please. Don't let me die.*

She glanced up to see that Kian had come to stand beside her.
He was silent a moment, watching her, and then asked, "Did you
know him?"

"No." Isolde shook her head. "I don't think I'd even spoken to
him before today."

Kian nodded. "A good death."

"A good death?" Isolde could smell, still, the stench of

Bedwyr's bowels breaking at the moment of death, could still feel in her own mind the echo of Bedwyr's pain. She managed to choke back the words that rose to her lips, though, and instead drew in her breath. "Are you all right?" she asked.

"Me? Oh, aye. I'm well enough." Kian lowered himself with a grunt onto the log beside her and rubbed his sword arm. "Stiff, of course, but aren't we all?"

He drew from his scrip one of the little wooden carvings he worked at in moments of rest. A thrush this time, Isolde saw, plump body balanced on fragile, delicate legs, small head cocked as though listening.

Kian pulled the knife from his belt, then started to work at the feathers of the thrush's tail, the carving balanced against one knee—though she saw he also lifted his head from time to time, scanning the trees around them for any sign of alarm, and he kept his sword out, laid ready on the ground by his side.

The way of the world, Isolde thought, with a brief twist of bitterness, or maybe just the way of men, that a bloody ambush and sword fight to the death can do more to heal Kian than any skill or power of mine.

Still, watching him chisel at the thrush carving, Isolde felt some of the bitterness ebb away. His hands were steady, the line of his mouth relaxed. And this was the first she'd seen him take out his carving since his return to Dinas Emrys with Madoc, four days since.

Kian was a warrior, first and last. And knowing that he could still fight, one-eyed or no, would of course have done much to banish the lingering ghosts of torture from his mind.

Isolde was silent a time, watching the shavings of wood drift down to form a little pile at Kian's feet, and then she asked, "Do you think it was only chance the Saxon party happened upon us when they did?"

"Just a stray war band? Out scouting and happened to see our campfire's light?" Kian looked up, rubbing his chin with the back of his hand. "Could be, I suppose."

"But you don't think it was?"

Kian shook his head, for the moment letting the knife rest idly against his knee. "Doesn't feel right. Besides, war bands don't do their scouting at night—not without they've good cause." He paused, then bent to flick another tiny sliver of wood from the thrush's tail. "We were lucky to get away with only three men down. Likely lost a lot more, but for the drink."

"Drink?" Isolde repeated.

Kian gave a snort and nodded. "Christ, yes. Could smell the ale on 'em from forty paces away." He paused and tucked his chin, staring down at the ground as though searching for words before glancing up at Isolde. "Takes a lot for a man to attack an enemy he knows is armed, you understand," he said at last. "No matter how many times he's done it before."

He shifted position, his gaze suddenly distant as he stared into the spring-green trees. "I remember my first battle—first time I saw a shield wall of Saxons standing there across a field. Screaming curses. Beating those drums of theirs. I was standing there, sweating like a hog and praying like I'd never prayed in my life. That if God just got me through this, I'd take the cowl and become a monk. That I'd never take His name in vain again as long as I lived."

Kian paused and glanced at her again, one corner of his mouth twisting in a crooked smile. "There's few that don't believe in God before a battle. And even fewer that do believe in Him after the fighting's done. Still—" He shook his head. "Thought I'd die before I took a single step towards the Saxons."

It was almost the longest speech Isolde had ever heard Kian make in all the five months she'd known him. "And what did you do?" she asked.

Kian's shoulder jerked in a shrug and he took up his knife again. "Knew if I turned tail and ran I'd only be cut down from behind. And I thought, Well, if I'm to die, I'd rather know who killed me. So I charged. Fought. Lived through it to see another battle, another day, and another year."

He was silent, thumb moving idly along the blade of his

knife, his face remote once more. "You'd think it'd get easier—but it doesn't. It's the same for every battle—every time. There's that moment just before when you'd give anything you've got to be able to turn around and run like hell."

Kian shook his head. "So you get yourself stinking drunk, if you can. Nothing like ale to make a man feel—well, if not like God Himself, at least like His first cousin once removed." He laughed shortly. "And if you can stay drunk enough after the battle's over, you've a chance of keeping the nightmares away."

They were both quiet, listening to the murmur of voices from up ahead. Madoc's prayer was ended, and they were checking the horses, preparing to move on. Isolde thought of Marcia—Marcia, who would almost certainly be dead as well by the time they returned to Dinas Emrys. *There was treason before,* Marcia had said. *And there'll be treason again.*

"And you think this was an ambush and not just a chance attack?" Isolde asked.

Kian was silent again, squinting down at the tip of the thrush's wing, then he shrugged again, his single eye meeting Isolde's. "Could be I'm wrong. And come to that, I hope I am, because I don't like the look of things if it's true. But that's what I'd have said. Someone knew what day and which direction we'd be taking back from Ynys Mon."

TRYSTAN STRETCHED OUT ON THE THICK carpet of fallen leaves beneath an oak tree, his back propped against the gnarled trunk. Not as comfortable a bed as the old hermit—a white-haired Christian holy man, not a god—had offered him the night before. But since he'd tried to kill the poor bloody fellow, he couldn't in all conscience have stayed.

Trystan grimaced, recalling how he'd come awake to find that the man he'd got by the throat was not one of his Saxon captors but his host, plump, elderly, and gasping with terror. The old man had been almost comically relieved when Trystan took himself off.

Trystan closed his eyes. Satan's hairy ass. All he had to do was let himself think about Isolde and that time, and the nightmares started up again.

Which was, after all, why he'd left five months before. His mind might be a bloody charnel pit with the memory of all he'd seen and done. But he could live with himself, more or less. If he got through each day as it came, allowed neither past nor future to creep in. Seeing Isolde again, though . . . knowing why he wasn't even worth her spitting on—

Trystan looked down at the mutilated fingers of his left hand. He ought to be a goddamned expert at getting through torture by now.

Come to that, it had been torture to leave as well. At least he'd known Kian would be with her. Kian, who, the gods be thanked for his straightforward soldier's disposition, had honestly believed it his own idea that he should pledge himself to Madoc and so stay near Isolde.

Trystan allowed himself an hour or so's half-waking doze, then dragged himself to his feet. His eyes felt gritty with tiredness. But if he hadn't slept, at least the old hermit had offered him a salve and clean bandages for the cut in his side, and the fever seemed to be gone. And apart from that, he felt all right. Well enough to go on. Which was lucky, because it wasn't as though he had a choice.

He nearly tripped over the thing lying in his path before he'd seen it. A wolf-skin cloak. Matted blond hair. Bloodied war axe lying alongside. The hilt of a dagger sticking up from his chest.

All about, the ground was churned and muddied, and as his eyes swept the path ahead, he picked out another body sprawled under a tree on the opposite side. Must have been a fight here.

He shook his head. *Brilliant. A dead Saxon with a dagger in his heart, and you conclude there must have been a fight. Maybe that fever isn't gone after all.*

•   •   •

ISOLDE STEPPED FROM THE OUTER COURTYARD into the chapel, balancing in her arms a basin of water and a bundle of clean linen rags. The chapel at Dinas Emrys was cool and silent, though the courtyard outside was alive with the shouts of men as the added guards Madoc had posted scrambled to their posts. Twilight was falling, and the candles in the wall torches were lighted, casting a flickering light over the narrow room—and over the man's lifeless body that lay on a table before the high altar, roughly shrouded in a gray traveling cloak.

Isolde set the water basin down, soaked one of the rags, and began to make Bedwyr ready for burial, wiping the dirt and blood away from his white marble face. This, too, she had done many times before.

They had reached Dinas Emrys without further attack, though the nerves of all had remained on edge throughout the long ride, and as soon as he'd swung himself down from the saddle, Madoc had ordered scouting parties out to cover the surrounding countryside and be sure all was secure.

Now Madoc stood a little distance away with King Dywel of Logres, Cynlas of Rhos standing between the other two.

"Are you certain you want your son buried here, and not on your own lands?" Madoc asked.

Isolde had seen a sheen of moisture come into Cynlas's eyes hours ago on the forest track as he looked down at the body of his son, but his face now, though streaked with the dirt of travel, was still and hard and almost as lifeless as that of his son.

"When a warrior dies, you bury him and walk away. My son would care little for where his grave lies." Cynlas was silent, his gaze fixed straight ahead. Then he turned to Madoc and said, with sudden violence, "What I can't understand is why you continue to trust *her*."

Isolde's hands went still, and then she looked up to see Cynlas's gaze fixed on her. His face was still all but immobile, though oddly that only made his fury more keenly felt, as though a caged wild beast looked out from behind the frighteningly blank eyes.

Beside him, Dywel put a restraining hand on Cynlas's shoulder and spoke with the slightly awkward, toothless lisp. "My lord Cynlath. This is hardly the time—"

His voice was quiet, and Isolde thought how strange it was that again Dywel's should be the voice of peace. She'd seen his face in the forest as he fought the Saxon attackers with the rest, and had known that what Con had told her had been true. Dywel fought like a man possessed of demons, his handsome face so distorted by rage as to be all but unknowable, save for the head of tightly curling coal-black hair.

Now, though, it was Cynlas's mouth that contorted in a spasm of anger, and he shook off the other man's hand.

"Yes, you." Cynlas's voice had a harsh, metallic edge, and his hands were balled into fists as he took a step nearer Isolde. "You were wedded to Marche, as King Goram said. You knew where Marche was. How do we know you're not a traitor? Sent here by Marche to betray us all?"

Isolde, standing beside the body of Cynlas's son, with the touch of his lifeless flesh still at her fingertips, found she couldn't resent Cynlas's suspicion—or even be angry at his tone. Though she was suddenly aware of just how tired she was, her every muscle stiff and aching from the long day's ride. It seemed a lifetime ago that she'd sat in the ferryman's round coracle and felt the salt breeze on her face as they crossed the sea back from Ynys Mon.

"You're quite right," she said to Cynlas. "You have no reason to trust me—none. And if you believe I'm a traitor, I know there's little I can say that will change your mind. But I can promise you that if Marche had known I'd be one of the party riding back from Ynys Mon—if he'd had any part of the attack today—I'd be lying here, dead, next to your son. And that I can't possibly say how much I wish I could have saved Bedwyr's life."

For a long moment, Cynlas's eyes held hers. And then, without warning, the grim immobility of his face shattered, twisted in a spasm of pain, and he sank down on one of the chapel's wooden benches, his head buried in his hands.

Both Madoc and Dywel stood looking down at the other man as his shoulders shook. Dywel shifted his weight from one foot to the other, hands clasped behind him, as though he were wishing himself anywhere but here, and after a moment he said, his voice sounding slightly embarrassed, "Always better for a man to theek vengeance than to grieve."

Madoc's eyes, though, were grave and pitying, and Isolde could see him hesitate as though wondering whether Cynlas would only take a word or gesture from him as an insult.

But before Madoc could either move or speak, Cynlas had drawn himself stiffly upright, dragging a hand across his red-rimmed eyes and drawing a ragged breath.

"I beg pardon, Lady Isolde." He spoke stiffly, and with an attempt at dignity that might have been pathetic in a man less self-assured, but his gaze was very direct. "You gave my son a quick death, and a clean one—the kind of death every man hopes to meet. And you eased his passing. I am in your debt."

Isolde's face must have mirrored her shock at the words, for Cynlas said, almost fiercely, "You didn't think I'd believe, did you?"

"No," Isolde said. "I didn't."

Cynlas jerked his chin in confirmation. Beneath the shock of russet hair, his face was still fiercely controlled, but his voice, when he spoke, was low and rough with feeling. "You said, Lady Isolde, that you couldn't say how much you wish you could have saved my son's life. But you needed no words—the look on your face as you spoke told me clearly enough."

He passed a hand across his face again, and Isolde saw a long, jagged scratch on his wrist that had trailed dried blood onto his sleeve. "I've a reputation for temper, I know—and well deserved it is, as I'd be the first to say. I don't suffer fools—I don't coddle weakness. And I don't"—his jaw hardened, and Isolde thought he gave the briefest flicker of a look in Madoc's direction—"forgive those who have crossed me or done me a wrong." Cynlas paused, then let out his breath, his eyes again fixed on Isolde's. "But I'd make a poor king, Lady Isolde, did I not recognize the truth when it hits me in the face—or looks out at me from a woman's eyes."

Almost, Isolde would have wished he'd stayed angry. Suspicion was somehow easier to bear than trust just now. She felt a lump come into her throat, but she let Cynlas take her hand, and said, "Thank you, my lord Cynlas."

She remembered all Bedwyr's restless, belligerent energy at the feast on Ynys Mon. And she could still hear the echo of his voice. *Lady . . . don't let me die.* And do all fighting men actually believe they hope for such a death, she thought, or is that only a bed tale to comfort children when they cry?

The words almost choked her, but she made herself say, "If you think that I made Bedwyr's death easier, then I'm glad."

And then she turned, taking up the wet rag once again and rubbing the blood and dirt gently from Bedwyr's hands and arms. The three men stood in silence for a time, and then Madoc cleared his throat, turning to Cynlas again. "I know this is a poor time for such a question, but I must know. What did Goram mean when he spoke of your having lost another son?"

Glancing up, Isolde saw a tide of color sweep up Cynlas's neck then ebb away, leaving his face starkly pale against the russet hair, and for a moment she thought he would refuse to speak. But then he let out his breath, something of the stiff, immobile mask creeping once more over his face.

"It was three years ago—nearly four, now." Cynlas looked down at his hands resting on his knees. The knuckles of the right hand were grazed, and he rubbed at them absently before going on.

"Goram and his men had been raiding the settlements along our shores. Small surprise, there." Cynlas's mouth thinned. "Every spring brings more of the sea wolves to our shores. We try to guard the coast—but we've not forces enough to cover the whole. And they strike fast—sail into shore their boats. By the time we've got troops there, a whole settlement's burned to the ground. The men slaughtered like so many sheep. The women and children taken in fetters to be sold as slaves."

Cynlas paused. "My son—my eldest son, Gethin—insisted we'd only put a halt to the raids if we moved to the attack instead of constant defense. Carried the fight onto Goram's shores. And to carry out the campaign, he contracted with a band of mercenaries—masterless men for hire to the highest pay. I was against it. An allegiance bought is an allegiance just as easily sold to someone with a fatter purse. But Gethin was bent on his own way. He engaged the services of the band I speak of. Wild men. Mongrels and half-breeds. Saxons—Britons—men of Ireland and Gaul. Their leader—"

Cynlas stopped again, his eyes moving once more to the body of his second son, his jaw tightening, as though he forced himself to speak the words through his clenched teeth. "Their leader was such a one. Saxon to look at, though his speech was that of a man Briton-born. He said he could guide our ships to Goram's shores. That he knew Goram's country—knew what Goram's defenses would be." Cynlas's mouth stretched again, and he gave a short, mirthless bark of laughter. "He was telling the truth there, at least.

"We arrived in Ireland. Made camp on the crest of a hill. A good position for battle, as my son's mercenaries pointed out. We pitched our tents and posted a guard just as the sun was going down."

Cynlas broke off once more and was silent so long that Dywel asked, "And then?"

Cynlas looked up. "And then?" he repeated. He gave another short, harsh laugh. "And then we woke the next morning to find the mercenary dogs decamped in the night and gone. And Goram's army massed at the foot of the hill. The whole campaign was a fool's trap—and we'd walked straight in. Been sold out by men who change allegiance as other men change their whores."

Cynlas's eyes were still fixed on Bedwyr's body but had

darkened as though, lost in memory, he scarcely saw even his dead son. "Nothing to be done but fight. We charged—and it was a slaughter. Two hundred and more of our men were killed. A hundred more taken captive—Gethin was one of those. I called a retreat—drew back to the crest of the hill. Sent a messenger to Goram, offering to ransom my son and the others of my men he held. That was at sundown. All that night we waited—watched the Irish campfires and waited for Goram to respond. And at dawn we got our answer. Goram had built a gallows in the no-man's-land between our two camps."

Cynlas stopped. Isolde saw his hands clench again, but his voice, when he went on, was flat and all but expressionless. "He hung my messenger first. Then the men-at-arms. He kept my son for last. The gallows was some distance away. But I knew Gethin by the color of his hair. Red. Like my own."

For a long moment after Cynlas ceased speaking, the chapel was silent, the only sound the men's voices and the occasional bark of a war hound from the courtyard outside. Then Madoc cleared his throat. "I'm sorry," he said. "If I'd known, I would never have asked you to join the delegation to Goram."

Cynlas's face quivered briefly, then hardened once more. "What Goram did was war. Men are taken, men die. It's the way battles are waged. But the mercenary dog who betrayed us—"

Cynlas paused, then said, in the same flat tone, "Him I would know again. And one day I will find him and pay him for the deaths of both my sons and my men."

And then he straightened his shoulders and turned to Madoc, his weathered face still granite hard, though his eyes were fixed and bright once more. "The deaths of both my sons must have a purpose, my lord Madoc." His tone made the words almost a threat. "Otherwise they are not to be borne."

Chapter Five

ISOLDE STOOD A MOMENT, LOOKING down at Bedwyr's face, and thought as she often had before that any claim of death resembling sleep was another bed tale for children. Bedwyr's face was peaceful, all trace of pain smoothed away by death's hand, but she would never have mistaken him for a man asleep. She had finished here, though. The young man's body was washed and dressed in clean breeches and an ermine-trimmed tunic and shrouded in a long white cloak. Ready for burial.

She had thought the silent chapel empty, save for Bedwyr and herself, but as she turned to go, she saw a man seated on one of the benches at the far rear of the room, his face in shadow. She was too tired for either fear or surprise, only took up the basin and bundle of dirtied rags and started down the chapel's central aisle. Night had fallen, and the chapel was lighted by the wall candles alone, but as Isolde moved towards the door, he rose and she recognized his form.

"My lord Madoc. I thought you'd gone with King Cynlas."

Madoc made her a brief bow, then fell into step beside her. "I had. He abruptly remembered, though, why I was about the last man at Dinas Emrys he would have chosen to share his grief, so I returned. And besides, he's best on his own just now."

Madoc remained silent as they stepped from the chapel into the outside courtyard. The fortress' main gates lighted by a pair of burning resin torches, and the night sky was gray and luminous with rain clouds. Here and there, along the looming bulk of the outer ramparts, a helmeted sentry stood alert, spear and shield at the ready, staring out into the night.

"I wanted to speak with you in private, Lady Isolde. If you would."

"Of course." Isolde was too tired as well to wonder about what Madoc might wish to say. But even so, his first words took her by surprise.

"Do you believe, Lady Isolde, in a life after this one?"

Isolde raised a hand and rubbed the aching muscles at the nape of her neck. "You waited in the chapel all this while to ask me that?" Then she stopped. She could still see Bedwyr's lifeless face every time she closed her eyes. "I've just come from preparing a man's body for burial. And if you ask me whether I felt anything of his presence—whether I felt anything was left of Bedwyr but a kind of empty husk—I'd have to say no. But then—"

Isolde paused again, her gaze on the luminous sky above. "Sometimes I've felt as though . . . as though the world were an endlessly spinning wheel that sometimes—just rarely—stops and rests on a balance. So I don't know. Maybe that is a god— or someone else beyond the veil to the Otherworld—thinking about me?"

Madoc looked at her curiously and then said, "Do you have faith in the gods, Lady Isolde?"

Isolde was silent a moment before answering. But this was, after all, why she made herself see Marche in the scrying waters time after time. Because she wanted to believe herself meant to use the power of seeing Marche for Britain's defense. Because she would rather believe that there was a purpose in the Sight's having flooded back to her now.

She looked up at Madoc and said, "Hope, maybe, if not quite faith." The silence rested between them a beat, and then she said, "Why do you ask me, though? You believe in the Christian God already. And doesn't your holy book promise heaven to all believers?"

"So it does." Madoc's broad-set shoulders jerked impatiently.

They were passing beneath a pair of wall-mounted torches, and by their flickering orange light Isolde saw the bleakness carved into Madoc's scarred face. "The Bible also says, *Thou shalt not kill*. And in such times as these, that sometimes seems to me about as much use as telling a man to take a piss into a strong wind."

He pushed a hand through his wiry dark hair, his mouth twisting in a quick, mirthless smile. "You know, I thought of taking the cowl and becoming a monk when my wife died three years ago. Instead—"

He broke off, and then said with a brief, bitter laugh. "King Arthur's the lucky one. Eternally riding out at twilight to wreak vengeance on his enemies. While the rest of us poor mortal fools are left to battle amidst the wreckage he left behind."

Isolde thought as she had once before of the Old Ones, who had built their own timber halls in this place long before—and had killed a king by the triple death every seven years, so that his blood might water the earth and renew the land. Maybe, she thought, watching Madoc's scarred face, not so much has changed since that time after all.

Then Madoc shook his head as though throwing off the thought. "But to answer your question, no. I didn't wait in the chapel just to drivel on about the fate of the dead. What I wished to speak to you about was the meeting on Ynys Mon."

They were passing the work buildings—the armorer's and smith's sheds, bake houses and weaving rooms, all dark and deserted at this hour of the night. Madoc gestured to a stone bench, sheltered by an overhang of thatched ramparts. "Will you sit?" he asked. "Or had you rather be inside, out of the rain?"

The rain had slowed to little more than a fine, light mist, and the air was warmer than it had been, with the earth-scented promise of spring. Isolde shook her head. "No, this will be fine." She sat down, drawing her cloak about her, and then looked up at Madoc. "I'm sorry for what I said—for losing my temper with King Goram and Hywell, I mean."

Madoc seated himself, leaning back against the wall behind them and shook his head. "Don't be. It would have made no difference what you said. My own guess is that Goram's mind was made up before ever he set foot on Ynys Mon."

In the time she'd known him, Isolde had seldom seen Madoc so much as smile, but now he gave a sudden laugh, sounding all at once younger and without the usual burden of cares. "Besides, I'll have to say I enjoyed seeing Goram and his old goat of a druid shown up for the liars they are." He shook his head. "The look on Hywell's face. I thought he'd dirty that disgusting robe of his."

Then Madoc sobered. "But no. That wasn't what I wanted to say, either." He paused and was silent a beat, then turned to Isolde. "King Goram sent me a messenger this morning—before we left Ynys Mon. Saying that he had reconsidered yesterday's refusal and naming the price of his allegiance."

"I see." Isolde was silent. "I don't suppose I need to ask what that price was."

"No."

Isolde waited until she could trust her voice enough to speak. "Is this, then, what you want from me?" she asked. "That since the council has ruled my marriage to Marche invalid, I now wed King Goram to secure an alliance?"

Instead of answering, Madoc watched her a moment and then said, his voice very quiet, "I am truly sorry, Lady Isolde, that you were ever forced into marriage to Marche."

There was genuine sorrow, genuine pity and understanding

in his black eyes. Isolde's muscles tensed, and she gritted her teeth, telling herself that Madoc didn't deserve to have her snap back that he should save his sympathy for when it was wanted or might do any good.

She might loathe being pitied almost as much as she hated to feel as though she was pitying herself. But Madoc had been unconscious, nearly dead of the burns that marked his face on the night she'd married Marche. She could hardly blame him for not having come to her aid.

So she said, quietly, "It was no fault of yours. And you saved my life afterwards, my lord Madoc. I've not forgotten that."

"Perhaps." She thought the pity was still there, darkening Madoc's gaze, but then he shook his head. "But in any case, I gave you my word, Lady Isolde, that I would not force you to marry against your own will." He stopped and sighed, rubbing a hand across the back of his neck. "Though if I'm honest, maybe I would ask it of you. Not gladly—but yes, if I had any faith that Goram would honor such a pact, I might beg you to put your own feelings about the match aside. But I wouldn't take Goram's word that his own breath reeked—much less believe him when he says he'll send his forces to our aid if only I hand over you and Camelerd first." Madoc laughed shortly. "It would be liking giving a wolf house-room in your hen yard. Let Goram take Camelerd for a toehold in Britain and he'll have his war parties raiding every part of the land within reach. But all the same—"

Madoc broke off and shook his head. "All the same, I must have a reason—a credible reason—for refusing the match. One that doesn't depend on my own unwillingness to trust Goram any farther than a child could throw a warrior's spear. Otherwise, the refusal will be taken as insult—one that would turn him from a neutral force to an enemy. And God knows, we've enough of those." Again the silence rested between them, and then Madoc went on, "I had thought, with your permission, to tell him that you were betrothed already. To me."

In the mist-filled shadows, Madoc was a little more than

a deeper shadow on the bench beside her, his outline broad-shouldered and tall. Isolde realized that she must have jerked back involuntarily, because before she could answer, he said, his voice both wry and, she thought, a little sad, "All right. You needn't tell me your initial response to the idea." He stopped and looked away from her a moment before asking, "Is it because of this?" His hand lifted, indicating the burn marks on his face, all but invisible, now, in the dark.

Isolde found herself touched by the gesture and the unex-pected vulnerability it betrayed. She said, quickly, "Of course not. You mistake me, my lord Madoc. I was . . . taken aback, that's all."

Something in the quality of Madoc's silence made Isolde think that he'd recognized more in her reaction than simple sur-prise. He said nothing, though, and after a moment, she went on, "But asking the council to accept me as your queen can only weaken your own position as High King. You saw yourself just now how quick Lord Cynlas's suspicions were to rouse."

"But still you won his trust."

"This time." Isolde remembered standing in the chapel with Cynlas and the body of his son, and half wishing that he might be angry with her still. Why? Because of Bedwyr? Or maybe be-cause after seven years of being suspected and doubted at every turn, it felt almost dangerous to think that she might sometimes be able to relax her guard?

"But I was High Queen once before, my lord Madoc," she went on. "From the time I was thirteen until five months ago when Constantine was killed. I know exactly the council's re-sponse—most will never be able to look at me without seeing my father, Britain's traitor, or remembering King Arthur, dead at Camlann."

Beside her on the bench, Madoc frowned, and then said, as though choosing his words with difficulty, "I know I myself said a number of ugly things, Lady Isolde. Made accusations against you. I'd hoped you might have . . . not forgotten. But forgiven them, perhaps."

Madoc's voice sounded so unhappy that Isolde felt a pang of compunction and said quickly, "I have forgiven them. And I'm grateful to you for your offer—more than I can say." She turned to look up into Madoc's face, his dark eyes just a gleam of reflected light. "But you're the High King—perhaps the only man who can ensure Britain survives beyond a few months more. I can't ask you to risk all that just for the sake of protecting me— you must see that. It was you the council chose High King when Marche turned traitor. And rightly so. Britain needs you."

"Britain needs me?" Madoc's voice was tinged with irony, and he shook his head. "Maybe. But I've stood at the graves of many other men who thought themselves invaluable to Britain, these last years. That's beside the point, though. You . . ." He passed a hand across the back of his neck, sounding suddenly younger once again. "I'm doing this badly. I—"

He broke off, as though searching for words. "I've few friends, Lady Isolde—fewer, since I took the throne as king. And it's a hard life—and a rough one—spending day after day caught up in battles and raiding parties and war. I'm accustomed to it by now. It's all I've known since I was old enough to raise a sword. But still, I've wished . . . what I mean is that it would be good to have . . . someone to come home to, after the battle was done." He stopped again, then said, in the same quiet tone, "I would be . . . very happy, Lady Isolde, if that could be you."

Isolde felt her mind go momentarily blank with the shock of the words. Because until now, she'd not have said that Madoc, at heart, either liked or trusted her any more than his councilmen. She could feel, though, in Madoc's words the ache of desperate loneliness and grief for the wife he'd lost in childbed, three years before. And she knew how much it must be costing him to lay bare his innermost self to her this way.

"I am . . . honored that you would ask this of me, my lord Madoc. Truly. I—"

She had to stop, because despite the compassion she felt for the man beside her, a sharp stab of panic pulled tight in her chest and made her want to jump up from the bench and get away—anywhere else but here. This was one of those times when she wished more than ever that it didn't hurt so much, now, to recall the words Trystan had spoken to her years before.

The stars will still shine tomorrow, whatever happens to me here.

Isolde said suddenly, "You never asked me how I could know Hywell and his gods were wrong about where Marche is now."

"No." It was too dark too see Madoc's expression, but she could hear the flicker of a smile in his words. "I'm learning, you see." And then, before Isolde could respond, he said, "You needn't . . . you don't have to give me an answer now. I can give you until morning—I can't send word back to Goram until then in any case. So just . . . think on it for tonight."

"SHE'S NOT LIKE TO WAKE AGAIN, is she?"

Isolde looked from Marcia's still, tallow-pale face to Garwen, sitting and spinning in her chair by the bed. She shook her head. "I doubt it, no." She looked down at Marcia again. The rise and fall of her breathing scarcely lifted the blankets that covered her chest, and her pocked, sharp-featured face was for once relaxed, lines of spite and anger and tension smoothed as though by some unseen hand. "At least she's beyond pain."

Garwen bowed her head in agreement, making the heavy jeweled ornaments in her ears flash in the firelight that was the only source of illumination in the room. The soft orange glow was kind to Garwen's face, as well, softening the marks of age and bringing her nearer that Isolde had yet seen to the lovely young woman she must have been years ago.

"Do you want me to sit with her awhile? If you want to rest—"

But Garwen shook her head, fingers still deftly fashioning a smooth, slender thread of pale cream-colored wool. "No, I will stay. Maybe I'll doze a bit here beside her. But I'll be here, whether she knows it or no." She looked up at Marcia. "Poor child. As you say, she's already passed beyond us. But no one should die alone."

For a moment, the only sound in the room was the hiss and crackle of the fire, and the soft whirr of Garwen's spindle. Then Garwen looked up at Isolde again and said, "I knew your mother, you know. Gwynefar."

After the long day's journey and Bedwyr's death, Isolde had been half drifting in a haze of fatigue, and Garwen's sudden words caught her completely off guard. She couldn't even think of any answer to make, and after a moment Garwen smiled. "You're very like your grandmother Morgan—I expect you've heard that before—but you've your mother's eyes."

Isolde found her voice. "I've heard that as well." She paused, uncertain whether to ask the next question—uncertain even whether she wanted to. But Garwen, as though reading her thoughts, smiled again. A slightly grim smile, this time, and quite unlike her usual one.

"If you are wondering how Arthur's mistress came to be acquainted with Arthur's wife, I can tell you that more than besides you have wondered as well. But Arthur was ever a man unable to see through but one pair of eyes—his own. And if it suited him to keep his whore and his lady under one roof, then he was not to be persuaded that it might not suit the rest of us as well as him."

For a moment, Garwen's voice sharpened almost into anger, but then she sighed, looking down at the spindle and thread lying idle now across her lap. "Though God help me and may God forgive me, I loved him well. Too well, perhaps. He was stubborn, he could be hard, even cruel, sometimes. But he was also—" Garwen broke off, pressing her lips tight together, her large, misty blue eyes glimmering with unshed tears. But then she blinked, shook her head, and focused her gaze again on Isolde. "You never knew your mother, did you?"

Isolde shook her head. "No. She fled into a convent and died there almost as soon as I was born. Arthur had returned to

Britain. She was afraid to face him, after what she'd done—that was the way my grandmother told it, at least."

"And you blamed her for it, perhaps?"

Isolde had been staring into the fire, but at that she looked up to find Garwen watching her, head tilted a bit to one side. Isolde shook her head. "No. I never blamed her."

Her mother had never been much more to her than a name in the bard's tales. Gwynefar of the white hands and golden hair. Beautiful queen or traitorous harlot, depending on the tale.

Isolde could still hear the suppressed contempt that had edged her grandmother's voice on the rare occasions when she'd persuaded Morgan to speak of her. But she'd always known, too, that beneath the contempt Morgan had nursed for all weakness, her grandmother had concealed a half-unwilling pity for Gwynefar.

Isolde watched a log flare red and then crumble to ash, sending out a shower of sparks over the hearth. She thought of herself, thirteen and left utterly alone after Camlann, sold into marriage with Con by the king's council for the sake of peace. Gwynefar had been scarcely any older when she'd been wedded to Arthur—a warrior nearly twice her age, instead of the good-hearted if awkward boy of twelve Con had been.

She thought, too, of herself on trial for witchcraft, after Con's death. Forced into marriage with Marche because it was that or die.

No, she couldn't blame her mother for any of the choices Gwynefar had made.

She looked up at Garwen. "I've heard some claim that Camlann would never have been fought if not for her. That Arthur would still be alive and Britain still whole. But I never believed it. Men fight because they choose to—not because of a woman's honor or the lack. And besides"—her mouth lifted in a small smile—"besides, if she'd not chosen to wed Modred, my father, I'd never have been born. How can I fault her?" She shook her head. "I used to wish, sometimes, that I'd had the chance to know her. Especially when I was small. I used to pretend that she'd not really died—that it was only a tale made up to keep her safe from Arthur. And that she'd come riding up on a white horse to see me one day. But I never blamed her or felt anything but pity for her for all that had happened."

There was a moment's silence, and then Garwen said quietly, "She used to pray every day for a child when I knew her. It was her greatest grief that she never bore Arthur an heir." Garwen's eyes turned distant, her face softening as she looked back across half a lifetime's worth of years. "But all the same, she was kind to me, always, even though I'd given Arthur the son she never could. She never slighted me—never made me feel she despised or resented me for what I was. And she loved Amhar, my boy. I can still see them playing together with a set of wooden horses one of Arthur's men had carved. She was very beautiful, Gwynefar. She had the loveliest smile and the most beautiful hair—like spun gold."

Garwen was silent a moment, gaze still faraway. Then she blinked again and turned back to Isolde. "Did Modred truly love her, do you know? Or was marrying her only a means to the throne?"

Slowly, Isolde shook her head. "I've wondered the same. But I've no idea. My father never spoke of her that I can remember. I suppose that might mean that he loved her very much—or not at all."

Garwen let out a breath and picked up her spindle and thread again. "Well, I have always hoped he did—I hope it still." The firelight gleamed on her gold necklaces, the heavy brooches and jewels. And just for a moment, she and all her finery looked not absurd at all, but regal, like the queen of one of those same impossible tales. "Everyone deserves to know that kind of love at least once in a lifetime."

Isolde blinked an unexpected press of tears from her eyes. She wasn't sure even who the tears were for. Garwen . . . Gwynefar . . . Marcia . . . Morgan. She'd be completely disgusted if she were crying like a child for herself. As though weeping ever made a road easier to walk or a burden easier to bear.

She felt her gaze drawn back towards Marcia's face, still and pale as the linen sheets on which she lay, already wandering half-way between this world and the next. And she thought of Bedwyr, dying a choking, blood-soaked death on a bed of dirt and dried leaves.

"Perhaps everyone does deserve it," she said softly. "But I think it's very rare anyone actually finds that kind of love. And getting to keep it must be rarer still."

AS IT HAPPENED, HE MADE IT over the outer wall without being spotted by any of the guards posted at intervals along the narrow walk. Nice, he supposed, to know that he'd not lost the skill—if inconvenient, in this case. He could hardly go crashing around the fortress for the rest of the night, hoping he'd eventually run into Isolde. Best get it over with, then.

He had to practically hit the three guards stationed at the main gate over the head to get their attention, then spend what seemed a short eternity answering their questions and cross-questions about the story he'd told. Finally, one of the men—a beefy man with a black mustache and beard—went to summon help, leaving his two fellow guards behind.

The men left behind were younger than the third. In the light of the torches above, they looked pink and scrubbed, with wispy, straggling beards, and they shifted uneasily from one foot to the next, keeping their spears directed at Trystan's chest. A nervous man being a greater danger than an angry one, Trystan was keeping still, and wouldn't have said he'd moved. But abruptly one of the guards glanced at Trystan's sword belt, then lunged forward, the tip of his spear jabbing over Trystan's heart.

"Don't try to draw your sword."

Trystan felt a trickle of blood start under his shirt and let out an exasperated breath. "Oh, for the love of a flaming goat. I had time to kill you both and do a dance on your graves before you noticed me getting over the wall. Even now I could probably slit one of your throats before the other one got me in the back. So do you want to draw lots, or can you just take me at my word and put the spear away?"

ISOLDE STEPPED OUT FROM THE NARROW stairwell out onto the ramparts. She had been exhausted enough to fall asleep almost as soon as she reached her own bed, but she'd woken sometime about the middle watch of the night and lain staring into her darkened room, unable to sleep again. And so she'd dressed by the light of the glowing embers of her fire, taken up her traveling cloak, and come up here.

The rain had stopped, and the night sky cleared to a deep, bottomless black, hung with a net of stars. The shapes of the surrounding mountains were just visible as hunched, craggy shapes, vast and looming, as though they'd indeed been the backs of slumbering dragons, as in the old tales.

Isolde walked to the parapet and looked out, letting the night breeze tug at her loosened hair. She'd told Madoc that she'd felt nothing of Bedwyr's spirit having survived death or crossed into a world Other than this—and that was true. But all the same, standing here alone in the darkness atop the mountain fortress, she could imagine she heard the voice of those who had gone before and were now west of the Sunset Isles, or wherever the land of the dead might lie.

The voice was not Myrddin's—neither the enchanter of the harper's tales whose eyes saw the future and whose spells could trap the wind in knots of cord. Nor even the white-haired druid man she had known. For her, at least, Dinas Emrys spoke in a voice that held the smooth, rippling cadence of a stream, bubbling up from deep within the earth and spoke of tales told, not by bards, but by women spinning wool or singing their children to sleep.

Tonight Dinas Emrys seemed more than ever a place of the Old Ones, who had on these hills raised ramparts long ago crumbled to earth. Who had carried bronze spears against the cold iron weapons of invaders who built in stone—and who had long, long since been driven away, to dwell as little more than a memory in the hollow hills.

The voice in her ears now seemed filled with those memories, a tale of loss and grief now long since vanished into the swirling mists of time. Though it might of course be, she thought, that *voice is inside me, and I'm only imagining its echo on the moun-tainsides.*

Isolde leaned against the stone parapet and remembered Cynlas, standing beside the body of his son, demanding of Madoc—and, she thought, of whatever presence might dwell in the chapel, too—that there be a purpose in his son's death. And then she turned her face upwards to the night sky and thought, one by one, of all those she'd watched torn away from life these last years.

Morgan, her dark hair turned white and her face all but un-recognizable, swollen with the black running sores of plague. Myrddin, lying in a pool of his own blood, his throat cut by Marche's guard. And Con, resting in his oaken coffin, gold coins weighting his eyes.

Isolde pressed her eyes shut. What had Madoc said? *I've seen eyes like yours—looking back at me from an enemy's face across the divide of a shield wall.*

She thought of Con at twelve, just after they'd been wedded, a tall, broad-shouldered boy with a shock of baby-fine brown hair, clear-eyed and brave and desperately afraid he'd prove un-worthy of his place as Arthur's heir. She could see him again, now, his face pale against the pillows, laughing up at Myrddin as she reset the stitches in the wound he'd carried back from his first battle. A wound that could easily have killed him if it had turned to poison. Or if it had been a hand's breadth closer to his heart.

From somewhere far below, Isolde caught the murmur of men's voices, carried to her on the clear, silent night air. Some of the sentries, maybe, breaking up the boredom of their watch by a drinking song or a game of dice. Isolde listened a moment, then turned away, sinking down so that her back rested against the stone parapet, drawing her feet up and hugging her knees.

She'd been thirteen when she'd been wedded to Con. Just after Britain had been broken on the battlefields of Camlann. When King Arthur had died at Modred's hand, a father slain by his own traitor son.

Did Modred truly love Gwynefar? Garwen had asked. She didn't know—likely never would know, now. And she wasn't sure whether to hope for her mother's sake that he had or no. But she had known that Con had loved her, in his way—for all he had a different plump, pretty maidservant in his bed for every turning of the moon.

She'd never let herself think of loving Con, though. By the time they'd been wedded, she'd had her heart shredded by grief so many times that she'd built a darkening wall in her mind to shut out both memory and pain. But then, even so, after he was dead and buried, the yawning ache inside her chest had told her that she must have loved him, after all. As a comrade and friend—and maybe as a younger brother, too—more than as a husband. But she'd loved him all the same.

Isolde opened her eyes, feeling her chest begin to tighten with the same panic she'd felt with Madoc on the stone bench below. The thought of being wedded to King Goram had made her skin crawl and brought a familiar sickness to the pit of her stomach. But in a way, the idea of marrying Madoc was worse. Because she'd felt nothing like love for Con when first they'd been wed. But even that had been no protection when he'd died. And Madoc was a good man—as Con had been.

In time, she thought, I might come to love Madoc as well.

And then she bowed her head as another memory broke over her and hung in the still night air like the silent echo after thunder. *A hurt that never stops bleeding*, Garwen had called losing a child. And even now, Isolde could see with aching clarity the tiny, waxen face and flowerlike hands of her stillborn baby girl. Could feel under her fingertips the swirling fuzz of hair on a fragile, rounded skull.

And she could feel, still, an echo of the pain that had racked her, fierce as the birthing pangs themselves that had seemed to tear her body in two. Another shiver shook her from head to foot. Just at that moment, she could understand the panic of a wolf who gnaws through his own leg to escape a hunter's snare.

There were the herbs, of course. The same ones she had used with Marche five months before. But they didn't always work. Marcia, Isolde thought, probably knew about those herbs, as well.

Isolde rested her forehead against her upraised knees and tried to stop the cold shaking inside her. She could always enter a convent, as her mother Gwynefar had. Plead devotion to the Christ as reason for rejecting Madoc and Goram both.

Isolde pressed her eyes more tightly shut. She might never have blamed Gwynefar for making the choice she had, for fleeing the world and leaving her baby daughter behind. But all the same, for her to likewise flee into the convent's sanctuary now was so patently the coward's choice that even thinking it made her sneer at herself.

Yes, she thought. You could enter a convent and be safe behind its solid stone walls. And Camelerd would be divided, carved up among the men of the king's council. Men who might rule well and justly—or might prove of the same ilk as Goram or Marche.

An image of the burned and plundered settlement rose before her mind's eye, and Isolde raised her head, staring unseeingly out at the night sky. I could enter a convent, she thought. And then someone else could explain to the people of Camelerd that their homes had been burned and their children enslaved and their villages pillaged because Isolde, the lady of Camelerd, didn't want to bear another child. Or love anyone, ever, ever again.

HOW LONG ISOLDE HAD BEEN SITTING there she didn't know, when a step close by made her start up with a jolting heart, straining her eyes to see into the shadows. She scrambled quickly to her feet, then relaxed as she recognized the bard Taliesin, brother to Dywel of Logres, who had played for the feasting on Ynys Mon. Beneath a dark cloak, Taliesin wore still the tunic and breeches of fine cream-colored wool, and the fabric seemed to glow pearly white in the moonlight. He walked with a limp, the left leg dragging slightly behind, and as he came closer, Isolde saw that his left foot was crippled, clubbed, and turned inwards, with a boot of fine dark leather crafted specially to fit.

He saw her and made a slight bow before limping slowly across the remaining distance between them to stand at her side. He was silent a moment, looking out over the parapet as Isolde had done, then turned.

"My lady Isolde. We have not met formally, I don't believe. I am Taliesin, brother and bard to King Dywel of Logres."

Isolde let him bow again over her hand, trying to gather her scattered wits into something like order, then said, "I enjoyed your playing on Ynys Mon greatly. You have a rare gift for song."

"A rare gift." There was a note of mockery in Taliesin's voice, and Isolde saw in his face the same smoldering bitterness she'd noticed before. He gestured with one soft, white hand to the crippled left foot. "I suppose you might put it that way. If I can't fight at my great ox of a brother's side, I can at least journey with him to battle and watch the killing and the rending of men into small bleeding bits. And then go home and turn it all into a song."

Isolde's glance moved to the heavy gold torque about Taliesin's neck, the small jeweled and gilded harp he wore strapped at his belt. She'd said nothing, but the bard was quick to see the look, and he gave a faintly grating laugh.

"Yes, you're quite right. It does pay well. My brother's warriors take care to pay me handsomely and to stay in my good graces if they want to be shown favorably in the songs I compose. How a man is remembered in this life is at least as important as what he actually does."

Taliesin turned his face upwards to the night sky, the moon running silver threads through his sleekly oiled beard. "So, Lady Isolde. What trouble brings you out in the darkest watch of the night to sit under the stars?"

Isolde heard again snatches of men's voices below, coming, she thought, from the direction of the fortress's eastern gate.

"No trouble," she answered at last. "I came to sit quiet for a time, that's all."

"And to be alone, no doubt." The faint note of mockery was audible in Taliesin's voice once more, but his eyes were steady on Isolde's face, with a grave, thoughtful look that belied the tone. He was silent a time, watching her, and Isolde shivered, feeling as though his cool, dark gaze were reading, weighing, and judging her on some private balance or scale all Taliesin's own.

Then the bard reached for the small gilded harp at his side. "And since I've intruded on you, I owe you a gift. A song. To atone for my presence here."

He swept out his cloak and knelt down, resting the instrument on his knee, raised his head once more to the sky, and began to play. The notes were soft, silvery clear in the night stillness, like drops of crystal rain. And then he opened his mouth and began to sing, his voice neither grating nor mocking, but sweet and soft and very true, the song seeming almost a part of the moonlight all around.

"In a time that once was, is now gone forever, and will come back again soon, a young maid's lover was stolen from her by the Fair Folk to pay their seven year's tiend to the gods of the earth."

Isolde leaned against the stone balustrade and let the words wash over her. The story was an old one, and one she knew, of a maid cast out by her father and mocked and scorned by all, for she was to bear her lover's child—but her lover was vanished, nowhere to be found.

But the maid's love for her man was strong and true. She would not believe him inconstant, and though it was autumn and winter's bitter chill coming on, she set out to search for him, across hills and wide valleys, the forests and fields. And whenever she doubted or grew so weary she thought she could not go on, she would feel the child's tiny flutter of life inside her. And she would take one step more.

At last, then, she caught sight of her love. He was sadly altered from the man she'd known. His face was blanched and thin, his clothes in tatters, and his hair wild and long. The maid knew him, though—knew him at once, despite the change in his look. And she threw her arms around him for joy of finding him alive.

But her arms slid through him as through the empty air. And her man stepped away and told her what had befallen him. That he had been made captive by the Fair Folk, a mortal sacrifice to pay the tiend to their gods at Samhain.

> *And pleasant is the fairy land,*
> *But, an eerie tale to tell,*
> *Aye, at the end of seven years,*
> *We pay a tiend to hell.*

And the maid wept to hear her love's tale. But then she dried her tears and said that she would save him, if such a thing might be. And her love sighed and said that there was a chance— just one. But that he could not ask it of her. It was too great a trial, too hard. But she begged him to tell her, with the tracks of tears still on her cheeks and her hands clasped over the child in her womb. And at last her man told her what she must do.

And so on the night of Samhain, when the veil between the Otherworld and this lifts, the maid watched the Fairy host ride past her along the road. She let pass a steed as black as night, and one brown as earth. And then came a man mounted on a steed as white as snow, and she knew him for her love and caught his hand to pull him down.

And all about her, the Fair Folk screamed in fury, but she held fast to her love, put her arms about him, and would not let go. And then, the man's form she held began to shift and change. His skin grew scaled and slimy, his body writhed, and she clasped a great, hissing, thrashing serpent in her arms, its fanged mouth opened wide.

And the maid's heart pounded in terror, but she repeated to herself what her man had told her, for he had known the magic of the Fair Folk and what they would do.

> "They'll turn me in your arms, lady,
> Into an esk and adder,
> But hold me fast, and fear me not,
> I am your babe's father."

And so she held the serpent fast. And again felt the form in her arms begin to change, until she held a great, snarling bear. The beast struck at her with its claws and roared with rage, and she could smell the blood of a kill on its mouth and fur. But again she held fast, and the bear's body began to shift and change.

And then the maid held in her arms a glowing, red-hot iron rod that burned her arms and hands until she almost screamed aloud with the pain. But she held in her heart the memory of her love's own face, the feeling of his true self held fast in her arms. And she would not let go.

And another great howl of rage went up from the Fair Folk,

so that a chill of fear ran up the maid's spine. But she could feel the burning iron rod in her arms shifting, changing again. And then it was her own man she held in her arms. And the Fair Folk were vanished, nowhere to be found. For she had won him free.

TALIESIN STOPPED PLAYING, AND FOR A moment, all was utterly still, not even a breath of wind stirring the night air. *Sometimes—just rarely,* Isolde had said to Madoc, *I've felt as though everything stops and rests on a balance. So maybe that is a god—or someone else beyond the veil to the Otherworld—thinking about me?*

"Thank you," she said. "That was—"

A cry from down below made her break off. A shout of alarm, coming, she thought, from somewhere along the fortress's outer palisade. When she looked back at Taliesin, she found him watching her again with the same measuring look—a look that made her feel as though his gaze lifted her up and then set her back down in not quite the same place she'd been before.

Isolde thought suddenly of Myrddin. Myrddin, who had never in his life worn gold rings like Taliesin's or been anything but bony-shouldered and thin—but who sang as Taliesin did and had walked with the dragging gate of lameness as well.

The moment seemed to stretch out between them. When at last Taliesin spoke, his voice, like the mountain itself, seemed to hold the chiming cadence of a stream flowing from deep underground.

"Yes," he said. "You should go."

THE FLARE OF TORCHES IN THE great courtyard was dazzling after the darkness atop the ramparts. Isolde stepped out from the stairwell, blinking at a knot of Madoc's guardsmen grouped near the main gate. She'd reached the courtyard almost at the same moment as Kian, who stepped from the shadows of the passage leading to the hall where the men ate and slept.

"Do you know what's happened?" Isolde asked him.

Kian's single eye was bloodshot, his hair rumpled, and his clothes and sword belt looked as though they'd been snatched up and flung on without care. He shook his head.

"No idea. Heard someone sound the horn for an alarm, that's all I—"

The rest of his words, though, were lost to Isolde. Her eyes had adjusted to the light, and she saw, amidst the group of Madoc's guards, another man. A man dressed in a plain linen shirt, breeches, and a forest-green traveling cloak instead of the blue and gold of Madoc's men.

He was tall and strongly built, his face lean and hard, with a thin, flexible mouth. His eyes were startlingly blue, set deep under slanted golden-brown brows. And he looked more impatient than either angry or afraid, despite the spears Madoc's guard held pointed at his chest. There was a line of annoyance between his brows, as of temper rigidly controlled, and Isolde thought he looked tightly strung, as if there were a task he had laid on himself to accomplish and now begrudged the men around him this delay.

For the space of several heartbeats, Isolde stood staring, frozen in place. Beside her, she heard Kian suck in his breath and say in a voice blank with shock, "Sweet bleeding Jesus."

And at the same moment Kian spoke, her own lips formed a name without any conscious thought. "Trystan."

Chapter Six

"THAT MAN—WHO IS HE?"

Isolde turned to find that Cynlas of Rhos had come up to stand beside her and was speaking to her, his voice urgent and hoarse. She felt as though a wall of water had crashed over her, temporarily blocking both hearing and sight. With an effort, Isolde kept her voice even and unconcerned. "A messenger from my own lands, my lord Cynlas. As he—and as I—said just now. And lucky to get through Marche and Octa's patrols on the borderlands. I've had no word of how Camelerd fares for some months, now."

She'd listened as Trystan told his story, his voice sounding distant and far off in her ears. And in the same distant way, she'd heard her own voice making appropriate responses, offering confirmation of the story Trystan told in response to Madoc's questions.

Madoc had listened, asked a question or two, and Trystan had answered easily enough—though Isolde had the impression he was exercising a deliberate, tight-muscled control to maintain the look of ready calm.

Now Cynlas ignored her response, giving an impatient shake of his head. "That's not what I mean. Where does he come from? How long has he been in your service?"

Isolde felt a faint warning tug of premonition and glanced round, looking for Kian. He had melted away, though, almost as soon as he'd caught sight of Trystan's face and hadn't returned during Trystan's brief account to Madoc and the rest of who he was and why he had come to Dinas Emrys. And now Kian still was nowhere to be seen among the men grouped about the courtyard.

Isolde looked back at Cynlas. "Why do you ask?"

Cynlas's throat worked before he looked up, blinking, like a man waking from black nightmare.

"I—" His voice was still hoarse, and he licked his lips before beginning again. "I spoke in the chapel, Lady Isolde, of the mongrel dog who betrayed us and cost me the life of my eldest son. I said one day I would find him again. And so I have. This is the man."

Isolde had been expecting Cynlas to say something about Marche—or about their time at Tintagel, five months before. For a moment, she could only stare at him, registering distantly that this was one shock too many for her mind to absorb in what was beginning to seem an endlessly long day.

Then, before she could speak, Dywel of Logres broke in. He wore, still, his mud-stained riding clothes, and though his eyes looked puckered with weariness, his curling hair was tidy, his cloak straight.

"No," Dywel said. "I know this man—I've seen him before, at Tintagel. Just after Marche's betrayal. A messenger in the service of the lady Isolde, captured and tortured by Marche's men."

Dywel glanced towards Madoc. "You remember—you saw him as well. Don't you agree?"

Madoc had been giving orders to the captain of his guard, but at that he glanced up, frowning. "You heard me greet him as such, didn't you? I'd scarcely have let him inside if I'd not known him."

Cynlas looked from Dywel to Madoc to Isolde, and then back towards the door of the guest hall where Trystan and his escort had now gone from sight.

"I could swear it's him," he said. He sounded less certain, though, his brows drawn together in a bewildered frown. "I could have sworn . . ."

He trailed off, and Dywel shook his head, clapping a hand on Cynlas's back. "You're fixed on the man from telling us all about him earlier, that's all it ith. Come on. There's likely a cup of ale left in the fire hall."

Cynlas passed a shaking hand across his eyes. "Maybe I'm mistaken. It's been a . . ." His words trailed away once again, and his broad shoulders slumped as though with defeat. "Maybe I'm wrong."

Watching Cynlas's righteous fury collapse in on itself, Isolde felt a moment's pity for him, even in the midst of all else. He must, she thought, have been so thankful to think that he'd found someone to fight instead of mourn.

Before he could speak to ask any more, though, Isolde said, "I beg you would excuse me, my lords. The hour grows late, and my messenger will be waiting. I bid you all good night."

THE FIRE IN ISOLDE'S WORKROOM WAS unlit; the herb-scented air felt chilly and damp as she stepped inside. The flare of torchlight from the passage outside was enough for Isolde to find the tin-derbox beside the brazier and kindle a small flame, then light the room's single oil lantern as well. She hung the lantern back on its hook in the wall and slipped out of her traveling cloak, only then turning to where Trystan sat on the corner bench, leaning back against the wall as Kian had done, days ago.

He shifted slightly under her gaze, then straightened in sur-prise as the movement knocked something from the bench to the ground with a metallic chime. He bent to pick it up.

"What—"

The first shock of seeing him was wearing off. Even still, though, Isolde looked at the object he held blankly before she recognized Garwen's Latin-inscribed iron ring and remembered that she'd taken it off her finger when salving Kian's wounds and forgotten it here.

"It's meant to trap devils," Isolde heard herself say.

Trystan glanced from the ring to her, one eyebrow cocked. "So you just—what? Hope your devil speaks Latin?"

Isolde felt a smile tug at the corners of her mouth. "I suppose." Then she sobered and added, "Garwen gave it to me. She was Amhar's mother—you remember Amhar?"

A brief stillness came over Trystan's face, and then he nodded. "I do. A wicked shot with a bow and arrow. Good with a sword, too."

His voice hadn't altered, but Isolde wondered whether he'd fought in the battle where Amhar had died. He might have. Trystan would have been—Isolde tried to think back—fourteen, she thought, when Amhar had died by his own father Arthur's hand. Old enough that he'd been fighting with the rest of her father's army for nearly a year. With that still startling clarity she could see herself at eleven or twelve, trying her hardest not to cry every time he rode away. And then laughing and begging him to take her out fishing or hunting with him when he returned.

Isolde wondered for a moment whether it was Trystan's presence that made the memory especially clear, the breath of longing for everything about the years before Camlann unexpectedly strong. Because Trystan was likely the only one she knew who would still remember that time, too. Nearly everyone else was gone—killed at Camlann or dead in the year of plague that had followed.

"I've—" Isolde began, then caught herself, her eyes on Trystan's face. He was thinner than he'd been five months before, his face leaner, the angles of temple and jaw more well defined. His skin was sun-browned, making his eyes seem even more intensely blue, and his gold-brown hair was longer, tied back now with a leather thong. She could still trace in his features, though, the boy she'd grown up with years before, and it brought an odd, unsteadying shiver to feel that Trystan was now at once both a stranger to her and as familiar as the searingly bright flashes of memory that still caught her off guard.

And what had she been about to say? *I've missed you?* That, Isolde thought disgustedly, is something I might have said to him at eleven or twelve, when I still believed with all my heart in an oath of friendship sworn in blood. But hardly now.

She'd changed in the last seven years. Of course she had. So had Trystan. And now she felt . . . surprise seeing Trystan again. And relief, too. Because for all she'd known otherwise, he might have been dead, lying facedown in the mud or bleeding on a far distant battlefield, sightless eyes staring up at the sky. But she felt something else, too, beneath the relief and the shock. Something that flowed with a hissing warmth through her veins but that she couldn't quite name.

The silence between them lengthened, and Isolde was the first to break it, pouring ale into a cup as she'd done for Kian days ago. "Here. Take it. You look as though you haven't eaten or slept in days."

Trystan looked down at the cup of ale she put in his hand, then shrugged, and tossed it back in a single draft. "I may feel like it, too, but it wasn't quite that bad."

Isolde's eyes went to the bandage tied around his right hand. "Are you actually wounded—or was that only an excuse for speaking to me alone?"

Trystan, too, glanced down at his bandaged hand. "What? Oh, that." He shook his head. "No, it's nothing. Slipped a couple of finger joints out of place, but I put them back myself. It's fine, now." He reached to pour another cup of ale from the jar, then asked, almost as though he'd read her thoughts, "Is Kian here?"

"He's—" Isolde started, then stopped. She was remembering Kian's hand going, as though by reflex, to the patch over his eye as soon as he'd recognized Trystan outside. And then Kian had melted quietly away outside, before Trystan could pick him out of the crowd, as though he dreaded seeing the younger man. As, Isolde thought, he probably does. Any man maimed in battle dreads having the damage noticed for the first time—and I owe it to Kian, she thought, not to speak of his capture behind his back.

"He's safe," she said. "Risen to one of Madoc's most valued fighting men."

Trystan's head tipped in a brief nod of acknowledgment, and there was another moment's silence. Then Isolde asked, "So why have you come?"

Trystan let out his breath, setting the cup of ale down, and said, his voice evenly controlled, "Because Hereric's wounded. Or dead by now. I don't know."

Isolde remembered Hereric's broad Saxon face and slow smile, his big, gentle hands that spoke for him, since his tongue could not. An escaped slave, Trystan had thought him. Though no one could say for sure. Hereric, simple as a child, never spoke—even in gestures—of his past.

She asked, "Wounded—how?"

Trystan leaned one shoulder against the wall, raised the cup, and drank again. "We were attacked. Five days ago. A war party—I don't know whose they were. No insignia, but their weapons were good quality. Professional fighting men, not just chance bandits."

Trystan was never—had never been—easy to read. But growing up with him, Isolde had known his face as well as she knew her own, had learned to recognize what it meant when he sat as still and as casually as he did now and spoke in such an evenly controlled tone. Seven years ago, she thought, I'd have said he was furiously angry—either at the men who did this or at himself for not stopping them.

Or because he was here, about to ask aid from her? Isolde felt the hissing, unidentifiable feeling spread once more through her veins as she thought, He must be hating this.

Aloud she asked, "And Hereric was wounded?"

Trystan rubbed a hand tiredly across his face, then nodded. "Took a blow to the arm. It's broken—badly so. I had to leave him on the boat. He's too weak to move."

"I'm sorry," Isolde said. And she was. It hurt her to think of Hereric frightened and in pain. "Is he alone?"

Trystan shook his head. "Not alone. I paid an old fisher-woman to stay with him—make sure he had food and drink. The gods know whether she'll just take the money and walk away. But she seemed stupid—so maybe she's honest as well. The two often go hand in hand."

"And you came here. Looking for me?"

It was hardly a question, but Trystan nodded again.

"I don't understand, though," Isolde said. "There must be other healers."

Trystan jerked one shoulder impatiently. "Of course there are—the surgeons who serve the war leaders and lordlings of these parts. And can you imagine their faces if I walked in and asked them to please set the broken arm of an escaped Saxon slave? That's assuming I could even get near enough to one to ask. Men like us aren't exactly welcome in every corner of the land."

"I suppose not." Isolde wondered for the first time how Trystan and Hereric had come to be moored so close by. What would bring two mercenaries, their swords for hire to the highest bidder, to the coast of Gwynedd at all?

Trystan's blue eyes were steady on hers, though, and he said, his voice quiet, his face completely serious now, "Please, Isa. Will you help him?"

The words rang oddly in Isolde's ears, but it was a moment before she realized that was because he'd used the old childhood name. She thought, Trystan is probably the only one left alive who would think to call me that now.

She said, "You don't have to ask. Of course I will."

And then she went suddenly still, shocked into immobility by idea that had struck her like a dash of cold water across the face. She thought, It might be possible. It might—if Trystan agrees. And if he does—

Trystan's gaze still rested on hers. Slowly, Isolde said, "I'll do everything for Hereric that I can. And if I asked you for help as well, would you give it?"

Trystan's brows rose, and he was silent a moment before replying. Then: "Is this the price of your care for Hereric?"

His tone was neutral, but even still Isolde felt anger coil and harden in her chest—and in the same moment realized that the unnamed feeling had been anger, all this time. Not so much at what Trystan had said, but because Trystan, her childhood companion, oath-sworn friend, protector and playmate and brother she'd never had—

Because he had left five months ago. Would have slipped off without even saying good-bye, if she'd not forced that much out of him, at least.

Which isn't, she thought, entirely fair. Just because we grew up together—were friends at thirteen and fifteen, seven years ago—doesn't mean Trystan owes me anything now. The anger refused to die away, though, and she demanded, "Do you honestly think I would do that? Ask you to bargain with Hereric's life? You know me better than that."

For a long moment, Trystan was silent, his gaze on her face, a look she couldn't quite read at the back of his blue eyes. And then he nodded. "Maybe I do."

The room was dark, save for the lantern's glow, deepening the shadows about his mouth and eyes. Trystan leaned forward, elbows resting on his knees, and then he said, "All right. Tell me what you need."

Isolde let out her breath. "Do you know Cerdic of Wessex's country? Could you cross safely through his lands?"

Trystan's brows lifted once more, but he said, "I suppose so. It's an unstable country—there's always raiding and fighting along the borders. But if need be, yes."

"Fighting," Isolde said. "You mean the hostilities between Cerdic and Octa of Kent?"

"Cerdic, Octa, and whichever of their warlords take it into their heads to steal cattle or burn a village."

"You've seen it firsthand?"

Trystan tipped his head in a brief nod.

"Which of them did you fight for?"

One corner of Trystan's mouth curved again. "Not for Octa, or I'd not be able to safely cross through Cerdic's lands."

Not for Octa. Until she heard him say the words, Isolde hadn't realized she'd instinctively tensed in anticipation of his response. Not that she knew enough about Cerdic of Wessex to judge him preferable to the Kentish king. Cerdic might have been her father's ally, but she'd never met or even seen him that she could recall.

Modred, as she'd told Kian, had never had much attention or thought to spare for her, his only daughter—though she thought he'd loved her, in a distant, abstracted way. But for all her life, before Camlann, he'd been at war with Arthur. Modred had been constantly on campaign, leaving Isolde and Morgan in one garrison or another. She'd scarcely seen him, her own father, much less his allies from those years.

"Does Cerdic know that you're . . ." Isolde stopped, caught off guard by how hard it was to say Marche's name. "That you're his grandson?"

She'd thought Trystan might be angry at the question—and a shadow did flicker across his face, but only briefly. Apparently, whatever ghosts the mention of Marche's name raised either were laid or were such constant companions that by now he hardly spared them a glance.

"Tell Cerdic that I was the son of Marche—the traitor who cost him victory at Camlann?" Trystan raised the cup of ale to his mouth and drank again. "He'd not have trusted me with a table knife, let alone a sword if he'd known that. Besides, it was Cewlin—one of Cerdic's warlords—I fought for, not Cerdic himself. I scarcely saw Cerdic, and never to speak to." He frowned. "But you knew that already, didn't you?"

Isolde nodded. "You told me at Tintagel, yes."

She was silent a moment, watching Trystan's face, patched with shadow by the lantern's flickering light. She could feel how easy it would be to fall back into her old childhood way of speaking to him—almost as easily as though she talked for herself. And yet, it was still hard to join her memories of the Trystan she'd grown up with to the man she'd met five months before. A man with the first joints of the fingers on his left hand gone and the brand of slavery on his neck.

Trystan shifted, stretching his booted feet out towards the glowing brazier, and gave her a quick, direct look from under his slanted brows. "So what does my having fought as a mercenary for a Saxon warlord have to do with what you want from me now?"

It was very late—or very early. Isolde could see the garden outside the window beginning to lighten with the approach of dawn. She rubbed her eyes. "First, let me tell you what's happened in the last days."

Trystan sat in silence, the cup of ale in his unbandaged hand, while Isolde told him. She left out Kian's story of the reward Marche had offered for Trystan's capture. Because she might have a rule for herself about not flinching away from mentioning Marche's name. But she absolutely couldn't face the thought of speaking with Trystan about him tonight.

She told him, though, of the meeting with King Goram, of Marcia's warning of treason—and of the morning's ambush as they traveled back from Ynys Mon. Despite her efforts, her voice faltered slightly when she came to Bedwyr's death, and she looked up to find Trystan watching her.

"I'm sorry," he said. "Not that you need me to tell you, but there was nothing else you could have done for him."

Isolde looked away. "No."

"It's—"

But the control Isolde had been hoarding all throughout the long day abruptly snapped, and she cut him off. "If you're about to say it was a good death, then don't. There's no such thing. Death is ugly. Brutal and sordid and ugly. Always. Every time."

She realized that there were tears on her cheeks, and she scrubbed them furiously away.

Trystan made a brief movement, as though he were about to reach out for her. And Isolde felt a twist of something like panic at the realization of how much she wanted him to. As though she truly had been ten years old again, and he could still put an arm around her when she cried. As if she could lean her head against his shoulder and forget all that troubled her—surrender it all into his hands.

Trystan checked the motion, though, instead shaking his head. "No. I wasn't going to call it a good death. Bleeding to death is a filthy, unpleasant way to go, and I don't suppose Cynlas's son liked it any better than the other men I've seen die that way. I was only going to say that it's always a dirty trick of fate when you've got to kill a man to be kind."

Isolde nodded. Trystan's words had scarcely been ones of comfort, but even still Isolde felt a clenched knot inside her chest begin to ease and loosen a bit. This was why she'd missed Trystan with an ache that was almost physical. Because he understood; he always had.

But that was all. The warmth that was flooding through her veins didn't have to mean anything more. Anything but that it was good for once to feel that she could trust and rely on someone, good not to feel so completely alone.

But Trystan had left—disappeared once before. He would surely sooner or later leave again.

And then, abruptly, Isolde remembered Cynlas's words in the courtyard outside. Though Trystan had given no sign in speaking Cynlas's name that the King of Rhos meant anything more to him than another man.

"Do you—"

She checked herself, though, before she could finish, and waited a moment, wiping the last of the tears from her cheeks with the heels of her hands and then drawing a steadying breath. "What I wanted to ask was this: you fought for Cewlin, Cerdic's man. Could you get to wherever Cerdic is holding court now?"

Trystan looked up sharply, brows drawn. "Why?"

"Because I want you to take me there. Cerdic was my father's ally—he has as much reason as Goram to hate Marche. And he's Octa's enemy as well, for all the rumors are that Octa is now seeking to end the fighting between them. Goram has rejected an alliance between his armies and ours. But we still need more men—more supplies—if they're not to be crushed. Cerdic is the best and clearest choice."

Trystan was still frowning, absently scraping his thumbnail against the side of the cup. "And you want me to take you—you alone, without a guard—across the Saxon war lands? Get you inside Cerdic's court so that you can propose an alliance to him?" He shook his head. "Powers of hell, Isolde, if you're set on killing yourself, I can think of easier ways."

Isolde shook her head. "It makes sense, Trys. Any war band trying to get past Octa and Marche's forces would be caught—slaughtered. And how far do you think a formal king's delegation would get speaking to Cerdic of alliance?"

"As far as Cerdic chose to throw them, before he ordered their heads staved in with an axe. All right, true enough."

Isolde nodded. "But a party of three travelers—you and Hereric and I—might get through Octa and Marche's patrols. Especially if we made part of the journey by boat, sailing around the coast. And then, I'm Modred's daughter. Cerdic wouldn't think me a threat."

Trystan was quiet a long moment, blue gaze fixed on her face, and then he said abruptly, "What aren't you telling me?"

"What do you mean?"

He made an impatient movement with one hand. "Isa, I knew you when you spoke with a lisp because you'd lost your two front teeth.

Maybe you're stubborn enough to pretend there's nothing else troubling you. And maybe I'm cross-eyed enough with lack of sleep to believe it—or pretend I do. But if I'm going to get in the middle of this, you'd better tell me the whole if you want us both to survive."

Why didn't that occur to me? Isolde thought. That if I can read him, he'd be able to read me as well? She remembered him teasing her when they were growing up because she could never keep her temper—and because her every thought showed plain on her face.

The memory made her feel strangely safe—and yet almost frightened at the same time, as though she'd been swept into a fast-moving river current far beyond her power to control.

She nodded, then said, "All right. Though it doesn't change anything—not really. It's only that Goram did offer Madoc an alliance at a price—that price being marriage to me."

She thought the line of Trystan's jaw might have hardened, but apart from that, his expression didn't change. "And you don't want to wed Goram?"

"Would you?"

Trystan cocked an eyebrow at her again. "It's the hell of an unlikely prospect that I'd ever have the choice to make. But I know what you mean. And no, in your place I wouldn't give Goram a kick in the teeth, much less a marriage vow. But what do you want?"

"Since when have a woman's wishes had the smallest influence on whom she weds?" Isolde stopped and shook her head, raised her hand and let it fall. "No, that's not fair. Madoc refused the offer. I suppose if I thought Goram would actually honor the alliance, I'd have to agree. But I don't trust him any more than Madoc does."

Trystan sat without speaking again. Then: "And you think Madoc would agree to your making the journey to Cerdic's court instead?"

"Honestly? I don't know. But our position is desperate enough that I think he will. And he trusts me . . . more than he once did."

"I'm sure he does."

Something in Trystan's tone made Isolde look up sharply, but he said nothing more, and after a moment, she went on. "But I can hardly tell him what I propose doing unless you've agreed to lend your aid."

A line of thought appeared between Trystan's brows. "You'll do what you can for Hereric?"

"I said I would."

"Sorry." Trystan rubbed a hand along the length of his jaw, and Isolde realized just how tired he must be. "I know you did." He looked up. "All right. You can tell Madoc whatever you choose to account for how your messenger happens to know his way through the Saxon war lands. And I'll take you to Cerdic."

Isolde let out a breath she hadn't realized she held. "Thank you."

"Thank me when you've actually made it to Cerdic's court and back alive." Trystan pulled himself to his feet, and Isolde saw him hold back a grimace, as though the movement hurt. She asked, "Trys? Are you all right?"

"Fine." Trystan picked up the sword and cloak he'd laid at his feet. He stood watching her a moment, frowning a bit, a look she couldn't quite read in his blue eyes. And then he asked, "What about you—are you sure you're all right?"

The question caught Isolde completely by surprise, and to her horror she felt another of those utterly stupid presses of tears behind her eyes. She blinked, absolutely refusing to cry just because for the first time in five months—maybe longer—someone had looked at her, really looked at her, and asked how she was.

"Fine," she echoed Trystan. "I'm fine."

Trystan seemed about to speak, but then he shook his head and said only, "Then I'll go, now. I'd best be getting to that bed in the guest hall Madoc offered before someone wonders why you've taken so long to rewrap an injured hand."

·   ·   ·

TRYSTAN CLOSED THE DOOR QUIETLY BEHIND him. Then he leaned back, letting his eyes slide briefly shut, and wondered whether he was indeed losing his mind to agree to what Isolde asked. Though the gods knew he'd wanted to say yes badly enough. To have the chance of seeing her, being alone with her, for weeks on end.

God, after living without her these last months, the thought had been like coming on a stream of sweet, clear water when dying of thirst.

He could still see her, gray eyes smudged with shadows but very steady and clear, telling him in a frighteningly controlled voice that if she'd thought it would do any good, she would have agreed to marry King Goram. Well, that shouldn't have surprised him. She'd never lacked courage.

And the best of luck to you and the nine companions of Arthur, he thought, if the very thought makes you want to get your hands around Goram's neck and squeeze.

A vision of her face swam up against his closed lids: delicate features and flawless lily-white skin, soft red mouth, and wide, thickly lashed gray eyes. God, she was beautiful. Like silver moonlight. Like some distant glimmering star.

And about as far out of his reach. He could still feel the cool brush of her fingers against his as she'd handed him the cup of ale. It had run through every nerve in his body.

Gods, it had taken every last scrap of his self-control not to reach for her, pull her towards him, into his arms. And he was planning on being alone with her for a weeks-long journey?

Trystan let out his breath. He'd do as she asked. Get her safely to Cerdic's court. Cerdic, who, the gods help him, was his own blood kin. Even the thought made a shudder ripple through him, an echo of the all too familiar shaking that always followed one of the dreams, and for a moment he felt the hilt of a knife in his hand, slippery with blood.

Trystan swore at himself under his breath. But as well to remember it. If only to fix clearly in his mind exactly why he couldn't so much as touch Isolde or speak the word *love* in her hearing.

Not that she'd want him to.

Trystan waited a moment, focusing on breathing until he had himself under control. Then slowly and dispassionately he laid the steps out in his mind, as though this were any of the other missions he'd carried out in the past for one lord or the next—whoever offered the highest pay. That was how jobs like that worked. Concentrate on the pragmatics and put everything else out of your head. Get back to Hereric. Hope he was still alive. Do as Isolde asked. Get her safely across Wessex and back. So that she could be wedded. Not to Goram, but to some suitable man. Maybe even Madoc himself—he'd seen how the man looked at her in the courtyard outside, with a look on his scarred face that had made Trystan want to strangle him as well.

So bloody much for pragmatism. Wearily, Trystan pushed off from the door panel. He'd best be off. It would be dawn soon, and he still had to make it back to the guest hall without being seen.

MADOC OF GWYNEDD WAS SILENT A long moment before he spoke. Then he asked, "And this messenger of yours—he knows the Saxon lands?"

After Trystan had gone, Isolde had sat by the hearth in her room until the rose-colored morning light showed over the eastern mountains. Then she'd changed her crumpled and dusty gown for one of pale blue wool with an over-tunic of light gold, brushed and rebraided her hair. She'd found Madoc in the king's receiving room, at table with Dywel of Logres and several of his fighting men, Cabal asleep on the hearth, tail curled around him and head on his paws.

Madoc had dismissed the men, and Isolde had taken the place he'd indicated, a wooden chair with a high carved back opposite Madoc's own, the table with the remains of the men's morning meal of ale and bread spread out between them. Madoc had waited for Isolde to speak first, holding his shoulders straight, almost as if in anticipation of a blow. And Isolde, watching, had felt a stab of compunction as she realized abruptly that he thought she'd come to answer his proposal of marriage from the night before.

He'd listened with a grave face as Isolde spoke, though, repeating the arguments she'd made to Trystan hours before.

Now Isolde nodded in answer to Madoc's question—the first he'd asked since she began. "He knows the country of Wessex, yes."

Madoc frowned, brows drawn. "A dangerous journey," he said. "You would put yourself at great risk in undertaking such a task."

"No more than you do in facing Marche here."

"Perhaps." Madoc moved one shoulder, dismissing that. "But have you thought what will happen should you arrive at Cerdic's court? You may be Modred's daughter—the child of Cerdic's old ally—but you're also a Briton noble. Constantine's former queen. And we both of us know how the Saxons deal with their enemies' wives."

Isolde started to speak, then stopped as Cabal woke with a snuffle and scrabbled to his feet, coming to sniff at Isolde's hands. Isolde scratched his ears, then looked up at Madoc. "I do know. And I know, too, there are many, many terrible ways to die. But whatever Cerdic and his warlords might do is no worse than would happen to me should Marche and Octa prevail."

"You've great courage, Lady Isolde."

"No more than you do," she said again, "facing Marche here."

Madoc didn't answer at once. His eyes, deep-set and dark in his ravaged face, were on Isolde's, and it seemed to her that there was a shadow of sorrow in their depths. "Perhaps."

He got abruptly to his feet. "Come outside." The words were abrupt, and he shook his head, adding, "Your pardon. I should have said, will you walk outside with me for a time?" He glanced round the room with its rush-strewn floor and heavily carved table and chairs. "I've been so long on campaign that I always feel suffocated indoors."

THE GUARDS STATIONED OUTSIDE THE RECEIVING room came to attention when Madoc opened the door and made to fall into step behind him. Madoc waved them back, though, and he and Isolde walked alone along the passage and out into the courtyard, with Cabal trotting at their heels. They passed the workrooms, as they had the night before—though the smith's and armorer's sheds were busy, now, filled with metallic hammering and the hiss of steam as red-hot iron was plunged into water to cool. When they reached the water cistern, set close to the fort's outer wall, Madoc paused. The sun was rising, burning off the morning's mist, and the air felt fresh and clear and warm with the promise of spring.

Madoc kicked lightly at the cistern's stone cover with the toe of his boot. "It's here Merlin is supposed to have had his vision of the dragons. Prophesying Britain's victory over the Saxon hordes."

A yew tree grew just to the side of the cistern, its branches covered with the first golden-green buds of spring—and covered as well by hundreds upon hundreds of knotted scraps of cloth. In less dangerous times, travelers had journeyed miles to tie their rags to the branches of the tree at Merlin's holy pool in hopes of blessing or answer to prayer. A good harvest, cure of an ailment, a child for a barren woman's womb.

Isolde nodded. "Yes, I know."

"You believe it?"

Isolde fingered one of the small scraps of cloth—a tattered blue that might have been torn from a woman's gown and had now begun to fade with the rain and sun. "Believe in the dragon story? No. Believe that we've a chance of victory?" Isolde lifted one shoulder. "I have to. So do we all."

"I suppose so." Madoc sighed and crossed his arms, looking

up at the stretch of sky, clear and for once almost cloudless above the fortress's outer stone wall. "Though I sometimes feel as though a great tide of darkness is rolling over the land. Maybe Arthur held it back for a time—but even he could not drive the dark away in the end."

Madoc was silent, and then he shook his head, turning back to Isolde. "You wish me, then, to propose your being appointed emissary to the king's council?"

Cabal had sat down at Isolde's feet, and she scratched his ears, then shook her head. "No. But then neither do you wish to propose such a thing."

Madoc sighed again and rubbed a hand across the back of his neck. "And why not?"

She could see the understanding, though, in his eyes and knew he didn't need her answer. Still, she said, "Because you don't believe that yesterday's attack was random chance. No more does Kian. No more do I."

Madoc looked away. From the practice yard behind them came the clash of weapons as the fighting men drilled with staffs and swords. Then, slowly, Madoc moved his head in affirmation. "Treason."

"Yes."

Madoc let out his breath, moving his shoulders as though seeking to ease the burden of a heavy load. He was quiet a beat, then abruptly nodded at the big dog, now resting his brindled head against Isolde's side. "Take Cabal."

"What?"

For the first time, a brief flash of a smile lightened Madoc's face. "If you're to journey to Wessex, take Cabal along. He'll be some protection to you, at least. And he'd be useless left behind, knowing you were gone. He only follows my orders on sufferance at the best of times."

And then the smile faded, leaving his scarred face looking all at once older than his thirty years. "I don't like it," he said. "I like it even less than I did suing King Goram for aid. But a king can't worry overmuch about his own conscience." Madoc's mouth tightened, a note of bitterness creeping into his voice. "Any more than he can worry over-much how well he's going to sleep at night, thinking of what he's done."

He shook his head, looking down at his own hands, the fingers splayed, the nails still rimmed with black from the ride the day before. "How many men have I killed? How many widows have been made on my orders these last months? How many children orphaned, whose only blame was to be in an ungodly wrong place at an ungodly wrong time?"

He stopped, folding his hands into fists and locking them behind his back. "As you yourself said, Cerdic would slaughter any party of men I sent to him on sight. But a woman alone—the daughter of a man he once held as a brother in arms—yes, you might stand a chance of gaining his ear long enough to hear the alliance you propose. And if I've admitted already I might have asked you to marry Goram, did I trust him to keep any bargain he made, then I can hardly scruple to ask you to risk your life on a journey across the Saxon war lands."

He paused, eyes on the cistern's stone covering, then asked, "Do you wish a serving woman to accompany you?"

Isolde looked up, surprised. "A serving woman? Oh, for propriety's sake, do you mean?" She hesitated, then shook her head. "No. You may say that I've taken one, if you wish—when you give out the story that I'm gone to Camelerd. But it's a dangerous journey, as you said. And I'd rather my own reputation be blemished by traveling in the company of two men than see an innocent woman killed or captured by Saxons." She stopped, then smiled briefly. "Besides, that sort of gossip would be more of an improvement than anything else over what's been whispered about me before."

Madoc's face lightened as well, but he shook his head again. There was a silence in which Isolde could hear the steady metallic hammering from the smith's forge behind them, and the baying of a pair of war hounds, set to fight by some of the men. The hairs on Cabal's neck rose, and Isolde rested a hand on his back.

Then Madoc said, "The question I asked of you last night, Lady Isolde—"

His voice had turned gruff, and Isolde thought a faint wash of color had crept into his face, though the livid scars made it hard to tell. She felt suddenly as though an iron hand were gripping her heart, but she said, steadily, "Keep it, my lord Madoc. Until I return. You can tell King Goram that I've undertaken to journey to my own lands, to be sure the defenses there are as strong as may be. That will do for a story to give the rest of the king's council as well. And then when—if—I return . . ." she stopped. "Ask me again."

She thought the shadow of sadness had returned to Madoc's dark gaze, as though he'd heard more in her words than she'd meant him to, and she felt another twist of compunction. But then, slowly, Madoc bowed his head. "As you wish." He looked up, meeting Isolde's look once again and said, in a different tone, "And will you tell me now who he is, this messenger of yours?"

Isolde went still. "You know that already."

"I know who you claim him to be."

With another man, Isolde might have stretched the truth or invented a lie. But Madoc, she thought, deserves better than a tale he'd likely not believe in any case. So she said nothing. A faint breeze stirred the scraps of cloth on the yew tree's branches, and after a moment Madoc sighed.

"Tell me this at least. You trust him enough to place the success of this mission—and your own life—in his hands?"

Isolde slipped her arm about Cabal's neck, hugging the big dog lightly to her as the pieces of her talk with Trystan reassembled themselves in her mind. She thought again of Cynlas's blanched, rigid face and hoarse voice, claiming him for the mercenary who'd betrayed his eldest son. *You know me better than that,* she'd told Trystan. And she would have said that she knew Trystan, too, better than to believe him the man Cynlas thought.

But she'd not asked him when she'd had the chance, sitting with him in her workroom. If she were honest with herself, she'd not asked him because she was afraid of what the answer might be. Trystan had changed. He must have.

Because the Trystan I knew, she thought, wouldn't have left five months ago. Or at the very least, he would have found a way to send her word, so that she'd not be left not knowing whether he was alive or lying dead somewhere facedown in a muddy ditch. Neither would he have sought a living as a Saxon spy. Isolde thought of all the men whose wounds she'd stitched these last years—all those she'd helped die as she had Bedwyr— and wondered how many might be alive today if Trystan hadn't gained intelligence for the enemy side.

The thought made her a little sick to her stomach. But it wasn't entirely fair. She'd long since passed a point where she could believe Britain's fighting men blameless in the seemingly endless war. And it was certainly unfair—and more than that, dishonest—to blame Trystan for having been in a Saxon war- lord's pay, when it was for exactly that reason that she could now call on him for help in reaching Cerdic of Wessex.

And she could still see the damaged fingers on Trystan's left hand, the Saxon mark of slavery at his neck. And she thought again of her father's man Emyr, tortured into madness by Octa of Kent, whom Morgan had simply put to sleep as she might a suffering dog.

It was only in the bard's tales that a hero walked through cruel trials unchanged. In life, men's bodies were maimed and scarred, their spirits broken or turned bitter by what they'd en- dured. Isolde had been healer to more of them than she could count, and she knew how very, very rarely did such men pick up the shattered pieces of themselves and walk on with their spirits not unscarred exactly, but at least whole.

Though that didn't mean that Trystan hadn't done what Cyn- las claimed—or worse. Only that it wasn't entirely fair to blame him if he had.

Beside her, Cabal whined, and as though the sound had been a signal, Isolde made up her mind. If she couldn't judge Trystan on the past, she could judge him on the journey they'd shared five months before. She'd doubted Trystan then, and it had nearly cost him his life—though he'd still risked himself again and again without hesitation to save hers. She watched the fluttering scraps of cloth dance in the breeze, seeing—the memory hit her like a slap in the face—angry lashes on Trystan's back, black-crusted burns on his skin. My fault, all of it, she thought.

"Yes," she said, meeting Madoc's dark gaze. "I trust him enough."

To her surprise, Madoc asked nothing more, only nodded again and said in a quiet voice, "Then I wish you godspeed on your journey, Lady Isolde. And a safe return."

For a moment Isolde thought he would touch her. She felt a cold tightening in the pit of her stomach, but held still, ordering herself not to flinch or pull away if he took her hand. Unfair to Madoc, she thought, when he would inevitably think it was because of the scars on his face after all.

But instead Madoc frowned, brows drawn, and shook his head. "It's strange, though." He spoke more to himself than to Isolde. "I'd swear I'd seen the man before, too. Not just those months ago at Tintagel. But years ago. At Camlann."

BOOK II

BOOK III

Chapter Seven

TRYSTAN SAT WITH HIS BACK against the gunwale. He'd moored for the night under a grove of willow trees, and the light of the moon sifting through the branches above cast wavering shadows over the sailboat's deck. He broke the seal on a jar of wine and took a swallow, suppressed a shudder as the burning liquid ran down his throat, and wondered just how long he would be able to keep this up. Long enough? Maybe. With the luck of Satan and all his devils.

The dog Cabal lay on the deck at Trystan's feet. Ordinarily, he refused to leave Isolde's side, but tonight, to Trystan's surprise, the big dog had stayed out with him when Isolde went into the cabin to be with Hereric. He'd thought Cabal asleep, but now the animal stiffened, suddenly, his ears lifting, and rose, scenting the air.

"What is it, boy?"

Cabal whined, shifting his weight from side to side and thrusting his nose under Trystan's arm. Trystan set the wine jar down. "Something wrong?"

The cry from the cabin had him upright and on his feet

almost before he realized, and in another moment he had crossed the deck and jerked open the cabin door. The interior space was narrow, just large enough for a bed, a row of storage bins, and a pallet spread on the floor.

"Isolde?"

She'd been sleeping on the pallet; the single oil lamp burning showed the imprint of her head on the woolen blanket. Now, though, she was sitting bolt upright, her dark eyes wide and fixed, her whole body shaking. She made no response, and he dropped to his knee in front of her and put a hand on her shoulder.

"Isa?"

She stiffened instantly at his touch, and he heard her breath catch as she came awake, her eyes losing their fixed, glassy look and gradually focusing on his face. The black hair was loose on her shoulders, and she raised a hand to push it out of her eyes, then nodded shakily.

"I'm all right. I—"

She froze, suddenly, then drew back a little, mingled disgust and anger beginning to flicker in the wide gray eyes. The wine. Of course. He must fairly reek of the stuff.

"Trys?" Her voice sounded a little shaky still, and she rubbed a hand across her eyes again. "Is there something—"

Trystan allowed himself a silent inward curse. In a single movement, he had dropped his hand and pulled himself to his feet, turning away.

"I'll be outside."

Once on deck, he leaned against the gunwale, as he'd been before, then picked up the wine jar and took another swallow, grimacing again. And if she didn't despise you before this, he thought wearily, she certainly will by the time this journey is done.

Cabal had followed him out of the cabin, and now the big dog padded over to butt his head against Trystan's shoulder. Trystan absently scratched him behind the ears and drained the last few swallows of wine.

"What do you think, boy? Long enough to get through Wessex and back?"

Cabal flopped to the deck beside him, his head resting on his paws, and Trystan set the wine jar down. "Yes, right," he muttered. "Barely a week out of Gwynedd and already I'm talking to a dog."

ISOLDE WATCHED THE CABIN DOOR CLOSE. Her skin was clammy, and the memory of the dream still clung, sticky as a spider's web. Tonight, as she'd lain in the great carved bed and listened to the approaching footsteps, she'd known it was Madoc she waited for, not Marche. *I must have screamed, too,* she thought. *Or Trystan wouldn't have heard and come in.*

She shuddered, then pushed back the coarse woolen blankets and went to kneel beside the small basin of water on the floor, feeling a cowardly relief that she need not, this time, try to see what settlement or farm Marche and his troops had now sacked and burned. This time it truly had been only a dream.

She splashed water on her face, shockingly cold against her clammy skin. Then, as the dream's panic subsided, she sat back on her heels, her gaze falling on the cabin door Trystan had shut behind him when he went back out on deck.

Why, she thought, *didn't I think of this?* She knew why, though. She'd been so thankful for an excuse to escape, to delay agreeing to marry Madoc, that she'd not realized fully until setting out what the journey would mean. That she would be all but alone with Trystan, day after day.

It was harder even than she might have thought. Sitting with him while the strained silences between them stretched on and on. Watching him drink himself into a heavy slumber night after night.

Is there something wrong? she'd been about to say before he'd left. Which was an idiotic question, really. Because clearly there was. The Trystan she'd known had rarely even touched wine. But even if she'd managed to finish, she knew with a bone-deep certainty that he wouldn't have answered. She'd tried a few times before to ask him why he drowned himself in wine night after night. And always he'd avoided giving any answer at all—changing the subject or discovering some task about the boat that needed his immediate attention.

Isolde felt a flare of anger, hot and unexpectedly painful, at the memory of his wine-drenched breath, though it helped to drive away the lingering memory of the dream that twisted like a knife blade under her ribs.

And then feeble motion from the roughly made bed in the corner made her turn, and the sight of the man who lay there was enough to banish anger and fear both. Hereric had always been a big man, with massive, powerful shoulders, and a broad, fair-skinned face, the blond hair and light-colored eyes clear marks of his Saxon birth. Now, though, the flesh seemed to have shrunk, pulling tight across the heavy bones, and his eyes were sunken.

The bone of his forearm had been shattered below the elbow by a blow from a wooden club, and when Isolde had first seen it, was stuck in jagged, blood-smeared points through the mangled twists of muscle and sinew. She had set and splinted it, bandaging the whole with linen soaked in garlic and honey. But in spite of all she tried, the fingers on that hand were turning black, and streaks of angry red were spreading up from the elbow, a little higher each day.

Isolde took up a pottery cup of milk, poured a little into a spoon, and then held it to Hereric's lips. He only turned his head fretfully away, though, the liquid dribbling down his cheek.

She wiped up the spilled liquid, then once more took up cup and spoon, and began in a low voice, "Cuchulain was marching from the field of battle, when a young woman appeared before him, clad in a mantle of many colors, her face as beautiful as the dawn."

She'd lost count of the number of stories she'd told for Hereric this way in the nine days since they'd set sail from Gwynedd. She doubted Hereric heard, but the sound of her voice quieted him, sometimes, when his head turned restlessly on the pillow and he groaned aloud in pain.

"*I have heard tales of thy bravery, Cuchulain,*' the maiden said. 'And I have come to offer you my love.' But Cuchulain replied shortly that he was worn and harassed with war, and had no mind to bother with women, beautiful or no. 'Then it shall go hard with thee,' the maiden said. 'And I shall be about thy feet as an eel in the bottom of the ford.' Then she vanished from sight, and he saw but a crow sitting on a branch of a tree. And Cuchulain knew that it was the Morrigan he had seen.'"

The tale of the great hero Cuchulain was one of the longest she knew, with battles and beautiful maidens and sea voyages enough to last a bard many nights in his lord's fire hall. Isolde went on with the story, keeping her voice to a soothing murmur as she held the spoon to Hereric's lips again.

Again Hereric turned his head and the milk was spilled, but the third time she managed to slip the spoon between his lips, and she saw the muscles of his throat contract as the liquid went down. What must have been an hour later, though, the muscles of Isolde's wrists and arms aching with holding the spoon steady, and Hereric had swallowed only twice more. At last he whimpered like a tired child when she brought the spoon to his mouth, and she couldn't bring herself to force him any longer.

She set the cup and spoon down on the floor beside the bed and instead took up the vial of poppy syrup. She put her hand on Hereric's forehead, steadying him, and managed to trickle a few drops between his lips.

"It will help with the pain," she told him softly, though she knew he was far beyond understanding.

Isolde stood looking down at Hereric, watching as his breathing deepened and slowed, seeing the sickly gray color stealing like nightfall along the line of his jaw. And she wondered whether it was only chance that had made her choose a tale of the Morrigan—the death maid, who flew over a battlefield in raven form and chose the men who would fall.

She closed her eyes, and as she often did when she faced a patient she feared was beyond her power to heal, tried to summon up an image of her grandmother. Tried to imagine what Morgan the enchantress would do or say if she were here.

She could see her grandmother's face vividly: her long snow-white hair, her fiercely proud, still beautiful face with its delicate, fine-cut features and flashing dark eyes. A wave of longing caught her, sharp enough to stop her breath. Goddess mother, she wished Morgan were actually here. She would have been desperately glad, just now, to have an older authority to whom she could defer. Or at least her grandmother's listening ear.

What haven't I thought of? she asked the shadow Morgan silently. *What else can I try?*

Isolde could almost imagine she heard an echo of her grandmother's voice in the soft, lapping whisper of water against the boat's hull. *Herbs themselves cannot heal. They can only remind the body of the feeling of health, so that it heals itself.*

She could almost believe she saw the shadow Morgan she'd conjured from the air take a step nearer the bed and give a gentle shake of her head, a shadow of sadness or pity crossing her dark eyes. *When the body has forgotten health for too long, all herbs will be powerless to help.*

Isolde let out her breath. Now she knew she was purely imagining her grandmother's presence here. Morgan might have loved her, might have taught her the healer's craft and the ways of the Sight. Might have been the most skilled healer Isolde had ever known. But she'd never in her life seen Morgan either gentle, pitying, or sad.

The shadowy Morgan firmed her mouth as she turned from the bed back to Isolde, her dark eyes stern. *Stop hiding your head under the blankets like a frightened child. You know very well there's only one hope left for this man.*

Isolde might almost have smiled, if the image of Morgan hadn't been overlaid with one of Hereric's ashy gray face and shattered arm. *Well, that sounds more like you, at any rate.*

Hereric did have only one hope left. She did know. One last measure she might try to save his life. And she had no idea—none—how she was going to tell Trystan.

But it couldn't be tonight, at any rate. Now Hereric seemed to have fallen into a deeper sleep. Isolde rose, stretching muscles stiff with bending over the bed, went to open the cabin door, and stepped out onto the deck. She paused, drawing a long breath of the clean, cool air. The sky was a deep, fathomless black, as yet untouched by dawn, and the night was silent save for the steady lap of the water against the boat's side and the soft creak of wood and rope as the boat rocked gently in the current.

They had sailed around the southern tip of Demetia to reach the coast of Cornwall, at the point where the River Camel joined the Severn Sea. Now they were making their way upriver, the winds carrying them against the current towards Camelerd. The moon was a silver crescent overhead but bright enough that Isolde could make out Trystan, lying asleep on a pile of old sails near the prow of the ship.

Cabal, visible only as a lean, dark shadow, padded towards her to snuffle into her hand, and Isolde ran her hand over his back, then abruptly went still, her whole body tensing as she strained to listen. The sound she'd heard came again. Above the lap of water against the hull, she caught the steady creak, dip, and splash of oars.

Isolde reacted instinctively, even before the conscious part of her mind had registered that no fisherman would be on the river at this hour of night. Almost instantly, she was across the deck and kneeling at Trystan's side. She didn't dare risk speaking aloud, and so she took him by the shoulder and shook him.

Trystan didn't stir. He lay sprawled, one arm flung out along the deck, and Isolde saw the empty wine jar lying on its side near his outstretched hand. She gritted her teeth and shook him again, harder, but the jolt of fury was overshadowed a moment later by cold fear, as she felt the boat rock on its moorings and heard a thump, followed by the shriek of wood against wood. The other boat had come alongside.

Isolde felt panic hit her like rain driven on a gusting wind, and she looked quickly round the deck, willing herself to think. Her eye fell on the mooring ropes, stretching out over the side, and in another moment she had snatched the knife from Trystan's belt and was up and sawing at the ties. The first rope broke with a snap, and she felt the boat lurch beneath her feet so that she lost her balance for a moment and nearly fell. From somewhere behind her, she heard a splash and an angry shout that ran like ice up her spine, but she forced herself not to look round, starting on the second rope instead. It broke as well, and she felt the boat spin out into the current and begin to move.

Bracing herself against the side, she turned at last, then froze. A man's figure crouched on the deck across from her, a black shadow against the night sky. It was too dark to see his face, but he wore a leather war helmet and had a sword and two knives at his belt. And then, as Isolde stood still, her blood running cold, a second shadowy form hauled himself up over the gunwale, landing on the deck with a thump and a muttered oath.

Both men had seen her. Slowly, they started to advance, moving with arms outstretched and legs braced as the boat, now free of its moorings, lurched and swayed in the river's flow. Both men had drawn their weapons, and the moonlight ran silver along the blades of their upraised swords. They came at her, faces too much in shadow to see more than palely gleaming eyes.

Isolde felt a scream building inside her, but she forced it back, making herself stand motionless against the rail. Her gaze flicked from one man to the other, trying to gauge the space on either side of the human wall they formed. Not far enough for her to get past. They'd have her in a moment if she tried. Her hand was clenched on the knife, hard enough to drive the hilt's ridges into her palm. And then, out of nowhere it seemed, Cabal was launching himself at the nearest man, catching him square in the chest.

They fell to the deck with a crash that shook the boards under Isolde's feet, the man's shoulders striking first, followed a moment later by the back of his head. It must have knocked him unconscious, for though Isolde heard him give a low groan, he lay still and unmoving and made no effort to rise. Cabal twisted up from where he'd landed and in a flash was between her and the second man, the fur on his neck standing on end, teeth bared in a snarl.

The man's sword flashed, and Isolde heard Cabal give a high, sharp cry of pain, but he didn't draw off, only stood with his head down, forelegs planted wide and a rumbling growl sounding deep in his chest. Isolde's heart was pounding hard enough to make her vision blur. But this was the second time within a seven-night she'd faced violent attack—the second time she'd stood with Cabal between her and an upraised sword, waiting for a blow to fall.

And she wasn't afraid. Her eyes stung and her chest felt as though she were breathing fire instead of air. But somehow, she'd passed beyond fear to pure, simple fury. At the man before her for hurting Cabal, at Trystan for being too drunk to wake, and at the stupid, pointless waste of dying this way, not even knowing who her attackers were or how they had found her and why.

She adjusted her grip on the knife, breathing quickly, ordering herself to think. *Think.* Her mind flipped uselessly through possibilities—none of them standing a chance of saving her life or Cabal's. The boat was still rocking under her feet, making it hard to keep her balance. And hard for her attacker to stay upright as well.

She waited until a lurch of the boat had made the man before her stagger. No time to think—hardly even any time to take aim. She threw the knife, hard and fast. Not at his body—he wore a leather war shirt that she doubted the knife would penetrate—but at his leg.

The blade caught him in the upper thigh, and Isolde heard

his howl of pain. He staggered again, and then the leg collapsed under him, the sway of the boat making him fall as hard as the first man against the deck. This time, though, Isolde had time only for a sharply in-drawn breath before the attacker struggled upright, regaining his footing, and came at her again with a shout.

He'd lost his grip on his sword—Isolde could see it lying on deck a short distance away. Maybe half a heartbeat, though, Isolde thought, before he draws one of the knives at his belt. She threw herself forward, kicking out at the man's injured leg, but another lurch of the deck beneath them made her lose her balance, robbing the blow of its force. Instead the attacker's hand shot out, catching hold of her arm and dragging her to him, pinning her back against his chest.

She could smell the man's sweat, feel his breath hot on the back of her neck. Her heart was racing, but the tide of fury was still running hot and strong through her veins. Isolde drew back and then drove her elbow into the man's stomach, as hard as she could. The blow caught him by surprise; he'd not expected her to fight back. He grunted and doubled over, partially releasing his grip on her, and she lashed out again. This time her elbow caught the attacker full in the face.

She heard a crunch and another howl of pain, and knew with a sick certainty that she'd broken the man's nose. But this time his hold on her had loosened enough that she was able to jerk herself free and twist away, breathing hard.

TRYSTAN SAW ISOLDE THROW HERSELF FORWARD at the attacker, heard the crunch and the gasp when she broke the man's nose. It got her free—but not for long. One hand clapped over his face, the man lunged at her, catching hold of her by the wrist and dragging her towards him again. Snarling, Cabal launched himself forward, but the man kicked out, catching the big dog a savage blow to the belly with the toe of his boot, and the snarl changed to a yelp of pain.

Trystan's hand reached reflexively for the knife at his belt a moment before his mind registered that it was gone. His sword was where he'd left it, by the pile of sails he'd used for a bed. No time to get it, either. The other man had drawn his knife and had it at Isolde's throat, his other hand gripping her by the hair, forcing her head back.

A red mist seemed to come down across Trystan's eyes. There was a sword, lying just at the attacker's feet; Trystan could just see the gleam of metal in the moonlight. Probably a good thing his head was still swimming with the effect of the wine. You never wanted to think before trying a stunt like this one.

A voice in the back of his head told him he was likely to die swearing at himself for stupidity after all—and get Isolde killed, into the bargain. But even then he was throwing himself to the ground, grasping the sword, and then rolling up to block the slashing blow of the other man's knife with the flat of the blade.

The impact sent waves of shock vibrating up and down Trystan's arm. But the man had loosed his grip on Isolde; Trystan saw her wrench herself free again, stumble, and then come up with her back pressed against the rail.

Trystan turned back to the other man, shaking off the feeling that all this had to be some wine-induced nightmare. It was too dark to see the attacker clearly—but he'd gotten used to taking an opponent's measure quickly. This one was a big man, and clumsy with it, Trystan judged.

As though to prove the point, the other man lunged forward, slashing with the knife, and Trystan twisted aside, landing a hard kick to the other man's knee that sent him sprawling. He staggered, flailed wildly as he tried to recover, then went down, and as he struggled to rise, Trystan hit him across the back of the neck with the sword hilt. The man collapsed with a groan, sprawling facedown on the deck.

Only then did Trystan register what he'd only half noticed

before. The pitch and sway of the deck beneath his feet had stopped. They'd run aground against the riverbank; he could see a sea of reeds, swaying shadows in the night darkness, just beyond the rail. Isolde was still pressed back against the rail, and in an instant Trystan had caught her by the shoulders, the lurch of sickness in the pit of his stomach making him forget his rule of not touching her. "Are you all right?"

In the moonlight, her face was a pale oval, the gray eyes huge and wide. She nodded, though, and Trystan passed a hand across his brow, controlling the urge to either shake her or pull her into his arms. "Shades of hell, Isa, what in God's name were you thinking of?"

"What do you mean?"

"You're unarmed, facing an opponent with a knife? You run— you lock yourself in the cabin. You don't throw yourself at him and break his goddamned nose so that he's going to kill you or die trying."

Her answer came quick as a slap, her voice angry and hard, and she pulled herself away. "I was thinking that I'd rather die fighting back than cowering in a corner like a rabbit and waiting to be killed."

He saw her hand move to her throat, and knew she was remembering the bite of the attacker's knife. "I was thinking that since you were too drunk to do more than snore, I was the only one who could put up a fight. And besides, what were you—"

But her teeth had started to chatter, and she had to clench her jaw shut to stop. Even so, Trystan could see the shivers of reaction that shook her from head to foot. His hand moved towards her, but he stopped himself. Try to put an arm around her or touch her again and he'd probably get his nose broken as well. Not that he could blame her.

Too drunk to do more than snore. If she didn't despise you before this, he thought, she certainly will by the time you reach the Wessex borderlands. Though if that was the worst that happened, he supposed he could be heartily thankful.

Trystan turned to the two unconscious men sprawled across the deck. Out of the corner of his eye, he saw Isolde move, too, dropping to kneel beside Cabal, who lay panting beside the cabin door.

"Is he all right?" Trystan asked after a moment.

"I think so." Isolde's voice still sounded tight, but she did at least answer. She ran her hands gently over the big dog's coat. "I don't think his ribs are broken—only bruised. And there's a cut on his shoulder, but it's not deep."

Trystan nodded, then toed the body of the man he'd fought, rolling him onto his back. His face was smeared with blood from his broken nose, black in the pale light of the moon. But no badge or other marks—nothing to tell where he'd come from or whose man he was. For a moment, Trystan saw again the man's hands, holding the knife to Isolde's throat, and his own hand went to the hilt of the sword he still held. But it was a long time since he'd cut an unconscious man's throat. Besides, he'd enough on his conscience already.

Trystan let out his breath, then hefted the man up onto one shoulder, carried him to the railing, and then heaved him over the side. The water was shallow here; unless he rolled onto his face and drowned before he woke, he'd likely survive. Trystan did the same for the second man, then turned to find Isolde watching him, her arms still about Cabal's neck.

"What are you going to do?" Her voice still sounded slightly shaky, but she'd stopped shivering. Trystan thrust away the image of her with the knife at her throat. For the first time, he gave his full attention to the question of who these men had been and where they'd come from. A random attack? Not bloody likely.

He shook his head, wiping the sweat from his brow with the back of his hand. "Get us as far away from here as possible, for a start. After that, I don't know."

· · ·

ISOLDE LET HER HAND FALL FROM Hereric's brow and sat back, biting her lip. The fever was rising. Slightly, but unmistakably. The Saxon man's skin felt hot and dry to the touch, and looked painfully stretched over the broad bones of his cheeks and brow. Though at least he hadn't wakened when they'd carried him ashore from the boat. Trystan had carried him, and Hereric had groaned and tossed his head fretfully with each step. Isolde had held her breath until Trystan had splashed his way through the shallows and lowered the big man at last onto solid ground.

Now Isolde made an effort to push away the awareness of Hereric's fiercely agonized pain. She'd managed to trickle another dose of the poppy syrup between his lips; there was nothing else she could do for him now. She straightened from where she knelt at Hereric's side and wrung the water out of the hem of her gown before joining Trystan beside their campfire, sullen and smoking, since what wood they'd been able to gather had been either rotted or damp.

Cabal padded over and settled himself at her feet with a sigh, and Isolde checked the bandage she'd wound around the cut on his back. Still dry. The wound hadn't been deep, and she'd not even needed to stitch it to be sure it would heal cleanly.

Dawn was breaking, showing as a faint band of orange on the horizon, showing the sea of swaying reeds and patches of mud all around. They'd come some little way into the marshy swamp that surrounded this stretch of the river on all sides. The air was dank and smelled of mud and marsh gas, and clouds of stinging insects buzzed overhead. The boat they'd had to leave behind, at the water's edge, beached and keeling over on its side so that the steering rudder, broken on a sand shoal during the wild voyage downriver, showed plain.

"Is the rudder badly damaged?" Isolde asked, breaking a silence that had lasted nearly since they'd stepped ashore.

Trystan shrugged and reached for one of the skins of water they'd brought from the boat. "Nothing that can't be mended.

Say a day, maybe, for me to get it fixed. Maybe only half a day. I'll be able to tell better once it's light."

He squinted at the eastern horizon, where the band of orange was broadening into fiery gold. There was another silence, and then Isolde said, "They were professionals—paid fighting men— who attacked us last night."

Trystan took a swallow of water, eyes still on the eastern sky. "Common bandits don't wear leather armor or fight with swords," he agreed. He lowered the waterskin, securing the metal cap once again. "No random attack, either. It was murder they meant, plain and simple." He stopped and glanced at her. "Any idea whose men they were?"

Isolde shook her head. "Not for sure. Marcia did speak of treason, though, on the king's council."

"And you think someone on the council got word that you were traveling to Cerdic and sent his guardsmen to stop you?" Trystan absently rubbed at a smear of mud on the back of his hand and frowned. "I thought no one but Madoc knew your intent."

"I thought so, too. But it's either that, or—" Isolde stopped.

Beyond that one single outburst just after the attack, she'd not spoken of what Trystan's drunkenness had nearly cost. Drunk or no, he'd still saved her life, with that insane dive for the attacker's sword. The memory of it still turned her cold.

She might still have been angry—or rather, more angry—a faint tingle of disgusted fury still vibrated in every nerve. But when they'd faced each other across the unconscious attacker's body, Trystan's look had called back a memory from years before. Meeting his eyes, she'd remembered the boy who stood in the practice yard with a set, stony face and threw a knife at a leather target over and over, because he'd not been able to stop his father beating his mother again.

And unless he's changed more than I think, Isolde thought, *there's nothing I could say that he's not already saying to himself.*

And now, sitting with him amidst the rushes, drying their clothes by the smoking fire and listening to the buzz of the insects all around, she tried to make up her mind whether to finish what she'd just begun to say.

Isolde looked over at Trystan. His breeches were still muddied at the hems, and there was a bruise on his jaw. He sat with his arms resting on his knees, the linen of his shirt pulled tight across the broad muscles of his shoulders, and his eyes strayed from time to time to Hereric's motionless form.

Slowly, Isolde shook her head. "No, nothing." Trystan was, too, she saw, holding his right hand slightly awkwardly, as though the fingers ached, and she gestured. "Do you want me to tie that up for you?"

Trystan had been watching Hereric again. In the silence, the harsh rasp of the injured man's breathing was almost as loud as the rustle of reeds stirring in the breeze. But at Isolde's question, Trystan glanced down at his own fingers, then shook his head. "This? No, it's nothing. Last night maybe didn't do the fingers I dislocated before any good. But it's fine. Tie it up and I won't be able to work on the rudder."

He took another swallow of water, then got to his feet. "I'd better scout around for some wood to use." He cast a glance around the hastily assembled campsite. "You'll be all right here on your own?"

"Of course." Isolde hesitated then said, "Trys? Those men—they came on a boat. I heard the oars."

Trystan nodded, and answered the unspoken question, picking up his knife from the ground and sheathing it in his belt. "They'll search for us—bound to. Unless we're both wrong, and it was just a chance attack by bandits. But we came a good way downriver. And now the reeds would hide the boat and this camp both from anyone still on the river. So there's no more reason for them to look here than anyplace else." He looked up again at the lightening sky. "Better put the fire out, though, before the smoke gives us away."

• • •

'WHEN THE FIRE HAD BEEN EXTINGUISHED and Trystan had gone, Isolde sat down beside Hereric, drawing her feet up under the still damp skirts of her gown. *Either the night's attackers had been under orders from a traitor on the king's council,* she'd been about to say, *or else they were from Marche. Acting in hopes of his reward.*

But when it came to the point of speaking them aloud, the words had stuck like rocks in her throat.

Beside her, Hereric made a soft, fretful sound and turned his head restlessly against the blankets she'd spread under him on the ground. Isolde took up the waterskin and dampened a rag, then started to wipe off the Saxon man's face, wondering whether she only imagined that his tautly stretched skin felt hotter yet.

At first, back at Dinas Emrys, she'd been too shocked by Trystan's arrival to face the thought of telling him that his father was searching for him. And then, later . . . later she'd said nothing because they'd hardly spoken since leaving Dinas Emrys. Because Trystan was drinking himself into a stupefied sleep every night. And, more than that, maybe, she'd said nothing because it would have meant speaking of Kian, returning to her captured and battered bloody and with a hollow socket in place of his eye.

Isolde remembered the last time she'd spoken to Kian, before starting out with Trystan for Hereric and the boat. She'd gone to her workroom, to pack the salves and simples she'd need for the journey, and found Kian there, waiting for her on the corner bench, arms crossed on his chest. He'd refused her offer to change the dressings on his eye, though.

"Don't trouble yourself, it's well enough. Just came to say good-bye. Heard from Madoc what you planned."

"He told you the whole?" Isolde asked.

Kian shrugged. "Gave me the story he's giving everyone else. Bloody unlikely Trystan would appear out of a blue sky so that he could take you to Camelerd, though."

Isolde nodded. Kian, at least, deserved the truth. So she told him everything and watched his face tighten when she spoke of Hereric's injury. He said nothing, though, even when she'd finished, and after a moment Isolde asked, "Are you angry with him? Trystan, I mean. Because he didn't tell you himself that he's Marche's son?"

"Angry?" Kian had been frowning down at his own boots, but at that he looked up, plainly surprised. "Why should I be angry? Can't remember ever telling Trystan the story of my life, either—or mentioning who my father was." He hunched his shoulders. "That's the way we lived—no past, no future, just get through each day as it comes."

"Do you want to see him, then?" Isolde asked. "Before we leave?"

Kian was silent. His gaze was fixed once more on the floor, but Isolde could see his inner struggle in the tight set of his shoulders. And after a moment, he shook his head. "No, better not. I—" He broke off, and reflexively touched the leather patch over his missing eye. "I . . . well, better not, that's all."

Now Isolde set down the damp rag and drew the blankets up over Hereric's chest. Kian would know Trystan, she thought. Maybe even better than I do, by now. And even she could guess what Trystan would feel if he knew what Kian had suffered because he'd been recognized as Trystan's companion of five months before. And tell Trystan about it now, Isolde thought, let him guess that last night's attack may have been more of the same, and he'll almost certainly go one step further.

She could still feel the crushing weight of what she'd felt seeing the bloody marks of torture on Trystan's back—the torture he'd endured at Marche's hand, but her fault. And Trystan would be able to put the pieces together as well as she could herself. If last night's attackers had been driven by the thought of Marche's gold, the men who had attacked and hurt Hereric might have been as well. Tell him about Marche's offered reward, Isolde thought, and Trystan will hold himself accountable—even more than he does already—for Hereric's broken arm. And not only that, but for Kian's lost eye as well.

Hereric groaned and stirred again, trying to rise, and Isolde put a hand on his forehead to sooth him. In a low murmur, she started to tell the story of the daughters of Llyr, one of the countless other tales she told for the injured man these last days. The words were so familiar that she scarcely needed to think about what she said, though—and as she sat watching the labored rise and fall of Hereric's chest, and looking down at the streaks of red climbing up the broken arm, Isolde set aside all thoughts of Trystan and Marche—for the time being, at least. Because now she had to acknowledge what she'd feared all along. Though she'd not told Trystan this, either. But she couldn't save Hereric's arm—he was either going to lose the arm or die.

THE SUN CLIMBED HIGHER IN THE sky. Isolde wiped Hereric's face again with water, managed to coax him into swallowing a few mouthfuls of honey wine, and set up a makeshift tent from a pair of blankets to keep him in the shade. She poured water into her cupped hands for Cabal to drink, gave him a torn-off piece of stale bread, and checked the big dog's bandages again, finding them still dry and the cut in his back scabbing over cleanly. Some time in the middle of the day, she slept a little, still sitting at Hereric's side— but only lightly, because her every muscle was tight, continually waiting and listening for some sound or sign that the men who had attacked last night had found them again.

Dusk was falling and the evening shadows drawing in by the time Trystan returned. Hereric was tossing restlessly again, but all the same, Isolde had been watching for Trystan, looking up every few moments to scan the surrounding reeds. Even still, she hadn't realized how worried she'd been until she saw Trystan walk into the small circle of their camp and felt an almost dizzying rush of relief.

He moved wearily, his steps a little dragging, and Isolde could feel—

Nothing.

Startled, Isolde tried again, watching Trystan and reaching for the space where she felt the echo of Sight. She could feel, still, the grinding throb of Hereric's pain and the prickling heat of his skin. But nothing at all from Trystan—though he still held his right hand motionless, as though guarding against hurt. And watching him move to take a place nearby on the ground, she realized that she'd only guessed that morning that he'd injured his hand in the fight. And that back at Dinas Emrys she'd had to ask him whether he was wounded at all.

Reaching with his left hand, Trystan took the cup of honey wine she poured for him, and Isolde studied him again. Save for the stiff right hand, he showed no other sign of injury, and she could see his gaze traveling round the small clearing, ticking off the details of their surroundings and keeping watch as she had done for any sign of alarm. But the nothingness she felt watching him wasn't just the simple absence of pain, but as though a shadow had fallen, blotting out her connection to the Sight itself.

Before she could do more than wonder what further strange twist of the Sight this might be, Trystan spoke, nodding towards where Hereric lay on the ground, his face looking like bleached bone in the fading light.

"How is he?"

A cloud of the stinging insects were swarming around the bandages on Hereric's broken arm, and Isolde waved them off. "He's all right," she said. "The fever's rising, though. I'll be happier when we can get him up off the damp ground. Were you able to mend the rudder?"

Trystan slapped at one of the buzzing swarm that had landed on his arm, swore, and then shook his head. "No. I'm sorry. It's a bigger job than I thought—and there's not much in the way of wood around here that's not rotted through with the damp."

"I'm sorry," Isolde said. "About the rudder, I mean."

Trystan shrugged, his gaze still traveling round the camp, his head tilted as though he were listening for something far off. "Not your fault. Maybe tomorrow I'll have better luck, but I'm afraid we're stuck here for tonight."

He jerked his head towards where the big dog was asleep on another blanket near the remains of last night's fire.

His eyelids were slightly reddened with sleeplessness—or maybe, Isolde thought, with the effects of all the wine he'd drunk the night before. But his jaw had hardened, and his tone was expressionless and flat. *Not your fault*, he'd said, but Isolde wondered abruptly whether he did blame her for the broken rudder.

She seemed to hear above the twilight stillness the shriek of wood on wood as the other boat had drawn alongside, and see again in the deepening shadows of the two armed men clambering over the guard rail. She shivered. Even now, she couldn't think what else she might have done but cut the mooring lines—but still, that was why the boat lay beached and damaged now. She couldn't either call it entirely unfair if Trystan did blame her—though she knew the small spark of anger she still felt would kindle and catch fire once again if it were true.

Seven years ago, she would simply have demanded an answer, even if it meant the start of an argument. Now, though, with them back to exchanging brief, stiffly polite words whenever the occasion absolutely demanded that they talk—as they'd done since this journey began—she couldn't make herself ask. It was a pointless question, after all. At best, she thought, I'd only dredge up a memory of Trystan's drunken sleep that would make me angry and not able to trust him all over again.

"That's all right," she said instead, matching Trystan's tone. "It's—" She glanced round them. "It's a good place to camp."

From somewhere amidst the reeds, a cricket started to sing, echoed a moment later by the shrill cry of a marsh bird. Trystan watched her a moment, his blue eyes shadowed by the gathering dusk, and then a smile tugged at the corners of his mouth. "A good place to camp?" he repeated. "Even for you, that has to be the most unconvincing lie I've ever heard."

Isolde pressed her lips together, then gave up the struggle and laughed. She pushed a stray lock of hair back from her brow. "All right. This is, without question, the most uncomfortable place I've ever spent the night—and I include nights I've spent in a hospital tent on the hill above a battlefield, with two dozen wounded men in my care. But at least we've been safe here, so far. How's that?"

Trystan's mouth relaxed in a rare, unguarded smile, and Isolde felt something twist tight in her chest. Something she had to push far, far away. "Better," he said. "I—"

Before he could finish, Hereric groaned again, this time struggling to sit up and then screaming in pain as the movement jarred his broken arm. In an instant, Isolde had sprung up to kneel beside him, putting a hand on his good arm and speaking in a low, soothing murmur, trying to ease him back down. This time, though, her voice didn't seem to reach Hereric. He jerked away from her touch as though frightened, screamed again, and then without warning struck out with his good arm. In health, Hereric was strong as a draft horse, with broad shoulders and arms banded with muscle. Even weakened by fever as he was, his blow was enough to knock Isolde backwards.

Trystan, too, had risen at once and dropped to the ground on Hereric's other side, and now caught hold of Hereric's arm before he could swing again.

"Is that how you treat a lady when she's trying to help you, man? Be your own fault if she gives you up as a bad job."

Trystan's face was stark, his mouth grimly set as he watched Hereric's agonized struggles. His tone, though, was easy, good-humored, and almost unconcerned, and Hereric's frantic movements subsided. Slowly, Hereric turned his head, his bleary, fever-bright gaze finding Trystan's face, and his breath went out in a sobbing rush as his good hand fumbled to make a series of his word signs.

"That's all right." Trystan clapped Hereric lightly on the back. "Just lie back, now, and we'll have you well in no time."

The bunched muscles of Hereric's shoulders relaxed, and he let Trystan ease him back down onto the blankets.

"Here," Isolde said quietly. She had poured a measure of the poppy mixture into a cup of wine, and now put it in Trystan's hand. "Can you get him to swallow some of this?"

Trystan slipped an arm under Hereric's head and shoulders, holding the cup to his lips, and bit by bit the wine and poppy went down. When about half the cup was gone, Hereric let out another sigh and his eyelids drooped closed. Trystan took his arm away, lowering Hereric's head and shoulders once again.

He watched the injured man's slow, steady breathing for a moment, then turned his head to look at Isolde. "Did he hurt you?"

Isolde touched the place on her cheek where Hereric's blow had caught her. There might be a bruise there in the morning, but only a faint one. She shook her head. "It's nothing. He must have thought I was the one causing the pain in his arm. It happens, sometimes. At least he knew you, though."

"I suppose." Trystan sat back on his heels, turning again to look down at Hereric's face. The darkness was drawing in around them, deepening the shadows about the Saxon man's sunken eyes.

"What did he say to you?" Isolde asked. "Or rather, sign?"

Trystan grimaced. "Said he was sorry—he'd not recognized me at first. And that his arm hurt so much it was making it hard to think."

Isolde hesitated, but only for a moment. Trystan had to be able to see the truth as well as she. And besides, she couldn't keep simply adding to the list of topics she was stopping herself from speaking to him about. She drew in her breath. "Trys, he's not going to get better unless he loses that arm. We're going to have to take it off—and soon. I don't think it can wait even a full day more."

Trystan straightened with a jerk and looked at her across

Hereric's motionless form. "Do what?" And then, as Isolde started to answer, he shook his head. "Take off his arm? Out here? That's madness. Do you know what the chances are of a man surviving an operation like that?"

"Of course I do. I know exactly what the dangers are. But it is a chance of surviving, at least. Without it, he's none at all."

Trystan's mouth tightened. "A chance of what? Life as a one-armed mute? I'd sooner cut his throat now or have you give him a brew of something that would finish him off. He'd be better off dead."

"Maybe you think he would—but you can't make that choice for Hereric. It's his life. Only he can say for sure."

Trystan shook his head again. "Hereric earns his way by his sword—and his hands. As I do. Take that away, and what has he got left?"

Isolde suddenly remembered Evan, a bony, long-faced man with a drooping mustache who had been one of Con's bodyguards. Evan had lost a foot to an arrow wound gone bad, and had dragged himself from his sickbed and tried to drown himself in a water butt afterward. And for the entire three weeks he'd lain in Isolde's care, he'd snarled curses at her morning, noon, and night for pulling him out of the water and saving his life. That was another of those times she'd had to fight to keep from losing her temper with one of the wounded in her care—horribly sorry for Evan though she'd been.

Now, facing Trystan in the chill, gathering darkness of the marsh, Isolde's mouth twisted. "Yes, I know that argument. I sometimes think that's all men know how to do—fight and hurt and hack each other to pieces with their swords. So you think Hereric is only of use as long as he can kill? Take that away, and you might as well put him down like a wounded dog?"

Trystan held himself very still, and Isolde had the impression that he was working to keep anger in check as well. "That's not what I meant."

She'd rarely known him to lose his temper when they'd been

growing up together, either. He might get angry, but he'd always manage to keep himself under tight control. Now Isolde wished he would simply shout back at her. Seeing Trystan's effort to maintain his calm only made her angrier still.

"Maybe not," she flashed back. "But you're not God—nor yet even Hereric's blood kin. You can't decide on your own whether he lives or dies."

A muscle jumped in Trystan's jaw. "What about you? Haven't you ever wished you left well alone and let someone die—because all you'd done was just prolonging their agony a little more?"

Isolde's breath caught, and she realized, with a brief twist of irony, that she had ended up blazingly furious—and half able to believe Trystan the man Cynlas had thought him—after all. "That's a horrible thing to say."

"But it's true, isn't it?" Between them, Hereric flinched and muttered in the depths of his drugged sleep, and Trystan drew in his breath. When he went on, he spoke more quietly, though his voice was still hard and deadly calm. "Isa, Hereric's already had his tongue cut out—and it left him as simple as a six-year-old child. You want to see what's left of him after you cut off his arm?"

Isolde shook her head. "Trys—" All at once, all the fear and strain and exhaustion of the past night and day seemed to rise up and crash over her in a wave, and to her horror, she felt tears come into her eyes. She blinked them savagely back, keeping her gaze locked on Trystan's. "I'm a healer. I can't just sit by and let Hereric die if there's a chance I can act to save him. I can't."

Trystan watched her, still looking as though he worked to keep his voice even and quiet. "And that's what being a healer means? You'll grant Cynlas's son a quick death, but not Hereric?"

Isolde's temper flared again. "It means, at least, that I wouldn't give up on a friend because I was too much of a coward to take the chance on saving his life."

For what seemed an endlessly long moment, Trystan's eyes met hers, his face giving away nothing of whatever he thought.

Then, abruptly, he let out his breath and dropped his head into his hands.

For the space of several of Hereric's labored breaths, Trystan sat unmoving, so still he might have been carved in stone while the night stillness thickened all around them. Then, slowly, he raised his head. His face was still expressionless, but his eyes had the same look Isolde had seen in men newly returned from battle, who'd seen their companions cut down on every side.

Trystan drew in his breath, then said, "When?"

Something in his voice made even the last spark of Isolde's remaining anger die out and a cold chill brush against the back of her neck. Impulsively, she reached out and touched Trystan's arm. She said, "Trys, I didn't mean—"

His forearm was warm, even in the raw, predawn chill, and she felt a jolt run through her at the touch of his skin against hers, strong enough to tighten her heart. Quickly, she took her own hand away.

For what seemed another endlessly drawn-out moment, Trystan's eyes met hers, and she wondered whether he'd felt something of what she had. But then he shook his head and said, "It's all right. I know what you meant. Just tell me what you'll need for Hereric."

Chapter Eight

Isolde bent to check the bindings of soft rags she'd used to tie Hereric down. She'd managed to dose him with a few swallows of poppy-laced wine, and he slept, but not deeply. Not deeply enough that he'd stay unconscious once they began.

Trystan set down the lamp he'd lighted on the ground beside Hereric, and Isolde glanced up. They were in an abandoned fisherman's hut that Trystan had happened on in his search for wood the previous day, an hour's slow walk upriver from where they'd abandoned the boat. Part of the hut's thatched roof was falling in, and the door was gone, but it was shelter, of a kind. And the hut stood beyond the marsh on drier ground—though the wattle and daub walls were still crumbling with damp and smelled faintly of must and decay.

They'd spent the day in moving enough supplies here to last a few days, since Hereric would need time to recover before he could be moved. Isolde had helped Trystan fashion a carrying sledge for Hereric from an old blanket, and Trystan and Cabal had taken it in turns to pull him through the reeds to this place.

Now it was near nightfall, and Cabal kept guard outside, lying in front of the open doorway. Isolde sat back to glance round the hut's single small, square room. The floor was of beaten earth, packed hard as stone with years, and the place was empty save for a pile of old fishing nets in the corner, the strings half rotted through, and the roughly built wooden sleeping shelf where Hereric now lay.

Isolde looked up at Trystan. "Are there any settlements nearby? I didn't notice."

Trystan shook his head. "Nothing close. I saw a curl of smoke in the sky towards the east, but it was some ways off—half a day's walk, at least, I'd say."

Isolde nodded, and turned back to study Hereric's face, yellow as old tallow in the lamp's flickering light. The ominous smear of green-gray still ran the length of his jaw, and his mouth ominously colorless and slack. Isolde could hear what her grandmother would have said at such a bedside. That already the Morrigan hovered over this man, beating her raven wings, marking him for her own. At best, Isolde thought, she might have burned a pine bough to free the soul and speed it on its way.

For a moment, Isolde let herself look full in the face the fear that despite what she'd said to Trystan, this was the wrong choice after all. That Hereric would die, and they—she—would have put him through agony to no good cause. Then, deliberately, she locked the fear away. She'd chosen this course; there was no room for doubts now.

Trystan, to judge by his face, must have done the same. His eyes looked smudged with tiredness, but their gaze was clear and still as he stood looking down at the unconscious man.

"I'll make the first cuts," Isolde said. "And then I'll need you to take over when it comes to getting through the bone."

Without taking his eyes from Hereric, Trystan nodded. "Here." He handed her his bone-handled knife. "I put a new edge on it earlier. It's as sharp as I can make it."

Isolde took the knife, holding it in her hand a moment,

balanced across her palm. She'd done this before, many times, these last seven years. But still Kian's voice echoed briefly in her ears, repeating what he'd said about facing battle. *You'd think it'd get easier—but it doesn't. It's the same for every battle—every time.*

Since Hereric had taken so little of the poppy, Isolde drew out from her box of medicines a small glass vial of a hemlock and ivy decoction. Swallowed, the dose would be enough to kill—but inhaling the fumes could keep a man unconscious a short while. She unstoppered the vial and poured the contents over a clean rag, then handed it to Trystan.

"Hold this under his nose, and I'll begin."

EVEN WITH THE HEMLOCK AND POPPY, Hereric screamed. Deep, searing cries that at first echoed off the hut's crumbling walls, then grew weaker and hoarser as his voice gave out. By that time, Isolde had finished her own part and was holding Hereric as still as she could so that Trystan could make the cuts through bone. She could see Trystan flinch, convulsively, with every cry Hereric made, and rivulets of sweat run down into his eyes, but his hands were absolutely steady as he gripped the knife and sawed quickly through the blood-smeared bone.

Isolde's own skin was clammy with the effort of blocking out the awareness of Hereric's pain, but she took the Saxon man's face between her hands and spoke softly. "Nearly over, now. You've borne it bravely. Nearly done."

When it was over, reaction would set in, and the man whose face she held would be Hereric once more. But for now he was only a man with a broken arm. A series of bloody tasks that must be done, one by one, if a life was to be saved.

Trystan held the red-hot blade against the bloody stump that had been Hereric's arm and Hereric screamed again, his body going rigid, the muscles of his neck and throat standing out like cords. But it was over. Trystan set the smoking knife down and raised a hand to dash the sweat from his eyes. Isolde saw that, now that it was all over, the hand shook, briefly, but when he spoke his voice was steady as before.

"I'll go outside and bury this lot." He gestured to the blood-soaked mess by the bed. "If you'll stay with Hereric."

He looked so completely shut-off, so controlled and un-reachable and utterly *alone* that Isolde couldn't stop herself. She reached out, laying her hand over his. "You did incredibly well, Trys."

He looked slowly from their joined hands up to her. Their eyes met, and at that moment Isolde would have given anything to know what he was thinking. But then he shook his head, a swift shadow crossing his blue gaze. "Thanks. Though I'm not so sure Hereric would agree."

TRYSTAN STOOD MOTIONLESS, DRAWING IN LONG breaths of the chill, damp night air and waiting for the fit of shivering to run its course—like the racking chills of a fever, but stronger. Then he turned and went back inside. Isolde had bandaged the stump of Hereric's arm in clean wrappings and drawn fresh blankets up over his chest. She'd washed the worst of the blood from her hands and arms as well. Now she was sitting motionless against the wall by the bedside, her arms locked around her knees, her gaze fixed on Hereric, the flickering lamplight picking out the tears on her cheeks.

Trystan cleared his throat, then asked, "Are you all right?"

"What?" Isolde brushed at her eyes, then looked blankly at the moisture on her hand for a moment, as though she'd not realized she was crying until now. "Oh." She shook her head. "I always cry afterwards when it's someone I know. It's nothing."

Trystan hesitated again, then dropped to the floor beside her, leaning back against the wattle and daub wall. There was a moment's silence and then she said, "Hereric should have a few days' rest before we try to move him. Will that give you time enough to fix the rudder?"

"It should." Trystan called up an imagined map of the surrounding landscape. "We're maybe a seven nights' journey from the Wessex border now."

Isolde twisted a little to look up at him. "You're still willing to finish the journey, then?"

Trystan rubbed the space between his eyes. He was trying to avoid looking at Hereric's motionless form on the bed, but he asked, "Why wouldn't I be?"

Isolde bit her lip. "It's just . . . I'm not sure I've actually done Hereric any good, and—"

Trystan caught himself before he could reach for her. "Don't say that. I thought we'd already agreed we weren't making that kind of bargain. You feel you have to get to Wessex and Cerdic. I gave you my word I'd take you. Nothing's changed."

Isolde scrubbed a hand across her cheek again. "I'm sorry. I know. It's just—" She turned to look up at him, wide gray eyes huge in her pale face. "Do you think Cerdic will even listen to me?"

Trystan sighed. He knew she'd not thank him for a facile lie. "I don't know. He's a name for being a hard man—but a just one. A good soldier, in his day, a fine leader of his war band. And he's not a fool. He's a keen mind, as well as a strong heart for war. I'd say there's at least a chance he'll listen to what you have to say."

Isolde nodded. "I suppose I have to hope so. I just—" She stopped, biting her lip again, and then said, her eyes still on his face, with a look in their depths that made his heart twist in his chest, "I just can't help feeling as though I've dragged you and Hereric all this way and subjected you to all the dangers we've faced for what's doomed to be a lost cause."

He hadn't meant to touch her. It was his arm moved of its own accord, going round her before he realized what he'd done. "That doesn't sound like you."

That made her smile a little. "It doesn't, does it? I know. It's only that—" She broke off, turning to look at Hereric's gray face and bandaged stump of an arm. "It's only that every time, after an operation like that, I think, If I ever have to do that again—but then I have to. Because I'm a healer, and sometimes it's the only way, and—"

She must have been even more shaken and exhausted than he'd realized, because a shiver shook her, and then she leaned against him, unselfconsciously resting her head against his shoulder.

The part of Trystan's mind that wasn't still trying to block out the memory of Hereric's screams asked exactly how long he thought he was going to be able to keep some kind of a grip on his self-control, sitting with her like this. But he nodded. "Like with Hereric. It was the only way, Isa. Don't blame yourself."

Still, his left hand clenched involuntarily, and he heard Isolde draw in a sharp breath.

When he looked down, she was staring at the scarred fingers, her face gone a shade paler even than before. "So that's why you didn't want . . . and I said . . . oh, Trys, I'm so sorry."

He'd learned long ago that lying to Isolde was a waste of breath. Trystan didn't bother to ask what she meant or try to deny it. He tipped his head back, watching a coil of smoke from the lamp drift towards the ceiling, and said, after a moment, "Do you have to do that?"

"Do what?"

"Read my mind like that."

Isolde glanced up, a brief ghost of a smile touching the corners of her mouth. "I suppose I've had plenty of practice. Trying to make you talk always was like dragging river reeds up by the roots."

She was still leaning against him; above the reek of blood from the rest of the room, he could smell the sweet, floral scent of whatever she'd used to wash her hair. "Well, you could usually talk enough for ten, let alone two. If I had a measure of wheat for every story and fire tale you made me listen to, I could feed an army through the winter."

He heard her smother a yawn; she must be as tired as he was. But then she laughed. "I know. You used to tell me I could talk the hind legs off a goat."

"Did I? It's a wonder you ever bothered with me at all."

She shifted, resting her head against his shoulder again. "Oh, well, you weren't always that bad. You told Mara that she had pretty hair. That was kind."

Trystan rubbed his eyes with his free hand. After two all but sleepless nights, they were beginning to feel gritty with fatigue. "Who?"

"You don't remember? She was the daughter of Andras, my father's armorer. My age—eleven, or twelve, maybe. And she used to be teased, often—because she had bad skin and teeth that stuck out in front. And you knocked the boy down who was laughing at her, and you told her she had pretty hair. I remember, because I'd never heard you pay any girl a compliment before—however much they all giggled and made eyes at you. But I thought it was a very kind thing to do."

Trystan shrugged. Outside, the wind was whistling around the corners of the hut, tugging at the thatched roof above. "I was sorry for her, I suppose. And as I recall you weren't all that pleased with me at the time. I cracked a knuckle in the fight, and when you were tying it up for me, you said you'd skin me alive if I was ever stupid enough to get into another fight like that. I had to teach you how to throw a knife just so you'd speak to me again."

Her laugh was the one he remembered from years ago, bubbling up out of nowhere, clear and musical as her speaking voice. "I remember. I'd been begging you to teach me for months, but you'd always refused."

"Yes, well. If you'd cut your fingers off, I'd have been the one explaining just why I'd thought it a good idea to teach the king's daughter knife throwing in the first place."

Isolde laughed again, then was quiet a moment. Her eyes strayed again to his scarred hand. Trystan braced himself for her to ask for the whole story, but all she said was, "I truly am sorry, Trys."

She pulled back slightly, twisting so that she could look up at him, putting one hand on his cheek. Her raven dark hair was slipping out of its confining braid to curl around her face, and in the orange glow of lamplight, her face looked milk pale, her eyes the color of the ocean at dawn. "Will you promise me something? Promise me that even if Hereric . . . even if he dies, you won't blame yourself for tonight either? Hereric would know—really know—that you'd never hurt him willingly."

Her voice always made him think of sweet, cool water. Trystan closed his eyes. Then, through the haze of his own weariness, he heard himself say, "When I was in the quarries—in the slave camp—the guards used to . . . I was lucky to get off with a couple of finger joints gone. Usually they took hands—or arms—both of them, most of the time. Sometimes it was a punishment and sometimes—sometimes it was just for fun. Because they were edgy or bored or just plain angry as sin that they were stuck pulling guard duty at a filthy quarry in the middle of nowhere. They'd always do it nearby, so that the rest of us could hear. And then they'd group the ones without hands, without arms, together, in a kind of a cage and stand around laughing themselves sick while the wretches grubbed around in the dirt for whatever food was tossed in—trying to pick it up with their teeth, because of course they couldn't get at it any other way. The guards never gave them much. Just enough to keep them alive while their bodies rotted from the outside in."

When he looked down, Isolde was still watching him, the gray eyes wide, what little color had ebbed back into her face entirely gone. Trystan forced himself to stop speaking. "I'm sorry—I shouldn't have told you."

"Don't be stupid." She gave an impatient shake of her head, her voice almost angry. "I'm glad you did. I just . . ." She stopped and looked up at him again. "I wish I'd been there as well."

Trystan caught himself before he could say something that couldn't be taken back. *Remembering you was the light in the darkness. I'd live all of it over again just to hear you laugh once more.*

Powers of hell, he thought. You sound more like that damned harper's song by the day.

Instead he said, "So that you could have suffered, too? A lot of good that would have done." He paused and was silent, watching another curl of smoke from the lamp spiral upward, hang suspended a moment in the air above their heads, and then dissolve into the shadows of the thatched roof. Then he said, "I used to tell myself your stories, sometimes, though."

"Did you? I'm glad." She paused, then twisted to look up at him again. "I—"

And then she stopped, her eyes widening as though in shock or surprise, her gaze turning suddenly blank. She didn't speak, though, and after a moment, he asked, "Is something wrong?"

She shook her head slowly. "No. It's nothing." She was silent again, then, "Trys, what happened at Camlann? How did you come to be taken as a slave?"

"I—" Trystan's head came up with a jerk. Hell's rear gate, what did he think he was doing?

He felt as though he'd been asleep and had come awake suddenly to a kick in the chest. Even as the obscenely graphic memory boiled up inside him, even as his heart started to pound and a cold sweat broke out on his body, that detached, sneering voice at the back of his mind told him that he'd asked for this, letting himself get as close to her as he had.

Reflexively, he jerked away and saw Isolde's eyes widen again, and a look, part startled, part something that might have been pity or hurt or anger pass like a shadow across their depths.

"Trys?"

He turned away so that he wouldn't have to see her face. He'd managed to lie with a reasonably convincing air of relaxed boredom with an enemy knifepoint at his throat. But he was heaven damned if he could think of a single thing to say now.

"Do you trust me?" he asked finally. He heard the slight hesitation before she spoke and told himself he'd asked for that as well.

"Yes," she said after a moment. "Yes, I trust you."

Trystan got to his feet and forced himself to look down at her, briefly. "Then don't ask me to answer that."

ONCE OUTSIDE THE HUT, TRYSTAN SAT motionless on the blanket he'd spread out on the ground—so that he could keep watch, he'd told Isolde. He waited until all movement inside had stopped. Isolde would leave the lamp burning through the night, in case Hereric woke. But she'd spread a blanket for herself on the beaten earth floor so that she could catch what rest she could before he did. Trystan tilted his head back to look up at the ice-pale network of stars above. A clear night, at least. Unlikely that there would be rain. He gave Isolde time to fall asleep, debating with himself.

The thought of being caught unready by another attack was like chewing and swallowing broken glass. But there'd been no sign of pursuit all day. And now his muscles felt vaguely as though he were dragging himself along underwater, his eyes throbbing. He was approaching the limit of the time he could go without rest and still be alert enough to work on the rudder again in the morning. And if he tried staying awake and then dropped off anyway—

Wearily, Trystan reached for the pack of supplies he'd carried from the ship, found the skin of wine, flicked open the cap, and took an explosive swallow. The liquid ran like sour fire down his throat. You'd think one of these nights I'd start to like the filthy stuff, he thought.

He didn't know what made him turn. Maybe she made some slight sound that caught his ear. But when he looked round, Isolde was standing in the open doorway of the hut, watching him. It was too dark to see her face, but he knew her eyes were on him. She stayed like that, absolutely motionless, a slender shadow against the yellow glow of lamplight at her back. And then she stepped back, turning away, and was gone back inside the hut without a word.

THE SUN WAS JUST BREAKING OVER the horizon when Isolde looked out of the hut. The morning air was cool and damp, and she could see curls of silver mist rising over the sea of reeds that stretched between her and the river. Cabal had been sleeping curled on the blanket Isolde had spread for him near the door, but he woke at the sound of her passing by. He sat up, snuffling into her hand, and Isolde ruffled his ears and ran a hand over his back before stepping outside.

Trystan lay almost exactly as he had two nights before, one arm flung out, an empty wineskin lying by his side. The silver cap had come unfastened, and a last trickle of wine had pooled on the dirt, looking almost like blood in the harsh morning light. Isolde stood a moment, looking down at him, then dropped to sit beside him.

She'd slept a bit, wrapped in her traveling cloak and dozing lightly enough that she'd hear Hereric if he stirred or woke. But she'd not undressed, nor even taken off her shoes and woolen stockings. Even still, she was cold, and she drew her cloak more closely about her, keeping her eyes fixed on Trystan's face. This time he was less deeply asleep; after only a few moments his eyelids flickered, then opened.

His gaze was bleary at first, then cleared to startled awareness, and he jerked partway upright. "Is something wrong?"

"No."

Trystan let out his breath, and Isolde waited while he shook his head, then dragged himself upright to lean against the outer wall of the hut. He didn't speak, though, and after a moment's silence Isolde looked from him to the empty wineskin.

"You must have the devil's own headache," she said.

Trystan had shut his eyes again. "He's welcome to take it

back, then." Then he seemed to come to himself, for he started and shook his head again. "Is Hereric—"

Isolde shook her head. "No. Hereric's as well as can be hoped, I think. I gave him another dose of the poppy a short while ago, and he's asleep. It's too early to say any more."

Trystan nodded, then winced, and Isolde held out the cup she'd brought from inside.

"Here. Drink this."

Trystan's gaze was slightly wary, as though expecting her to say something more, but he accepted the cup, then drew back as he started to raise it to his mouth. "What in God's name is this? It smells like an ill-cured goat hide."

"It tastes worse. But it will help."

Trystan glanced up at her again, then tossed the cup back, a convulsive shudder running through him as he swallowed. "Jesus. Next time I'll stand the headache."

There was another moment's silence, and then Isolde said, "Trys, what's wrong?"

She saw him stiffen, then deliberately relax, his head still tilted back against the wall, his eyes sliding closed once more. His jaw was stubbled by a day's growth of beard, and he had still a smear of blood on his temple from where he'd wiped his brow the night before.

"What do you mean?"

"I know you. You hate drunkenness. Do you think I don't remember? Because of—"

Isolde stopped, then forced herself to go on. "Because of your father and what he used to do when he was drunk on ale or wine. And I have never, ever known you to put a friend at risk if you could help it. On the worst day of your life, you wouldn't do that. You've changed, maybe, but not that much. So what is it? Why are you doing this to yourself?"

Isolde thought something passed, swift as a shadow across Trystan's face. "I—" But then he stopped and shook his head.

They sat without speaking a moment more until at last Isolde said evenly, "Something else I just have to trust you on?"

Trystan started to speak, then stopped. Isolde saw him un-clench his hands, and then he shook his head again. Then all at once he sat bolt upright and froze, his gaze fixed on something over Isolde's shoulder. And, turning, Isolde saw it as well. A roil-ing black column of smoke, rising from the riverbank beyond the sea of reeds.

Isolde's blood ran suddenly cold, and she said, her voice sounding strange in her own ears, "The boat."

"It has to be." Trystan was on his feet, now, his eyes still fixed on the pillar of smoke, and his face was grim. "The smoke's com-ing from the exact spot where we left it. And there wasn't any-thing else there that could burn—not to make that much smoke."

Isolde swallowed. "That means—"

"They've found it—whoever 'they' are." Trystan was still a moment longer, then abruptly turned to Isolde. "How much damage would we do to Hereric if we move him now?"

"You think they'll find us, then?"

"I think if they've gone to the trouble of burning the boat, they're bound to look. And we're not all that far away. If you tell me it's death to Hereric to leave, I'm willing to take the chance and stay. But I don't like the odds on our getting by without being discovered." Trystan glanced up at the lightening sky. "It's not even as though it will be night soon. They'll have all day to search."

Isolde looked back into the hut. The pale sunlight slanting in through the door was enough that she could make out Her-eric, motionless on the sleeping shelf, his broad face gray in the hut's relative dimness, the bandaged stump of his arm lying atop the blankets. She shook her head helplessly. "I don't know. You're asking me if moving Hereric now could kill him—and I'll tell you honestly, I think it could. The shock of last night, and then traveling so soon after—" She stopped. "But then if we're discov-ered, he'll die in any case. We all will."

She could smell the smoke now, sharp and acrid amidst the more familiar scents of mud and must and damp. Isolde shook her head again, then looked up at Trystan and said quietly, "I don't know that there is a good choice, here—but I'll agree to whatever you decide. You know Hereric better than I do. What would he want?"

Trystan pushed a hand through his hair. "Christ's wounds, make it easy for me."

"I'm sorry."

Trystan let out his breath. "No, sorry. Not your fault." He was silent a moment, staring once more across the marsh towards the rising column of smoke. Isolde knew the inner debate he must be holding, but his face gave no sign of it. His gaze was steady and absolutely calm, with the same look she'd seen the night before as they worked over Hereric. And it was barely a moment before he turned. It came to Isolde that he must have faced decisions like this one many times before. So would any man who'd known battle and war.

"I think we should go."

Chapter Nine

ISOLDE STOPPERED THE VIAL OF hemlock decoction and slipped it into the pocket of her gown, then turned to bend over Hereric once more. He lay slack on the makeshift carrying sledge, and his gaze remained unresponsive, the pupil fixed, when Isolde gently lifted the lid of one eye. Isolde sat back, pushing a lock of damp hair off her face.

They were in a small glade of trees where they'd stopped a short while ago. It was raining, a chill, penetrating drizzle that dripped through the branches above, soaking their hair and clothes; Isolde's cloak was heavy and sodden about her shoulders, and underneath the outer layer of wool, her gown was growing damp as well.

In a way, though, the rain was a blessing. It was by now nearing midday, and hours since they'd left the abandoned fisherman's hut, and so far they'd seen no sign of pursuit. They'd met with no one at all, either—not even a stray sheep or goat. Though Isolde had seen, off in the distance, the remains of a burned-out settlement, the roofless huts sticking up like a row of black, broken teeth against the leaden sky. If she judged right, she thought they must be nearing the border of Atrebatia, where the fighting and raiding by Cerdic's war parties would have been worst. The knowledge made chill prickles run down Isolde's spine, and kept her turning her head, straining for any sight or sound of alarm. For now, though, even the column of smoke from the burned boat was invisible, as was the river itself, blotted out by the billowing sheets of rain and fog.

"How is he?" Trystan's voice made Isolde look up to find that he'd come to stand beside her. He'd given up his own cloak for an added covering for Hereric, and his shirt was soaked through, plastered to his skin.

Isolde straightened, stepping back to sit down on a fallen log. Cabal trotted over to settle beside her, and she put one hand on the big dog's head, grateful for his warmth. "Unconscious—for now, at least."

Hereric had woken just as they reached the shelter of trees, screaming and trying to throw off invisible attackers, his fevered eyes wild. Isolde had tried to coax him to swallow another dose of the poppy-laced wine, but he'd fought her and then collapsed, retching, onto the carrying sledge. He'd not even recognized Trystan. At last Isolde had found the hemlock in her medicine stores, holding a saturated pad under Hereric's nose as before until finally he lay still.

Now, looking down at Hereric's rain-streaked form and remembering his frantic screams and blank, terrified eyes, she felt a lump of ice settle in the pit of her stomach. She concentrated, focusing on Hereric's broad, ashy pale face. She could still feel the steady, wrenching throb of his pain, but nothing else. No way to tell, she thought, whether he's only fever crazed or whether the horror of last night has damaged his mind.

Either way, though, he couldn't stay out in the cold rain, and she looked up. "Trys, where are we—" she began. And then she stopped with a bitten-off cry as a sharp stab of pain bit into her ankle. She looked down in shock, and was in time to see a winding, muddy brown form, patched with a stripe of interlocking diamonds down its back slide off into the underbrush to her right.

With a growl, Cabal made to bound after the snake, and Isolde caught him back just in time. "Cabal, no!" She held him tightly by the collar, and the big dog whined in frustration, then subsided, settling back beside her on the ground.

"Was that—" Isolde began.

Trystan had jerked upright at her cry, his hand moving by reflex to the hilt of his sword even as his eyes found the place where the snake had vanished into a clump of grass. "An adder." He turned back to Isolde. "Must have had a nest under that log—they don't usually attack like that. Where did it bite you? Let me see."

He dropped to kneel at Isolde's side, and drew his knife to cut her stocking away, baring the place where the snake had struck, just above Isolde's ankle. Already the flesh was starting to swell, and was throbbing with a fiery pain that made Isolde bite down hard on her lower lip.

"They're poisonous—although their bite isn't fatal. Not usually, at least. Hurts like the devil, though."

"I know," Isolde said.

That won another brief smile from Trystan, but then he sobered, tilting his head back to look up at her through the rain. "The poison should be bled out—as soon as possible."

Isolde nodded. "I know," she said again.

"Do you want me—" Trystan began, but she shook her head. "No, it's all right—I've done this before." She'd treated adder bites, though never on herself. But Con's huntsmen had sometimes come home with snakebites. Not enough to kill, as Trystan had said. But the venom could make a whole arm or leg swell.

Isolde's vision was starting to shiver, making the sullen gray sky above seem to press down on them and the thick screen of dripping green leaves all around seemed suddenly menacing and close. The forest floor of dead leaves and sodden scrub, too, seemed to tilt on a crazy angle. Beside her, Cabal whined anxiously, butting his head against her arm, and Isolde put a hand on his head again. "It's all right, Cabal. Good dog. Lie down, now. There's nothing wrong."

Cabal obeyed, slumping unwillingly onto the muddied ground at her feet, and Isolde shut her eyes against another stab of pain. Then she asked Trystan, "Can you reach my medicine bag? It's over next to Hereric." She gestured to where Hereric lay on the carrying sledge under the comparative shelter of a towering pine tree.

When Trystan had handed her the bag of supplies, Isolde found her roll of clean linen bandaging and knotted one just above the snakebite. The pain was making a clammy sweat break out on her skin, but she studied the puncture marks briefly and then said, "Give me your knife?"

Trystan handed her the blade and Isolde took it, set her teeth, and then made two quick, intersecting cuts across the bite. Blood spurted from the wound, and Isolde looked away, dropping the knife and pressing her hands hard against her eyes.

"Isa?" Trystan asked after a moment. "Are you—"

Isolde focused on drawing first one breath, then another, telling herself that she'd never fainted in her life and wouldn't now. "No, it's all right." She shook her head, her eyes still closed. "It's just the snake's venom. I remember hearing it makes you dizzy, sometimes."

"Here." Trystan found a jar of mead, broke the seal, and handed it to her. "Drink some—you'll feel better."

Isolde took a few swallows, then handed the jar back to Trystan. "Thank you. I'll be fine." She looked down at the cut above her ankle. The blood was still running freely, and she squeezed it gently, trying to expel as much of the poison as she could, then bound it up with another clean bandage. When she'd done, she looked up at Trystan, trying to ignore the rivers of fire that were running up her calf and the strange shivering still at the corners of her vision. She must not have made the cuts deep enough to draw all the venom. Or else she'd been too slow and the poison had already spread.

"What are we going to do? Hereric can't stay out in this rain much longer. He needs a fire—and a roof overhead."

Trystan nodded. "I know." He turned, scanning the thick screen of surrounding trees, wiping a trickle of rain from his face. "If you can face going on a bit farther, there's a place over that way"—he gestured off to the right—"that should do."

Isolde looked up in surprise, then shut her eyes again as the movement brought a wave of dizziness. "How can you know that?"

"I was in these parts once before—years ago." Trystan was still squinting off into the distance, frowning as though comparing the trees and rocks that marked the landscape to whatever memory he'd called up from that time. "But I think I can find the place again. It's an old Roman ruin. And we should be safe there for the night. The Saxon war bands won't go near anything Roman built. Not even the old Roman roads."

Each separate drop of rain felt like an icy needle pricking her skin. Isolde was shivering under her wet clothes, trying to keep her teeth from chattering, but she asked, "Why not?"

Trystan shrugged, hunching his shoulders against a sudden gust of rain; the wind was rising, blowing from the southwest. "The old ruins are *wearge*—cursed, or so the stories go. But I don't know that I've ever heard why or how." Isolde shivered again, and he held out a hand. "Can you stand?"

With Trystan's help, Isolde got unsteadily to her feet, but then swayed and would have fallen if Trystan hadn't caught her around the waist and held her up. She blinked, trying to clear the shivering darkness from her sight, fighting back the waves of nausea that were sweeping through her. A tiny corner of her mind told her that sickness, too, was a common effect of an adder's bite—though the knowledge didn't stop the lurch of her insides. "I'm all—" she started to say, but Trystan cut her off.

"No you're not. Here, sit back down." He lowered her gently back onto the fallen log, keeping one arm about her shoulders to steady her. "I'm going to hitch Cabal to Hereric's carrying sledge. He can pull Hereric, and I'll carry you. It's not that far."

Isolde couldn't summon up the energy to argue. She felt her muscles tense at Trystan's touch, but was warmer once he'd lifted her into his arms. She closed her eyes, trying to lock the throb of the snakebite away in a far-off compartment of her mind, thinking instead of all the men whose wounds she'd treated who had borne far worse agony than this in silence, without so much as a moan. She could feel the steady beat of Trystan's pulse under her cheek, and she started to count the beats, trying to imagine herself a boat, floating above the sea of pain. Amazingly, she'd almost drifted off to sleep when Trystan's voice pulled her back and made her open her eyes.

"Here we are."

Isolde blinked. The building must, she thought, have been a Roman villa once. Home of some retired commander of the legions of Eagles that had abandoned Britain to its enemies more than an old man's lifetime ago. Now, seen through the misting rain, the place looked almost Otherworldly, the graceful stone columns cracked and twined with climbing vines, the roof hidden by the spreading trees that had grown up all around.

The building must have been vast, when it was newly built, but only a single wing remained standing. The rest had tumbled into ruins that stretched back and away amidst the trees and underbrush, and what once must have been a carefully laid garden was overgrown with weeds, the paving stones half buried or cracked. At the far end of the remaining wing, the original heavy oaken door hung crookedly on its hinges, and Trystan pushed it open with his foot before carrying Isolde inside. She felt his muscles tense as though in anticipation of what they might find, but the place was ringingly empty, smelling faintly of must and damp leaves.

"Will you be all right here for a bit?" Trystan asked. "I want to get Hereric and Cabal inside."

Isolde found she still couldn't summon up the energy to

speak, but she nodded, and Trystan set her down so that she could lean back against the wall. Isolde closed her eyes, listening to the sound of Trystan's retreating footsteps and trying hazily to recall everything she knew of adder bites, to gauge how long might it be before the effects of the poison started to wear off. By morning, at least, she thought, and felt a stab of anger at herself. Stupid, stupid, stupid, she thought, not to have seen the snake. Or not to have made the cuts deeper or let them bleed more.

She forced her eyes open, and looked round the room, dimly lit by the gray afternoon light that filtered through the open door. The walls had once been plastered and whitewashed, though some of the plaster had fallen into crumbled heaps on the floor. And the floor itself must have been beautiful once. It was overlaid, now, by a layer of dust and dirt, but she could see that it was made up of hundreds of colored tiles that formed a pattern like that of a woven basket even underneath the grime.

The door swung open again, and Trystan carried Hereric inside, Cabal following close at his heels. Trystan had spread a pair of blankets on floor across from Isolde, and now he lowered Hereric onto the makeshift bed. The Saxon man's head lolled back, his muscles utterly limp, and his flaxen hair was plastered to his face by the rain. Isolde's throat felt swollen and dry, but she swallowed and forced herself to ask, "Is he all right?"

Trystan nodded. "No worse, at any rate, I don't think."

Their voices echoed strangely in the empty space, the room's high ceiling tossing the sound back at them. Isolde struggled to sit up, biting back a gasp at the fiery throb in her ankle. "He should drink something. I can—"

"That's all right. You stay there. I'll do it." Trystan found a waterskin amidst the rest of the supplies he'd carried in. He unfastened the cap, lifted Hereric's head and shoulders slightly, and held the spout to Hereric's mouth. Isolde, watching from across the room, saw the water run out of Hereric's slack mouth and down his chin, soaking into his beard.

Cabal padded across the tiles floor to Isolde, settling next to her with an exhausted sigh. Isolde ran a hand down his back, then swallowed painfully again. "He didn't take any water, did he?" she asked.

Trystan was still facing Hereric, but she saw him shrug. "Maybe a bit. It's hard to tell."

He sorted quickly through their supplies until he found tinder and flint, then turned to the center of the room, where Isolde now saw a kind of makeshift hearth had been fashioned from some of the fallen building stones. Cursed the old Roman ruins might be, but they weren't the first travelers to make camp here. There was no hole cut in the tiled roof above, but the windows were small and set high in the lime-washed walls, and would allow the smoke to escape without letting in the rain.

The heat of the fire Trystan built took the damp chill from the air, and Isolde finally stopped shivering and started to feel warm in her sodden clothes. Cabal, worn out after pulling Hereric's carrying sledge, was snoring lightly beside her, and despite the pain of the snakebite Isolde started to feel drowsy also, her eyelids heavy and sore. She shook her head, though, forcing herself not to fall asleep again.

"Can you reach me my medicine bag again?" she asked Trystan. "I should do a better job of cleaning the knife cuts now that we're out of the rain."

Isolde found her supply of vinegar brewed with rosemary and goldenseal. She untied the bandages on her ankle, unstoppered the vial, and poured a measure of the liquid over the angry-looking cuts. The sting of the vinegar made her eyes tear and a clammy sweat break out again on her skin. She gritted her teeth, soaked a clean linen pad with the mixture and pressed it hard over the cuts, then repeated the procedure twice more. The third time she caught her breath and bit her lip, and looked up to find Trystan watching her. The firelight shadowed his face and ran reddish gold along the stubble of beard on his jaw.

"You know, you could just scream if you want to," he said. "There's no one to hear."

Isolde still felt dizzy and slightly sick to her stomach, but she managed to raise her eyebrows and say, "Screaming makes it hurt less?"

One corner of Trystan's mouth curved in a brief, half-unwilling smile. "Yes, well, you've got me there. Here, let me do that." He took the clean bandage Isolde had started to tie over the cleansed ankle.

His gold-brown hair was still damp with the rain, small droplets of rainwater still trapped on his eyelashes. The firelight gleamed on the lean, strong lines of his face, and his touch on her skin was warm and sure. And all at once, as their eyes met, Isolde felt something enter the room—something that crept in like sea fog and tightened her every nerve. She started automatically to pull away. "It's all right—I can manage."

Trystan didn't let her go, but he made an exasperated sound that at least broke the moment. "Isolde, for once in your life will you admit you can't do everything on your own? You may be a fine healer, but you probably pull your own hair out whenever a patient like you lands in your care."

Isolde's vision had started to shiver and darken again. Trystan's face was half in shadow, half lighted by the fire. She leaned her head back against the wall, letting her eyes slide closed, trying to ignore the shivers of warmth that spread outwards from the touch of his hand on her ankle.

"That's good, coming from you. You could have had a severed hand when you were younger, and I'd have had to knock you unconscious to so much as get within reach of it with a bandage." She drew in a breath as Trystan tied a knot in the strip of linen, then said, "You're right, though. I do hate being ill or hurt. That's probably part of why I'm a healer."

Trystan finished knotting the bandage and sat back. "Let me give you something to drink. You should take some water or something, at least."

Her mouth did feel painfully dry. "All right."

She let him help her to sit up again, let him guide the cup

of water he'd poured to her mouth, his hand over hers. She drank the whole cupful but shook her head when he asked if she wanted more. "No. Thank you, though."

The pain was receding slightly, and Isolde forced herself to say, "Trys, all this is my fault. I should have—"

She had to break off as a hot prickle of tears started again behind her eyes. Isolde blinked, ordering herself to stop. If she'd been careless enough to be bitten by the adder, she absolutely refused to dissolve now into tears. That was something else she might have forgiven herself when she was ten, but not now.

Trystan must have seen, though—or else she looked even more ill and pathetic than she'd thought—because he came to crouch down next to her. His hand moved as though he were about to smooth her hair back, but then he seemed to check himself and said, instead, "Your fault? That a snake bit you? You can't blame yourself. Besides, haven't you heard about an adder's bite being good luck?"

Isolde smiled unsteadily, raising a hand to scrub at her cheek—and tried not to wish he'd touch her, put an arm around her so that she could lean against him. "You just made that up. And stop being so nice to me—you'll make me feel sorry for myself."

Trystan smiled, one eyebrow raised. "All right. Give me a moment, and I'll think up some names to call you."

Isolde smiled again as well, then she shook her head and sobered as she met Trystan's eyes, on a level with hers. She felt that same prickling awareness start to creep into the space between them again, and she went on quickly, "I didn't mean just the adder bite. I meant to say that I'm sorry for . . . for your boat. And because I'm not caring for Hereric now, when he needs me. And—"

This time, Trystan did touch her, brushing a stray lock of hair lightly back from her brow. Quickly as he took his hand away, Isolde still shivered. "I'll sit up with Hereric," Trystan said. "You can tell me what to do. Although"—a flash of bleakness crossed

Trystan's intensely blue eyes—"I'm not sure there's anything either of us can do for him now beyond just waiting to see if he survives. But as for the boat and the rest—you were honest about the risks when we started out. I'd have had to be God's own fool not to know there was danger of something like this happening."

Guilt caught Isolde like a knife-sharp gust of wind—powerful enough that she forgot any unaccustomed currents in the room, forgot everything but the wish that she could sink through the stone-tiled floor. Or at least faint after all. I should tell him about Marche, she thought. I have to, now. Her throat felt dry and tight, though, and she couldn't somehow make herself speak the words.

She shook her head. "You know," she said instead, "I'd understand if you . . . if you wanted to leave. To just take Hereric and go."

"And leave you here? Alone? Are you out of your mind?" Trystan shook his head, but then his expression softened as he looked at her. He took her hand, folding his fingers over hers. "Look, I'll make you a bargain. If you won't let me feel guilty for taking off Hereric's arm, you can't blame yourself for the boat's being burned. Or because you can't cure an adder's bite with a snap of your fingers and get up to take care of Hereric now." He shook his head again, a brief smile edging into his eyes. "Christ, Isa, God probably asks less of himself than you do."

Isolde gave a choked-up laugh. "I—" She stopped short, hearing what she'd been about to say. She felt the blood drain from her face, and Trystan caught her, steadying her with an arm about her shoulders.

"Do you want to try to eat something?" he asked. "Or some of the poppy brew you gave Hereric?"

Isolde shook her head. The strong, solid warmth of Trystan's arm around her, the rise and fall of his chest as he breathed, the hiss of the rain on the tile roof above their heads all seemed to weave themselves together and settle around her like a golden web, at once the cause of her panic and yet oddly the only thing that held it somewhat at bay. So she sat still, letting herself lean against him for just a moment. Then, when she could trust her voice enough to speak, she drew slowly away.

"No, that's all right," she said. "Maybe I'll try to sleep for a little while. Wake me, though, if Hereric needs anything more."

TRYSTAN LEANED BACK, STARING ACROSS AT the patchwork of dancing shadows the fire cast on the opposite wall. The room was silent, save for the pop and crack of the flames, the sound of the rain, and the occasional snuffle from the dog, asleep at Isolde's other side. After a time she said, "Trys? Have you any idea who the men who attacked us might be? I mean, did you see anything on them that might give a clue as to what lord they served?"

She was lying curled on her side under the covering of her cloak, her eyes fixed on the fire. The light gilded her pale skin and twining gold threads through her hair. Trystan forced himself to drag his gaze away and shook his head. "Nothing like that. I did look. But no. Someone bound on keeping you from reaching Wessex and negotiating an alliance with Cerdic, I'd say. You've no idea yourself who that might be?"

He heard the soft rustle as Isolde shifted a little. "Not really. If it's a traitor to the council, it would almost have to be Cynlas of Rhos or Dywel of Logres. They were there, at Dinas Emrys, when we left. They could most easily have learned of our plans. But I don't know which of them is most likely. And there's no way to tell, now. We've no way even of knowing what's happened at Dinas Emrys since we've been gone."

She stopped. Glancing down, Trystan saw a shadow cross the wide gray eyes, and said, "Don't worry for Kian. He can mind for himself. And he's been in worse places by far."

Isolde let out her breath. "I know. It's just—" And then she stopped, a strange look passing across her face. "Can you always guess what I'm thinking as well?"

Trystan shrugged. "Not always. Sometimes."

She was silent, seeming to hesitate, and then she said, "Trys? Do you think you could come over here and just . . . lie down next to me for a little while?" A shiver racked her, and she curled up more tightly under the cover of her cloak. "I'm so cold—I just can't get warm."

Shades of hell. Trystan wondered briefly whether the adder that had bitten her could have been some petty god or wood spirit in disguise. One with a particularly malignant sense of humor, who had set all this up as a way of driving him completely out of his mind.

Isolde was still shivering, though, her teeth starting to chatter as well. All right. It wasn't as though he were still sixteen years old. He could do this. Just think about wild dogs or knives or cleaning and gutting fish. Anything but what Isolde had just asked.

He said, "If you like."

Trystan got up and moved to lie down beside her. Staying on top of the cloak that covered her. Not that it helped by much, because he could feel her still through all the layers of fabric, slender and small and fine-boned. He felt the warmth of her breath on his neck as she sighed and relaxed, the shivering slowing and then finally coming to a stop.

"Thank you."

Trystan didn't trust himself to speak, so he didn't answer, and Isolde was silent so long he thought she'd fallen asleep. But then she spoke again, her voice quiet in the high-ceilinged room.

"This place must have been beautiful once."

Trystan turned his head to glance round the decaying room at the crumbling lime-washed walls, cracked columns, and dirty tiled floor. "Cost someone a good deal to build, at any rate."

"Yes, it must. All this marble and carved stone."

She was silent, and he felt her shift again, then draw in her breath as though in pain. The adder's bite had to be hurting like fury, but she'd said nothing of it, and Trystan knew better than to bother asking how she felt. She'd been like that, always. Incredibly stubborn and unbelievably tough. Right now she'd probably get up and run if he'd said they had to.

She turned her head, looking round the room as he had, the softness of her night-dark hair brushing his cheek.

Wild dogs. Knives. Cleaning and gutting fish.

"My grandmother used to spit whenever she spoke of the Romans or their legions, I remember," she went on. Even exhausted and in pain, her voice had a soft, musical lilt. "She would have agreed that places like this one were cursed. She used to say it was the fault of Rome that the old gods had fled from Britain and left a space open for the Christian God to steal in. That it was because of the Romans that all the old songs were forgotten and no longer sung. And that we'd lost the connection to the land and couldn't drive the Saxons back when they came to these shores. Because the land was no longer ours to hold."

"Did she?" Trystan asked.

Isolde nodded. "She used to say that a great darkness was rising, ready to sweep over Britain. And that even Arthur wouldn't be able to hold it back in the end."

"Yes, well." Trystan shifted position a bit. "She was right about Arthur, at any rate."

She was silent. He could feel the steady rise and fall of her breathing beside him. "Trys?" Her voice sounded soft and a little sleepy, and she reached out from beneath the cloak to touch his hand. "I'm still sorry I dragged you along on this journey. But I'm so glad you're here."

Trystan held himself in check, focusing on *not* thinking about the way the feel of her lying close against him like this ran like flame through every fiber in his body—or about the way her lips would feel if he turned his head and touched his mouth to hers. Before he could even think what to say, her eyes had drifted closed. He felt the rhythm of her breathing change and knew she had finally fallen asleep.

He lay still a moment, drawing a little away and propping

himself on one elbow so that he could see her face, tracing the glimmers of golden firelight running across her pale skin, the curve of her long dark lashes resting against her cheeks. Then he swore at himself, rose—carefully, so as not to wake her—and found an extra blanket to put over the cloak under which she already lay. And then he crossed to where Hereric lay like a dead man, putting half the room's length between him and Isolde.

Not that it helped. He could still feel the warmth of her breath against his neck. Feel her, light and slender in his arms, the sweet weight of her head resting on his shoulder.

Trystan shut his eyes and wished he had a bucket of icy water to dump over his head.

Well, at any rate, he should have no trouble staying awake tonight.

HOURS HAD PASSED, AND TRYSTAN WAS still sitting beside Hereric— and still awake—when Isolde gave a sudden cry as though she'd been stabbed and sat bolt upright. Her eyes were open, but their gaze was unfocused, staring and wide, still lost in the grip of the dream. Trystan crossed and knelt beside her, touching her arm and feeling a shudder run through her from head to foot. She turned towards him, hiding her face against his shoulder and clutching at his shirt.

Definitely still asleep, then. Awake, she'd have thrown herself off a cliff before she clung to anyone like this.

After a moment's hesitation, Trystan put one arm around her, steadying himself against the floor with his free hand. "It's all right. I've got you. You're all right."

He felt another shudder shake her, and then she woke with a gasp.

"Trystan. What—"

"You were asleep—dreaming."

"Dreaming." She sounded dazed, still, but then she caught

her breath and pulled herself abruptly away. Cabal had woken
as well at the sound of her cry and now butted his head against
her shoulder with a soft, high-pitched whine. Isolde quieted him
with a hand on his neck, though Trystan had the impression
that the movement was more a reflex than anything else. She
drew a shaking breath, then smoothed a stray lock of hair away
from her face and shook her head, pressing her eyes tight shut
as though still trying to break free of the dream.

"It was just a nightmare." Her voice wavered slightly, and
Trystan saw her throat contract as she swallowed. Trystan ignored the irrational pulse of fury behind his eyes and made
himself move back a step or two. Any closer, and he didn't trust
himself not to reach out to her again. When she went on, the
words were steadier and she turned her head with a visible effort,
meeting his gaze. "I'm all right, now."

ISOLDE LAY ON HER SIDE UNDER the combined weight of her cloak
and a rough woolen blanket, her eyes closed. She could feel
Trystan's eyes on her, though, and she dug her nails hard into
her palms, forcing herself not to shiver or shake, because Trystan
would see. *Don't ask,* she willed him. *Don't ask. Believe I'm asleep.*

Whether or not he believed it, she didn't know, but he did
finally turn away, returning to Hereric's side. Isolde knew she
should get up and join him, make sure Hereric was all right and
needed nothing more, but she couldn't make her muscles work.
The adder bite in her ankle was no longer as painful as it had
been, faded to a dull, pounding ache instead of a fiery throb. But
still Isolde couldn't make herself leave the shelter of her makeshift bed.

Nor could she sleep again. She could feel the clinging residue
of the dream like a layer of cooking grease smeared over her skin.
That was familiar, by now—but it was worse, much worse this
time, with the memory of Trystan's touch burning in every part
of her body like a brand.

Why did that never occur to me? she thought. That Marche is Trystan's father?

She'd known it, of course—she'd always known, in the same way she knew Trystan had blue eyes and gold-brown hair. But that was a far distant cry from the stomach-clenching aware-ness that gripped her now. She'd salved the bruises and cracked ribs Trystan had won trying to shield his mother from Marche's blows more times than she could possibly count when they were growing up together. But even still, somehow she'd always man-aged to keep them separate in her mind.

She'd managed, too, these last five months, to keep Marche out of her thoughts, save for the nights when the dream came. Even when she summoned him in the scrying water, heard his thoughts, she'd kept him locked away in a tight cage of her own making, not even allowing a picture of him to form in her mind. Now, though, he seemed a palpable presence in the room, as real as though he'd clawed his way out of her dream and come to stand before her, somewhere on the tiled floor between her and Trystan.

A black-haired bear of a man, broad-chested and powerfully built, with a square-jawed face and strong, solid bones. Maybe handsome once, though age now had coarsened him, leaving his skin weathered and scored with broken veins, his dark eyes puffy and tired-looking, puckered with fatigue. Still, nothing out-wardly at least to distinguish him from a hundred other fighting men—save maybe for something that moved, very rarely, beneath the surface of his dark gaze.

Isolde shut her eyes more tightly, as though that could block out the thought, but she couldn't stop herself from imag-ining it, seeing the firelit scene play out in her mind as though it had actually happened that way. She imagined hearing Trystan ask her what the nightmare had been. And then hear-ing the words crawling against her will from her own mouth, and seeing the look on Trystan's face once he knew what she'd dreamed.

It didn't matter how much she might wish Trystan closer to

her. It could never, never be now. Marche—Trystan's father—would always be there, standing in between.

Isolde thought for a moment she was going to be sick, but she clenched her jaw shut, tightening her hands and lying absolutely still. She didn't cry, either. Partly because Trystan would hear. Partly because crying would feel like giving the victory to Marche, and because she hated the feeling that she was wallowing in self-pity when she was hardly the first or the last woman to feel this way. But partly, too, because the hollow ache that filled her was somehow too raw and painful—and too deeply lodged in her chest—for tears.

FINALLY, THE FIRE TRYSTAN HAD BUILT died down to glowing embers, and the room began to brighten with the first gray light of dawn. A headache had settled behind Isolde's eyes, but she sat up, ignoring the lurch of her stomach. Trystan had been bending over Hereric, but he looked up as Isolde stirred.

"How is he?" Isolde asked.

Trystan lifted one shoulder. "Well, he swallowed some of the poppy an hour or two ago, at least." His blue eyes looked smudged with tiredness, and there were lines of fatigue about the corners of his mouth.

"How do you feel?" Trystan asked.

"Better." Isolde got unsteadily to her feet. Her ankle hurt, but less so than it had the night before, and she found it would take her weight. The dizziness, too, was gone. "Is there somewhere nearby I can wash?"

Trystan nodded. "There's a stream that runs across a corner of the gardens outside. Do you want me—"

"No!" The word came a shade too quickly, and Isolde drew in her breath. "No, that's all right. I'll find it. Someone should stay with Hereric in case he wakes."

Outside, she leaned against one of the cracked stone columns.

The air was damp and clean feeling after the night's rain, and the sky was clear, banded with the orange of the rising sun. Cabal had padded after her when she'd stepped out through the door, and Isolde scratched his ears, holding tight to his collar to keep him by her side. She closed her eyes but found herself remembering Trystan's face, shadowed by the firelight of the night before, feeling the brush of his fingers smoothing the hair back from her brow. Lying close beside him and finally being warm—and feeling completely, frighteningly safe.

The rustle of a breeze in the branches of the surrounding trees seemed to whisper an echo of Garwen's weeks-ago spoken words. *Everyone deserves to know that kind of love at least once in a lifetime.*

Isolde jerked her thoughts back and tried to fill her mind instead with the memory of Trystan drunkenly asleep beside the empty wineskin. She half wished that he had drunk himself to sleep again last night, as well. She would have clutched at being able to be angry just now.

Instead, she thought, I'm going to have to spend day after day and night after night with him until the journey's end. When just being in the same room with him this morning had made her skin prickle as though with the jabs of hot knives and her lungs burn as if she were trying to breathe water instead of air.

She felt steadier, though, after she had bathed her face and hands in the icy water of the stream she found running between mossy banks among the trees. If there was still a hard, cold knot in her chest, the panicked, shaking feeling had eased. Isolde combed her hair out with her fingers and then braided it tightly again before sitting down on a rock to untie the bandages on her ankle. The wounds still looked red and angry, but the swelling had gone down, and the streaks of red around the snake's bite were starting to fade.

Isolde had brought her medicine bag; she cleaned and salved the cuts, then retied the bandages. She let herself sit still a moment longer, watching Cabal splash in the shallow water, making wild bounding leaps after the schools of minnows that darted to and fro near the surface and snapping at the water with his jaws. She stared at Cabal so long her vision blurred. Then she rose and summoned the big dog with the low whistle he'd been taught by Con.

TRYSTAN WAS WIPING HERERIC'S FACE WITH a damp cloth when Isolde returned.

"Here, let me." She took the cloth from Trystan and knelt at the Saxon man's side, putting a hand on his brow. His skin was still dry and hot, but at least no hotter than the night before. Hereric stirred, twitching restlessly at her touch, and gave an indistinct, fretful sound, though his eyes remained closed. Isolde checked the bandages on his arm, but they were still dry; as Trystan had said, there was little she could do for him beyond waiting to see whether his body was strong enough to fight free of the fever's leeching grasp.

Trystan had found brown bread and water amidst their supplies, and he handed Isolde both a cup and a round of the bread. It was hard and dry, but dipped in the water it softened enough to chew. Isolde shared her portion with Cabal, then forced herself to swallow a few mouthfuls.

They'd not yet spoken of any plans beyond the most immediate ones, but now Isolde looked across at Trystan and said, "Trys, what are we going to do? We can't keep on pulling Hereric on a carrying sledge."

"I know." Trystan tore off a piece of his own round of bread, looking down at Hereric. His eyes were still shadowed by weariness, but his look was the same one Isolde had seen the day before, shutting out all thought but straightforward consideration of the immediate questions at hand. He looked up at her. "Can you make any kind of guess at what the chances are he'll live through this?"

Isolde's gaze went to Hereric's still form. It was almost a relief to let her mind slip into the familiar channels of healing and treatment, death or life for a man in her care. "He's young," she said slowly. She realized as she spoke that she'd never considered how old Hereric might be before. There was something almost ageless about him, the warrior's powerfully built body without and the child's mind within. Now, though, studying his broad, flaxen-bearded face, Isolde thought that he couldn't be more than five and twenty, and maybe even younger still.

"Young and strong," she said. "That will count in his favor, sick as he is now."

She stopped and focused again on Hereric's face, concentrating, letting the awareness of pain she'd been blocking out flood in. Pain . . . and beneath it . . . Isolde closed her eyes in an effort of concentration, trying to grasp at the feeling that flashed and slid away through her hands like the darting minnows in the stream.

"He's in pain," she said at last. "In pain, and he doesn't know why or what's wrong. He knows we're here—or at least that he's not alone. But he's afraid to wake, because he knows the pain will be worse if he does." She swallowed, then added, in a steadier tone, "I'd call his odds . . . even. Maybe a bit less if we move on, a bit more if we stay here."

Trystan said nothing, but he looked at her questioningly, one eyebrow raised. Isolde could have ignored the look. But her head was still aching, and she found she was too tired to bother trying to evade the question or lie. Not that it likely matters in any case, she thought. She could remember asking Trystan in honest bewilderment when she was six and he was eight whether he didn't hear other people's thoughts sometimes or catch glimpses of the future in water, too.

She broke off another piece of bread for Cabal and said, "I can hear his thoughts—or not hear, exactly, but share them, in a way. Not always. I can't tell what you're thinking now, I mean. But I can feel anything that has to do with injury or sickness or pain."

A faint line appeared between Trystan's brows. "Is that why you asked me whether I'd hurt my hand in the fight two nights ago?"

"Partly." Isolde lifted one shoulder. "But even without the Sight, I'd be a dismal healer if I couldn't tell when someone was favoring one hand."

She waited, but Trystan looked neither surprised nor uneasy, only weary, still, his brows drawn as though his thoughts followed some inward track of their own. Isolde asked, curiously, "You don't think that's strange or frightening?"

One corner of Trystan's mouth lifted, though she thought the smile was slightly grim. "Not if you can't read my every thought, at any rate." Then he shrugged and cocked an eyebrow at her. "Besides, I'm going to be afraid of the girl who used to spit apple seeds at me across the garden wall?"

Isolde smiled a bit despite herself. "I'd forgotten about that. I always won when we made it a contest."

"Only because I let you." Trystan's smile faded, and he took a swallow of water, then said, frowning slightly once again, "All right. As to making plans—you still want to get to Wessex—to Cerdic."

It wasn't a question, but Isolde nodded. "I suppose so. I mean, yes, of course I do. I must, or all this really has been completely in vain. But we can't move Hereric—not now. And we can't stay here long, can we?" She rubbed the space between her brows. "I'm sorry—maybe I could see a way forward if I hadn't been bitten by an adder last night. Or if I weren't trying to block out feeling Hereric's pain."

Another grim smile tugged momentarily at Trystan's mouth. "I doubt it. I'm not facing either of those things, and I'm not having much luck." He took another swallow of water. "I can't see how we're to go on overland." Isolde thought a brief shadow of regret might have passed across his face at the thought of the boat, but it was gone in a moment, and he went on, "It's one thing to sail along the coast. But traveling through the border lands, we're dead or captive as soon as a stray war band or guard patrol crosses our path."

Trystan shifted, leaning back against the lime-washed wall, his glance flicking round the room, ending on the ashes of last night's fire. He was silent a moment, then looked up, meeting Isolde's eyes. "I can see only one way to go on from here. I don't like it, because it means I'll have to leave you and Hereric for a day or two on your own, with only Cabal for a guard. But it might gain us safe escort into Cerdic's lands."

He stopped, and after a moment, Isolde said, "Go on—what do you mean?"

ISOLDE MADE HERSELF TEAR HER GAZE away from where Trystan had vanished into the surrounding trees—though she couldn't stop their final exchange of words from ringing in her mind. Just before he'd turned to go, Trystan had stopped, his eyes straying back to the ruined villa where Hereric still lay.

"Isa, if Hereric doesn't—" He seemed to check himself, and Isolde knew he was stopping himself from saying, *If Hereric doesn't survive.* He shook his head as though to clear away the words. "If he gets any worse, will you tell him from me . . ." Trystan stopped again, his gaze still resting on the villa's cracked columns. "Tell him—" And then he broke off and shook his head again. "Oh, never mind. You'll know what to say. Just"—he looked back at her, then, his eyes resting on her face—"Just take care, all right? Keep safe."

And Isolde had swallowed the tightness in her throat and nodded. "And you."

Now Trystan was gone to seek out the band of broken men— warriors unsworn to any lord—he'd lived wild within these parts some four years before. So he'd said—which was more that he'd ever told her of what his life had been after Camlann, after the mines.

And Isolde was left here with the realization that had struck her like a slap across the face with the flat side of a sword: that if four years ago, Trystan had been fighting as a mercenary among a gang of masterless men, it dovetailed all too neatly with what Cynlas had believed at first sight of Trystan's face.

And if that were true—and if Cynlas had swung back to his first conviction, decided after all that Trystan was the man who'd killed his son—he would almost certainly have set himself to find out where Trystan and Isolde herself had gone. And he might well have found out, Isolde thought. No secret can be kept absolutely safe for long.

Isolde felt doubt slide like a knife blade through her skin, even she went back inside, went to kneel once more by Hereric's side. If that should be true, she thought, it might be neither Marche's men nor a traitor to the king's council who set on us three nights ago and burned the boat—but instead Cynlas of Rhos, bent on blood payment for the life of his son.

Do you trust me? Trystan had asked when he'd refused to answer her question about the aftermath of Camlann. And I do trust him, Isolde thought. Whatever happened to him seven years ago, she would still trust him with her life now. Where the cold doubt crept in was when she asked herself if she could trust him with Britain's survival as well.

She could feel the frighteningly strong pull of wanting to believe she could trust him—like being caught in the current of a fast-moving river. But wanting and knowing were two different things. And she'd been thirteen the last time she'd known— really known—Trystan. She'd never dragged from him an answer about why he turned into a lolling drunkard at night, either. Much less how he'd come to be living wild on the edges of the Saxon war lands with a band of lawless mercenary fighting men.

Isolde picked up the waterskin and a damp rag, and began to wipe Hereric's face, concentrating on moving the cloth with smooth, even strokes across the fevered man's skin. But even so, she couldn't stop the memories flashing across her mind like jagged strikes of lightning across the night sky. Cynlas of Rhos's hoarse voice and furious gaze . . . Trystan's face, going abruptly and utterly still at the mention of Camlann . . . the reek of wine on his breath . . . the steady beat of Trystan's heart under her cheek last night as he'd carried her here.

The memory of what she'd almost said to him last night beat like frantic bird's wings at the corners of her mind as well, but she refused to let that at least in. She poured more water over the wet rag, making sure to dampen every corner and fold, and thought, I'll journey to Wessex. And if I live to return, I'll be wedded to Madoc. Madoc, who is the only hope I have of protecting the lands I was born to rule.

Madoc, who was a good man and who needed her—or at least needed some woman to make him a refuge and a home. Isolde thought, you'll marry Madoc. And if you feel sick now at the thought of sharing any man's bed, not all men are like Marche. Con wasn't. In a year or two, you'll maybe not be able to help loving Madoc as you loved Con. And so you'll wait for him to return from war, as you waited for Con. And wonder whether he'll be killed in this battle, this time—or the next—or whether he'll be carried home with a wound it's beyond your power to heal. And maybe in another year you'll give him a child—a baby son, maybe, with his father's black hair and eyes—who might live or might die and take another piece of your heart.

Isolde forced her hands to relax their grip on the damp cloth, willing the tide of panic back. Because even that, she thought, would still be safer than letting yourself even think the words you stopped yourself from saying to Trystan just in time.

Chapter Ten

TRYSTAN LEANED FORWARD TO THRUST a branch deeper into the fire. "We have an agreement then?"

He looked up to find the man opposite him sitting with eerie stillness, his eyes on Trystan's face. The hut was hot; Fidach had to be sweltering under the weight of the bearskin cloak he wore, but he'd not taken it off, nor even unfastened the heavy bronze brooch that held it closed.

"Are you doubting my word?"

His voice was soft, but there was an undercurrent of a threat in the tone. Trystan squelched a flicker of impatience at the man and his bloody games. This was neither more nor less than what he'd expected: a sparring match of words, the steps as fixed as those of a sword fight. Play his part, he thought sourly, and he just might stand a chance of walking away from here with a whole skin.

He lifted one shoulder. "Always hard to believe a man's telling the truth when you know you'd lie in his place."

For a moment, Fidach was silent, still as a serpent about to strike, his face expressionless above the collar of the fur robe. Then, abruptly, he threw back his head and gave a shout of laughter. "Well said, my friend. Very well. I may be lying—as may you. But for the moment we pretend we both speak the truth. You will undertake the job I outlined. I will fetch this girl—your sister—and keep her safe until you return." Fidach paused, his smile thinning and turning faintly wintry on his narrow, sharp-featured face. "If you listen to rumor, you'll know, at any rate, that her virtue will be under no threat from me."

ISOLDE SAT BACK ON HER HEELS, looking down at Hereric's immobile face. Four days had passed since Trystan had gone. And if the thought that he might never return was still a prickle of fear at the back of Isolde's mind, she had by this time managed to isolate it, keep her thoughts focused on the immediate tasks of getting through each moment of the day. She couldn't help Trystan, a lone man against whatever war parties he might have met with on his way. But she could keep fighting for Hereric's life.

Over the last days, she had slept only in short snatches, sitting up with Hereric day and night, coaxing him to swallow spoonfuls of broth or water, bathing him with water from the stream in an effort to bring his fever down. She had talked to him, offered words of reassurance, rubbed his remaining hand between hers, told him how much she and Trystan wanted him to live, and tried to kindle in him the will to fight for his own life.

Hereric, though, still lay in a deep, fever-stupefied slumber, his face the color of firewood charred to pale ash. He was no worse than he'd been four days ago, but neither had he gained any ground. He simply hung in some shadowed middle ground, suspended between life and death, his breathing rasping and slow, the pulse in his neck light and thready and hectically fast.

Now it was midday but raining again, so that the abandoned villa was dimly lit, the colors of the tiled floor flattened to a uniform dusty brown. And all about them, she seemed to feel a grim, somber presence that made her remember what Trystan said about

Saxons avoiding Roman dwellings for fear of the ghosts. She had by this time explored more of the ruin during the odd times when Hereric slept, searching for anything that might be of use.

She'd discovered nothing of real value to them, but she'd found herself wondering about whoever had built this place and lived here. The god killers, as her grandmother would have called them. And standing in the remains of what must once have been the kitchen and looking at a huge clay bread oven—or finding in the garden a cracked marble urn, with a circle of marble dancing girls supporting the central bowl—Isolde wondered what the men and women who had eaten the bread from the oven or planted flowers in the urn had thought about this wild, wet, mist-filled landscape. Had they been certain that they'd conquered it, with their heavy marble buildings and arches built in stone? Or had they been frightened sometimes by the power of the gods they'd driven away—the small, nameless gods of the rocks and trees and streams?

Now, sitting once again beside Hereric, Isolde rubbed the stiff muscles at the base of her neck, then took up the spoon and bowl of broth, beginning yet another tale in a low, soothing murmur.

"Cuchulain replied shortly that he was worn and harassed with war, and had no mind to bother with women, beautiful or no. *Then it shall go hard with thee,* the maiden said. *And I shall be about thy feet as an eel in the bottom of the ford.* Then she vanished from sight, and he saw but a crow sitting on a branch of a tree. And Cuchulain knew that it was the Morrigan he had seen."

And then Isolde stopped short, hearing her own words and realizing that she'd unconsciously begun the story of Cuchulain and the death maiden once more. She gritted her teeth together so hard her jaw ached. Then, deliberately, she drew in her breath and began again, this time a silly, comic tale about a pair of dim-witted brother giants, Idris and Bronwen, who lived so far away from each other—one in the south, and one in the north—that they decided to build towers from which they could stand and shout at each other across the miles. Isolde could dimly remember laughing at the story when she was very small. And childish or no, it was better than beginning a tale of curses and doomed foretellings yet again.

Hereric's head only lolled back, though, when she touched the spoon to his mouth, the broth dribbling uselessly out and down his chin. After a dozen or more tries, Isolde let out her breath and sat back again, tears of frustration pricking her eyes. Out of habit, though, she kept on with the tale, even as she watched the labored rise and fall of Hereric's chest and tried to think what next to do.

"It happened, though, that the giant brothers had only one hammer to use in building their towers. They would throw it across the mountains between them, taking turns in the work."

And then she stopped dead, her skin prickling, wondering if she'd only imagined what she'd just felt. She drew in her breath and started again, keeping her eyes fixed on Hereric's brow.

"And since Bronwen was a selfish giant—and slow witted, as all giants are—he would call for the hammer back as soon as he'd thrown it to Idris, his brother."

Isolde broke off again. She had felt it—she was sure of it this time. Just a faint, a very faint stirring, like a spring plant pushing its way up through the winter-hardened soil. Isolde remembered what she'd told Trystan. That Hereric was in pain and didn't know why. That he knew he wasn't alone, but was afraid to wake.

Since the Sight had flooded back to her, she'd used it to feel pain, to read thoughts if it might help her understand where an injury lay. She'd never tried to speak to any of the men in her care that way. Now, though, she took Hereric's hand and closed her eyes. Since he'd seemed to respond to the story, she went on, her voice a low murmur as she tried to reach out in her mind towards that faint stirring she'd felt from Hereric.

At first she met with only blackness, blackness and the crushing pain. But then she felt it again. A soft, pitiful cry in the dark, like the call of a motherless lamb lost on the moor. Isolde tightened her grasp on Hereric's hand, as though that might help her hold on to the spiderweb-fine strand of connection between them.

Isolde drew in her breath, keeping her eyes still closed and blocking out everything else—the sobbing sound of the wind outside, the patter of rain on the roof, Cabal's soft breathing from the blanket she'd laid out for his bed, the musty smell of damp leaves and smoke from the fire. With every part of her concentration, she focused on reaching out towards Hereric's faint, stirring cry, feeling as though she tried to catch mist in her clenched hands. Sweat prickled on her ribs and back under her gown, but she kept on, stretching out a hand towards Hereric in her mind, focusing every scrap of her energy on twining into her outstretched thoughts what she would tell Hereric if he could hear. *I know there's pain, but you are brave and strong. Take a step towards me, I know you can.*

Without any conscious decision, she went on with the tale, working to pour into her spoken voice what she wanted Hereric to hear. The message made an odd counterpoint to the comic words of the tale, but she kept speaking.

"Finally, Idris lost his temper, and threw the hammer back at his brother with all his strength."

Be brave.

"And where it landed, you can still see a scar in the earth, called Pant y cawr, the giant's hollow."

This is not your time to die.

"And without a hammer, the two foolish giants couldn't go on with the building, and so in fits of temper, kicked down the two towers they'd begun."

Here, take my hand.

"And all that's left now are two heaps of boulders, one in the south, and one in the north."

Isolde spoke the final words, and then a shock went through her, like a sudden gust of wind or the beat of a mighty drum that echoed through her every nerve. She gasped and opened her eyes. And found that Hereric's eyes were open as well, bleary and pain-dulled, still, but fixed on her face. For a long moment, their eyes held, and Isolde sat absolutely still, not even letting herself breathe. And then, very slowly, a spreading smile curved Hereric's mouth and he let out a sigh like a tired, contented child.

• • •

ISOLDE SAT IN THE OPEN DOORWAY, looking out at the rain-wet, over-grown garden. The sky had cleared, and the moon and stars were out, silvering the tangled vines and the branches of the trees. I ought to be thankful, she thought. And she was, if cautiously so—thankful and grateful, both, as well as so bone tired she could hardly make her eyes focus.

Bit by bit and with her help, Hereric had drunk a cupful of the broth and kept it down, had taken wine mixed with poppy and fallen asleep. The danger wasn't yet entirely passed. His face was still flushed with fever, the bones protruding sharply through the skin after all the flesh he'd lost in the last weeks. But for the first time since they'd taken the broken arm off, Isolde felt hope, at least, that she'd made the right choice.

Now, though, with Cabal and Hereric both asleep inside, Isolde felt a cold, hard weight pressing into her chest. Two days, Trystan had said when he left, or three at the most, and he would return. This, though, was the end of the fourth day, and still he'd not come back. And with part of her fear for Hereric lifted, the knowledge that Trystan might well never return at all was growing harder to ignore.

Isolde leaned her head against the door frame, watching a pair of black-winged bats swooping and fluttering just above the trees. She drew in a breath, let it out, then rose and walked to where a pool of rainwater had collected atop one of the garden's broken paving stones.

She hadn't told Trystan about Marche before he'd gone—hadn't warned him that his father was seeking him throughout the land. Remembrance of her recurring nightmare had slithered over her and stopped her tongue every time she'd so much as thought of mentioning Marche's name. Or rather, remembrance of what Trystan would surely despise her for if he knew.

He might be sorry for her—because of his own memories. Because of who his mother was. But however much against her will, she'd given herself to Marche. To save her life, had lain with him for one horrible night. She wouldn't blame Trystan if he saw that as a betrayal of every part of their friendship from years before. But she'd been coward enough not to want to see his face if he did.

Now, though—

Now, tonight, her conscience gripped her by the back of the neck and asked whether she wished to bear the blame for Trystan's capture and death because she'd been too much a coward to use the one weapon she possessed that might have helped him escape.

Isolde knelt by the shallow puddle, feeling the damp from the ground start to seep into her skirts. She closed her eyes and drew in another breath of the night air, scented with the smell of wet earth and the burgeoning plants all around. Then she looked into the pool.

The surface looked almost black, glimmering in the moonlight and reflecting back a patch of the star-studded sky above. Isolde saw her own face . . . and nothing else. She steadied and slowed her breathing, focused her thoughts. From somewhere nearby, she heard the mournful call of an owl, the sound brushing like cold fingertips against her skin. The owl's call was an omen of death, so the tales said. Ever since the faithless, beautiful Blodeuwedd murdered her husband for love of another man and was turned into an owl for her crime.

Isolde wondered fleetingly whether she was too exhausted from her efforts with Hereric for a vision to come to her tonight. But then an image flashed across the surface with the suddenness of a sparking hammer strike on forged steel. Two men, seated at a wooden table in a fire-lit banqueting hall. Marche, his harsh, blunt-featured face so haggard that Isolde wondered with the part of her mind still her own whether he was wounded or ill. And another man, one Isolde didn't know. A Saxon, broad-shouldered and taller than Marche by half a head and more, and wearing a heavy necklace of gold and a silvery wolf's pelt for a cloak.

The Saxon man had a broad brow, a nose that had been broken and inexpertly set, and a mouth full of broken teeth. His blue
eyes were so pale as to be almost colorless, and his full blond
beard and the long flaxen hair that fell past his shoulders were
threaded with gray. Beneath the beard, his lips looked tight, and
his colorless eyes were cold.

"I ride south at dawn. Meet Cerdic. I hope for your sake, he
agrees." The man spoke with a thick, guttural accent so heavy
Isolde could scarcely make out the words. All fear, all thoughts
were gone now, save for the images appearing on the surface of
the pool. She let her breathing slow further, further. Imagined
herself drifting closer and ever closer to the water, as though the
glimmering moonlit surface was only a fine filament of a barrier
between herself and the two men. Closer . . . closer . . . until she
felt—

*Rage. Rage filled every part of her. Stabbed through her stomach
like a red-hot skewer. Stuck like burning embers in her throat. Because
she couldn't draw a knife from the table and carve the sneering threat
off Octa of Kent's face. Because Cerdic, the crawling worm, might refuse. She felt rage because—*

Because he, Marche, was coldly, deadly afraid.

And then, with another lightning-swift flash, the image on
the water was gone, and Isolde was left shivering as the cold
sweat dried on her skin and drawing in breath after shuddering
breath of the cool, clean night air.

"IS SHE PRETTY, THIS SISTER OF yours?"

Trystan glanced round the circle of men grouped about the
campfire. Darkness had fallen, and someone had brought out a
skin of wine, even viler than the stuff he'd been drinking. Even
the fumes would have felled an ox. The man who'd spoken was
Ossac. A bull-chested lump of a man with gooseberry-pale eyes
and a slack, wet mouth. Trystan had the unpleasant sense of a

swarm of insects crawling down his spine. Son of a goat, he had to be out of his mind. He didn't move, though, and he kept his voice easy and pleasant as he answered. "Pretty? Very. And at least as good with a knife as I am."

He shifted, leaning back on one elbow, and then with a quick flick of his wrist sent his own knife flying. The blade flashed silver in the firelight, struck the earth with a thud, and came to rest, hilt quivering, in the patch of ground above Ossac's inner thigh.

A gasp went round the group, followed by laughter and several raucous shouts. Trystan saw Ossac pale, and then a wash of angry color crept up his thickly muscled neck. He started to speak, but Trystan cut him off, letting his gaze travel slowly around the circle of men.

"That," he said, still speaking pleasantly, "was purely showing off. It doesn't even begin to cover what I'll do to the first man who so much as looks at her with an expression I don't like in his eyes."

ON THE MORNING OF THE SIXTH day, Isolde left Hereric asleep and went out into the sunlit garden, Cabal following close on her heels. Hereric was growing stronger. She no longer had any doubt that he would live. He was still thin, wasted from the fever and too weak even to sit up on his own. But he was drinking broth and the herbal draughts she gave him, and the fever had broken at last the night before. This morning, when she'd laid a hand on his brow before coming outside, his head felt damp and cool to the touch, and the stump of his arm was healing cleanly and well. She could safely leave him while she went to the garden stream to bathe.

The sun was shining this morning, and for the first time the breeze felt warm with the promise of spring. Isolde let her fingers brush against the dew-wet branches of shrubs and trees as she made her way back from washing in the stream. The pain from the adder's bite was nearly gone, the cuts on her ankle scabbed over to thin red lines, and she stopped at the cracked remains of an old sundial, half obscured by grass and a covering of dead leaves. There was a motto carved in Latin around the edge of the sundial's face. In the rain, she'd not been able to make it out, but now, with the sun out, Isolde could just read the words: Fert Omnia Aetas. *Time bears all away.*

She'd washed her hair in the stream, and now she wrung the water out of the end of her wet braid, thinking of the sword blade, green and rusty with age, that she'd glimpsed at the bottom of one of the deepest pools. The sword of a dead warrior, maybe, gifted to the waters so that he might bear it again in the Otherworld. Or a man's sacrifice of his most valued treasure, that the gods of the stream might hear his prayer. This place might have been the home of a water and forest god, once. Before a Roman noble had built his great villa here. Maybe the Old Ones had carved their swirling signs into the rocks and trees or thrown the severed heads of their enemies into the rippling stream.

Isolde looked out into the shadows of the trees all around and found herself counting the days ahead. How many days until Hereric might be able to stand, to walk on his own. How many days—she flinched away from the thought but grimly made herself finish—how many days they should wait here for Trystan before finally admitting that he would likely never return.

Then, beside her, Cabal growled deep in his throat and bared his teeth, the fur on his neck bristling as he stared, as Isolde did, into the surrounding trees. Isolde felt a cold prickle all along her neck and arms as her mind flashed through the possibilities. *A raiding Saxon war party. A band of masterless men. One of Marche or Octa's patrols.* She put one hand on Cabal's collar, holding him at her side, her free hand going to the hilt of the knife she carried in the pocket of her gown.

Not, she thought, that it will do me the slightest good if there is more than one man.

And then, as though the very thought had conjured them out of the trees and stones, men began to appear, stepping out of the forest to form a loose half circle around her. Isolde's heart was pounding, and her gaze went rapidly over them, taking in their bearded faces, their matted hair, their clothing stitched from tattered patchworks of animal hides. All were armed, with bone-handled swords or knives or axes at their belts, or with bows and feather-fletched arrows strapped to their backs.

Isolde took an instinctive step backwards, towards the ruined villa. Then one of the men detached himself from the group and spoke.

"You are Trystan's sister?"

He was a tall man, dressed in a cloak of what looked like an oiled bear's pelt with the skins of a dozen or more other animals stitched over top, gray and brown and deep black furs glossy in the morning sun. He had a lean, almost cadaverous face, his skin transparently pale and with hollows under his cheekbones and deeply set eyes. His nose was hooked, his mouth narrow and tight, giving his features a predatory cast, and he might, Isolde thought, be somewhere about thirty or thirty-five. His eyes were of a curiously light brown, and his hair and beard were likewise brown, and as matted as the other men's. Above the beard, though, he bore the swirling blue tattoos of the Pict countries on the crest of each cheek.

His voice when he'd spoken had been clipped and hard, and Isolde thought she now caught a flash of hostility in the leaf-brown eyes as his gaze met hers. This was something she'd not thought to ask Trystan before he left: what story he planned to give the band of broken men when he found them again.

She steadied her breathing, though, and answered the question with barely a perceptible pause. "Yes, that's right. You are—" She cast her memory back for the name Trystan had used. "You are Fidach?"

The man gave a short nod of acknowledgment. "I am. And these"—he jerked his head at the circle of men behind him—"are my men."

Isolde looked from Fidach to the men at his back. There were, she saw, maybe fifteen or twenty in all, watching her with tight and watchful faces, the same shadow of hostility she'd sensed from Fidach in their eyes. Cabal, too, must have sensed antagonism or at the least ill feeling, for he bared his teeth in another rumbling growl, the fur on his neck still bristling.

Fidach's gaze dropped to the big dog, and something in his look made a cold slither run down Isolde's spine. She put a hand on Cabal's neck. "It's all right, Cabal. Good fellow." Then, from the man before her, she asked, "Where is Trystan now?"

Fidach had already half turned away, but at the question he gestured curtly towards the surrounding trees. "South. Not far. He sent us to fetch you."

No reason, Isolde thought, to trust that he spoke the truth. Even still, Isolde felt a wash of relief, as though a knot inside her had suddenly slipped free. The men behind Fidach, though, had been shifting uneasily and muttering amongst themselves as their leader spoke, and now one of them stepped forward. He was an older man, forty or forty-five, with a head of matted reddish hair, a sloping forehead, and one eye inflamed, red, and oozing a yellowish discharge.

"I don't like it." He spoke in a deep, heavily accented voice, addressing Fidach. "There's no place for a woman in this band."

Instantly, Fidach swung round on him. The red-haired man was a hand's breadth beneath his leader in height, but far more heavily built, with broad bands of muscle stretching across his chest and powerfully built shoulders and arms. Still, Isolde saw him flinch, visibly, before Fidach's stare. Fidach's face was expressionless, as he stood a moment, looking down at the other man. Then, indifferently, almost carelessly, he raised one hand and brought it down across the other man's face in a smashing blow that sent him sprawling to the ground.

Fidach turned to the other men. "You know as well as Esar here the bargain I made with Trystan. Does anyone else question my decision?"

Another stir of uneasiness went round the group of remaining men, and then a murmur of denial. "Good." Fidach spoke over his shoulder to Isolde, though without looking in her direction again. "Get yourself ready. We leave at once."

Chapter Eleven

I SOLDE FELT A TOUCH ON her arm and turned her head to find
Hereric watching her with a worried frown. His remaining
hand moved in a rapid series of signs.

Isolde not eat?

Isolde nodded. "Yes, I'll eat. Thank you, Hereric."

She took a mouthful of the round of bread one of Fidach's
men had given her and Hereric to share. It was slightly burned
on one side and was flecked with bits of gravel from the grinding
stone that she kept having to pick out with her fingers before she
took a bite. Isolde chewed, swallowed, and told herself grimly and
for the dozenth time since they'd left the abandoned villa that
questioning whether she'd chosen right was like asking whether a
man would rather be run through with a sword or a knife.

She could, she supposed, have refused to accompany Fidach
and his band. But she and Hereric couldn't have risked staying
much longer where they were. And—so far, at least—they were
safer with a group of armed men about them than they would
have been on their own. Isolde took another bite of bread and
glanced at Hereric, sitting beside her on the ground and leaning
back against a fallen log.

Above the flaxen beard, his face was still pale, his eyes sunken by illness. But there was no flush of color on his cheeks or any unnatural brightness in his eyes that would mean the fever had returned, and so far as Isolde could tell, the day's journey didn't seem to have done him any other harm. He was still too weak to walk, so two of Fidach's men had been carrying him between them in a sling fashioned from a pair of sturdy branches and a blanket of stitched-together goat hides.

They had traveled through dense forest, following no track that Isolde could see and had met with no one at all on the way. Still, the signs of the raids and warfare that had ravaged this region were plain. Occasionally Isolde had seen a patch of blackened ground that marked a burned settlement, and once they'd crossed an open field where a long-ago battle must once have been waged. The dead had been buried shallow in one mass grave, and the soil over them had started to erode away, so that here and there among the grass a white bone jutted out of the ground: a tapered thigh bone or a smooth, rounded skull.

The men of the outlaw band murmured uneasily among themselves as they passed the old battlefield, and Isolde saw several make signs against evil or mutter charms meant to keep ghosts at rest. They passed the burned settlements, though, without a second glance. Isolde wondered whether that made it less likely that they had done the burning themselves or more. She might know next to nothing, yet, about Fidach or his men. But lands torn by constant fighting and war drew bands like this one. Bands of the outlaw, the mad, and the discontented who preyed on the lawless countryside like ravens on carrion.

Now there was only the deep, brooding stillness of the forest all around; Isolde might have been alone in the world, save for Hereric, Cabal, and Fidach's band. The very stillness and isolation seemed to drive home the fact that she'd just put all three of their lives into the hands of these men.

They were stopped in a small patch of clearing surrounded by towering oak trees, Fidach having called a halt to rest and eat. Isolde had been surprised at that; Fidach had all the marks of a man who drove his men hard, and she'd not have expected him to grant them the luxury of a meal at midday. But the men were now grouped a little distance away from where she and Hereric sat, passing a skin of ale around their circle and sharing out more of the coarse brown bread. They ate in silence, and Isolde thought that the mood among them was sullen. Or maybe this was how they always behaved when so closely under their leader's eye. Fidach snapped out orders, and the men—all of them, seemingly—sprang to obey. So far, Isolde had seen few of them even meet their leader's gaze, much less argue or answer back when he spoke.

Her gaze went briefly to the red-haired man Esar's face, still smeared with blood from his broken nose. Small wonder, Isolde thought, if none of the others voiced an objection to her presence here, whether they agreed or disagreed with Esar. None of them had so far approached or spoken to Isolde, either. But now, sitting beside Hereric she could feel them watching her, exchanging muttered comments and smiles that made her fight not to draw her cloak more tightly about her shoulders.

Cabal was lying at her feet, and she let him finish the remains of the bread, just as Fidach's voice called out for the journey to resume. Isolde rose, brushing crumbs from her skirts, and Hereric's bearers came to lift him into the carrying sling once more. They were a pair of young men, and Nubian, Isolde thought, with coal-black skin and long hair divided into hundreds of tiny braids. Their faces were so alike that Isolde thought they must be brothers—or even twins—with high cheekbones, knife-sharp features, and thickly lashed brown eyes.

Both gave Isolde quick, curious glances as they lifted Hereric between them, and one smiled, teeth flashing white in his dark face. Hereric seemed to know them. Back at the ruined villa, he'd greeted them both with a slow, delighted grin and a few hand signs, and the young men had responded with greetings in what Isolde thought must be their own tongue.

Two nights ago, when the fever had broken and Isolde had

first told Hereric where Trystan had gone, she asked him what he knew of Fidach's band. But the answer had told her nothing but what she already knew. *Hereric . . . Trystan . . .* a sign she thought might have been *travel . . . years ago.*

Maybe if she'd known more of Hereric's language of gestures, he might have been able to tell her more. Or if he'd still had the use of both hands. Since the fever had broken, he'd been communicating with her in simple signs, and every so often he would raise the stump of his arm as though about to form a sign that required both hands, and then stop as though momentarily bewildered. And each time it happened, Isolde would hold her breath, her whole body tightening as she waited for grief for what he'd lost to sweep over the big Saxon man.

But it never had. Every time, Hereric would look from the bandaged stump to his good hand and shrug. Then his broad brow would clear, and he would look up at Isolde and form a sign he could still make. And Isolde would breathe again and think that if whatever hardships he had known in the past had stripped Hereric down to some simple, childlike inner core, that core was also immensely strong.

"Lady?"

The voice made Isolde draw in a sharp breath and turn to find that one of the group had detached himself from the rest and come to stand beside her. He was a big man, and older than most of the rest, some forty or forty-five, his body heavyset and with a paunch spilling over the top of his belt. His head was balding, fringed by scanty nut-brown hair, and beneath his face was jowly and round. Hardly a handsome man, but his brown eyes were gentle, his voice hesitant and deep.

But before he could speak again, one of the rest of the group—a tall, thin man with black hair and a tattered beard—cupped his hands about his mouth and called out something towards them in a tongue Isolde didn't recognize. She could, though, make a fair guess at the meaning of the words, since the man before her blushed furiously, a tide of color sweeping up his short neck and flooding his face. He shook his head, though, like a bull twitching away from a stinging fly.

"Sorry, lady. Don't mind that lot. Not used to having a woman in the group, that's all."

Isolde ignored the sharp little stings of tension dancing up and down her spine, and said, "Do you know, I'd gotten that." Then, because she wanted to put as much distance as she could between herself and any rumors these men might have heard of the High Queen Isolde—and part, too, because she felt unaccountably sorry for the man before her—she added, "You don't have to call me Lady. Just Isolde will do."

The man continued to look uncomfortable. "Thank you, la—well, thanks. That's right kind of you. Name's Eurig." He made a movement as though about to offer her his hand, then changed his mind and rubbed the back of his neck, flushing again. "Just wanted to say . . . to tell you that you don't have to worry none. About the rest of the men, I mean. You're safe with us."

Cabal was standing close at her side, and though his ears were cocked and the muscles beneath his brown-and-white coat bunched, he'd not yet bared his teeth or growled. Isolde said, slowly, "Thank you."

Eurig ducked his head and looked embarrassed once again. "Don't mention it. Promised Trystan I'd look after you a bit, till he could come back, that's all."

Several questions seemed to crowd themselves into Isolde's mind all at once, but she forced herself to choose just one. "Where is Trystan now?"

Eurig's face reddened once more, though, and he muttered, looking at the ground, "Not far. He'll meet up with us soon, I reckon, with a bit of luck." He gave Isolde one last quick glance from under his brows, then turned away. "Best be getting on, now, la— Isolde. Fidach won't be pleased if he sees us talking instead of getting ready to move again."

.   .   .

'DUSK WAS FALLING WHEN 'FIDACH AGAIN called a halt. They had crossed from the forest into wet, marshy ground, patched with fields of reeds and stunted bushes, with silvery pools of open water glistening between the tracts of black boggy ground. Here and there a gnarled, misshapen tree clung to one of the tiny islands of dry ground.

A fog had come up, wreathing the landscape eerily in drifting silver threads, and the air was filled with a muddy, decaying smell. Up ahead, Isolde could hear Fidach snapping out orders, though she could see only the vaguest outline of him and the rest of the men. She turned to Eurig. He'd not spoken to her again all throughout the long day's walk—none of the men had—but she'd noticed that he was never more than a handful of paces away from her and took care to position himself between her and the rest of the band.

Now he had come once more to stand at her side, and Isolde asked him, "Are we to camp here for the night?"

Eurig shook his head. "Not here. Fidach sent scouts ahead to made sure the encampment's safe, that's all."

The scouts must have found all secure, for a short while later Isolde again heard voices from up ahead, and then Fidach's voice, shouting that they could move on. Darkness was closing in, and Isolde had continually to watch where she stepped to keep from slipping off into one of the holes of sucking black mud that littered the path. When at last she did look up, then, the settlement before her seemed to have appeared by some eldritch art of enchantment out of the drifting mist.

It was a crannog: a grouping of round, reed-thatched huts raised on oak piles above the swampy ground and connected by a network of swaying rope-and-wood causeways. Lighted torches had been set at intervals along the causeways and above the doors of several of the huts, forming bright glowing orbs amidst the patchy fog. Talking amongst themselves and shouting across the narrow bridges, the men began to disperse themselves among the small thatched buildings.

Eurig stepped first onto one of the precarious walkways, then belatedly looked round and offered a hand to Isolde. She shook her head, though, holding tight to the rope guardrail with one hand as she followed, her other hand grasping Cabal's collar. The wooden slats beneath her feet shook and creaked under their combined weight, and Cabal whined, stepping with reluctance from one plank to the next. The causeway held, though, and Isolde stepped off onto one of the small wooden platforms that formed the foundation for the round-built huts.

Eurig had stepped silently to one side, his homely face slightly nervous in the flare of torchlight, and Isolde saw that Fidach himself awaited them, standing motionless beside one of the platform's pair of dwellings.

"You'll sleep here."

He gestured to the nearer of the two huts—empty, it appeared. Through the open doorway of the other, Isolde saw that Hereric lay on a rough pallet just inside the hut, his two bearers already gone. She nodded. "Thank you."

Fidach ignored the thanks and stood watching her, as though expecting her to say something more. Isolde realized that he was waiting for her to ask about Trystan. Some instinct, though, stopped her tongue—a certainty that the man before her would seize on the first sign of weakness she let herself show. She kept silent, and after a moment she thought a flicker of amusement appeared in his leaf-brown gaze, as though he'd read her thoughts and understood the reason for her refusal to ask.

Then, in an instant, the look was gone, and Fidach's glance flicked disinterestedly from Isolde to Cabal, standing close at her side. His gaze rested briefly on the big dog and then traveled back to Isolde.

"I'll take the dog. He'll be useful in keeping away wolves."

Isolde's skin prickled unpleasantly. She was tired and hungry both, and the whole scene—the buzz of the marsh insects, the pointed roofs of the huts, the flickering light and creaking sway of the platform beneath her feet—all felt suddenly unreal, like something out of nightmare. As though in leaving the Roman villa, she'd stepped from one world into the Other or somehow out of time.

She answered calmly, though, keeping both anger and fear from her tone. "No. Cabal stays with me."

Fidach's face darkened. "Are you saying you don't trust my men?"

At some time while they'd been talking, Eurig had gone, vanishing down another causeway into the mist; she and Fidach were alone. Isolde kept her hand on Cabal's collar and ordered herself not to react to the tone or look away from Fidach's gaze. "Should I?"

Fidach was silent a long moment, watching her. The anger had gone from his face, leaving it expressionless, cold, and hard. He wore, still, the fantastical robe of many-hued furs, and looked, with his tattooed cheeks and hooked nose, like an Otherworld creature himself. Isolde thought too that his face looked oddly flushed in the glare of the torchlight, with a sheen of sweat brightening the swirling blue marks on his cheekbones. Then, abruptly, he threw back his head and gave a harsh bark of a laugh.

"No. You shouldn't. You'd be a fool to trust a single one of them any farther than you can see."

ISOLDE STOOD IN THE DOORWAY OF the hut, listening to the shrill cry of a night bird outside. Her whole body felt gritty and dirty with the day's travel, but she was hesitant to undress enough that she could wash. From the huts of the crannog surrounding her own, she could hear men's voices, faintly muffled by the drifting fog, and the occasional startlingly clear laugh or shout that made the hairs on the back of her neck prick. And she'd found no latch on the hut's leather-hinged door.

In the end, she pushed the door shut and told Cabal to lie down across the threshold. Fidach must have ordered the supplies she and Trystan had brought from the boat so many days ago deposited here; everything—blankets, food stores, the bundle that held her clean clothes—lay in an heap on the floor. Isolde found a half-empty waterskin, unlaced her gown, and stripped to her shift. She washed quickly, scrubbing her face, her arms, and her neck. Then she found her single remaining clean gown, dropped it over her head, and lay down on the straw pallet, her heart beating fast and hard.

The hut was windowless, but there was a smoke hole cut in the center of the roof, allowing enough moonlight to enter that she could just make out vague shapes in the darkness: Cabal, curled by the door, the room's single low table, a storage basket, and a rickety stool. There were no blankets, but she had her cloak for cover, and the night wasn't cold. She couldn't sleep, though, despite the ache of weariness behind her eyes. No reason, she thought again, to trust Fidach and believe that Trystan would soon join them here. But then no definite reason, either, to think he'd lied. She closed her eyes and tried to imagine Trystan and Hereric living in this place, years before, amongst these men.

She and Hereric had shared the meal of bread and stew one of the men had left in their hut, and Cabal had finished off the remains. She'd thought of asking Hereric whether his bearers had told him anything of Trystan—or of Fidach's plans for them. But Hereric had been so tired by the journey that he was almost nodding off over his food, and it had seemed like cruelty to ask him to search for signs that he could still form and that she would understand. Instead, she'd checked his bandages and given him a draft that would help him sleep, since she knew the healing arm still caused him pain. And then she'd left him, knowing that she would hear him if he woke or cried out in the night.

Now Isolde shifted on the lumpy pallet, feeling blades of straw pricking her even through the wool of her gown. And then she jerked upright, her heart giving a sickening lurch, as the sound of a soft footfall came from just outside the door of the hut. In an instant, she had thrown off her cloak and was on her feet, her fingers closing round the hilt of the knife she'd left within easy reach on the floor. Moving as silently as she could, willing the boards under her feet not to creak, she edged towards the door, then eased it open—only partway, but still the man standing outside jerked back, biting back a cry of surprise.

Some of the torches were still burning, casting enough light that Isolde could see his face: Eurig, eyes wide with shock, one hand clapped to his beefy chest.

He let out a breath. "Great Arawn's manhood, you gave me a jump."

Cabal had woken at the sound of the opening door, and now bounded forward, teeth bared in a snarl. Isolde kept one hand on his collar but let the big dog move between her and Eurig. She took a breath and tried to steady her racing heart.

"Why are you here?" she asked. "What do you want?"

Eurig looked from Cabal to Isolde, and he rubbed a hand over his bald head, glancing all about them and whispering as though afraid of being overheard. "No harm—believe me. I meant—mean you—no harm."

"Believe you?" Isolde repeated. "You know, I've found when anyone says that, it generally means you'd be seven times a fool to take their word."

"I . . ." Eurig's gaze dropped to the ground, and he looked so wretched—like a dog expecting to be kicked—that Isolde relented. Because despite Fidach's words, she found she did instinctively trust Eurig—partway, at least.

"Tell me why you are here, then," she said.

Eurig's eyes flashed gratefully to her face, and he swallowed. "It's Piye."

"Piye?"

Eurig nodded. "That's right." The words came in a whispered rush. "He's one of the men that carried Hereric today. Piye and Daka. Twins, they are. But now Piye's sick. And Trystan said as how you were a rare skilled healer. And me and Daka thought—"

He swallowed again. "We thought as how maybe you'd help him. On the quiet, like. Because if Fidach finds out, it'll be all over for him. For Piye, I mean."

Isolde studied Eurig's round, homely face and gentle brown eyes. His gaze was still shifting nervously about the crannog, and she could see a glitter of perspiration on his brow. Slowly, she asked, "You mean that Piye would be cast out if Fidach found out he was ill?"

Eurig's head moved in jerky confirmation again. "No place for a man here who can't hold his own in a fight. He'd be cast out—and even then he'd not be long lived. Fidach doesn't let any man stay alive that can find this place, if he can help it."

Isolde kept silent a moment, still holding Cabal between her and Eurig. If she hadn't yet entirely decided to trust Eurig, she found she could believe what he told her of Fidach—believe it readily. Her mind flashed for a brief moment to Trystan, and she wondered how he had managed to get free—plainly carrying the knowledge of how to find Fidach and his men again.

She pushed the thought aside, though, trying to make up her mind about the man before her. On the one side of the balance was her instinctive liking of Eurig. And on the other side was the certainty that if she'd wanted to lay a trap for herself, this was exactly the kind she would have devised: a plea for help, with a sick or wounded man to bait the snare.

Eurig cleared his throat. "We could pay, maybe. If you'd see what you can do."

Isolde's eyes rested on those of the man before her. The moment stretched out. But wherever Trystan was now—whenever he returned—any allies she could find among the group would be valuable. Isolde came to a decision. "You don't have to pay me," she said. "I'll come." She put a hand on Cabal's head. "Cabal, stay and guard Hereric here."

Cabal whined softly at seeing her follow Eurig down one of the causeways, but he was a war dog, well trained to obey. Glancing back over her shoulder, Isolde saw him settle himself, paws outstretched, ears alert and at the ready, by the door of the hut. Then she turned back, keeping her eyes on Eurig's broad back as he led the way towards another of the round thatched huts.

"FALLING SICKNESS."

All was silent outside, the sound of men's talking and laughter died away as Isolde stood looking down at the prostrate man, lying on a straw pallet much like the one she'd just left behind. Piye's eyes were wide and terrified in his dark face, and though he hadn't moved since Isolde entered, she could see the rapid rise and fall of his chest and the rigid stiffness of the way he held himself, as though poised for flight. Daka, too, looked tense and strained, and kept shooting quick, wary glances at Isolde from the corners of his eyes.

Piye's fit had passed by the time Isolde and Eurig had reached the hut the brothers shared, but his brother had told her—grudgingly, it seemed to Isolde—what had happened. She had asked Piye, first, how he felt, but Daka had shaken his head. "He not know your tongue. I speak for him instead." Daka had a deep, musical voice that made Isolde think of the thrumming beat of a great drum. "A bad spirit come to him. Take him. Throw him on the ground. He fight with it." Daka's arms sketched the frantic movements Piye had made. Then he shrugged. "Finally, spirit go."

Daka and Piye's hut was much like the one where Isolde had left Hereric and Cabal, save for the array of knives, hunting bows, and arrows hung on the walls. A single small oil lamp burned on the floor beside Piye, showing her the three men: Eurig, pale-skinned and anxious, Daka and Piye, their coal-black faces so alike as to be mirrors of one another down to the suspicious fear in their eyes.

Now Isolde moved to kneel beside Piye, and instantly he jerked back, pressing himself against the wall of the hut, his eyes flying upwards to where a hunting knife hung just above his pallet. Daka, too, made a quick, convulsive movement, as though about to catch hold of Isolde's arm and hold her back—though he checked himself before actually touching her.

He turned to Eurig and said something, rapidly and low, in what Isolde thought must be his own native tongue. Probably, *How do you know we can trust her?* Or something of that kind. Before Eurig could answer, though, Isolde looked from Daka to Piye and then back again. Her scalp was prickling, but she had come here, had decided to trust Eurig, had chosen her course. So she set aside all thought of fear, keeping her gaze firmly fixed away from the weapons hung on the walls.

She spoke to Daka, since Piye's look was uncomprehendingly blank, his eyes dazed even amidst his fear.

"It's all right," she said. "I'm not going to hurt him. I only want to examine him, to see if there's anything I can do to help."

Though if what she suspected was true, and it was the falling sickness that had struck Piye, there would be very little that she could actually do. Daka hesitated a long moment, then gave a wordless nod of agreement, gesturing her to go ahead.

Piye sat as though carved of stone while she listened to him breathe, looked into his eyes, and felt the pulse of life in his throat. She could feel, though, how tightly strung he was, sense the control he was exercising not to leap up and run from the hut or burst into speech. Isolde thought briefly of starting one of the old tales, as she often did with patients afraid or in pain—or as she'd done with Hereric so many times over the last days. But if Piye didn't speak the Briton tongue, and Daka only barely, hearing her murmur a flood of unfamiliar words might be only another cause for fear.

Thinking of Hereric, though, made her wonder whether she might be able to reach Piye as she had Hereric. So as she worked over him, she focused on speaking to Piye in her mind, forming with her thoughts what she would say to him if he could understand her words. She imagined Piye's fear as almost a separate, breathing presence in the room with her and the other two men, imagined herself stretching out a hand to that fear, soothing it softly into sleep.

The effort was harder than it had been with Hereric—maybe because she knew Piye so much less well. Isolde's head started to ache, and her eyes felt gritty with fatigue. But slowly, slowly Piye's taut muscles started to relax. By the time she at last sat back on her heels, Piye's eyelids had started to droop and his head had fallen forward on his chest as the exhaustion that usually followed fits like his started to overtake him.

Isolde watched him another moment, then turned to look up at Daka. "Has this happened before?"

The young man seemed to hesitate, his long-lashed dark eyes still wary, as though seeking to take Isolde's measure. Then he inclined his head. "Happen six—maybe seven times before."

Isolde nodded.

"Can you do anything for him, lady?" Eurig asked.

Isolde's eyes had gone back to Piye, but she said automatically, "Isolde."

Eurig ducked his head, his face flushing. "Sorry. Just don't seem right to call you that, somehow. Plain to see you're a cut above the likes of us here."

"I wouldn't say that."

She was thinking that at least these men had risked their chief's formidable anger in aid of their friend. And she had absolutely no power to help Piye, who despite the confusion of fear she still felt from him was now half asleep, slumped back on his pallet of straw.

Isolde drew out from her medicine bag a vial of lady's slipper and valerian decoction, and worked to shake off an inevitable wave of anger at her own helplessness. She'd learned long ago that there would always be those like Marcia or Bedwyr or Piye here that she was powerless to aid. But still she felt the same every time.

She started to hold the glass vial out to Piye, but he jerked back again, eyes flaring wide, and beside her she felt Daka go rigid, too.

"Don't be afraid." She spoke directly to Piye this time, hoping that he would understand the intent, if not the actual words. "It won't hurt you. Here—look." She unstoppered the vial and took a sip of the draft herself. The mixture of herbs was cool and slightly spicy on her tongue. "You see—it's safe to drink. It will help you go to sleep, that's all."

Piye looked from her up to his brother, and it seemed to Isolde that his eyes held a question. The silence stretched out in the small, lamp-lit space. Then Daka said something in their own tongue, and Piye let out his breath. He reached to take the vial from Isolde, raised it to his lips, and swallowed before sinking back against the straw pallet once more.

"That draft—cure him? Drive out evil spirit?" Daka asked her, after Piye had drunk.

Isolde felt another twist of anger at herself—and guilt, this time as well, because she could see the hope warring with disbelief in both Piye's and Daka's eyes. The god's touch, her grandmother had called the falling sickness, because fits like Piye's sometimes brought Otherworld visions, flashes of Sight. But whether it was a sign of attacking demons or was a gift of the gods, Isolde knew that there was nothing—nothing at all—that she could do to heal it or stop its striking Piye down again.

"I'm sorry," Isolde began. And then she stopped, a sudden memory flashing across her mind's eye: herself in her workroom at Dinas Emrys, packing what she would take on the journey with Trystan. She'd been putting jars of salve and vials of herbal simples into her medicine bag. And then her eye had lighted on the crude little iron ring Garwen had given her. And because she'd not wanted Garwen to find it after she and Trystan were gone—and be hurt, because Isolde hadn't kept it by her as she promised—she'd dropped the ring into the bag.

Now, in the dimly lighted hut, with its weapons of war hanging all about them on the walls and the eyes of the three men fixed on her face, Isolde opened her medicine bag again, sorting quickly through the array of bottles and jars. And the ring was there, sifted to the very bottom.

It was partly impulse that made Isolde pick it up, impulse born of the way the hope in the brother's eyes had caught in her chest. She took up the iron ring, holding it on her palm. "I'm sorry," she said again. "I can't cure Piye's sickness. No healer that I know of can. But this—" She stopped, then spoke steadily, reaching this time towards both Piye and Daka in her mind, imagining her words reaching through to the deepest root of their fear. "This ring is a charm against all evil. Make sure he wears this, and he'll be certain to triumph if the shade attacks him again."

It was almost frightening how readily the three men trusted her. Maybe it was the power she'd tried to pour into the words. Or maybe they were all simply so desperate that they clutched at any hope at all, like a drowning man clutching a floating spar. Whatever the reason, Daka's fingers closed round the ring, and he said, his deep voice turning slightly husky, "Thank you."

Piye was asleep almost before Daka had pushed the ring onto the smallest finger of his brother's right hand. Then Daka straightened and turned back to Isolde. The lamplight gleamed golden on the chiseled plains of his dark face, throwing glimmers of golden yellow into his eyes. "And—" He stopped, glanced from Eurig to Isolde, and then back again, the hint of wariness creeping back into his deep voice. "You not tell Fidach?"

That, at least, Isolde could answer truly, and she shook her head. "No. You have my word."

Daka bowed his head in grave acknowledgment. "Thank you," he said again. For a moment, his dark gaze rested on his brother's face, the face that was so much a mirror of his own. When he looked back at Isolde, she thought she caught a glimmer of moisture in his eyes. "Piye is my brother," Daka said. "Hurt to him hurts me as well." He made Isolde a slight bow, oddly formal in the round, cramped little room. "I thank you, lady," he said. "For us both."

Isolde nodded, because she would undo any good to Piye if

she denied that she'd done anything at all. "You're very welcome," she said quietly. "Both of you."

Daka watched the slow rise and fall of his brother's breathing a moment more, then let out his breath and turned to Eurig. "Better be getting her back, now. Safer she be in her own place."

Eurig nodded and rose to his feet. "You're right there." The eyes of the two men met, and it seemed to Isolde that a wordless communication passed between them.

"Safer for you—or for me?" she asked.

There was a silence in which the hut was filled with the sounds of Piye's breathing and the chirp of crickets from the marsh outside. Eurig and Daka both seemed to hesitate, and then at last Eurig said, "Aye, well. Safer for all of us, maybe. But you don't—" He stopped, looking awkward. "I mean, you don't have to worry none. I meant what I told you before. None of the rest would lay a hand on you. Even Esar—he's the one Fidach clouted for objecting to your being here—wouldn't dare."

Unexpectedly, Daka grinned at that, teeth flashing in his dark face. "Not after what Trystan say he do to the man that try it, anyway." He glanced towards Eurig. "You ever be trying to fight Trystan?"

"Oh, aye." Eurig rubbed the bridge of his nose with his thumb. "Like fighting smoke. I know."

He made as though to turn to the door, but before he could, Isolde stopped him, looking from one to the other of the two men. "Will you tell me, now, where Trystan is?"

Another silence followed, another wordless communication between Eurig and Daka. Then, finally, Eurig let out his breath. "We would tell you, if we could. But we're under oath—all of us—not to speak of it. Not to you. Not even amongst ourselves, like. But—" Eurig passed a hand over his bald head. "Don't seem right not to tell you anything. You being Trystan's sister and all."

It gave Isolde a shock to hear him say it, to realize that of course the rest of the men would believe the story Trystan had given Fidach. Eurig, though, apparently saw nothing out of the way on her face, for after a moment, he went on. "I'll tell you. Can't see it would do any harm for you to hear this much: Trystan's off on a job for Fidach. A mission, like."

"A mission?" Isolde repeated. Then, with a tightening feeling about her heart, she asked, "Is this the price Fidach demanded for his help—for allowing a woman amongst the band?"

Slowly, and as though unwillingly, Eurig nodded, and Isolde asked, "And this job—this mission—is it a dangerous one?"

She felt half sorry for asking the question, Eurig's discomfort was so transparently clear. But right now she wanted too desperately to know every scrap of intelligence he could give her to do anything but wait in expectant silence for him to go on. Eurig looked helplessly from her to Daka, as though seeking aid, and at last Daka said, "Could be danger. Will be, I'd say."

Eurig's gaze was fixed on the floor, but at that, he looked up at Isolde. "Trystan's good, though. None better at this kind of thing. He'll come back, right enough. And besides, we . . ." He stopped, then added, awkwardly, "We'd look after you, you know. If anything—well, if anything happened to Trystan. He made us swear it before he left. But we'd all—" He sketched a gesture that included himself and the two other men. "The three of us, I mean, we'd all have done it anyway. Even if he hadn't."

The strain of the long day must have been wearing on her even more than she'd realized; Isolde felt the breath freeze in her lungs at Eurig's words. And she actually bit her tongue to keep from losing her temper, from telling Eurig furiously not to speak—not to even think—of such a thing. Eurig meant well, after all. He was trying to be kind.

So she forced her tight hands to relax, and instead said simply, "Thank you."

LYING AGAIN ON THE ROUGH STRAW pallet in the hut she'd been allotted, Isolde drew her cloak about her and stared unseeingly out into the dark. Something rustled and squeaked in the thatched roof above her head, and she was grateful again for Cabal's presence, the knowledge that the big dog lay now across the threshold of the single door. She kept trying to tell herself that in cases like Piye's, where she could do no good towards healing the ailment, it was better than nothing if she could at least allay terror. That the Sight was a blessing if it let her reach towards the sick or afraid.

She couldn't entirely believe it, though. Closing her eyes, she tried to conjure up a vision of Morgan's face in the dark. *Was there anything more I could have done?*

The imagined Morgan shook her head. *Of course not. You know as well as I do that the gods' sickness has no cure.*

Isolde shifted, turning onto her back. The feeling that she'd unfairly bewitched the men still clung to her—or that she'd played on the fighting man's readiness to clutch at all omens and protective charms. Such things were a way, she supposed, for men at war to live with the knowledge that they might die at any moment of any day. And in a way, she envied them their ready, clutching belief. It was only that after being swept up by the Sight's ebb and flow for so many years, she couldn't believe that charms or protection were ever as simple as a dried rabbit's foot or a ring set with a sheep's bone. Or at least that anyone—man or woman—could so easily bend to will the forces beyond whatever veil sealed off the Otherworld from this.

What do you think? she asked the memory of her grandmother's old but still lovely face in her mind. *Did I actually help Piye, or only trick him and the others into believing I had?*

She could imagine the shadow Morgan's wry smile. *Child, if you haven't learned yet that trickery is as real a part of healing as stitching wounds, I taught you nothing at all. However much we think we know of the herb craft and the healer's arts, we're still like those in the old tales—who climb what they believe a mountain only to find it the back of a sleeping dragon.*

Isolde let out her breath. *I know—but I still hate it.*

The imagined Morgan smiled again. *I know. You always did.*

Isolde thought of the ruined villa she and Hereric had left behind, with its cracked columns and beautiful tiled floor—and of Morgan spitting whenever she spoke of Rome—and of the abandoned glades and sacred pools on Ynys Mon. *So was there ever a time, before the Romans came and broke the power of Britain's gods—and the darkness started to sweep over the land—when healers did know how to cure ills like Piye's? When a healer might have done more for him than give him a cheaply made iron ring?*

Ah, well. As to that, only those old gods can say.

A sharp piece of straw was still poking through the pallet, pricking her neck, and Isolde shifted position again. She kept seeing Trystan picking Garwen's ring up off the floor of her workroom the night he'd first come to Dinas Emrys. And then herself, standing still and watching him walk away from the ruined villa days ago, his dark traveling cloak and gold-brown hair being swallowed by the spring-green trees.

And what about this journey? she asked her grandmother's conjured shade. *Is it completely futile to hope I'll succeed in persuading King Cerdic to ally with Britain against Octa and Marche?*

Expect defeat, and you have none to thank but yourself when that's what you earn. She could imagine Morgan's clear-sighted dark gaze, as unflinchingly direct as it had been in life, keen enough to see into every corner of her mind. *Britain needs you. So expect to succeed and then try.*

Isolde's mouth twisted a little in a humorless smile. *That's easy for you to say. If not for you, I might not be here at all. If you'd forgiven Arthur, and Camlann had never been fought.*

Just for a moment, the shadow Morgan was so vividly clear in her mind's eye that Isolde could almost believe her real. Could almost see the hurt in Morgan's dark eyes, hear the unaccustomed pain in her voice. *Is that really what you believe?*

Even in imagination, Isolde couldn't truly be angry with the fiercely tender old woman who she'd always known had loved her as much as any mother ever could. *No. I'm sorry. It wasn't your fault. But I wish you hadn't had to die. I wish you hadn't had to leave me, all those years ago.*

The shadow Morgan bent towards her, and Isolde almost—almost—could believe she actually felt a brush of soft fingers, featherlight, across her cheek. *So do I, child. So do I.*

ISOLDE SLEPT—SHE WAS TOO EXHAUSTED not to. But she woke with a gasp sometime in the darkest watches of the night, her heart racing, with a dream that she held a severed boar's head in her lap still vivid in her mind. She sat up, pushed the damp hair back from her brow, and tried to steady her breathing. But she couldn't entirely drive away the clinging horror of this dream, any more than she could readily escape the one of Marche when it came.

Instead, she found herself staring up at the patch of starry sky visible through the smoke hole in the reed-thatched roof and imagining the sea of black, sucking mud spreading all around this place. *We'd look after you, you know,* Eurig had said. *If anything— well, if anything happened to Trystan. He made us swear it, before he left.*

She'd been almost relieved in a way when Trystan had gone. Relieved, at least, that she'd not have to face seeing him day in and day out for a time. But she hadn't told him about the bounty Marche had offered for his capture. Simply because she'd been too much a coward to bring herself to mention Marche's name.

And now, with her hands still feeling the warm stickiness of the bloodied boar's head in her dream, she couldn't shake the certainty that Trystan was in danger. Tonight—this moment, now. The feeling pressed like a stone weight over her heart, making it an effort to draw breath.

And there was absolutely nothing she could do for him. No way of going back and giving him warning of the danger he might face. Still, Isolde found herself closing her eyes and whispering into the surrounding night, almost as she had to the memory of Morgan she'd conjured from the dark, "For once, be careful—please. Please keep yourself safe and come back."

TRYSTAN CAUGHT HIMSELF JUST BEFORE HE stepped into the sucking pool of mud, swore, and added drowning in a quagmire to the list of idiot ways he could die tonight. He'd left the forest behind, climbed the rocky slope up to the flat table of the moor, and now was crossing through one of the patches of bog that littered the place. And he had to be getting close, at any rate. The stench of burning metal from the smelting fires was starting to catch in the back of his throat.

He focused on one of the distant granite tors, jutting up from the ground and silvered in the moonlight. He tried thinking of Isolde—and Hereric—and getting this bloody job over and done so that he could get back to them. But that led him straight back to where he didn't want to go.

Trystan flexed the scarred fingers of his right hand. Listening to Hereric scream while they took off his arm. Breathing in that burning metal smell day and night. Breaking his back from sun up to sun down with crushing the rocks that carried the tin ore. Staying alive, trying to get through one breath, one bloody heartbeat at a time. And at the same time wondering whether hell—or wherever else he might end up if he was dead—wouldn't be preferable to life.

There was another idiot way he could die. Having one of the guard patrols catch him heaving his guts up in a ditch.

At least he'd been able to sleep without drinking himself into a stupor last night. Though the memory of nightmare was still quivering along every nerve, setting his teeth on edge.

Trystan shook his head to clear it, then froze, swearing under his breath. *King Arthur's hairy left—*

As though the thought of guard patrols had conjured him

out of the air, he saw a man ahead, maybe three spear casts away, leather helmet, bossed shield, and short sword plain in the moonlight. Yes, right. It would be almost the full of the moon.

Trystan held absolutely still. Then he allowed himself another muttered oath. The other man's head had turned, and by the sudden tensing of the guardsman's shoulders, he knew he'd been seen.

Chapter Twelve

ISOLDE WOKE TO THE SOUND of a beating drum and for a moment couldn't remember where she was. Dawn was breaking, and she lay blinking at the dimly lighted walls of the hut around her before memory came flooding back. Fidach and his men . . . the journey through the marshes . . . the crannog . . . her visit to Piye and Daka's hut the night before.

She could hear nothing from Hereric's hut, so she rose, washed her face and hands with the last of the water from the waterskin, then combed and braided her hair. The water was beginning to smell of the goat hide it had been carried in for so long, but it helped to clear away the lingering dullness left by her night's broken sleep.

The drum was still beating, a slow, steady pulse that seemed to be building in both speed and sound and mingling with the sound of men's voices, laughter, and shouts. Isolde was about to venture outside when a hesitant tap came at the hut's door, and opening it she found Eurig standing outside. His round, jowly face was stubbled by a day's growth of wiry dark beard, and his eyelids looked faintly reddened, so that she wondered whether he'd slept at all after seeing her safely back from Piye and Daka's hut.

He carried a bundle that he held out to Isolde, raising his voice a little to be heard above the drums. "Here, this is for you. I'd thought to just leave it outside if you weren't awake yet, but seeing as how you are, well—"

Isolde took the bundle and found that he'd brought her a blanket, slightly musty smelling and lined with what looked like a wolf's pelt, and a battered tin washtub of incredible age, the metal beginning to corrode around the rim.

"It's so you can have a bit of a wash, like, if you want to," Eurig said. "And the blanket's for the bed, o' course. I thought . . . well, living here not being quite what you're used to—"

He trailed off. Isolde could have said that she scarcely remembered what it was like to bathe in anything but an icy stream or sleep in a real bed. But she was touched by Eurig's gesture and the thoughtfulness that had prompted it.

"Thank you," she said sincerely. "You're very kind."

Eurig's ears reddened in embarrassment and he waved the thanks away, his gaze dropping to his own feet and his voice sinking to a barely audible mutter. "It's nothing—no trouble."

He was, Isolde thought, truly kind. And neither slow-witted or simple—only painfully shy, with her, at least. It made her wonder how he'd come to be here, a member of this band of broken men.

Before she could ask, Eurig cleared his throat, though, and said, "Fidach's asking to see you. That's the other reason I came."

Isolde thought that *given orders* was more likely than *asking*, but she only nodded. "Thank you," she said again. "I'll go as soon as I make sure Hereric's all right this morning."

Something of what she felt must have been visible on her face, though, for Eurig said after a moment's hesitation. "Do you want—would you like me to come with you? Fidach said as how you were to come alone, but—"

Remembering the look in Fidach's eyes the night before,

Isolde wished for a moment that she could ask Eurig to come along. She knew she couldn't risk Eurig's incurring his chief's wrath for her sake, though. And even apart from that, something in her sensed that it would be a mistake for her to let Fidach know she'd been afraid to come alone.

So she shook her head. "No. But thank you, though. Just tell me where to go, and I'll see him on my own."

Eurig nodded. "Aye, well. Probably best, at that." He paused, eyeing her uncertainly, rubbing the bridge of his nose with the back of his thumb. "And you needn't worry that . . . well, that—" A dull red crept into Eurig's face, and he seemed to grope for words. "You needn't be worried that Fidach will . . . er . . . that he'll be too much taken with you or try anything on. He's not . . . well . . ." Again Eurig seemed to search for the right words. Finally, he seemed to give up, for he let out his breath and said, bluntly, "He's not one of them that favors women. Not any-where—but especially not in bed."

THE MORNING MIST WAS GONE, AND a watery sun was shining over the bog when Isolde came out of Hereric's hut. She had checked to be sure the fever hadn't returned and that his bandages were still clean and dry. She had eaten, too, of some of the bread and hard, dry cheese that Eurig had brought for them to share. And while they ate, she had hesitated, then asked Hereric again for anything he could tell her of Fidach and his men.

She'd not been able to make much of his answer, though—there were too many of his finger signs she didn't know and too many more that he could no longer form. And she'd not wanted to take a chance on upsetting Hereric by letting him see her frustration at just how little she could understand, and so she'd only nodded and tried to smile. The most complete string of signs she'd been able to put together had been: *Isolde . . . Hereric . . . stay here. Trystan . . . come.*

Now Isolde turned towards the building Eurig had pointed out to her: another round, reed-thatched hut, but larger than the rest and positioned at the center of the network of bridges and dwellings, this one built on an island of dry ground instead of a wooden platform. The pulse of drumbeats had stopped some time while she had been with Hereric, and now, as she made her way along the swaying causeway that led to Fidach's hut, the rest of the crannog seemed deserted, lifeless, and eerily quiet amidst the black slippery ooze of the bog.

The door to Fidach's hut was ajar, and as soon as Isolde approached the threshold a curt voice she recognized as Fidach's bade her to enter. She ducked through the low doorway, then stood just inside, waiting for her eyes to adjust to the dimness. The air inside felt close and hot and smelled of wood smoke, as though a fire burning all night had only recently been put out.

Pale yellowing shapes stood out against the shadowed darkness of the curved walls, and after a moment Isolde realized that the room was hung with row upon row of grinning skulls. Not all of them human—she saw several wolves' skulls and at least one of a bear—but the effect might still have raised a shiver along Isolde's spine if she'd not been so certain that that was the intent. Or if the man who sat in the center of the room hadn't been watching her so closely, waiting for her to react.

As it was, she held herself very still, concentrating on slowing the rapid beating of her heart, on allowing nothing of fear or uncertainty to show on her face. Fidach occupied a place beside what Isolde now saw was a central hearth, the ashes of the recent fire still sending up tiny wisps of smoke. His chair was of some carved dark wood, crowned with the rack of a stag's horns, and he sat quite still, his tattooed face indistinct and pale in the gloom, like yet one more age-yellowed skull.

Then: "Be seated. Please."

Isolde took the place he indicated, a wooden stool beside his own, drawing the skirts of her gown tightly about her to keep them from dragging in the ash. She wished for a moment that she'd not thought it best to leave Cabal with Hereric—but she'd been all but sure that bringing the big dog with her would be as much a mistake as allowing Eurig to play escort would have been. So instead, she folded her hands together in her lap and studied the man before her.

Fidach had left off the great fur robe today. Isolde's vision had by now adjusted to the dim light, and she saw with a moment's shock what the fantastic cloak concealed: Fidach's body was gaunt to the point of emaciated, his arms and legs thin as dry tree branches, the bones of his shoulders jutting sharply through the dark woolen tunic he wore.

He was watching her as well, the pale, oddly bright brown eyes flicking rapidly over her from head to foot. Then, with a faint, rasping cough, Fidach cleared his throat. "So. Have you been hearing about how I bed with goats and young boys?"

The sharpness of Fidach's voice, the look in his eyes was a test of a kind. Isolde shook her head. "No. But if it's true, I suppose I'm lucky that I'm neither a boy or a goat."

A thin smile tightened the edges of Fidach's mouth, and he was silent a long moment. Then abruptly he leaned forward and asked, in a louder, harsher tone, "And have you promised Piye you'll not betray his malady to me?"

Even knowing the words were meant to catch her off guard, Isolde couldn't quite stop herself from starting with shock. When she had her breath back, she asked, "Why should you think that?"

She thought something stirred in the depths of Fidach's leaf-brown gaze—something that might have been amusement, or it might have been anger. "I know everything that goes on in this camp. And you would be well advised to remember it. Nothing is secret from me here."

Isolde remembered the terror in Piye's eyes the night before, the strain on his brother's face, and she had to work to keep from showing the wave of mingled anger and revulsion that swept over her. She wanted more than anything to be out of this dark, smoke-scented hut, away from the rows of skulls that grinned from the shadows like hungry ghosts. Away from this man with his painted cheeks and light, maliciously amused eyes.

Fidach, though—whether he liked beasts or young boys or neither or both—was master of this place. As much a king here as Madoc was at Dinas Emrys. And whatever Isolde thought of Fidach himself, her life—and Hereric's—lay at the moment in his hands. So she drew in her breath and ordered herself to keep silent, waiting for Fidach to go on.

He watched her a moment, and then his thin lips parted in a smile, revealing a row of broken gray teeth. "Knowledge is power. And I like power." The smile broadened. "I like it a great deal. Only through power can men taste the wine of the gods." Then, when Isolde still made no reply, he said, a flicker of irritation crossing his sharp-featured face, "Well? Have you nothing to say?"

Isolde didn't answer at once. For seven long years, she had survived by pretended witchcraft. By now she could read faces—and voices—well enough to make a guess at the kind of man Fidach was. A tyrant, she thought. One who despised those who feared and cowed before him. Most tyrants did.

"I would say," Isolde answered, "that one has only to look at the men who are granted earthly power to know what the gods think of the gift."

For a long moment, Fidach's eyes met hers, his gaze expressionless as stone. Then, abruptly, he threw back his head and laughed, the harsh sound echoing in the confining stillness of the hut. "You—"

The laughter had changed to coughing, though, and he had to stop, his emaciated shoulders shaking as he pressed a hand against his mouth and fought to control the fit. Finally, the tearing coughs subsided, and Fidach sank back in his chair. When he took his hand away from his mouth, though, Isolde saw there was a crimson smear of blood on his palm—and the sharp look he shot at her from under his brows told her that he knew she had seen.

"Well?" he said, after a moment. "You're a healer, so Trystan said. Have you a healer's medicine for me? A promise of a cure?"

Everything—the brightness of Fidach's gaze, the flush of color on his cheeks beneath the tattoos, the gauntness of his frame beneath the many-furred robe, her own surprise the day before when Fidach had called a rest at midday, and now the smear of blood on his palm—suddenly came together in Isolde's mind. If she'd thought about it, she would have realized it before. Or at the least sensed the pain in Fidach's chest, like red-hot iron bars about his lungs.

Slowly, she shook her head. "No. We both of us know you'll not see another turning of the seasons."

The anger that flashed across Fidach's gaze made her wonder briefly whether she would have done better to lie, but she knew that he would have known in a moment if she had. Then his features hardened and he laughed again, a harsh, unpleasant sound that stopped as suddenly as it began.

"You've courage, at any rate. There's not one of my men who'd dare look at me and say what you just have."

"Do they know?"

"They know I'm ill—but not *how* ill." Fidach gave another bark of laughter. "The whisper is that I've sold my soul to the devil, and he comes to ride me at night. That's why the flesh falls away from my body and my strength wanes. Though I would have sold my soul and gladly, if ever I'd had the chance. So perhaps it comes to the same in the end. And you know—" Fidach stopped, his eyes resting on Isolde's face, a thin smile still playing about his mouth. "Fear of death lies at the root of all men's other fears. No man fears battle itself—he fears that he will lose his life in the fight. No man fears simply the anger of his chief, should the chief find out . . . oh, for instance, that the man"—Fidach made an airy gesture with his hand that was belied by the hardening of his gaze—"that the man suffers from a falling sickness that makes him unfit to fight. No, what the man fears is that his chief, in anger, will condemn him to die because he is no longer worth the stench of his own dung."

Isolde stopped herself from flinching as he spat the final words, his voice turning poisonously sharp. "Perhaps," she said.

Fidach's smile was a brief acknowledgment that he knew she was ordering herself not to say anything more. His eyes remained fixed on hers, and, just briefly, she saw something stir at the back of his gaze. Something that made her think that his manner, his voice, everything about him was done with as calculated an effect as the skulls on his walls. Though what lay behind the manner and the hard mask of his face she had no idea.

"So a dying man has a choice," he went on. The look—whatever it had been—had gone, leaving his gaze icy hard. "He may fear everything—or he may fear nothing at all."

Isolde silently wished she could be sure of what game it was that Fidach played—and why he had summoned her here. She felt as though she were balanced on a rope bridge as fine as a hair, stretched across raging falls.

Fidach's mouth stretched in another thin-lipped smile, his face hardening and growing slightly predatory. "None of the men would believe you, should you try to persuade them that their chief will lie under the ground before the year's end."

Isolde met Fidach's stare with a level look. "Why would I try?"

Fidach didn't answer that but was silent a long moment, watching her. Then, abruptly, he said, "So you're Trystan's sister. Not much like him to look at, are you?"

The suddenness of the question caught Isolde off guard. Which is of course, she thought, exactly the intent. She drew breath and then said, with scarcely a perceptible pause, "No. But then we were born to different mothers." Let Fidach assume they did share a father. She knew from long practice that a half-truth was always more believable than an outright lie.

"I see." Fidach watched her intently a moment, then said, "And Trystan tells me he's three years the older?"

"Two."

Fidach's answer came like the ringing slash of a sword. "Trystan said three."

Isolde blocked out all awareness of Fidach's illness, the constricting pain in his lungs; any sympathy for this man would be not only unwelcome, but also dangerous just now. Watching him, she tried to imagine what Fidach had been before he'd come to this strange place of dark water and pools of sucking mud, before he'd built this room for himself with its rows of grinning skulls. She wondered whether he might have begun as the spymaster or interrogator of some warlord or king somewhere—or whether his methods of asking questions were simply the means by which he ensured that no secrets among his band of men were kept from him.

She said, as evenly as she could, "Maybe you're misremembering what Trystan said? I can't imagine he would have gotten that wrong. And he is two years older than I am."

She saw in Fidach's face a brief flash of acknowledgment that the trap he'd laid for her had failed. Then he bared his teeth in another smile. "Trystan's sister," he said again. "Good. You can tell me much about Trystan that I've always wanted to know."

ISOLDE SAT ON THE FLOOR BESIDE Hereric's pallet, watching the last of the sunset's glow fade from the western sky. The first stars were just beginning to wink out, and all about the marsh was filled with the sigh of the wind, the chirp of crickets, and the soft, occasional trill of a night bird. She passed the day in scrubbing the dust and dirt of travel from her own and Hereric's clothes— using the battered tub Eurig had brought—and then mending any rents and tears.

Now Hereric's tunic and breeches, and her second gown, stockings, and two shifts were spread about the floor of her hut next door to dry, and Hereric had fallen asleep after the evening meal of bread and thick stew they had shared. Eurig had brought them the food and had stayed to exchange a few words with Hereric. From time to time she'd caught glimpses of some of the guards posted here and there along the edges of the bog, forming what she thought must be a loose circle around the settlement. The guards wore gray and brown tunics and breeches that faded into the landscape, making them almost invisible. And apart from that, Isolde had seen no one since she'd left Fidach's hut. The whole network of huts and causeways had remained eerily empty and still.

She had left the door to the hut open to catch the last of the day's waning light, and from where she sat now, she could see Fidach's hut squatting like a great brown toad amidst the other, smaller dwellings of the crannog. Fidach had questioned her closely about Trystan and about the childhood they'd shared, and she'd responded with answers as true as she could safely make them. When at last Fidach had put an end to the interview, her neck muscles were aching with tension, but Fidach was—apparently, at least—satisfied that she was neither more nor less than what Trystan had claimed.

Now, looking across at Fidach's dwelling, Isolde remembered the outlaw leader's predatory, wolfish smile and thought that he was indeed not unlike the dominant wolf of a pack. He must be very afraid, too, despite what he himself had said about a dying man's having nothing to fear. A lead wolf holds his place only so long as his strength holds fast.

Isolde rubbed her eyes, then sat up abruptly as from some-where close by came a sudden raucous burst of sound: men's voices, shouts, and drunken laughter. And then, through the open doorway, she saw them, a group of perhaps twenty of the band, spilling from dry land onto one of the narrow rope bridges, weaving and swaying as they came, waving swords and heavy wooden clubs in the air. Their bodies—faces, arms, bare chests—were painted with swirling blue patterns like the heroes in the ancient tales, or like the tattoos on their chief's own face.

Cabal had been asleep by her side, but at the sudden noise he woke and was on his feet, fur bristling. Isolde put a hand on his collar to hold him by her side and instinctively drew back into the hut and shut the door. She was remembering the pulsing drumbeats she'd heard that morning and the desertion of the crannog today. Preparation for something—a raid, she thought, it had to be—and now a triumphant return.

For the space of several moments, Isolde sat without moving in the semidarkness of Hereric's hut, listening to the shouts and occasional snatches of song that reached her from outside and debating with herself whether to stay here for the night or go to her own pallet next door. She had almost decided to stay when a soft scratch sounded on the door, making her tense before she recognized Eurig's voice.

"Lady? Are you there?"

Isolde rose and cracked open the door. Eurig was there, as well as Daka and Piye, and at sight of her, Eurig let out a breath of relief.

"Saw you weren't in your own place." He kept his voice low, barely audible over the shouts and laughter coming, Isolde now saw, from Fidach's centrally placed hut. Extra torches had been lighted all around the perimeter of Fidach's small island, the leaping flames and smoky orange glow making the place look ever more otherworldly and strange. "Hoped it was only that you'd stayed with Hereric here."

"Is something wrong?" Isolde asked.

Eurig shook his head. "Might get a bit—well, noisy, like, that's all," he said. He paused, then added, "But if you want to go to your own bed, you'll be safe enough. The three of us"—he made a gesture that included Piye and Daka—"we'll make sure none of the rest get an idea to ... er ... trouble you with their company."

Isolde didn't bother to ask whether she needed a guard. The three men's faces told her they thought she did. She nodded. "Thank you." And then, as her eyes moved from Eurig to the other two, she noticed that one of the twins—Piye, she thought, from the iron ring he still wore on his right hand—had a stained bandage knotted about his upper arm.

"Are you wounded? Do you want me to see to that for you?" she asked.

Daka, standing at his brother's side, seemed to hesitate a long moment before translating the question in a low-voiced mutter. Both the young men's dark-skinned faces were impassive, all but expressionless in the gathering dusk, their long-lashed eyes studying her face.

Eyes still on her, Piye said something in an undertone to his brother. Daka replied in the same low-voiced tone, and Isolde saw Piye's fingers move as though by reflex to the ring she'd given him the night before. Then, almost as one, the two brothers turned back to Isolde, and bowed their heads in agreement.

"Cut on his arm," Daka said. "Not bad—he live. But some pain. If you can help, he be glad."

Isolde cast a look back over her shoulder at Hereric. She'd not given him any of the poppy tonight, but he still slept almost as soundly as though she had. He lay on his back, mouth slightly open, his breathing even and slow. She turned back to Daka and the other two men. "Come next door. All my medicines are there."

THE CUT ON PIYE'S ARM WAS long and ragged but not deep, and as Daka had said, not serious. Isolde made her examination by the light of a small oil lamp that Eurig had brought. Eurig had also stuffed a blanket into the gap between the floor and the door panel so that the light wouldn't show from outside.

"Not that any of that lot are like to notice, the way they're heading," he had said with uncharacteristic grimness. "But better to be safe than wish you had been."

Now, studying Piye's wound, Isolde still could hear the sounds of drunken song and laughter from Fidach's hut. Each burst of sound seemed to twitch through her every nerve, but she sat back, looking up at Daka. "You're right. It's not too bad. He should have it stitched, though, if it's going to heal properly. Can you tell him that I'll do it for him now, if he wants me to?"

Daka translated her words, and after studying her face a moment more, Piye nodded, giving her one of those grave, oddly formal bows and saying something in his own tongue that was clearly assent. Isolde cleaned the wound of dust and dried blood, then took out one of her bone needles and thread. Piye held himself utterly still as she started to stitch the wound, but she felt his muscles contract every time the needle pierced his skin and saw a glitter of sweat start on his brow. As Daka had said, the cut wouldn't threaten Piye's life, but it was still a constant, dragging pain.

Isolde was halfway finished before she realized that she'd slipped automatically into her habit of telling a story as she worked, had begun the tale without conscious thought, without even really hearing her own words. When she did realize it, she paused and glanced up first at Piye's face then at Daka's, to see whether her speaking made them uneasy. She saw nothing but taut control on both young men's faces, though, and so she went on, since the cadence of the words always helped distract her from the pain she inevitably caused as well.

The tale she'd begun was a sad one, of a man who one day at twilight stole the sealskin of a beautiful selkie maid when she danced on the shore with her sisters, as selkies do at that hour of changing between night and day. The selkie agreed to become his wife, for without her sealskin, she could not return to the sea. And she lived with him through many years and bore him fine daughters and sons. But always she looked longingly out towards the sea. And then one day, her daughter found a glimmering seal's skin hidden away in a chest in their home and went to her mother to ask what it might be. And so with a cry of joy, the selkie maid took the seal's skin from her daughter's hands and ran from the house, back towards the shore. She cried as she went, for she loved her children—and even her mortal husband. But still she went, for she loved the sea the more.

Isolde finished tying a clean bandage about Piye's arm as she spoke the story's final words, and for a moment the hut was silent, save for the continued sounds of revelry outside. Isolde hadn't been sure how much of the story any of the men followed, so she was surprised, glancing round, to find Eurig watching her. His gentle brown eyes were dry, but there was a look of such aching sadness in their depths that Isolde asked, before she could stop herself, "Are you all right?"

At once, Eurig's eyes fell, and he hunched his shoulders as though embarrassed. He cleared his throat, then said, "Fine—fine. It's a sorrowful ending to a tale, is all." And then, before Isolde could reply, he turned to Piye and Daka. "One of you'd better get down there"—he jerked his head towards Fidach's hut—"for a bit, at least. Stand out like black wolves in a flock of sheep, the pair of you. But if one of you goes down and moves around the crowd, chances are no one will notice you're not both there." He snorted briefly. "Most of them are probably seeing double by now anyway."

The brothers exchanged a quick, wordless look, and then Daka nodded and rose to his feet. "I go." He turned and gave Isolde another sober-faced bow, and said, "I thank you. We be in your debt."

When Daka had gone, Isolde started to tidy away the dirtied linens and pots of salve she'd used to clean Piye's wound.

"Eurig—" She glanced up at him. "How was Piye hurt?"

Eurig had been helping to wind a spare strip of bandages, but at that the tips of his ears reddened again, and he bundled the whole of the linen awkwardly into an untidy knot that tangled in his hands. "Don't know as how you want to hear that. Not a fit story for a lady's ears, maybe."

"Maybe not," Isolde said. "But I'd like to hear. Unless you're under oath not to speak of that as well?"

Eurig hesitated, then let out his breath, rubbing a hand across the stubble of beard on his chin. "No—nothing like that. It's just—well, it was a raid, that's all. No worse than most, I'll warrant, but no better, either. Fidach got word of the armies massing just south of here, and—"

He broke off as Isolde interrupted quickly, "Armies? What armies?"

The sharpness of her tone made Eurig throw her a quick, curious glance, but he answered, "Octa of Kent's forces. A day's ride away—maybe even half that, by now. Word out on the road is that Octa's come either to make alliance with King Cerdic or to make war on him and claim Cerdic's lands for his own."

"Cerdic," Isolde repeated. "Cerdic of Wessex, you mean?" Which is a stupid question, she thought, even as the words left her mouth, because what other King Cerdic could Eurig possibly mean?

Eurig nodded. "Aye, that's him."

"And the rumor is that he and Cerdic may be joining forces?"

Eurig shrugged. If he wondered at Isolde's interest, he gave no sign. "As to that—who knows? Fidach pays well to keep informed of what happens between them that hold power in these parts—has to, a man in his place. He says not a one of the warlords within ten days' ride from here could so much as wipe his—" Eurig stopped and glanced at Isolde. "Nose, without he gets to know of it, for all we're well hidden in this place here. But as to Octa and Cerdic making peace between them . . ."

Eurig paused again, brow creasing in a frown. "Not sure even Octa and Cerdic know for sure what's going to happen between them now. They've never trusted each other a hair's breadth, the two of them, that I do know—been at each other's throats since they came to power like a couple of dogs fighting over first share of a kill. Still—" He shrugged again. "Reckon stranger things have happened."

He stopped as Piye interrupted with a burst of speech in his own tongue. Eurig replied—slower and more laboriously than either Daka or Piye—in the same language the brothers used. Piye gave Isolde a long look in which she thought curiosity mingled again with that look that she couldn't quite name. Then Eurig said, "He heard us using Octa's name and wanted to know what we were speaking of, that's all."

With an effort, Isolde brought her thoughts back to the present and asked, "And that's how Piye was hurt? In a raid on Octa's armies?"

Eurig hesitated as though searching for a reply that would be fit for her ears. Then he seemed to simply give up, for his shoulders sagged and he nodded. "Aye. Caught a couple of Octa's scouts. Hurt them just enough to let them know they could be hurting a lot more. Then promised to let them live if they'd tell where Octa's supply wagons were and the kind of guard he had. Then they cut the scouts' throats and left them to rot."

"That's what Piye told you?"

Eurig lifted one shoulder. "Some. And I can guess the rest. That's usually how it goes. And if you're going to say it's a dirty day's work, I won't argue. But it's no dirtier than would happen to any of us if we fell into the hands of Octa's—or anyone else's—men."

"I'm sure that's true," Isolde said.

Eurig was silent a long moment, staring down at the floor, though Isolde knew that whatever he saw, it wasn't the rough wooden planks under their feet. Then he lifted his head, meeting Isolde's gaze. "I wasn't always outlaw. I was a man once—with a home. A wife. A son. Not that there's much of that left in me now. But—" He stopped. His shyness had all but fallen away, and for a moment, another man entirely seemed to look out through his gentle brown eyes. Then, in a flash it was gone, leaving him homely, lumpish, balding, and awkward of speech once more. He hunched his shoulders. "Well, just wanted you to know, that's all."

"Why do you stay?" Isolde asked. But that was another pointless question. Eurig—and for all she knew, the entire rest of the band—stayed because they must believe they could do nothing else. Men like Fidach's, broken men, were those disgraced by outliving their lord on the field of battle. Or breaking an oath of allegiance. Or escaped criminals or slaves.

Almost as though he'd read her thoughts, Eurig said, with a wry twist to his mouth, "Why do I stay? Because there's nothing else for me. Men like us"—he made a gesture that included himself and Piye—"not like we're going to walk into some lordling's hall and have him welcome us with open arms. Not without his noticing this, one fine day." Eurig pushed back the sleeve of his tunic, turning his arm to show his inner wrist. Two lines, crossed at the center, stood out black against the paler skin. A brand, the mark given for murder. "Or this." Eurig leaned forward, pulling down the neck of his tunic so that Isolde saw the brand on his neck. A dark, smooth oval. The same mark of slavery Trystan bore.

She said nothing, but Eurig, watching her face, nodded as though in confirmation. His voice changed, slightly, becoming somehow grimmer and hard. "Aye, Trystan was there, as well. At the mines. He's the one that got me free. Got me free and carried me on his back through the snow because I was too sick to walk—not that he was in much better case. And saved my life more times afterwards than I care to count. So you can see why he'd trust me to guard you as I would have my own family, while they were yet alive." He stopped, then added, in the same tone, "You can go to your own bed now and rest easy. No one gets past your door while I'm outside."

WHEN BOTH PIYE AND EURIG WERE gone, Isolde sat down on the hard wooden floor, absently running a hand along Cabal's back as the big dog came to settle beside her with an explosive sigh, resting his head in her lap. She didn't doubt that Eurig and Piye would keep watch outside her door tonight. Despite—or maybe because of—what Eurig had told her, she trusted them both. If either of them had wanted to harm her, they could have done it ten times over by now. And in the last moments before Eurig had turned to go, she'd abruptly become aware of the strength of his arms, the muscles of his shoulders, powerful as a bull's. For all his quiet voice and shy manners, she could see the value he would have in Fidach's band of fighting men.

Even so, though, she didn't go to bed or even lie down. She was thinking of what Eurig had told her of Octa and Cerdic. If Octa of Kent and Cerdic of Wessex had indeed sworn an oath of alliance, then she'd already failed in what she had journeyed all this way to do. Octa, Marche, and Cerdic between them would raise an army of spears and swordsmen that Madoc couldn't possibly hope to match or defeat. Britain would be crushed as surely as the tribes had been crushed underfoot by the Roman legions so many men's lifetimes ago.

There was still the faint glimmer of a chance, though, that peace between Octa and Cerdic was not yet made, or that Eurig had been misinformed. And that meant that she had to get free of this place, get away from Fidach, and journey the rest of the distance to Cerdic's court. Sitting in the lamp-lit hut, aware of the black, oozing mud and dark water that surrounded her on all sides, the thought seemed as possible as the story of selkies and twilight change she'd just told.

At least, though, she could put that worry aside; however impossible a journey to Cerdic might be, she could do nothing tonight. What she couldn't dismiss was her final exchange with Eurig, which kept ringing in her ears like the drumbeats she'd heard at dawn. Just as Eurig had turned to leave, Isolde had spoken again, making him pause with one hand on the door.

"I won't ask you to tell me where Trystan has gone," she had said. "Or what kind of job Fidach has given him. But will you tell me this, at least: would you have expected him to return by now, if the mission had gone according to plan?"

Eurig had turned back and looked at her across the dimly lighted space of the hut. Then finally, he let out his breath in another long sigh. "Aye," he said. "Don't reckon you're the sort that would take comfort in a lie. So I'll tell you plain. Aye, I would have expected it. Reckon Fidach would have, too—and that's why he had you in to see him this morning. See if he could find out whether Trystan was like to have just cut loose with—" He checked himself. "Just cut loose and left you here. Not that

I believe it," he added quickly. "But that's how Fidach would likely think, once he saw Trystan was slow in coming back."

Now, sitting by the guttering oil lamp, one hand still resting on Cabal's neck, Isolde knew that she didn't believe it, either. A part of her was surprised that she could be so sure—even kept probing her certainty for doubts, like touching a healing scar to see whether the pain is really gone. But she was sure—utterly and completely so. However Trystan had changed—whatever task appointed by Fidach he had set out to do—she knew without question that he wouldn't have abandoned her and Hereric here willingly. The fear that brushed like bat wings all along her spine was the one that had entered her thoughts the moment Eurig had mentioned Octa's name: that where Octa was, so Marche might be.

She had seen Marche last—or rather glimpsed him in the scrying waters—with Octa. Somewhere to the north of here, she thought, because Octa had spoken of riding south at dawn to meet with Cerdic of Wessex. He'd said nothing of Marche accompanying him. But he might have, she thought. He could be—what had Eurig said? Less than a day's ride away from here, even now.

Trystan, too, was somewhere abroad in these wild, war-torn lands—she supposed alone, for Eurig had said nothing of anyone's accompanying him on whatever mission he was on. And he doesn't know, still, Isolde thought, that Marche is seeking him. Because I never told him.

The hut's single room felt suddenly close and airless, as though the whole world had suddenly shrunk to only what was contained in these bare, cornerless walls. Still, Isolde made herself rise, drawing an aggrieved grumble from Cabal as she moved his head from her lap. The washbasin was where she'd left it that afternoon and still half full with the water she'd used to scrub their clothes. Moving to kneel beside it, Isolde felt a flicker of almost amusement at the thought about the strange assortment of vessels she'd scried in since this journey began, even as she dreaded what she would see this time. *A basin aboard Trystan's ship . . . a moonlit pool of rainwater . . . and now a battered tin washtub, grimy with the dirt and dust from travel-soiled clothes.*

She focused on the lamplight, shattered and reflected on the surface of the water here, she realized that for the first time she would welcome a vision of him if it meant an end to uncertainty. If she could know where Marche was—where Trystan was—tonight.

Isolde let her breathing steady and slow, emptied her mind of all hope, all expectation, all thought, until she was balanced as on a knifepoint of each breath she took, each beat of her heart. And, then . . . darkness. The darkness was so profound that for a moment Isolde thought no image had appeared at all. And then she started to make out shapes in the dark: a shield, a spear and sword lying on the ground. A rough camp bed. The inside of a war tent, maybe, she thought.

A man was hunched on the bed, his body clenched as though around some inner pain. Too dark to see his face. Isolde felt a moment's dread. But she'd come too far to turn back now. Closer . . . closer . . . she drew breath like a swimmer diving underwater. Then—

HER HAND WAS STUFFED IN HER mouth and she was biting down hard on her own flesh to keep from crying out. Pain . . . but she welcomed the pain. Pain was proof of life. Pain and rage. That was all she ever felt. For the rest . . . it was like being ravenously hungry, and having all food turn to ashes in her mouth. Drinking and drinking and nothing slaking the terrible, burning thirst. Because—

She bit down harder on the knuckles of her hand. Because what he wanted with a longing like a poisoned arrow twisting in his chest had been buried seven years ago under the ground at Camlann.

.   .   .

THE IMAGE BROKE WITH A SUDDENNESS that made Isolde gasp. The sound drew Cabal's attention, and the big dog burrowed his cold nose against her neck, whining softly. Isolde let him lick her cheek, grateful for the warmth of his fur, the rough prickle of his tongue on her skin. She was shivering, nausea rolling through her in waves.

For five months now she had been able to slide in and out of Marche's thoughts. But all that while, she'd slammed the door on even considering what she herself felt about Marche, the man. She'd refused even to consider feeling anger, because she didn't want even that added link with him, that extra presence of him in her mind.

But the more times she glimpsed him in the scrying waters—the more times she slipped into his mind, felt what he felt and heard his inner voice—

The more—goddess mother help her—she felt something like unwelcome pity stirring inside her. And that was even less welcome than anger would have been.

TRYSTAN STARED AT THE CRANNOG BLANKLY, wondering whether he'd actually reached the place at last or whether this was only some strange illusion. Some trick of vision conjured by the pain of his ribs. At least two were broken—cracked in the fight with the guardsman at the tin mines. A big man, he'd been, and clumsy with it. Not much of a fight at all, really. Just a matter of waiting for the guard to overbalance so that his own weight could be used against him.

Trystan shifted the weight of the leather satchel he carried, grimacing at the fiery stab that shot through his chest. Stupid, probably, that the pain in some measure assuaged his conscience for having taken the man's life. The fact that he was standing here swearing and sweating because his ribs ached like fury did the dead guard about as much good as a pair of boots did a snake.

"So, my friend. Back at last."

The voice at his elbow made him jerk round, one hand on his knife, then allow himself a profound wish that he hadn't as the movement brought another jolt of pain. Fidach. Of course. And probably it would be stupid as well to ask irritably whether he couldn't walk and talk like an ordinary mortal instead of creeping about like a bloody ghost.

Then again, Trystan must have let his own natural defenses drop, or Fidach wouldn't have gotten this close without his knowing it.

Fidach's eyes flicked over him, his glance cool. "You succeeded?"

Wordlessly, Trystan handed across the leather satchel filled with the gold of some local petty warlord. Payment for the tin he needed to smelt his bronze spearheads and knives.

Fidach hefted the bag with one hand, testing its weight, then nodded. "Very good. Though no less than what I expected of you, my friend."

"Good of you."

A faint flash of amusement in the pale brown eyes acknowledged the dryness of Trystan's tone. Fidach started to speak, coughed, then caught his breath and started again. "Your mute friend is recovering well. An unusual girl, your sister," he said. "A rare healer. And grown quite popular, too, among the men."

And it would certainly be truly and utterly stupid to grab Fidach by the throat, pin him to the ground, and threaten to choke the life out of him if Isolde had been hurt or harmed. But that didn't stop Trystan's hands from twitching with the wish that he could—or keep the blood from pounding blackly behind him eyes.

He'd had long practice, though, in schooling himself not to give wishes like that away. And he must have succeeded now because a flash of annoyance replaced the amusement in Fidach's gaze. He said, irritably, "Yes, she's won herself a following of devoted guards who watch over her like a pack of faithful hounds—much like that oversize beast of hers." A hint of venom crept into Fidach's tone. "They snap and growl when anyone else so much as comes near."

Breathe in. Breathe out. Trystan said, pleasantly, "You'll be pleased to be rid of us, then."

It was the wrong thing to say. Trystan knew it even as he heard the words leave his mouth. Fidach's smile broadened. "You know me well, my friend. Have you ever known me to let anyone go as easily as that?" His hand moved, and Trystan saw that under that ridiculous bearskin robe he wore a sword belt and long sword. "Let's make it a challenge, shall we? A match of blades. Beat me in fair combat, and I may even let you take your sister and leave this place alive."

Chapter Thirteen

ISOLDE STOOD FROZEN IN PLACE, watching as Trystan and Fidach spun in a dizzying circle, their blades clashing, locking, then scraping apart to meet with a ringing clash yet again. They were evenly matched—terrifyingly so—and in the lightning strikes of Fidach's blade, she could see how he had won and held the allegiance of his band of broken men. Despite his wasted body and fever-bright eyes, he moved with the grace of a dancer and the speed of a striking snake, so that Trystan had to work continually to block and parry each blow of Fidach's sword.

Isolde had seen Trystan fight before, while they were growing up and then again months ago. She knew the way he moved in a sword fight, the way he gripped a blade. This time, it seemed to her that his movements were stiffer than usual, lacking something of their usual quickness. His face was utterly still and calm, though, and his eyes were fixed on Fidach, reading the other man's every movement, gauging each step Fidach took, each twist of his shoulders or tilt of his body. They slashed for each other's chests, hacked downwards at arms and legs, thrust at each other's throats. And always Trystan was ready with a movement that mirrored and canceled Fidach's, always the swords clashed, screeched together as the blades slid towards the hilts, then sprang apart.

The rest of the band was grouped in a half circle about them, some calling encouragements to their chief, some cheering Trystan on, but Isolde scarcely heard them. Later, she might feel dizzying relief at seeing Trystan here, and alive. Later, she might think to wonder or ask where he'd been. For now, though, every scrap of her concentration was fixed on the play of swords between the two men. She couldn't even call to mind what Eurig had told her of the fight, when he'd come to her hut to give her the news that Trystan was returned. *Only in fun, like,* Eurig had said. *A fight to first blood, not to the death.* Watching, though, Isolde couldn't let herself believe it. The faces of both men were too focused and fixed, deadly intent written in every line of their bodies and every meeting of their blades.

Both were tiring. Sweat streaked Fidach's tattooed face and matted his hair, and Trystan's movements grew, not slower, Isolde thought, but more controlled, as though each slash of his sword required a greater effort than the one before. And then, suddenly, Trystan's foot slipped from under him and he started to fall, so that his arm flew out and he lost his grip on his sword.

Isolde's heart seized hard in her chest, and she heard several sharply indrawn breaths—and several more derisive calls—from the circle of watching men. Trystan's blade fell uselessly to the ground, and Fidach took a step forward, his own sword upraised, about to strike. Trystan had righted himself, but now faced Fidach without a weapon. For an endless moment, time seemed to hang suspended while the two men faced each other, one with his blade at the ready, glinting in the rays of the setting sun, the other unarmed.

Then, with the lightning swiftness of a serpent's strike, Fidach struck. Isolde's breath stopped. But somehow, incredibly, Trystan spun aside and kicked out, his booted foot connecting with the wrist of Fidach's sword arm and sending Fidach's blade flying to the ground. For another long moment, the two men faced each other, chests heaving as they fought for breath. Then Trystan put out his hand in a gesture of peace.

Fidach's face was impassive, his eyes unreadable as light brown stone. The next moment, though, he had thrown back his head and given one of his harsh, sudden bursts of laughter.

"Well fought. Well fought." He took the hand Trystan had offered, and the two men clasped wrists, pounding each other on the back. "I thought I almost had you there, my friend. We'll call it a draw, agreed?"

Trystan's reply was lost to Isolde as shouts and laughter went up from the watchers all around. Isolde hadn't thought Trystan even knew she'd been watching. But then he said something else to Fidach, clapped the shoulders of a few of those who pressed forward to offer congratulations, and turned, pushing his way through the group to where she stood.

Isolde moved without conscious thought—hadn't even realized she'd moved at all. One moment she was standing facing Trystan and the next her arms had gone round his neck and she was hugging him tightly the way she always had years ago when he came back from a battle or campaign. She felt his breath go out in a rush of surprise and thought he stiffened as though in pain. But his arms closed around her and he swung her up off the ground as he always had years before.

He smelled of earth and dried leaves and sweat from the recent fight. Isolde closed her eyes and for a moment was aware of nothing but the reassuring solidity of his arms, the fact of his presence: that he was here, alive. Not dead. Not a prisoner of Octa or Marche. Then two realizations crept in. The first was that Trystan's seemingly accidental slip and loss of his sword had been nothing of the kind, but a ploy calculated to throw Fidach off guard. The second realization was that they were now surrounded by Fidach's men.

Isolde instantly pulled free, but Trystan held her a moment longer, hands on her shoulders, looking intently down into her face.

"You're all right?" he asked.

Isolde nodded. "We're fine. Both of us—Hereric and I."

Trystan started to answer, but Fidach's voice broke in. "As you see, we have kept your sister safe for you."

Trystan stepped back from Isolde, wiping a trickle of sweat from his brow with the back of his hand, turned to Fidach, and said calmly, "And I thank you for it."

For a long moment, Fidach's eyes rested on Trystan's, and Isolde wondered whether it was only her imagination that the rest of the group seemed to tense in expectation, breath held. But then Fidach flung out his arms. "Come. You are safely returned. And not only safe, but successful. Tonight we feast in your honor. I insist."

ISOLDE SAT ON THE STRAW PALLET in her own hut, combing out her damp hair. She had waited until all sounds from the rest of the crannog had ceased, all the singing and shouts and laughter from Fidach's hut dying into silence. Then she had lit the hut's single rush light and washed in Eurig's battered tin tub, even unbraiding her hair so that she could rinse it free of dust and dirt. Now she was teasing out the tangles, wearing the shift, tunic, and skirt she'd washed the day before and feeling cleaner than she had since leaving Dinas Emrys.

A soft scratch sounded at her door, making her heart jump before she recognized Trystan's voice. "It's only me. Can I come in?"

Isolde sprang up and went to open the door. "Yes, of course. Come in. Down, Cabal."

The big dog had been asleep on the floor but had woken with a snuffle at Trystan's step outside the door. At Isolde's command, though, and recognizing Trystan, he subsided onto the floor, head resting on his outstretched paws.

Trystan slipped inside, and Isolde shut the door behind him. They'd not spoken all throughout the long feasting in Fidach's hut. The food—roast venison, bread, wild boar's meat, and jars of ale—had been spread out on the floor, and the men had sat in a ragged circle all around. Isolde had been placed between Eurig and Piye, and Trystan had been at the far end of the crowded, smoky room.

Now Trystan seated himself on an open space on the hut's wooden floor, and Isolde settled back on the pallet, curling her legs under her. There was a moment's quiet, and then Isolde said, "Hereric's recovering—he's nearly well now."

"I know. Fidach told me first thing. And then I looked in on him next door just before I came here. He was sleeping, but I could see he was better." Trystan looked down at his hands, then up again at her with a quick, crooked smile. "I'm not sure what to say. Just 'thank you' doesn't seem quite enough. But I do. Thank you."

Isolde shook her head. "You don't have to thank me. I'm just thankful that he's alive and with his mind still whole." She thought again of that night in the ruined villa, alone with Cabal and Hereric, when Hereric had first woken from the fever. The overwhelming rush of relief she'd felt when he'd formed a few signs, stumbling but coherent.

And then she felt a prickle of now familiar fear as she realized that the relief she'd felt then was only a pale, shaded echo of what she felt now at seeing Trystan here, within arm's reach of her and alive. Still. The dizzying thankfulness that had made her run to throw her arms about him was still warm in her veins.

Trystan shifted position and winced, his mouth tightening, and Isolde thrust the thought aside, asking quickly, "Are you injured?"

Trystan stretched out his legs, leaned back against the wall, and shook his head. "Just stiff. And a couple of bruises. That's all."

Isolde studied him, taking in the set of his mouth, recalling the slight stiffness of his movements during the sword fight. "Bruises," she repeated. Then remembrance struck her and she said, "I'm sorry—did I hurt you? After you fought Fidach—"

Trystan seemed to hesitate, but then shook his head again. "No, it's all right. You didn't hurt me. I was just surprised, that's all. You haven't done that since you were ten years old."

Isolde felt a flush creep into her cheeks, but she made herself smile a bit. "Well, twelve, maybe."

The rush light glinted on the stubble of gold-brown beard on Trystan's jaw, and Isolde, meeting his eyes, had another of those dizzying moments where Trystan seemed to waver back and forth between stranger and someone she knew as well as she did herself. Like looking at a shimmering reflection in a shallow pool. She said nothing, though, and after a moment Trystan said, "I'm sorry if I scared you. I needed a way to end the fight without actually winning."

Isolde had made herself look away, fearful that the unaccustomed, prickling undercurrents were about to enter the room again. She'd started to work the comb through the tangled ends of her hair again, but at that she glanced up. "You did slip on purpose, then? I thought so, but I couldn't be sure."

Trystan nodded. "I thought I'd better find a way to make it look like a draw. Not that I thought Fidach would kill me for beating him, but—" One side of his mouth tilted in a brief, grim smile. "I thought I'd be wiser not to try it. Fidach doesn't like losing any better than the next man."

"Less, I'd think." Isolde frowned, then asked, "How did you block his blow so quickly, though? You kicked the sword out of his hand as soon as he tried to strike—almost before."

Trystan was watching her as she combed through the ends of her hair; unbound like this, it reached nearly to her waist. At the question, he seemed to drag his thoughts back from a long way off and shook his head. "Oh, that." He shrugged. "Fidach's good. But he leads with his face—always has done."

"Leads with his—"

"Tenses his jaw—grimaces—every time he's about to strike a blow. Watch his face in a fight and you can usually guess at what he's about to do."

Isolde's eyes rested a moment on the rush light's flame, seeing again that savage, lightning-fast dance with swords. Then she closed her eyes to clear them of the image and said, turning back to Trystan, "You think we're in danger here."

Trystan looked up at her sharply. "Maybe. What makes you say it, though?"

Isolde set down the comb and started to separate the heavy curtain of her hair into three sections, working them smooth with her fingers until they were even enough to plait. The taut awareness that had brushed along her every nerve was gone—or at least held at bay. This was Trystan, whom she'd known as long as she could recall. Whom she did know better than anyone, and could speak to as easily as she did herself.

"I was watching you at the feasting tonight. You were eating left-handed—keeping your right hand always within easy reach of your knife."

"Was I?" Trystan glanced down at the knife he still wore at his belt, then rubbed a hand across his face. He looked exhausted, Isolde realized abruptly, and she wondered where he'd been all these long days. "That's more habit than anything else. Just a reflex, whenever I'm on edge." He let his hand fall, then said, "And as to danger, I don't know. I hope not. But—"

He broke off as a light, urgent tap sounded on the door outside the hut.

Instantly, Trystan was on his feet. He still moved stiffly, Isolde saw, and she wondered if he'd lied about not being hurt. He had the knife drawn from his belt, though, even as he crossed in a single quick stride to open the door. Isolde, too, sprang up and caught hold of Cabal's collar as the big dog woke and rose with a low, rumbling growl.

Then, as the door swung open, she let out a breath of relief at the sight of Daka and Piye, their ebony faces outlined by the silver light of the nearly full moon above. Though the relief lasted only until she saw their expressions: grim and set as two twin masks.

"Daka—Piye," she said. "Is something wrong?"

Daka glanced back over his shoulder as though checking for something, then turned back to Isolde. She thought there was something odd in the way he held himself, in the way he raised his voice slightly to answer and spoke even before ducking through the doorway of the hut. But his words were calm enough. "Nothing wrong. Only Piye's arm be bleeding again. Come to you, see if you can help."

Trystan, too, must have been struck by something strange in Daka's manner, for he stood still a moment, looking past them out into the night beyond. Then he gave the two brothers a swift, sharp look, all without relaxing his grip on the knife. He moved aside, though, letting Daka and Piye step into the hut's small space.

Piye had one hand pressed to the wounded shoulder, and Isolde saw blood-soaked bandage peeping through the gaps between his fingers.

"Sit down." She gestured to the pallet, then turned away to reach for her medicine bag. Trystan stood with his back against the panel of the door, Daka at his side. Piye sat as rigid and motionless as before while she unwrapped the saturated bandage from his upper arm. Then, as the final layer of wrappings fell away, Isolde stopped and looked up, first at Piye's immobile face, then at that of his twin.

"I don't understand. It looks as though the stitches I put in yesterday have been cut with a knife."

Her first thought was that Fidach had heard of her treatment of Piye and ripped out the stitches as some kind of punishment. But Daka's answer when it came surprised her even more.

"Yes, lady. I cut them before we come."

"You cut them. But why?"

The line of Daka's mouth hardened, turning his expression grimmer still than before. "Because better we have reason for coming to you tonight, if anyone sees us enter or leave."

Trystan had been watching the brothers in silence, but at that he cleared his throat and spoke for the first time. "What's happened?"

Daka turned to him. "Fidach. He plan to sell you to Octa tomorrow."

For a moment, Trystan's face was absolutely without expression. Then he said, "I see. How do you know?"

How do you know? Not, Isolde registered through the chill that gripped her, *Are you sure?* Plainly Daka and Piye were sure, or they'd not be here, risking themselves like this.

"Tonight. I see. Esar go—" Daka stopped, shook his head in frustration, then launched into a flood of speech in his own tongue, while Piye, from his place on the pallet, added a word here and there. Isolde caught the words *Fidach* and *Octa*, but apart from that, understood nothing at all. Trystan stood listening in silence, still with that utterly expressionless look on his face. Then, when Daka had finished, he said something in the same tongue—a question, Isolde thought—and Daka and Piye responded with another flood of words.

Finally, Trystan turned to Isolde. "He says that Piye was part of a raid on Octa's forces two nights ago. That they caught a pair of Octa's scouts, who gave them a story about a reward being offered for a black-haired woman traveling with two men, one Saxon, one Briton-born. They'd wit enough among them to realize that could fit the three of us—you and Hereric and me—well enough. Piye"—Trystan nodded in the young man's direction—"made the rest of the raiding party swear an oath they'd not speak again of what they'd learned. He said he owes you a debt, though he didn't say what the debt was."

Isolde felt as though the floor beneath her was crumbling into the oozing black mud of the swamp outside as she struggled to take in all that Trystan said. She was remembering the odd looks Piye had given her after his return from the raid—comprehensible, now. She shook her head, trying to clear her thoughts.

"No. He doesn't owe me anything. Not really. Only that—" She stopped and shook her head again. "Never mind. It doesn't matter, and I doubt we've time for me to explain. Go on." And then, as Trystan started to answer, she added, "I didn't know you spoke Piye and Daka's language."

Trystan stopped whatever he'd been about to say. His mouth twisted up briefly. "I don't. They're talking to me the way they would a two-year-old child. And they'd both of them likely be falling over laughing at my answers if the position wasn't so bloody serious."

At that, Daka's grim expression lightened as well, and he grinned, white teething flashing in his dark face. He said something under his breath, to which Trystan gave a short laugh. "He says claiming I've the skill of a two-year-old insults the child."

Trystan turned and answered Daka in the same tongue before turning back to Isolde, sober, now. "At any rate, one of the men—Esar, Piye says it was—apparently decided that Fidach's reward for information was worth more to him than the oath he'd sworn. After the feasting tonight, he slipped back to Fidach's hut alone. Piye saw him go and was suspicious enough to follow. He waited outside and heard what Esar told Fidach, and what Fidach said in return. Now Esar's gone—on Fidach's orders—to make contact with Octa and offer us to him. At a price, of course. They say—Piye and Daka—that they don't know any more than that." Trystan paused, then added, deliberately, "None of them, as far as I can tell, knows what Octa wants with us. Only that the pay was high."

Isolde, her eyes on Trystan's, nodded to show she'd understood the warning implicit in his words. *Say nothing else—not even to Daka and Piye.* The brothers already would be in danger because of what they knew. Letting anything fall now of Marche or Cerdic—or for that matter, who Isolde really was—would only make their risk that much greater.

Daka broke in, squatting down and gesturing to the floor. "I show you. Here. This be Octa's army camps." He drew out a small, round pebble from the scrip he wore at his belt and laid it on the wooden boards. "Here where we are now." He took out a second pebble and laid it to the left of the first. "And here—word is, this be where Cerdic is. Waiting talks with Octa. A—" He stopped, frowning as he groped for the words. "Holy place? House for Jesus-women?"

"A convent?" Isolde asked.

Daka nodded. "Yes. That be. Word is Cerdic and Octa meet there. Cerdic come already. His armies nearby."

For a moment the hut was silent. Then Isolde looked at Trystan and said, "We'll have to leave. Now—tonight."

Trystan's eyes were still on the crude map Daka had made, and Isolde had the impression his thoughts followed some distant inner track of their own. But he tipped his head in a brief, wordless nod.

Isolde's heart was beating unsteadily, but she said, "All right. You go and wake Hereric. I'll stitch Piye's cut again."

Daka started to protest at that. "No time—" But Isolde shook her head and said, "If you needed a credible reason for coming here tonight, you'd better leave with credible proof that your visit was as innocent as you say." She took up her medicine bag and handed it to Daka. "Here. Hold this for me. It won't take long."

ISOLDE PUSHED OPEN THE DOOR OF Hereric's hut. She had given Piye and Daka a chance to get well away before leaving her own place, using the time to put on her traveling cloak and pack what she would take. She had forced herself to focus on choosing what to fit into the small traveling pack she chose, concentrating on folding each item neatly inside, fighting the feeling that she had been plunged once more into nightmare.

Clearly, they could bring only what they themselves could carry, and so she had in the end packed only her bag of medicines, a change of clothes, and what food she could salvage from the supplies brought from the ship. Some dried meat, a slab of hard, crumbling cheese, a few leathery apples. Then she had given Cabal the order he knew for silence, taken hold of his collar, and slipped out into the night.

Now, as the door of Hereric's hut swung open, she heard the sound of Trystan's voice. The only light in the small room was from the flare of the torches set around the crannog outside. Isolde couldn't at first make out either man's face, only that Trystan was crouched on the floor beside Hereric's pallet. He was speaking in the Saxon language that was Hereric's own, so that Isolde caught only a word here and there. *Fidach . . . Hereric . . .* and then, *danger.*

Trystan sat very still, his gaze, as far as Isolde could judge, fixed on Hereric's face. But she thought he was working to keep his voice as calm and controlled as it had been. Hereric looked at him, then shook his head and made a series of gestures. Isolde's eyes were beginning to adjust to the dimness now, and she understood more of Hereric's reply. *Hereric . . . slow . . . Fidach chase . . . you go . . . Hereric stay.*

Trystan made a brief, jerky movement as of anger or frustration, though that, too, was instantly controlled. With the same still-muscled calm, he turned to face Isolde. "He says—"

Isolde's gaze was fixed on Hereric's face. "I saw. He said that he's still too weak to get away. That he'll slow us down too much if it comes to outdistancing Fidach's men."

And the awful thing, she thought, is that he's right. She could see in the set of Trystan's shoulders that he knew it as well. Without Hereric, they would stand a far better chance of getting away. With an effort, Isolde bit back the first words that rose to her lips—that Hereric had to accompany them. That he didn't understand the danger. That they wouldn't so much as consider leaving him behind. Whatever cruelties lay in his past had stripped Hereric down to a childlike inner core. She couldn't insult him further by telling him he didn't understand fully what he was saying now—or by refusing to allow him to choose his own path.

Swallowing, she turned to Trystan. "What will happen to him—if we do leave him behind?"

"I don't know." Trystan raised one hand, let it fall, and then shook his head. "He may be right, though. He could be safer here than if he goes with us. He's worth nothing to Octa—so Fidach would have no reason to use him as a bargaining piece. And Piye and Daka and Eurig would do whatever they could to make sure he wasn't harmed."

And if they were to leave, it must be soon. Trystan didn't say the words aloud, but she knew he thought them. She could see the wish for action, for haste in every taut line of his body—though he was holding himself still, keeping the urge under control.

Isolde nodded, answering the question Trystan hadn't asked. Their eyes met and held, and then Trystan turned back to Hereric. There was just light enough that Isolde could see Hereric's face: the flaxen-colored beard, the heavy-boned brow and cheekbones. The widely spaced blue eyes that looked out at the world always as though the soul behind them had been tested beyond endurance and retreated to a safe place, deep inside.

And then his accustomed slow, broad smile spread over his face. *Hereric stay. Isolde and Trystan go.*

Trystan was silent a moment, and then he said, gaze steady on Hereric's, "You're sure?"

Hereric's look was utterly confident, utterly calm as he formed another quick series of signs. *Isolde and Trystan find Hereric again. When safe to return.*

There was another long moment's silence while Trystan's eyes met those of the other man. Then Trystan held out his hand, and Hereric extended his arm. They clasped wrists, briefly but firmly. Then Trystan rose.

"We'd better be gone."

Chapter Fourteen

T RYSTAN LEANED BACK AGAINST A tree trunk and briefly closed
his eyes. Son of a flaming she-devil, his ribs hurt. *Ignore it.
Open your eyes and try to guess where the cursed hell you are by now.*

They'd left the crannog and the marshes behind hours ago.
And Trystan would have said they'd been lucky—save that he
mistrusted all luck like this. No one had followed, at any rate.
From time to time Cabal came bounding up at them out of the
darkness, then bounded off again. If the dog met with any search
parties or guard patrols, he'd give them some sign of alarm.

Now they'd entered a dense patch of forest, black as pitch save
for the faint, feeble light of the moon through the leaves that just
enabled them to see the shapes of the trees. Good for shielding
them from any pursuers. Worse for calculating positively the direction and distance they'd come.

"Trys?" He opened his eyes to find Isolde beside him, her face
a pale oval in the dark. "Is something wrong?"

"No—nothing." He wasn't even sure why he hadn't told her
about the broken ribs, save that denial was automatic by now.
That and he didn't want her coming within ten paces of him

when he was as tired as this, or he'd lose complete control of himself. As it was, he kept seeing her sitting across from him in the tiny round hut. Impossibly beautiful, with her skin glowing like pale starlight, her bare feet curled under her, and her loose hair falling to her waist in a shining curtain of raven black.

He kept reliving the moment when she'd thrown her arms around his neck—as she had in half a hundred impossible fantasies from the time since he'd first laid eyes on her again five months before. Not that it meant anything but that they'd been friends for years and that she was thankful to see him again. He knew that. Hell, if he'd been stuck in Fidach's mud pit of an encampment for the better part of a week, he'd have welcomed with open arms anyone who came to get him out as well.

Still, maybe at that he should be thankful for the broken ribs. If not for their aching stab, he would have forgotten all the reasons he didn't deserve to clean her boots, forgotten even Fidach's watching eyes. Another moment and he would have lowered his head and covered her mouth with his and—

And probably she'd now be back at the crannog, having decided to take her chances with Fidach's men rather than be alone with him this way.

Trystan swore at himself silently, closed his eyes again in anticipation of the pain, and was about to order himself to move when Isolde said a word that made his eyes snap open. She was at his shoulder, leaning to look up into his face, eyes wide in the moonlight.

"Don't lie to me, Trys. Not now. How badly are you hurt?"

It sounded as though she spoke through clenched teeth, and her voice wavered slightly. Please God, let her not start to cry—not even angry tears. Not that he'd blame her, but he'd be completely lost if she did.

Trystan slowly let out his breath. "A couple of broken ribs, I think."

She had moved into a brighter patch of moonlight so that he could see her face more clearly now. "A couple of broken ribs," she repeated. For a moment, she looked at him, blank-faced, and then she said, "Trys, I know I asked for it, but that is one god-damned bad answer if ever I heard one."

He should have known she wouldn't respond with tears. When had she ever cried at what couldn't be helped?

All the same, Trystan's mouth twitched, and then he started to laugh. It felt like iron spikes being pounded into his side, but he leaned against the tree trunk and shook helplessly. Then when he'd finally managed to stop, he opened his eyes again. "You never swear."

He could see an unwilling smile pulling at the corners of Isolde's mouth. "Yes, well. I do when I'm in the middle of a forest with Fidach and his men on one side of us and Octa's army on the other, and you have two broken ribs." Then she sobered and said, "Broken ribs—you realize there's almost nothing I can do for that? I could bind them up for you, maybe. But—"

Merciful God. Trystan shook his head. "Better not. It won't do that much good. And it would only slow me down if we have to fight or run." He tensed all his muscles, ordered himself again to ignore the pain, and finally managed to push off from the tree. "Let's move on and see if we can find somewhere to wait out the rest of the night. I don't want to take the chance on walking straight into some wandering war band in this dark."

"All right. Which way?"

Trystan scanned the forest around them. "There." He pointed. "You see that rise in the land just ahead? Head towards that."

The rise in the land turned out to be a rock-strewn hill, the slope ground for dozens of straight-limbed pine trees. The light from the full moon above was stronger here, and they were climbing quickly, Isolde ahead, Trystan behind. He had turned his head to listen again for any sounds that might show someone was tracking them, when a rock or loose branch must have rolled under Isolde's foot, because she lost her footing and fell backwards against him.

It caught him completely off guard, and sent them both

crashing to the ground. The wave of pain that shot through him as he struck the forest floor felt like a giant hand snapping him in two. When the pounding blackness that had darkened his vision cleared, he was on his back, the scent of broken pine needles sharp in the back of his throat, and Isolde was bending over him.

"Holy goddess mother." Her gray eyes were huge and liquid bright in her pale face, and her voice wavered slightly. "Oh, Trys, I'm sorry. I'm so sorry."

She was smoothing his hair back, brushing the dirt and dust away from his face, his chest. This time she did look close to tears. Trystan caught hold of her hand, and when he could draw breath enough to speak forced his voice to sound as close to steady as he could make it. "It's all right. I'm fine. No harm done—and don't say I'm lying again."

Isolde laughed shakily, scrubbed a hand across her cheeks, and shook her head. "I don't have to say it. I'd have to be blind, deaf, and feeble-witted to believe you. How bad is it? Do you think you can stand?"

"I think so." Trystan drew another breath. "Just—give me a hand."

It took three tries for him to drag himself upright with Isolde's help. By the second try he was sweating and shivering by turns and swearing under his breath.

"I'm so sorry," Isolde said again. She was crouched beside him on the ground, supporting as much of his weight as she could with a shoulder under his arm. "Yell if you want to."

"Yes, well." It took him several harshly drawn breaths to get the words out. "I would, but from all I hear, it doesn't do much good. Besides, I'd rather not get captured just now. Save at least one disaster for tomorrow."

She laughed unsteadily again, then when at last he was on his feet and standing, she looked up at him. "Trys, where do we go from here?"

·   ·   ·

WHEN SHE'D LET HERSELF BE LED to the great carved oaken bed, they left her, though she knew they would wait outside the door.

She dug her nails hard into the palms of her hands. It's only my body, she thought. I won't let him touch the rest of me.

She thought for a moment she was going to vomit, but she fought the sickness down, whispering the words through clenched teeth.

"You can face this. You have to."

In the darkness beyond the bed, she heard a door open—

STRONG ARMS CLOSED AROUND HER, PULLING her up out of the dream. Still gasping and shaking and feeling as though she'd been dragged free of the quagmire around Fidach's crannog, Isolde opened her eyes. Trystan had dropped to one knee on the ground before her and had one arm still around her shoulders, steadying her.

"All right. I've got you. You're all right."

For a moment, she couldn't remember where she was or what had happened. Then memory came flooding back: Piye and Daka's warning—the escape from Fidach—Trystan's broken ribs—

Belatedly, she pulled away from him, pushing a loosened curl of hair back from her sweat-damp brow. "I'm sorry—did I hurt you again?" Her voice sounded shaky, and she swallowed. "It was just . . . just a nightmare. I'm all right, now."

She drew further away, smoothed her hair again, and tried to steady her ragged breathing. They had found a clearing among the pine trees to shelter for the night. A small, hollowed-out patch of ground at the base of an outcropping of rock, where the dried pine needles made a soft, sweet-smelling carpet. Trystan's mouth had been tight with pain by the time he'd lowered himself to the ground, and Isolde had told him she would keep watch if he wanted to sleep. He'd shaken his head, though, giving her a brief flash of a smile.

"You'd have to drug me unconscious for me to sleep through the way my ribs are feeling just now. I'll stay awake. You rest, though, if you can."

So Isolde had lain down on the bed of pine needles, pillowing her head on her arm and drawing her cloak tight about her against the night's chill. Cabal still hadn't returned from his latest venture into the night-dark forest, and she'd tried not to be worried for him. He was a war dog, trained at hunting and tracking both. He'd pick up their scent and make his way back to them. She'd not expected to sleep. But she had. Obviously.

Now she could feel Trystan watching her and she willed him silently not to ask her anything more. *Don't ask. Don't ask. Don't—*

It must not have worked this time, though, because after a moment's silence, he said, "It's Marche you dream about, isn't it?"

Isolde understood in that moment how a rabbit caught in a the yellow-eyed stare of a wolf's eyes might feel. Beyond fear. Too hopeless to even try to run. She lifted her head. "How did you know?"

The moonlight was bright enough that she saw the small, mirthless smile tighten Trystan's mouth though his face was as grim and hard as she'd ever seen. "You're forgetting who my mother was. When you woke, you had the same look in your eyes that she used to, years ago."

Isolde's chest tightened as though a giant fist had clenched bruisingly about her heart, and a sudden stinging rush of tears burned in her eyes. *Don't cry,* she ordered herself. *Don'tcrydon'tcrydon'tcry—*

The silent order didn't work any better than it had with Trystan. Scalding tears spilled down over her cheeks, as though a dam had broken inside her, and she dropped her head, hiding her face against her upraised knees, trying without success to choke back the sobs that tore her throat. After a moment, she felt Trystan get up, come to sit down beside her, and put his arms around her. He held her very lightly—so lightly that even with the lingering remnants of the dream clinging to her, she didn't panic. He didn't speak, either, just held her while she cried and shuddered against him.

Finally, her sobs died away to wet, hiccupping gulps, and Trystan said, "Why wouldn't you tell me before?"

Isolde tried to sit up, drew a shuddering breath, and dragged both hands across her wet cheeks. Her head was stuffy with crying, and she felt utterly exhausted, drained and emptied and strangely numb. The threatening kind of numbness. When you know pain is coming, though it hasn't started to hurt yet. She locked her arms about herself.

"Tell you?" she repeated. "Trys, how could I? He's your own . . ." She stopped. Swallowed hard against the rock-hard lump lodged in her throat, willing herself not to start crying all over again. "He's your own father. The man who beat your mother—and you—over and over again when we were young. And I—I married him."

She stopped, gulped air again, pressed her hands tight against her eyes. "I—" She clenched her hands tightly together in her lap, looking down at her own interlocked fingers because even by moonlight she couldn't stand the thought of seeing Trystan's face. Not with Marche—Trystan's father—a living, breathing presence between them. Just as he'd been at the Roman villa, as though he'd crawled out of her dream.

Isolde heard the words spill out of her in a dull, exhausted rush like blood from a wound.

"The council had just chosen him High King. And men like Marche think, take a woman by force and you've mastered her—won. So I thought, give him that. Let him think he's beaten me, and—" Isolde stopped, squeezing her eyes tight shut against the tears that kept spilling down her cheeks. "But I've asked myself, over and over and over again, if I couldn't have thought of some other way—some other way of getting free from him. I—"

"Wait a moment." Trystan's voice was quiet, but something in his tone still made her break off, and against her will, look up, meeting his gaze. "Did you think—" He stopped. Shook his head. "You thought—you thought I'd blame you?"

Isolde couldn't make herself answer, but the truth must have been plain on her face, because he stared at her as though he'd never seen her before. "You honestly believed I'd blame you? Holy God, Isa, is that what you think of me?"

He sounded almost angry, but then he seemed to check himself. He rubbed a hand over his face, drew a deliberate breath, and seemed to force himself to speak calmly, his eyes on hers. "First of all, Marche of Cornwall is not my father. I stopped thinking of him that way a long time ago, before I was nine. I realized he was no father of mine. Not really. Whatever blood we share, he's no more to me than any other man. Except—" Trystan laughed shortly. "Except that he taught me most of what I know about dealing with pain."

Isolde flinched involuntarily, and Trystan said quickly, "I'm sorry. What I meant to say was yes, I hate that he hurt you. And if I thought it would do any good, I'd track him down and kill him for it. But blame *you*?" He shook his head, passing a hand across his face again. "Christ's blood, Isa, I've been facing battles since I was—what? Fourteen? You think I've never done anything terrible—anything I hated—because it was that or die?"

He let his hand fall back to his side, and leaned back on his elbows, looking past her into the night. When he went on, his voice was quieter. "You train for it—day in, day out, snow or sleet or pouring rain. How to fight with a sword. Handle a shield. Throw a knife. Ride a horse into battle. You practice every day until you can barely stand up you're so tired at the end of it all. But you keep going. You get better. Better able to aim a spear, wield a sword. And then you actually fight a battle one day. And you realize that all of it—your whole life—has been directed at just one thing: teaching you how to kill. And that that's all you know. How to fight to the death and win. Some days—" He shook his head. "Some days I can still see the faces of all the men I've ever killed. Every last one. And then—" He stopped. In the moonlight, his eyes were very blue. He spread his right hand, so that the mutilated fingers, the crooked scars were plain. "I was a slave in a tin mine, Isa. And you learn—and learn fast—that there's no law, no honor, no code that applies to you. There's only what you can live through and what you can't. Whether you're going to die or see one more day."

He stopped, folded his fingers, and let his hand fall back to his side. Isolde wiped her eyes with the heels of her hands and drew another shuddering breath. "How long were you there for?"

Trystan didn't answer at once, and she added, "I'm sorry. You don't have to speak of it if it troubles you."

Even in the darkness, she saw Trystan's mouth lift in a wry half smile. "Speaking of it doesn't trouble me half as much as it did to actually be there. It's just that I honestly don't know how long my time there lasted." A shadow crossed his face, and he looked past her again, out into the shadowed forest beyond. "First, I counted the days, the weeks. But after a while—" He broke off, one shoulder lifting. "After a time it was all the same. Nothing changing, day after day. By the time I finally got free, I couldn't even have told you how old I was."

For a moment, all was silent save for the sigh of the wind in the pine branches above and the soft night sounds of the forest all around. Then Isolde rubbed her eyes again and said, "Twenty-two. I'm twenty, so you'd be twenty-two."

Trystan's smile flashed out again, the tension leaving his face. "Thanks."

There was another moment's quiet, and then Isolde drew in her breath. "Trys—"

She stopped a moment, trying to make herself speak. "There's something I have to tell you. Something you should know." She stopped again, though, trying to think how to say what she had to.

Trystan's brows lifted. "Go on."

Whatever words she tried out silently in her mind seemed to lodge in her throat. Isolde shook her head. "I'm sorry. It's just I don't quite know how to tell you this."

Trystan let out a breath, half amused, she thought, half exasperated. "Isa, after the way we've spent the last few weeks, I don't think there's a hell of a lot you could say that would come as a shock. Just tell me—what is it? What's wrong?"

So she told him—told him everything. About Kian's capture and Marche's supposed plan for alliance with Cerdic of Wessex, and the price Marche had set on Trystan's capture. Through it all, Trystan listened in silence, his face unreadable. When she'd finally stopped speaking, he was silent a long moment, and then he said, "All right. I take it back." His voice was utterly, deadly calm, and Isolde couldn't tell whether he was angry or not. "So you didn't tell me before this because you were afraid I'd feel responsible for what happened to Hereric and—" Isolde could feel him working to keep his tone so tight with control. "Kian?"

"Well, wouldn't you?"

Trystan passed a hand across the back of his neck, then sighed. "Probably." One corner of his mouth tilted in a brief, wry smile. "That's the trouble with growing up with someone. They know too much about you."

"Yes."

Isolde waited, but Trystan said nothing else. After a moment, she said, "I am truly sorry, though. I should have told you right from the start. Are you angry?"

The line of Trystan's mouth had hardened, but he shook his head. "No. Or maybe I am, but not with you." Seeing Isolde's look, he gestured impatiently. "Would it have changed anything if you'd told me? Would I have done anything differently, these last weeks, if I'd known Marche was out for my blood? Would we somehow not have ended up here?" He swept out a hand, indicating the darkened forest of surrounding pines. "I doubt it. Besides—" He broke off with a short, harsh laugh. "I should have expected something of the kind. It's not as though I can claim I don't know what Marche is like."

Isolde saw his eyes go distant and knew he was seeing again Hereric's amputated arm. Imagining the empty socket of Kian's eye. Very tentatively, she reached out and touched the back of Trystan's hand. "I know it probably doesn't help much, but when last I saw him, Kian was . . . he was going to be all right. He's very strong. And he didn't want you to know he'd been hurt. That was part of the reason I didn't tell you sooner. I think he was ashamed of being captured that way. But I think I didn't want you to worry for him as well."

Trystan was silent a long moment, his eyes still distant, his thoughts following some inward track of their own. Isolde hesitated, then asked, "Do you blame him?"

Just briefly, she thought something hard and almost frightening crossed Trystan's face. It was gone in a moment, though, and he let out his breath and shook his head. "How could I? God knows I'd have done the same in his place."

He shifted position, sucked in his breath, and swore as the movement jarred his broken ribs. Isolde still met with only empty blackness when she tried to sense how severe his injuries were. But she hardly needed the Sight to guess at just how bad the pain must be by now.

"Trys." He looked up at her. Isolde hesitated again, then said quietly, "You really should rest. I've some of the poppy draft I used for Hereric left. Please, let me give you some so that you can get some sleep. I know," she added, as Trystan started to speak. "I know it's a danger. If anyone finds us here and you're too deeply unconscious to wake." There was a silence where she knew they were both remembering that first attack aboard ship—what now seemed like a lifetime ago. "But it's a danger, too, if you fall flat on your face tomorrow because you're too exhausted to go on. Please, get a few hours' rest, at least."

She'd expected him to argue further, but he swallowed the poppy draft she gave him without speaking again—proof, if she'd needed any, of how exhausted he really was. How he'd kept going this long she'd no idea. He stiffened when she came to kneel beside him, but took the hand she offered, letting her help him ease himself back onto the bed of fallen pine needles.

Isolde started to draw away, but he kept hold of her hand. The feeling of his palm against hers seemed to run through every part of her, filling her chest with a rosy warmth. "Isa, I—" The poppy draft was already starting to smooth out the lines of pain and tiredness in his face and blur his words.

"What is it?" As though of its own accord, Isolde saw her free hand moving to lightly touch his hair.

Trystan's eyes were already half closed, but he frowned, making an effort to speak through the effects of the poppy draft and his own fatigue. His hand came up, brushing Isolde's cheek, wiping a lingering trace of moisture away with his thumb. "I hope I never have to be as brave as you already are."

EVEN AFTER TRYSTAN'S BREATHING HAD DEEPENED and slowed into the rhythm of sleep, Isolde sat for a long time, looking down at his face. With the moonlight playing across the clear, determined lines of brow and jaw, he looked at once younger and slightly stern, his mouth set and his hair slipping free of the leather thong that laced it back. Isolde's own face still felt sticky with dried tears, and she wished she had water for washing. She settled for wiping her cheeks with a fold of her cloak, then wrapped her arms around her knees, watching the rise and fall of Trystan's chest as he breathed.

Isolde thought of all he'd just said to her. Of the way he'd listened. Of how he hadn't blamed her, or even pitied her, just held her while she cried.

Now she felt tired, still, empty, and utterly drained. And yet—

And yet for the first time—the very first time since that night with Marche nearly six months before—she felt as though the huge, looming boulder of memory had shifted inside her to a place she could bear. As though a wound somewhere deep had been cauterized. There might always be a scar, but the bleeding was stopped and the threat of poison gone.

At the same time, the fear that was pulsing through her veins with every beat of her heart was as cold and sharp as any she'd ever felt in her life.

As a rule, she hated dishonesty—hated, especially, the feeling that she was trying to lie to herself. Despite—her mouth twisted briefly—despite having done an extremely good job of it ever since that first night when Trystan had walked into Madoc's fortress at Dinas Emrys. Maybe even longer still.

She closed her eyes for a moment, thinking of the waves of longing for the past that had struck her from time to time these last months, ever since she'd chosen to remember the years before Camlann. She thought of the way she had—still did—miss the self she'd been then.

But she didn't even bother trying to persuade herself that what she felt now was part of that same longing for a time that was gone. She looked down at Trystan's sleeping face and locked her hands tight together in her lap to keep from smoothing his hair back again. Another wave of panic crashed over her, clogging her throat. And then she drew in her breath with a gasp as something hard and solid bumped against her arm.

"Cabal." The big dog had returned at last and now whined softly and butted his head again against Isolde. She looped an arm around his neck and ruffled his fur. "Good fellow. Good—"

And then she stopped. The worst of the wave of panic was ebbing away. And, like a tide leaving cast-up gifts of the ocean—driftwood or seashells or even pearls—she could see in this wave's ebbing wake a glaring truth.

Cabal had picked up a sticky blot of pine sap on the fur of his back, and Isolde worked at it absently with her fingers, all the while still looking down at Trystan. Already on this journey he'd seen his ship burned, had his ribs broken, and Isolde realized abruptly that she still didn't know how he'd been hurt or what it was that Fidach had asked of him as the price of aid. And now Trystan had been forced into leaving Hereric at Fidach's mercy.

They'd not spoken of what they would do when morning came. But—

Isolde saw again the smooth, round pebbles Daka had laid on the floor of her hut. One for Fidach's camp. One for Octa's army. And one for the house of Christian holy women where Cerdic was now, to the east of the crannog. The same direction she and Trystan had been heading since they'd left the marshes behind.

I could find it, Isolde thought. Even on my own. It can't be far.

Daka's guidance meant that she no longer needed Trystan to reach Cerdic. He couldn't be more than a half day's ride from where she was now. And as Isolde sat, resting her head against Cabal's neck and breathing in the sharp scent of pine, she saw the truth that the ebbing wave of fear had cast up on the shore and knew that she absolutely couldn't ask of Trystan anything more than what she already had.

If Cerdic and Octa had already sworn alliance between them, approaching Cerdic could lead them both straight into Octa's— and so Marche's—hands. Isolde could see taking the risk for herself. Gambling with her own life. Because if Cerdic and Octa did unite their forces, Britain was utterly lost. But she knew, utterly and absolutely, that she couldn't face the thought of gambling with Trystan's life, of knowing he was dead because of her.

She acted quickly, before her courage could drain away, rising to her feet, drawing her cloak tightly about her, picking up her medicine bag. And then she stopped. Because when he woke alone, Trystan wouldn't know where she'd gone—would search for her, maybe. And she had no way of telling him—

And then abruptly she was back in her workroom at Dinas Emrys, speaking to Kian about the childhood she and Trystan had shared. *We even worked out a secret language of signs—patterns we'd make on the ground with rocks or twigs or leaves.*

It took her a little time, stumbling and searching in the darkness to find what she needed: rocks, a pinecone, three smooth fallen branches. And she found herself laughing a little, a harsh breath of a laugh that tore at her still raw throat, because this was both completely childish and one of the most wrenchingly hard things she'd ever done.

She arranged the things in a pattern near where Trystan lay, where he would see them when he woke. *Gone. Don't follow.* And then her eyes went once more to Trystan's face, and an icy chill gripped her. He lay on his back with one arm up, his hand outstretched. Drugged asleep. Completely vulnerable should any attack—whether from man or wild animal—come.

For a moment, Isolde thought she'd have to stay after all. But that would risk Trystan's life just as surely. Awake, he would never let her travel on alone, however much he might wish he could.

Isolde's gaze fell on Cabal, padding in a half circle along the edge of the tree line, patrolling their small camp. She whistled softly. "Cabal, come here."

When Cabal stood before her, she took his head between her hands. Her throat felt tight, and she swallowed hard and rested her forehead a moment against Cabal's. Then she drew back, looking into the big dog's liquid dark eyes. Her heart still felt as though it were in the grip of some giant, constricting hand, but she forced herself to speak slowly and calmly. "Cabal, I want you to stay with Trystan. Don't let anything hurt him. Guard him until he wakes. Go on, now."

She gestured. Cabal threw one questioning look back at her over his shoulder, then obediently padded to where Trystan lay and settled with a soft sigh on the ground at his side. Isolde let out her breath. "Good dog."

Trystan stirred and muttered something unintelligible in his sleep. Slowly, Isolde rose and crossed to kneel at his other side. She watched him a long moment, watched the rise and fall of his breathing, saw in his face both the boy she'd grown up with and the man he was now. Before she could stop herself, she's reached out and lightly traced a line from his temple to his jaw with one finger. Lucky for her that he'd taken the poppy draft. Undrugged, he'd never have slept through that. He had a soldier's habit of coming awake at the slightest sound or touch.

"I—" Isolde started to say. Her voice cracked, though, and she had to squeeze her eyes shut against another hot, prickling rush of tears. Besides, she thought, if I couldn't say that before, I certainly can't now. So she made herself look down at him again, drew in her breath, then whispered softly, "Good-bye, Trys."

Then she rose to her feet and turned away.

BOOK III

Chapter Fifteen

WHAT YOU ASK OF ME is quite incredible."

Isolde bowed her head in acknowledgment. "Yes. I know it is."

The woman opposite her waited, head tilted, as though inviting Isolde to go on. Isolde said nothing, though, and at last she let out a little puff of breath between her teeth and drummed gnarled, blue-veined fingers on the wooden table between them.

Mother Berthildis of the Abbey of Saint Eucherius was an almost incredibly ugly old woman. She was small and plump, her head thrusting forward from rounded shoulders and a yellow, toadlike face set with very small, sharp black eyes. Those eyes now studied Isolde intently a moment before she said, "You know, if you would tell me why you wish an audience with King Cerdic—or even your name—I could easily present you to him."

"I'm sorry, but I cannot." Isolde shook her head. "For your sake, though, as I have said. Not mine. I would not endanger you by making you an accomplice to what business I have here. I don't imagine your position here is so secure that you can afford to take unnecessary risks with the lives under your charge."

Mother Berthildis snorted briefly through her nose. "Whoever you are, young woman, you've got that right. We were granted this charter of land by Cerdic himself. One of the conditions his wife, rest her soul"—the gnarled fingers sketched a quick cross in the air—"made when she wed him. She was a woman of the Frankish country, as you may have heard. And a believer in our Lord Christ. And when her father wedded her to Cerdic of Wessex, it was with the understanding that she would be allowed to practice her own faith. Surround herself with her own priests, hear the mass—and endow such churches and places of worship as she might see fit."

Her hand moved to lightly touch the wooden cross that hung on the breast of her plain black robes. "She came here often, did the lady Rotrud. To pray for her husband's soul. Not—" Mother Berthildis snorted again. "Not that it ever did the slightest good, that I could see. And no doubt the Heavenly Father in His infinite wisdom has His own purpose in denying King Cerdic entrance into the kingdom of His believers and saints. But still"—the keen black eyes fastened on Isolde—"it means that our position here is precarious, as you say. Cerdic has small patience with the church or the teachings of Christ—still less since his wife, the lady Rotrud died in childbed ten years since. At any point, he might choose to withdraw his support of the abbey—choose, even, to retract the charter that grants us our lands and the crops that keep us alive and fed. As abbess, I am charged with the care of the abbey, with the keeping of the thirty sisters who live and worship here, not to mention the souls who straggle in through our gates each day, begging for shelter or alms."

Isolde bowed her head again. "Mother, I know."

She had been one of those souls to enter the gates of the abbey walls that day, slipping in with a group of ragged families, men and women and hungry-eyed children, their belongings tied in bundles on their backs or packed into rickety carts. She had met with them on the road shortly after dawn that morning and had fallen in with their group, knowing she was safer as part of a band of travelers than on her own. The children had danced round her for a time, asking where she'd come from, begging for food or coins. But the rest had simply looked at her with dull, exhausted eyes that seemed not to see her at all or shot her sharp glances and then turned quickly away. Plainly afraid that if they acknowledged her—spoke to her—they might be called on for aid.

Daka had been right; Cerdic's armies were encamped all about the abbey. It had been sunset when Isolde and her fellow travelers had reached their destination, and she'd seen the neat rows of war tents on the hill beyond the abbey walls as she'd approached the gate. Within, too, the entrance courtyard had been crowded and bustling with confusion over the abbey's exalted guest. Servants, grooms, and stablemen—plainly Cerdic's own—ran this way and that, and perhaps thirty men-at-arms were stationed as guards about the outer walls.

Now it was early evening, and Isolde's whole body felt as though she'd been pummeled by stones. But she'd passed beyond weariness and into restlessness some hours ago. Her nerves felt stretched tight, and the strain of holding herself still on the hard wooden chair the abbess had given her was growing painful. Her thoughts—however much she tried to stop them—kept flashing back to Trystan. Seeing him asleep, as she'd left him in the forest the night before. Trying to imagine his face when he'd woken to find her gone. Wondering whether he'd been angry or only relieved.

With an effort, Isolde pulled herself back to the present, to the small, low-ceilinged chamber of Mother Berthildis's own quarters within the abbey. And the woman sitting opposite her, across a plain wooden table that held a platter of brown bread and two cups of wine. Mother Berthildis's eyes were fixed on Isolde's face, a deeper furrow crossing the finer lines on her brow. Then, at last, she nodded as though a decision had been made. "Very well," she said. "If you will not tell me about yourself, I suppose I may do it for you."

A lift of her eyebrow invited Isolde's response. Isolde said, "If you wish."

The abbess steepled her fingers, resting them against her upper lip and studied Isolde's face again. For all her toadlike ugliness, her black gaze was piercingly keen. Sitting under her scrutiny, Isolde thought, was like facing a blast of winter wind that knifed through cloak and clothing to the very bone.

When the abbess spoke, though, it was more to herself than to Isolde. "I see before me a young woman who will not give me her name or tell me from whence she has come. Her dress is of good quality, though—even if stained and dusty from a journey that has surely lasted some little time. And moreover, her manner, her voice—her every movement, in fact—speak of breeding and distinction. Plainly this is no common beggar girl in search of alms."

Mother Berthildis paused, and when Isolde said nothing, she went on, her slightly quavering old-woman's voice turning dry. "Since her eyes resemble two holes burned in a rug, I will hazard a guess that she has slept irregularly these last nights, if at all." She raised one eyebrow again. "You will tell me, perhaps, if I go wrong?"

"If I can."

The abbess was silent for a time, tapping her steepled fingers thoughtfully against her chin. "This young woman appears at my gates, asks to speak with me, confirms that King Cerdic of Wessex is a guest under my roof. She promises me that though she cannot tell me who she is or for what purpose she has journeyed here, neither will she lie to me or offer any untruths. And then, without further ado, she asks me whether she may drug Cerdic's guard tonight so that she may seek private audience with the king."

Mother Berthildis stopped, sharp black eyes resting on Isolde's once more, and again Isolde had the sense that the older woman's gaze looked through her, read her thoughts, saw every corner of her inner self. Clearly, though, she expected some response, and so Isolde nodded again. "Yes. That is what I ask."

The abbess gave another brief snort. "Not one to scare easily, are you? I've known strong men to crack and own up to a crime they'd denied when I looked at them that way."

Isolde smiled a little. "I'm sure that's true."

For a long moment, there was silence in the small, plainly furnished room. Then Mother Berthildis nodded abruptly. "Very well."

Isolde was so shocked that for a moment she thought sheer weariness was making her ears play tricks. "Did you just say—"

"I said very well." The older woman's voice was edged with impatience. "This is of some importance, is it not?"

Still stunned nearly speechless, Isolde nodded, and the abbess heaved herself to her feet. "Very well, then. Christ tells us to treat with kindness the benighted strangers who seek shelter at our doors." A trace of humor flickered momentarily across Mother Berthildis's lined face and she added, "Granted, this request of yours is likely not what He had in mind. But still, I believe in extending a hand to those in need. And"—again her intent black gaze swept Isolde's face—"and in trusting those I deem worthy."

The flash of unexpected sympathy or kindness in her dark gaze brought a sudden lump to Isolde's throat. But before she could speak, Mother Berthildis turned away, crossing to the room's single wooden shelf and lifting a heavy volume, bound in leather incised with a cross. She set the book on the table before Isolde, then turned to face her. "Will you"—all trace of the sympathy was gone, and her voice and face were suddenly fierce—"will you put your hand on the book of God's holy word and swear that the guardsmen will suffer no lasting harm from the draft you put in their ale?"

Isolde lifted her gaze to meet the abbess's. "If you wish it, I will. But since, as you say, I have promised not to lie to you, I must tell you that swearing on your holy book will probably not mean to me what it would to you."

For another long space of silence, Mother Berthildis's fiercely black gaze rested on Isolde's. And then, slowly, the abbess nodded her head. Likely, Isolde thought, I told her nothing but what she already knew, and the request was nothing more than another test of good faith. She made herself sit without moving while the older woman frowned, seemingly lost in thought. Then she nodded her head once again.

"Very well." Again the black eyes met Isolde's, but this time Isolde thought their look had softened. There might even have been a shadow of sympathy in their depths. "Will you swear, then, on whatever precious thing it is that you have left behind in coming here?"

Another of those knife-edged memories of Trystan's sleeping face flashed through Isolde. She closed her eyes against it just briefly, and against the press of hot tears that rose to her eyes. Let herself think too long on Trystan and she'd sit here weeping until every last scrap of the final reserves of strength she was drawing on had drained away.

She drew a breath, then looked back at the older woman and made herself speak as steadily as before. "I swear on what I have left behind—on all I hold dear—that Cerdic's guardsmen will come to no harm by my hand. They will only slumber and wake in the morning as from heavy sleep."

Isolde was expecting another silence, another penetrating look from the small black eyes. But instead Mother Berthildis nodded her head briskly. "Very well, then. The hospitality of the Abbey of Saint Eucherius is yours. And I will pray that whatever it is you would say to King Cerdic meets with a receptive ear." She stopped, and Isolde thought just the hint of a grim smile curved the thin trap of a mouth. "Though whether my prayers will be any more successful at touching Cerdic than those of his wife remains to be seen."

TRYSTAN LED THE WAY ALL BUT soundlessly through the night-dark forest, trusting in his companions to stay close. He probably ought to check that Eurig and Hereric were keeping up—for

Hereric's sake, at least. But he didn't trust himself to stay on the alert for danger, worry for his companions, and manage to block out the black pounding in his skull.

Yes, perfect. He might have known that a dose of poppy syrup would leave him with an even worse headache than wine.

Though at that, the headache was far better company than his own thoughts, beating like the black ache of a bruise. Ever since he'd woken and found Isolde gone.

Just for a moment, he wished Isolde were before him, not because he'd know she was safe as because he'd be able to take her by the shoulders and shake some sense into her. Powers of hell, what had she been thinking of?

Unless something had happened to her. A dozen images, each more stomach-twisting than the last flashed through his mind. With an effort, he pushed them away.

She'd left those signs for him to read. *Gone. Don't follow.*

Trystan pushed a branch aside before it could slap him in the face and wondered whether she'd actually drugged him on purpose so that she could get away. But only for a moment. Isolde was too brave for her own good, and she lost her temper in a moment at cruelty or injustice and broke her heart because she couldn't heal the whole goddamned suffering world. She wouldn't have done that.

Probably.

Trystan paused, eyes scanning the darkness, and wished the moon were brighter or the trees here less thick. Unless any guard patrols out tonight were carrying flaming torches, they were just as likely to walk slap into them.

He shook his head and started to move again, rubbing the space between his eyes. Isolde wouldn't have tricked him into swallowing the draft so that she could get free. Probably. At any rate, he was the one who'd been idiot enough to take the draft she'd given him, leaving her there alone.

He'd done it already a dozen times or more, but still he replayed everything in his mind, trying to imagine what in the nine caverns of hell could have made her get up and go off on her own. Something he'd said?

He'd managed not to give vent to the hot, unspent fury that even now was making the muscles of his arms spasm and his hands clench. Not much of it, at any rate. She hadn't needed the burden of that on top of everything else.

He'd told her Marche was nothing to him, now. Which was true. And yet he still couldn't escape.

It figured. It bloody figured that the son of a goat-rutting bastard would turn up now and poison his life all over again.

From somewhere up ahead, a branch snapped, and Trystan froze.

Voices. Speaking one of the eastern Saxon dialects. A band of Octa's men, most like.

He could feel Eurig behind him going still as well, sense him silently drawing the knife from his belt. In an instant, Trystan had gripped his own knife and turned to hold it at Eurig's throat. The other man stiffened with shock, but he was too well trained to do more than draw in a startled breath.

"Get Hereric out of this." Trystan said in a voice that was almost soundless, less carrying than a whisper.

Eurig answered in the same tone. "Are you out of your skull?" The moonlight was just bright enough for him to make out Eurig's expression of disbelief. "You think we're going to go off and leave you here to die?"

The voices were coming closer. Trystan heard the crunch of leaves under at least half a dozen feet. He pressed the knife a bit harder into Eurig's throat, though still not hard enough to break the skin. "Get him out of here. Swear it. Or I swear to every demon in the underworld that even dead I'll come back and plague you to the end of your days."

ISOLDE LAY ON HER BACK, STARING up at the plastered ceiling of the small novice's cell Mother Berthildis had offered her for as long

as she wished to stay. She had washed, tidied herself, eaten a little
of the meal of bread, dried apples, and cheese that the abbess
had given her. She had even rested briefly on the same straw-
filled mattress where she now lay. She'd been too much on edge,
still, to sleep, though, and after a time she'd risen and gone to the
kitchens as Mother Berthildis had instructed to collect the sup-
per tray prepared for Cerdic's guards.

The two burly, flaxen-haired guards had been absorbed in a
game of dice and had barely glanced at her as she'd delivered the
food and cups of ale—laced, now, with the remains of Isolde's
store of poppy draft, which she'd emptied into the cups on the way
across the abbey courtyard to the guest hall. And now she lay once
more on the rustling straw bed, marking the time by the shuffling
footsteps in the passage outside as the nuns went to the chapel to
pray.

Finally, when she judged the poppy would have had time to
take effect, she rose, her heart beating quickly, drew her cloak
about her shoulders, and stepped out again into the night.

As she entered the abbey guest wing, her stomach tightened
in anticipation of what she would find. But the poppy draft had
worked. When she reached the entrance to Cerdic's rooms, she
found both guards deep in drugged sleep, slumped down with
their backs against the wall, snoring lightly and with their spears
and painted shields fallen unheeded to the ground.

Isolde stood a moment looking down at them. Then she
stepped over their prone forms and pushed open the heavy
wooden door.

Inside all was in darkness, save for the light of a fire in the
hearth, but after the trip across the darkened courtyard, her eyes
were already adjusted to the night. She could just make out a
man's form seated before the flames, his face in shadow from the
light at his back. For a moment, the silence was so absolute that
Isolde could hear the beating of her own heart. Then a dry, old
voice spoke out of the shadowed dark.

"Well. It's been a long time since a beautiful young woman
sought my bedchamber at night. Might I ask who you are?"

. . .

'KING CERDIC OF WESSEX WAS AN old man. Nearly as old, Isolde thought, as Mother Berthildis must be. His beard was white, plaited into a single long braid that reached nearly to his breastbone. He wore his snow-white hair long, with several strands here and there plaited into braids whose ends were capped with gold. His hands, too, were stiff with gold warrior's rings, and the skin was parchment thin, blue-veined, and flecked with spots of brown. But what struck Isolde when she looked at the Saxon king was not the age carved into every line of his frame. What struck her like a blow to the pit of her stomach was how plainly, despite the gold, the braided hair, the battle scar across the bridge of his nose, the Saxon king's features mirrored those of his grandson.

The skin might be loosening over the bones of his cheekbones and firmly cut jaw, but Cerdic had the same lean features, the same slightly slanted brows as Trystan. And the same startlingly blue eyes as well. It had made Isolde slightly dizzy when she'd first entered the room—and wrung from her a twist of bitter amusement. Clearly, the fates were refusing to let her stop thinking of Trystan—or forget, even for a moment, that Cerdic's daughter had been Trystan's mother.

She had given already her account of who she was and how she had come to enter his private rooms. Now she sat on the hard wooden chair Cerdic had offered, waiting in silence for his response.

Cerdic had lit a lamp, carrying a burning taper from the hearth fire, so that the room about them was illumined by a flickering orange glow. It was a square-built room, very plain, with lime-washed plaster walls and a rush-strewn floor. But furs—silvery wolf and black bear pelts—had been hung to keep out the drafts, an immense curtained bed had been erected in one corner, and a set of drinking vessels worked in chased gold stood on the room's single table. Plainly, Cerdic had brought his own comforts with him to furnish the room for the duration of his stay.

Cerdic himself was now studying Isolde impassively, his lean face as well governed at concealing his thoughts as Trystan's had ever been. Impossible to tell what went on behind the guarded blue gaze or guess whether he was angry over this midnight intrusion into his private apartments. Impossible even, Isolde thought, to guess whether he believes me or no. The Saxon king wore a heavy, fur-lined robe over a linen under-tunic, and on his breast a heavy collar of gold set with deep red stones that shone like drops of blood.

When at last he spoke, it was in a voice that sounded rusty and faintly creaking with age. "Well then, Lady Isolde of Camelerd, what is it you would say to me?"

Something of Isolde's surprise must have showed on her face, because Cerdic waved an impatient hand. He spoke the British tongue with only a faintest guttural trace of an accent, reminding Isolde that if his father had been Saxon, his mother had been Briton, a princess of Gwent. A last relic of the reign of King Vortigern, who had sought alliance instead of war with the Saxon invaders.

"Lady Isolde, should you be fortunate—or perhaps I should say unfortunate—enough to reach my advanced age, you will find that strength is a thing that must be hoarded as a wolf guards its kill. You learn to dispense with what only saps the strength needlessly—anger, for example. The pleasures of the bed. And fear."

He paused, regarding her from under slightly hooded eyes, so that Isolde was reminded of a golden hawk looking down from a great height to the ground below. "I have no doubt that you are who you claim to be. I knew your grandmother—and it might be she standing before me. You are the lady Isolde, daughter of Modred, Arthur's heir. You have, by your own account, drugged my bodyguard and gone to no little trouble to gain audience with me. Plainly, then, what you have to say is of some import. I could bluster and shout about your invasion of my private rooms or about the treatment of my personal guard—though I must say that if they were fool enough to take food and drink from the hands of a strange woman, they deserve every part of what they get. But in any case, what would a show of anger on my part gain? Nothing. In the end, we would be in exactly the same place as we are now—I needing to hear what you have come to say before I can seek my rest tonight." He ended with a gesture to the tapestried bed in one corner of the room.

"You could, though, summon fresh guards and have me forcibly dragged out instead," Isolde said.

The quick, wry amusement that twitched at the corners of Cerdic's mouth was so much like Trystan's that her heart contracted painfully in her chest. "So I could," Cerdic agreed. "But if I have dispensed with anger, lust, and fear, I confess that curiosity proves stubborn still. I would sleep poorly tonight did I not know what has brought the daughter of my sometime ally Modred to my door."

For all this was the reason she'd come here tonight, the reason she'd set out from Dinas Emrys at all, Isolde suddenly felt entirely without words.

She made herself draw breath, steadying herself, consciously locking all thoughts of Trystan, of Hereric, and Fidach, of her own fatigue away. For all Cerdic's formal manner and dryly calm voice, the Saxon king's blue gaze and lean, hard-featured face spoke of a man accustomed to power and ill inclined to suffer either irritation or fools. She had this one opening, this one window of opportunity to make her case. If she failed—or if he simply refused to ally against Octa and Marche—she knew he would not grant her audience a second time.

"There is a rumor abroad," she said at last, "that you are considering an alliance with Octa of Kent—and so by extension with Marche of Cornwall. That it is for that purpose you have come here now."

Cerdic didn't answer at once. His brows drew together and he frowned as though weighing his words. Then he cleared his throat. "I am an old man. As I have said. And I have seen a lifetime of near-constant war. I fought Arthur at Badon Hill, and saw my armies broken and near destroyed. I fought at your father's side at Camlann and nearly lost both my kingdom and my life. Would it be any wonder, then, if I sought to make peace before I died? If I wished to live out my remaining years at home and not amidst the muck of the battlefields?"

Isolde shook her head. "No. But I would wonder at your choice of allies."

"You mean Octa?" Another faint smile just brushed at Cerdic's mouth above the plaited white beard. "Octa of the Bloody Knife? A man learns in battle to respect his enemy, Lady Isolde—if he is wise, that is. And I have fought Octa of Kent for nearly half our lives. He is neither an honest man, nor a good one. But he is a warrior to be feared. And as such, he has my respect."

"All that may be true enough," Isolde said. "But I was speaking of Lord Marche."

A brief shadow of something cold and hard passed across Cerdic's face, but his voice was unchanged as he repeated, "Marche?"

"Yes." Isolde willed herself not to flinch away, this time of all times, from speaking the name. "The man who killed your daughter."

"Ah." The sound Cerdic made was a soft exhalation of breath, no more. As though a pain he had lived with so long as to have almost forgotten had suddenly been eased. "You are certain?"

"Certain in my own mind. As certain as though I'd seen it done."

"Ah," Cerdic said again. The blue gaze turned distant for a moment, looking past Isolde at something beyond. "I wondered. I always wondered—though I could not, of course, be sure." He was silent, then shook his head, his gaze returning from the past to meet Isolde's. "I am glad to know this before I die. And I thank you for having brought this knowledge to me. But what you say changes nothing."

"Nothing?"

Despite her efforts, Isolde was unable to keep a hard edge from creeping into her tone, and she wondered whether Cerdic would anger. Instead he said, with no change of expression, "You have come to ask whether I would ally with Britain against Octa and Marche. That is your purpose, is it not?"

Anything but a direct answer would, Isolde knew, be a mistake. So she simply said, "It is. And will you tell me your response?"

Cerdic met her gaze directly. "My answer is no. Why should I?"

"Your own mother was Briton born."

Cerdic's shoulders twitched impatiently. "Yes, and she died bearing my squalling brat of a brother when I was five. I have a single memory of her—her slapping my face for breaking a jar of ale. A lifetime—an old man's lifetime—ago. My answer is still no. I will make no alliance with Britain. And should Octa's proposals in the days to come meet with my approval, I will make peace between us and swear alliance with him."

"Even though Octa is himself allied to Marche?"

Cerdic reached for one of the chased golden cups on the table at his elbow, poured wine, and drank deeply before replying in a voice that sounded flat, almost harsh. "Lady Isolde, even now, Octa's armies mass not a half day's ride from here. And in two days' time, Octa will ride here, to this abbey, to extend to me the hand of peace."

Isolde started to speak, but he raised a hand, cutting her off. "A hand of peace that nonetheless holds a sword. Should I refuse the offer of peace that Octa makes, his armies will attack. That is not simply a guess on my part, you understand, but the plain truth of what will occur. Born of my knowledge of Octa and his ways. I have had lands laid waste by Octa before. I have had his armies tear into mine like wolves at the kill. Cowardice has never been a weakness of mine—but neither am I a fool. And only a fool would feel no fear in the face of Octa of Kent's attack."

Cerdic paused, his lined face remote as a statue, his voice dry, precise, and calm, measuring each word. "The last time it came to outright battle between us, I saw a hundred and more of my men captured by Octa impaled on sharpened spikes along the road like a forest of corpses. I am told by one who was there that it took some of them two days to die. Now, my forces, too, are massed outside these walls, as you have seen. And in numbers and in fighting abilities, we equal Octa's strength. But only just. I cannot say whether we would win or lose. But what I can say with certainty is that a fight between us would be a slaughter. And I have already seen too many fields bathed in blood in my time. I have fought too many battles."

Cerdic stopped again, rubbing his thin, blue-veined hands together. "I have reached the twilight of my life, Lady Isolde. I no longer wish to kill—or to watch men killed in my name. I sometimes think the lives we take are irreversibly joined with ours. Some days I would swear I feel the weight of the men I have killed like a millstone round my neck. I would not make that weight any heavier than it already is."

The Saxon king stopped, again rubbing the joints of his right hand as though the knuckles ached beneath the heavy gold rings. In that moment, he looked neither like a golden hawk or even a king, but simply a tired old man who wanted nothing more than to drink his wine and seek his bed. "We Saxons understand two things, Lady Isolde: farming and war. We come to these shores hungry for land. We are ready to fight with axe and sword to make it ours. Now, though, I am fit for neither plowing the earth nor wielding a sword. I sleep poorly. Time hangs heavy on my hands. Time to look back across the years of my life. Feel the ache of countless old war wounds and live over again deeds done when I was young."

He gave another creaking sigh, then said, with sudden violence, "The gods protect you, Lady Isolde, from living long enough to think overmuch on who you are and what you have become."

Something in his tone made Isolde think suddenly of Morgan, staring with bleak eyes into the scrying waters on the eve of Camlann. A memory of Morgan's face rose before her, though the image was shadowy, less clear than it had been nights ago in her hut at the crannog.

Cerdic had gone on, shaking his head. "But I can see myself, now, with clear eyes—or clearer at least, than when I was young. I have little sentiment and a great deal of pride. I may have loved my daughter. I rather think I did. But I cannot clearly recall." He shook his head again, snowy hair brushing the collar of his robe. "I can scarcely call to mind what she looked like anymore."

Cerdic pressed his eyes briefly closed, and when he looked back at Isolde, the weariness and weight of age shadowed the startlingly blue gaze as well. "I was not yet thirty, Lady Isolde, when I came across the ocean to these shores, my men and all we owned packed tight into three stinking, salt-stained keels that smelled of ale and piss and vomit from the number of us aboard. I carved out a kingdom, watered its soil with the blood and sweat of my finest fighting men. And I have held that kingdom fast, throughout my lifetime. Now I am old. My bones ache. My sight begins to fail. The next time I board a keeled ship will be when my bones are laid aboard and burned on a funeral pyre to carry me to feast on boar with the warriors of Woden's hall. But I have yet pride enough that I do not wish my final act as king of Wessex to be an ignominious defeat. Should it come to a final pitched battle between us—should Octa's side win—Octa will ravage Wessex like a rutting boar. Make slaves of the children, slaughter the men, give the women to his army for whores. So, yes. Though Octa be an ally of Marche, who killed my child, I plan to accept the terms of the peace he offers. Should you live to be as old as I am, you may understand the choice—even find that you would do the same."

Isolde felt a cold wash of helplessness. *Expect defeat, and you have none to thank but yourself when that's what you earn,* the Morgan in her mind said again.

"Maybe," she said at last. "But I hope that I never live so long that I cannot see that a peace founded on an oath with a man like Marche will be rancid at its core."

But Cerdic only shook his head. "Perhaps. Yes, perhaps it is. But we have a saying, Lady Isolde. *Gæð??? a wyrd swa hio scel.* Fate goes ever as she shall. If the spinners that spin out the destiny of our lives have determined that Octa and Marche shall have Britain, they shall. Nothing you or I may do will stand in their way." He paused, raised the golden cup to his mouth again, then set it down. "I am sorry to disappoint you, Lady Isolde. I admire your courage. And the gods know I held your father in high regard and would a hundred times rather ally with him than with Octa and Marche. But Modred lies buried with Arthur at Camlann. And we who remain must live our lives and guard what is ours as best we may. My answer stands. Britain must stand alone in the fight against Octa and Marche."

There was a pause while Isolde searched for a response. And then, into the silence that had dropped between them like a stone, came the sound of someone pounding on the room's outer door. A moment later, the door flew open to admit a man—another of Cerdic's guard, he must be, by his leather jerkin and spear and the two knives he wore at his belt. He looked in blank-eyed astonishment from Cerdic to Isolde, then belatedly sank to his knees, head bowed.

"Forgive me, lord." Isolde knew enough of the Saxon tongue to understand that much, but had to guess at the rest of the words. By his gestures, though, he was stammering out that he had seen the unconscious guard outside the door and feared for Cerdic's life.

Isolde almost saw the weariness drop away, saw Cerdic don the mantle of kingship like a cloak as he rose to his feet. His voice held the clash of metal, and his eyes, as he looked down at the guardsman, were icy hard. He, too, had switched to his own native tongue, so that Isolde caught only a word or two here and there. "I . . . well . . . as see . . . explain . . . then go."

The guardsman was a young man, perhaps seventeen or eighteen, but no more. His fair hair was plaited into two long braids, and his beard was scraggly. He stammered out a flood of words of which Isolde understood only a bare handful. Something about a party of men, seeking shelter at the abbey. One of them injured—perhaps dead.

Then abruptly Isolde sat up, the shock of the guardsman's words momentarily darkening her vision and stopping her ears. If she'd understood the Saxon words right, the young man had just said that two of the men had skin as black as night and that a third man had only one arm.

It was a moment before Isolde realized that Cerdic had turned back to her and was speaking, using the British tongue once more. "I beg you excuse me, Lady Isolde. My man Ulf brings word of a party of men who claim to have been set upon by one of Octa's raiding parties. But by their looks and the weapons they carry, they are fighting men themselves—perhaps sent by Octa as spies. I—"

The rest of Cerdic's words, though, were lost on Isolde. Her every instinct was screaming at her to run—to get away before she could hear any more. But at the same time, she knew with sick certainty that she could do nothing but learn the truth, see with her own eyes what had occurred. Her throat had gone dry, and she had to swallow before she could make her voice work.

"Please," she said to Cerdic, and was distantly surprised to find that she was able to hold her voice steady as before. "Let me accompany you to these men. I'm a healer. If one of them has been wounded, I may be able to help."

CERDIC'S GUARDSMAN LED THE WAY PAST the row of abbey cells where Isolde had been housed. Cerdic walked with an old man's hobbling gait, his pace painfully slow, so that Isolde had to clench her hands to keep from shouting at him to hurry as they made their way towards the abbess's rooms. The same rooms where Isolde had sat with Mother Berthildis mere hours ago.

Now she felt at once as though she would snap in two if their walk lasted a single moment more—and at the same time she found herself wishing fervently that it might never end.

Then the door to the abbess's private rooms was swinging open, and she was standing frozen in the doorway, her every muscle locked in place, unable to move. A voice in her mind was saying over and over and over again, *Please, please, don't let this be real. Let this be a nightmare—a trick. Please, please, please, don't let this be real.*

A single oil lamp burned on the room's single table, casting yellow, flickering light over the low-ceilinged room. Eurig stood to one side, his round, homely face a tight mask of misery. Hereric was beside him, exhaustion in every line of his broad frame, his face wet with tears. Piye and Daka stood against the wall, arms folded across their chests, twin impassive, watchful guards. And on a low wooden bench, with Mother Berthildis bending over him—

He looked, Isolde thought, almost exactly as he had when she'd left him asleep in the forest the night before. Trystan's face was peaceful, his eyes closed. Save for the patch of blood that soaked an entire side of his tunic and an angry scratch across his temple, he truly might have been only sleeping.

Isolde felt strangely detached, as though she watched herself and all the rest of the scene around her from a great height. The voice in the corner of her mind was weeping, screaming, raging at the unfairness of it—that she'd left Trystan to keep him from being harmed. And now, not even a full day later, he lay before her, gravely wounded, or—

No, not dead. Isolde felt the tightly clenched knot in her chest loosen, if only a bit, and drew breath for the first time since entering the room. Scarcely even aware of having moved, she had flung herself down on her knees beside him and found the pulse of blood in his neck. Thready and terrifyingly faint, but there nonetheless. Trystan was alive.

Still with that odd feeling of standing back and watching from a distance what she did, Isolde heard herself telling Cerdic that these men were known to her—that none of them was in Octa's pay, and that she would vouch for them all. Making some kind of reply to the questions Eurig and the others asked. Answering Mother Berthildis in a voice that sounded tinny and hollow and far too steady in her own ears. *Yes, I'm a healer. Yes, please send someone to fetch my medicine bag. It's in the cell you granted me for the night. And thank you, yes, I'll need clean water and bandages as well.*

She watched herself checking Trystan for injury, apart from the obvious wound in his side. Gently press and move his arms and legs, feel for broken bones. Take one breath. Another. Keep her teeth clenched tight shut because otherwise the wailing in her mind would tear free of her chest and come out in a screaming sob.

Nothing was broken—save for the already cracked ribs—though when she stripped the filthy, blood-soaked garments from him, she saw that his whole body was marked with raw scrapes and angry, darkening bruises. The worst, though, was plainly the gash in his side—a sword cut, by the look of it—that had caught him just under the ribs. Deep and ugly, the wound had plainly bled a great deal. A wonder, really, Isolde thought, that it hasn't already proved fatal.

She swallowed and looked up at Eurig, who was standing closest to her. Mother Berthildis had departed in search of the water and bandages Isolde had asked for, and Cerdic, too, had gone, leaving his young guardsman Ulf posted outside the door. The Saxon king might believe Isolde was who she claimed to be, but plainly he'd not held power this long by failing to protect himself from the unnecessary risk of four strange men. Still, for the time being, at least, Isolde and the others were alone.

"What happened?" Isolde asked Eurig.

Eurig's gaze was fixed on Trystan's motionless form, and he shook his head, rubbing a hand over his bald pate before answering. "Fidach found out this morning that you'd gone, the pair of you. Near ruptured himself shouting when he learned you weren't anywhere in camp. He sent all of us—the whole band—out searching. Orders were to see you brought back to him alive. So us all"—Eurig sketched a gesture that included himself, Hereric, Daka, and Piye—"we took the direction we thought you'd have headed in. Figured we'd the best chance that way of catching up with you before any of the rest. We got to the woods west of here and split up. Hereric and me took one way—Piye and Daka the other. Wanted to give ourselves the best odds of tracking you. Hereric and I ran across Trystan and that hound of yours sometime about midday."

Isolde felt a pang of guilt as she realized it hadn't even occurred to wonder about Cabal. Her throat contracted as she swallowed again. "Cabal," she said. "Is he—"

Eurig shook his head. "No. Leastways, I don't think he was harmed. Although . . ." Eurig's voice trailed off, and he avoided meeting Isolde's eyes.

"Just tell me," she said. "Please."

Unwillingly, Eurig raised his gaze to Isolde's face. "Well, the plain truth is, he ran off after them that did this." He jerked his head in Trystan's direction. "So if he caught them—"

He didn't have to finish. Isolde nodded, willing away the thought of Cabal attacking a war party, falling under a hail of their spears, dying alone and in agony amidst the dry leaf mold of the forest floor. Of herself, leaving Cabal behind with the order to guard Trystan's life. Not now, she thought. Think of that now and you'll be no good at all to Trystan.

"Who did this?" she asked, when she could trust her voice. "Cerdic said it was a raiding party of Octa's men?"

Before Eurig could answer, though, Mother Berthildis, carrying Isolde's medicine bag, reentered the room, followed by another nun, in black robes and veil, who bore a basin of water and a roll of clean rags. They set medicines, basin, and rags down at Isolde's feet, and she soaked a cloth and started to wipe the dried blood away from Trystan's side. There was a comfort, of a kind, in the action. In the familiarity of tasks she had performed many, many times before.

The lost, desolate cry was still sounding deep inside her, and a cold, shaking feeling had settled in her chest. She ignored both, though, concentrating fiercely on the immediate tasks of cleansing the wound, wrestling her thoughts into the familiar track of the questions she always asked at such times as this: cauterize the wound or stitch it closed? Try to get him to drink wine or broth now, or wait until she'd done tending his wounds?

All the while, too, she was weighing the circumstances as feverishly as a miser counting his gold, adding up the odds for and against Trystan's chance of survival. In his favor was his health, his strength of constitution, his youth. She had known men to recover from wounds like his. But she'd also seen them die if the wounds turned to poison and fever set in. And against his odds she had to set the terrifying shallowness of his breathing. The blood he had plainly lost. The chill pallor of his skin.

In a way she was glad that whatever trick it was of the Sight still blocked her from reading Trystan; it would have been hard to work if she'd been constantly aware of Trystan's pain. But it was horribly frustrating as well. She'd grown used to the Sight as a guide when treating injury or sickness. Without it, she felt as though she were working blind.

Isolde realized abruptly that Eurig was speaking, telling her about the encounter with Octa's guard. She'd missed nearly the whole of his explanation and caught only the last. Something about how Trystan had taken on the five guardsmen alone so that Eurig could get Hereric—plainly in no condition to fight—to safety.

"Didn't so much as hesitate. Just went straight out and challenged them before they could spot Hereric and me. Didn't want to leave him, but he'd put his knife at my throat and made me swear I'd not leave Hereric's side. Even still, oath or no, I'd have fought with him—to the death, if need be. But he got the guards' attention and then ran like hell. Drew them off, away from us. Hereric and me followed—crashing about through the brush after them like a couple of wild hogs. By the time we caught up, Trystan had got them to follow him up a cropping of rock. There's a hill on one side and a kind of a cliff on the other. Me and Hereric were standing in the trees at the foot of the hill—saw the whole thing." Eurig's eyes darkened with the memory. "Octa's men had Trystan backed up to the edge of the rocks. He's wounded—even from a distance you could see the blood soaking his shirt on the side. But even still, he's holding them off. And then all of a sudden he throws down his sword. Just tosses it away. And he says, 'My life's yours. But give me a moment to pray before I die.' Something like that. And Octa's men, they just stand there a moment, looking at each other like they don't know what to make of that at all. But before they can act one way or the other, Trystan turns around and jumps off the cliff. Just—throws himself off, the same way he threw away his sword, if you can believe it."

Isolde was abruptly back in the stifling, smoke-filled confinement of Fidach's hut, answering Fidach's questions about the childhood she and Trystan had shared. *Was he always howling-dog crazy when it came to risking his life in a fight?* Fidach had asked her. And Isolde had answered, a brief half smile touching and then dying at the edges of her mouth, *Yes, he always was.*

So he'd thrown himself headlong off a cliff. That explained the multitude of scrapes and bruises. Isolde lightly brushed a reddening mark on his chest with one fingertip. Another miracle, she thought, that he didn't break every bone in his body or drive one of those cracked ribs through his lungs.

She looked up at Eurig again. "So what happened? Couldn't

Octa's guardsmen have gone back down the hill and around to where Trystan had dropped?"

Eurig nodded. "Well, and so they could. And they'd maybe have tried it. But there was a patch of thorny briars high as a man's head growing all about the base of the cliff. They tried hacking through them with their swords—spitting and swearing all the while fit to blister your ears. But they gave up after a time. Heard one of them say if he wasn't dead already, he would be soon, and it wasn't worth shredding their skins to finish the job now. So off they went. And me and Hereric"—Eurig nodded in Hereric's direction—"got through the briars and got Trystan free."

"You—" Isolde noticed for the first time the scratches that crisscrossed both Hereric's and Eurig's face and arms. "I can give you a salve for that, if you like," she said.

Eurig shook his head. "Thanks all the same, lady, but I reckon we can stand it for now. You just see to Trystan."

Mother Berthildis had been standing over Trystan, head bowed, but now she turned back to Isolde. "Is there anything further you need?"

Isolde, still kneeling at Trystan's side, looked about the room, at the fire in the grate, the washbasin, her collection of ointments and salves. She shook her head. "Nothing. Thank you, mother. But these are your rooms. Wouldn't you like—"

The abbess stopped her, though, with a firm shake of her head. "No. Humility is good for the soul, so we are told. Stay where you are, the rooms are yours. I shall go to seek a bed for the night in one of the novices' cells." She paused, small dark eyes softening as she looked down at Isolde's face. She touched Isolde's cheek, her hand cool and dry as parchment against Isolde's skin. "And I shall pray—for both of you."

Isolde rubbed her arms with hands that felt tingling and numb. She was sitting on the floor beside the bench where Trystan still lay. She'd done for him everything that she could: washed and salved the cuts and bruises. Cleansed and then cauterized the sword cut in his side, because that would stand the best chance of keeping the wound from turning poisoned.

She'd been wholly thankful, at that moment, as she held the hot knife to the wound, that the Sight didn't allow her to feel Trystan's pain. And at the same time, she'd felt the hard, clenched knot in her chest tighten again. Because Trystan should have been screaming when the red-hot metal touched his skin. And instead he'd only groaned, made a slight, feeble movement of his head, and then lapsed into unconsciousness once more.

Isolde had told the other men to get what sleep they could, since there was nothing they could do for Trystan by staying awake. But they'd refused, instead dividing the night into watches so that one could be awake and with her at all times. Eurig had taken first watch; he now sat on a low wooden stool near the room's small hearth, and occasionally made a slow circuit of the room, eyeing the door and window—checking, Isolde supposed, that all was secure.

Hereric, Daka, and Piye had retired to the inner chamber of Mother Berthildis's rooms, a small, square space with a rug, a chair, and a single narrow sleeping shelf. Isolde hoped they were asleep. All three had looked exhausted, and Hereric's face had been drawn and tinged with gray, reminding Isolde that barely a week had passed since he himself had lain hovering between death and life.

Hereric had turned at the last, before following Daka and Piye into the inner room, and looked intently down into Isolde's face. In the glow of lamplight, the tracks of tears on his broad cheeks had been plain. *Trystan hurt . . . Isolde help?* he had signed.

Of course I will, Isolde had said. Now, though, there was no more help she could give. She had tried, at intervals, to get Trystan to take some water or wine, but he'd swallowed nothing at all. Still, Isolde couldn't bring herself to move from where she sat beside him on the floor. She simply sat with her arms hugged about her knees, counting each of Trystan's terrifyingly shallow breaths.

Eurig had spoken to her hardly at all since the other three men had gone. Isolde was thankful for it. She kept dreading hearing one of the men ask her, *Will he live?* And then hearing her own voice answering with the words that even now pressed tight against her throat, *I don't think he will.*

Maybe in the morning she would manage to find some feeble thread of hope and cling to it. Now, though, in the darkest watches of the night, she felt as though she'd exhausted every last scrap of her reserves of courage and determination. She was left with a blank, gray, overwhelming tiredness and a bone-deep certainty that Trystan was going to die. And it would be all her fault, from start to finish, every single step of the way.

Eurig's voice broke in on her thoughts, making her start and look up. "Not really his sister, are you?"

Isolde found she was too exhausted to even try to lie. She said, simply, "How did you know?"

Eurig shrugged and even smiled slightly, though his brown eyes were soft with mingled sympathy and concern. "Well, for one thing, I'd a sister once. Fond of each other we were, too— when we weren't fighting like cats and dogs. But I never saw her look at me the way you were looking at Trystan just now."

Isolde said nothing, and after a moment Eurig went on, rubbing the bridge of his nose. "And maybe I'd have threatened to tear the liver out of any man that so much as looked at her in a way I didn't like—same's Trystan did with you. But if I'm honest, I'm not so sure I'd have walked straight back into my own private corner of hell for her sake." He gave her another brief smile. "Family feeling's well and good, but it only carries a man so far."

Isolde brushed tiredly at her cheek. "What do you mean?"

"Well, I suppose there's no harm in telling you now. I've broken so many oaths to Fidach in the last days that I should be dissolved into a pile of dust. But here I stand. That was the job Fidach made the price of our taking you in. Trystan had to go back to the mines—the slave's mining camp where him and me were prisoner—and rob the store of gold paid for their latest shipment of tin. Trystan—"

Eurig went on, saying something about Trystan, about his knowing the layout of the filthy pit of a mining camp better than anyone, knowing the movements of the guard patrols, how to get in and out without being seen. About what would have happened to Trystan if he'd been just a hair too slow, if the layout or the guard had been changed in the time he'd been gone.

But Isolde had stopped hearing. She was looking down at Trystan's lean, sun-browned face, still and almost relaxed as though in sleep. Her weariness was abruptly gone, leaving her mind feeling light and strangely emptied. Save for the last, lingering echo of a talk she'd had with Kian in her workroom at Dinas Emrys, what now felt like years ago.

This whole journey, she thought, since that time, has been running away of a kind. Running from Madoc's proposal. From the men who'd attacked the boat. From Fidach. Even, in a way, running from Trystan. Now, though, she'd reached the bottom, the end, the point where jutting land crumbled away into the sea. No more running. Nowhere left to run.

Slowly, Isolde rose to her feet and turned to Eurig, breaking in on whatever he'd been saying. "Will you sit with Trystan for a time? He won't need anything—there's nothing any of us can do for him just now. But I need to speak with King Cerdic again."

Chapter Sixteen

I SOLDE WENT BACK TO THE plain cell she'd first been granted.
Candle, washbasin, and pitcher of water were still there,
where she'd left them hours before. She lighted the candle,
emptied the basin, poured clean water in and set it on the hard
wooden sleeping shelf. Then she knelt beside it and looked down
at the shimmering surface.

She knew already what she planned to do—what she had to
do. But if Marche was there, one of Octa of Kent's encampment,
it would all be for naught.

So she sat very still, watching the broken sparks of reflected
light on the water's surface, letting her mind empty and her
breathing slow. And nothing happened. Nothing. No familiar
vision of burned-out huts. No image of Marche's face. Nothing
at all.

And then, in a lightning flash, a picture did appear: two men,
locked in fierce, deadly combat, blades ringing as they slashed
and struck at one another with their swords.

Their faces were grim and set, their strikes brutal as they
moved in a circling dance; plainly, this was a fight to the death.

The chests of both men heaved, and the younger of the two had a freely bleeding cut on one cheek. With a furious cry, the older man raised his sword two-handed above his head and charged. And then, with the same thunderclap suddenness, the vision was gone.

Isolde sat back, the beat of her own heart hammering loud in her ears, cold sweat drying on her skin. The vision was gone, but she could still see the faces of the two men as clearly as though they'd been before her still. Two men. One older, with long black hair and dark eyes and a coarse, heavily handsome face. The other younger, with strikingly blue eyes set under slanted brown brows. Two men, she thought. Father and son. She'd seen them—known them—plainly. Marche and Trystan.

And just as clearly, what she'd seen was not happening now, because Trystan was now lying only a short distance away, hovering between life and death. So the fight with Marche might have been a glimpse of the past or of the future yet to occur.

Or, Isolde thought, simply another of those huge jokes on the part of whatever controlled the Sight.

Drawing in her breath, Isolde leaned forward to look into the basin of water once more.

But nothing more appeared.

Isolde stared until her eyes ached, until her temples pounded, and her vision started to blur. She reached inside her for the space where the quivering strings of Sight were tied. But not even a flicker of an image broke the water's glimmering surface. Not even another flash of a sword fight between Trystan and Marche.

Definitely, she thought, another of the gods' malicious jokes. Oddly, though, she didn't feel angry—or even very surprised. Maybe she was simply too exhausted for resentment or shock. Or maybe, she thought grimly, it's only to be expected that every time I have to face real danger, the Sight leaves me with absolutely no help on which to rely.

Slowly, and still with that odd feeling of detachment, she

rose to her feet, blew out the candle, and turned to the door. She had still to see King Cerdic. This only meant that she now had no idea whether she would succeed or be doomed from the first.

THE FIRST LIGHT OF EARLY DAWN was creeping into Cerdic's apartments, leeching the room of color and turning Cerdic's fur-lined robe and sculptured old man's face to ashy gray and making the plaited white beard and braided hair stand out startlingly white. The Saxon king looked, Isolde thought, more than ever like Trystan—as Trystan looked now. As she'd left him, with the frightening stillness of a mortally wounded man creeping up his throat and across the line of his jaw.

Cerdic was eyeing her consideringly, ice-blue gaze fixed on her face. Finally, he cleared his throat and spoke. "You are asking a great deal, Lady Isolde."

Isolde shook her head. She pushed all memory of Trystan's broken body, his still face, and shallowly drawn breaths away, locking up unwanted emotion tightly in a small walled-off box in her chest. Later, she thought, you can go back to being agonizingly afraid for Trystan's life. Now even the thought of him was a stumbling block she couldn't afford.

"No. I'm asking you to give your word that you'll not threaten the lives of the four men who arrived here tonight—men whom I've already told you bear you no threat at all. In exchange for a way to avoid both swearing allegiance to Octa of Kent and a defeat at his hands."

Outside, she could hear the abbey stirring to life. Feet in the corridors, a high, sweet chanting from the chapel as the abbey sisters began the day in prayer. Cerdic's brows lifted, his lightly guttural voice, when he spoke, turning dry. "But you'll not tell me this miraculous plan?"

Isolde shook her head again. "No," she said steadily. "Not

until I have your word that the men I spoke of will meet with no threat from you or from any of your men."

Cerdic was silent a long moment, and then he rapped out a single word, with the suddenness of a sprung-arrow bolt. "Why?"

"Because if I die tomorrow, I want it to be with the knowledge that I've done all I can to see that these four men remain unharmed."

The Saxon king's brows shot upwards once again. "You expect me to believe you'll lead me to a defeat of Octa and Marche when you can't even preserve your own life?"

Isolde smiled thinly. "I said I would—almost—guarantee you a means of forcing Octa of Kent to back down. Perhaps even dealing his armies a crushing blow. That I myself would survive the attempt was never part of the bargain."

Cerdic watched her, looking down the length of his nose, making Isolde think more than ever of a golden hawk regarding some smaller, lesser bird down on the ground. Then, finally, he shook his head, setting the gold-capped braids in his hair swaying.

"No." He paused, his mouth also curving in a slight, thin smile. "I may have about me little sentiment and less affection. But I like you, Lady Isolde. And I loved your father well. I would not have his daughter's life added to the burden I carry of all the other lives I've taken in my time. Even for the chance of defeating Octa of Kent."

Isolde tensed her muscles and closed her eyes, rejecting the wash of defeat that threatened to overwhelm her. Not now, she thought again. Not now. Because if she gave up, watched Cerdic swear alliance with Octa and Marche, then Trystan's being hurt—even in thought, she wouldn't let herself say Trystan's death, as though thinking the possibility would make it true—was nothing but purposeless waste.

So she drew in her breath, looked across at Cerdic, and laid her very last bargaining piece on the table between them. "What about for the sake of your grandson?"

Cerdic's brows drew together. "Explain what you mean."

No turning back now. Her choice was made. "The man who was brought in wounded tonight. He is your daughter's son."

If the words came as a shock, Cerdic gave no sign. The papery skin around his eyes and mouth might have tightened a little, but that was all. He sat in silence another long moment, and then he said, with no change of expression, "Marche's son?"

"Your daughter Aefre's son."

Cerdic sat without speaking, without even moving, once again. Then at last he said, "I remember the boy. My daughter visited me just once after she was wedded. She brought her son to me. A well-formed, handsome lad. Brown eyes."

The obviousness of the trap Cerdic had laid was oddly steadying. Isolde folded her hands together in her lap, for once feeling not even a faint shadow of regret that she did now remember the years before Camlann. "I knew your daughter, Lord Cerdic—though I was only thirteen when she died. And I've known her son from the time I was born. Trystan's eyes are blue—like his mother's. Like yours."

Cerdic's expression still didn't change, but he let out a slow breath, the air hissing through his teeth. "I had to be sure, you understand. There are many who would claim kinship with a king, did they have a drop of my blood in their veins or no."

"Of course."

Cerdic made a quick, half-angry gesture with one hand, the gold warrior's rings gleaming in the early dawn light. "And you expect—what? That I should at once embrace this son my daughter bore to a traitor? Bypass my own son and make him my heir, maybe?"

The controlled anger in his tone, in the line of his mouth was like Trystan's as well. "No," Isolde said. "That kind of ending is for harper's fire tales. And Trystan—"

May not even live another day. She clamped her jaw tight shut, though, before she could say the words aloud. She drew breath and began again. "All I ask, my lord king, is that for your grandson's sake, you give me your promise that he and his companions will be under your protection. And then hear out what I propose. Because your daughter's son is—" Her voice wavered slightly, but she made herself go on. "A brave man. And because he once carried out almost exactly the gambit I would propose now."

Isolde had time to count five beats of her own heart before at last Cerdic inclined his head. "Very well," he said. "You have my word. Go on."

Cerdic listened in silence while Isolde spoke. At one point, he took two chased silver cups out, filled them with wine, and silently handed one to Isolde, but otherwise he remained as still as though he'd been carved from the same block of wood as his chair. Even after Isolde had stopped speaking, he sat immobile, keen blue eyes on her face.

"You propose then, to go—alone and unaided—into Octa's encampment. Pretending to be an escaped prisoner—a slave. You cannot say for certain whether Octa's recent ally Marche of Cornwall will be among those present. You think not and are willing to take the gamble that you are right. If you are wrong, Marche will recognize you at once and you will die. However, if you succeed in persuading Octa that you are an escaped slave, you will offer him false intelligence of my position here and maneuver Octa into making an attack that will end in his defeat."

Isolde's throat felt dry with talking. She raised the silver cup Cerdic had given her and took a swallow of wine. "Yes. That is what I propose."

Cerdic absently ran a finger around the rim of his own cup, frowning at the film of wine left on his skin. "And what you propose, Lady Isolde, is, to put it plainly, madness."

Isolde's hand clenched on a fold of her gown. "Does that mean you refuse?"

Cerdic was silent a moment more, eyes on the reddish brown liquid in his cup. Then he looked up, and, unexpectedly, his stern, hawklike face cracked in a smile. "On the contrary, Lady Isolde. I agree."

Isolde's breath went out in a rush, and for a moment the whole room seemed to tilt about her. As though from a great distance, she heard her own voice ask, "What did you say?"

"I said I agree." Cerdic raised a hand, stopping Isolde before she could speak, his brows drawing together once more. "I know. There are a dozen and more ways in which the scheme could fail. Marche may be there to recognize you, as you have already said. Octa may not rise to the bait. His forces could prove superior after all. But as I told you before, Lady Isolde, we Saxons like war. And I find, even at my advanced age, that I'm not so ready to give it up after all. If you can bend the odds of victory slightly in our favor, I would far sooner bury my sword in Octa's belly or split his skull with my war axe than make him an ally. After you left last night, I had time to think on what we each of us had said. And I realized I had begun to sound like some bleating Christian. Like one of the pious sisters here who prates and whines about forgiving our enemies and turning the other cheek so they can hit us again. Woden's bollocks, it's enough to make me wish I'd razed this place to the ground when my wife died, instead of having that yellow old crone of an abbess mutter her prayers at me and eye me like a dog slavering over a bone every time she passes me by. Hoping to make a believer of me and save me from the pits of hell, no doubt."

Cerdic's lip curled, and then he paused, studying Isolde, something hard and implacable crossing his blue gaze. "And besides—if a young woman who looks, to speak plainly, as though even I could snap her in two with one hand has nonetheless the nerve to propose this plan, I would not show less courage by failing to agree."

An edge had crept into his tone, and Isolde wondered whether the Saxon king did feel an insult in what she had proposed. In being forced, in a way, to hide behind a woman's skirts—or at least rely on a woman to win his fight. She couldn't find it in her to care, though, one way or the other. The wave of relief that had washed over temporarily blotted out all else. Cerdic had agreed. Why didn't matter.

Cerdic raised his cup of wine to his mouth again, then set it down and asked, "Will you take a guard? Some of my men?"

Isolde shook her head. "No. I'll be more likely to be believed if I go alone." She paused, her mouth twisting, then added, "And like you, I don't want to add any more deaths to my conscience."

Cerdic was still watching her, his lids slightly lowered, his head on one side, as though he tried to see some part of her not outwardly visible. "You realize," he said abruptly, "that you could be going towards your own death?"

A sudden image of Trystan, lying motionless and pale on the bench in Mother Berthildis's rooms flashed before Isolde. She pressed her eyes shut to clear the image—or try to—then said, with another twist of a smile, "Didn't you tell me just last night that fate moves ever as she shall, my lord king? And we all go towards our own deaths. Every day we draw nearer and nearer still. Some meet it sooner than others, that is all."

Cerdic opened his mouth as though to answer, then closed it again. "You leave tonight?" he asked instead.

"If you agree with me that that's best." Isolde paused. With the flash of Trystan's face, the space in her chest where she'd locked all unwanted emotion away was splitting open, fear—not for herself, but for him—again spilling free. She said, "There is one last promise I would ask of you, though, before I go."

Cerdic's slanted brows—so much like his grandson's—rose. "Go on."

Isolde swallowed hard. "As I said, I can't be sure whether Marche makes a member of Octa's party or not. But if I don't come back—if the plan goes wrong and I die, and if Octa's forces overrun your position here, I want you to promise me that you'll not let Trystan fall into Marche's hands. Kill him first."

EURIG WAS SITTING AT TRYSTAN'S BEDSIDE as Isolde had left him when she returned to the abbess's rooms. He looked up as Isolde entered, and she saw that his eyes were red-rimmed, his face lined with fatigue. Piye and Daka were awake as well, sitting against the far wall with their arms folded, their dark faces only slightly better rested than Eurig's.

"Hereric?" Isolde asked, as she came to stand at Trystan's side. He, too, looked exactly the same as she'd left him, his skin pale beneath the tan of living so much out of doors, his face utterly still. She told herself fiercely that she was only imagining a slightly longer pause between each of his shallowly drawn breaths.

Eurig shifted position on his hard wooden stool. "Still asleep," he said. "Reckoned we'd leave him be. If he's the only one of us that can get any rest, he may as well get as much as he can."

Isolde nodded. She laid a hand on Trystan's forehead. His skin was cool. No trace of a fever, at least. She folded her fingers tightly to keep herself from touching him anymore, from putting a hand to his cheek or brushing his hair back from his brow. Let herself start that and she'd lose what resolve she still had. She made herself instead turn away from his bed and look at the other three men.

"Will you all listen, then? I want to tell you about my meeting with Cerdic and what he and I have planned."

She told them the whole. When she came to telling them who she truly was, Eurig interrupted to say, "Knew you were a lady, whatever you said before." But save for that, he, Piye, and Daka listened in silence until she came to the end.

When she'd finished speaking, there was a pause in which the only sounds were of Trystan's breathing and the snap and crackle of the fire in the hearth. The three men exchanged a look in which a silent decision seemed to be made, and then Eurig said, "Piye and Daka go with you. Not in to meet with Octa—you're right that you'll stand the best chance of success there if you're on your own. But they'll go with you as far as Octa's camp."

Isolde opened her mouth to speak, but Eurig stopped her. His usual awkwardness had dropped away, and he said with sudden firmness, "No. Don't argue. If you're caught before you reach Octa, you can call them your slaves, your bodyguard—or two black devils you've raised from hell to do your bidding. Whatever you choose. But they go with you. Not going to do Britain or anyone else here a lot of good if you get your throat cut by guards or bandits before you get within sight of Octa."

Isolde felt a lump rise in her throat, and she swallowed hard. She looked from Daka to Piye and said shakily, "Thank you." Then she turned back to Eurig, closing her eyes briefly as she searched for words.

Again Eurig stopped her, though, seeming to know already what she'd been about to say. "Oh, aye. I'll guard him." He nodded towards Trystan's motionless form. "Anyone gets past me to do him harm, it's because I'm already dead."

There was a moment's silence, and then Eurig added, in a different voice, "Don't know whether it would occur to you—being a lady and all. But Octa's bunch are like to be a rough lot. Have you thought—"

The ready flush of embarrassment was creeping up Eurig's neck, and he cast a look of appeal at the other two.

"He mean," Daka said, "not many women in war camp. Not enough to go around. What if Octa's men see you, think better you warm their beds than go to their king?"

Isolde ordered herself not to look towards Trystan again. "I had thought of that," she said. "And I do have a plan. It will keep Octa and all the rest of his men from getting too close to me—and maybe keep Octa from setting any of his men to guard me. If it works."

Chapter Seventeen

ISOLDE BURIED HER FACE IN her hands, hiding her eyes—though she risked a brief glance at the man who stood looking down at her, his broad, stupid face a mask of indecision in the flare of torchlight above. Behind him, the army encampment stretched out across the night-dark plain, rows of sagging goat-hide tents grouped in clusters, with here and there a campfire casting an eerie pool of flickering orange. The whole was surrounded by a deep trench dug out of the soil, then an earth and timber stockade. There were only two openings in the stockade, both manned by guards. A well thought out and elaborately engineered defense, considering that Octa's purported mission here was one of peace.

Through the gaps between her fingers, Isolde watched the guard at this, the encampment's northern gate, frown ponderously. He had long, greasy, blond hair and across his shoulders he wore a wolf's pelt that had been improperly cured—if it had been cured at all. The stench was catching in the back of her throat every time she drew breath.

Isolde made an effort to master the raging impatience that

lapped at her, stopped herself from saying, *Will you just make up your mind? Get on with it, can't you?*

Instead, she let her shoulders shake as though with sobs. It would have been horribly easy to let herself give way to actual tears, when her every thought led like a circling path back to Trystan. When the very beat of her heart seemed to echo the terrifying pause before each rise and fall of Trystan's breath.

She had left Trystan lying under Mother Berthildis's watch, as unresponsive as before, as much poised on a knife edge between death and life. There was nothing more she could have done for him, though, even if she were still there, by his side. He still couldn't swallow even tiny spoonfuls of water or broth. And Mother Berthildis and the other holy sisters could sit with him as well as she, could try again at intervals to get him to drink and keep the fire alight so that he stayed warm.

Even still, every nerve in Isolde's body was screaming that she should be back by his side, even now, even in the midst of her fears of what she was about to face. But giving way to actual tears would be to risk washing away the marks that Mother Berthildis had helped her paint on her face, arms, and hands before she'd left the abbey with Daka and Piye. It had taken them nearly an hour, dabbing Isolde's skin with a mixture of thick oat porridge and dark red wine.

"What do you think?" Isolde had asked, when they were done.

The abbess had snorted briefly through her nose. "I think it looks like you've got wine and oat porridge dabbed in spots on your skin and pillow sewn under the belly of your dress." And then she'd paused, head tilted to one side as she frowned at Isolde from under drawn brows. "But yes. At night, with nothing but firelight, and the hood of your cloak pulled up—you'll look well enough like a woman who's caught the pox and is far gone with child. Especially to a lot of men. I don't suppose Octa's soldiers have done much sickroom nursing to know what a real pox victim looks like. Or that they've ever troubled themselves overmuch with noticing just how a breeding woman's belly looks. I think you'll pass."

Now, standing in the chill night air and pretending to cry for Octa's guardsman, Isolde could only hope Mother Berthildis had judged rightly—and wonder, as she repeated her plea in the stumbling fragments she knew of the Saxon tongue, whether this was the moment when the night's luck would turn. Because up until now, it had all gone with almost frightening ease.

She had left the abbey with Daka and Piye in the hour before sundown. Both of the brothers had gone warily, their knives drawn, their shoulders tight with watching and listening for any sign or sound of alarm. But they'd met with no one at all abroad as they made their way across pastured fields and a brief stretch of woodland to Octa's camp. They'd passed two small clustered settlements, but both had been deserted, empty even of livestock. Doubtless the families who lived in the huts had packed what possessions could be carried, roped together their cattle and goats, and fled into the surrounding hills, as much braced for trouble as Octa's camp appeared to be.

Piye hadn't even been struck by one of his fits. Just before they'd come within sight of the encampment, Isolde had seen him touch the iron ring she'd given him days before. He'd seen her watching, and had given her a quick, slanted smile that had made Isolde think he might have been half expecting a fit to strike him down.

She had wondered whether Piye's and his brother's nerves felt as raw as her own, set on edge by the unnatural hush and quiet of the countryside that felt like the silence before a clap of thunder. But she'd bidden them both good-bye in the shelter of trees that ringed Octa's camp. Dark had fallen by that time, so that their faces were only a deeper darkness amidst the shadows. Piye had said something, and Daka had translated in a whisper. "He say take care, lady. As do I."

They had offered to stay within sight of Octa's encampment, but Isolde had shaken her head, knowing that the danger for all of them would be far greater if they were found by one of Octa's patrols. Now, though, she felt an insidious, cowardly wish that she'd not refused their offer to stay. Because standing here, shivering as she waited for the man before her to decide whether to take her to his king, she would have felt a shade less alone if she could have imagined Piye's and Daka's eyes watching her from somewhere out in the surrounding dark.

But by now, she thought, they ought to be halfway back to the abbey. If they'd met with no trouble on the way. Halfway back to where Trystan—

Isolde jerked her thoughts back for what must have been the hundredth time and looked up at the big blond guard again, trying to sound as though she were choking back sobs, willing herself to push all thoughts, all memories of Trystan far, far back, at least for now.

If expectations of failure meant that you earned your own defeat, letting herself be distracted tonight would just as surely be to court her own death. Instead she cast about in her memory for the words that would convey what she wanted, wishing she knew more of the Saxon tongue. "Please. Octa be glad see me. Give you reward. Or—" She let her voice trail off doubtfully. "Octa not trust you? Not let you near enough to speak? Oh, please—"

She clutched at the guardsman's sleeve. As she'd hoped, the man's combined disgust and unwillingness to admit that he wasn't high enough in the king's regard to have Octa's private ear made him at last decide to act.

He shook her roughly off. "Get away from me, you poxy whore!" Isolde understood that much, at least. He turned and shouted something over his shoulder—an order, she supposed, for someone to replace him as guard, because after a moment a second man came up out of the shadows behind the first. The second man looked younger, with a nose that had been broken and never set. He cast a curious, sidelong look at Isolde, then took up a position at the gate, spear and shield at the ready. The first man said something to him, too low and quick for Isolde to make out, then turned back to her.

"You come with me."

. . .

HE WAS IN HELL.

It had to be hell, because it was so cold.

But his ribs still hurt like a ring-tailed devil. Unpleasant. But it seemed an unlikely punishment for his sins. And there was a voice somewhere. Chanting. What sounded like prayers. Which seemed wrong for hell, too.

Not bloody likely he'd have ended up in heaven.

His thoughts felt slippery—too slippery to come together. But he was sure of that much.

There was a crushing weight on his chest. And a pain that felt like being stabbed in a dozen different places by red-hot knives. God, there was no escaping it. Not that he could move. Or even open his eyes.

But there was something. Something he hadn't done. Something he had to remember. Some reason he had to get out of here. Wherever *here* was.

THE BLOND GUARDSMAN LED ISOLDE THROUGH the darkened camp, weaving a course through the churned and muddied pathways that separated the clusters of tents. The stench of the place was almost overwhelming—smoke and mud and human waste and the smell of too many unwashed bodies packed into too small a space. Finally, the guard stopped in front of a small, crudely constructed dwelling built of logs and meant, Isolde guessed, for housing prisoners, because it had a wooden plank door and a heavy crossbeam that when dropped into place would bar the door from the outside.

"In here. Wait."

He swung the door open, gave Isolde a rough shove that sent her across the threshold, then shut the door once more. From the pitch dark within, Isolde heard the bar being dropped across the door outside and fought down a primal wave of panic at being locked in—and blind. The darkness was so complete that she couldn't see her hand in front of her face, much less make out the details of the room.

Or even tell whether or not there was anyone else with her in this place.

That thought sent another jolt of panic skittering through her veins, and she forced herself to draw long, steadying breaths. She had Piye's knife, slipped into the top of her boot, but she didn't dare draw it just now. Not when the guard might be back at any moment, and her life and the success of this venture depended on appearing as absolutely no threat.

Instead, she made herself reach out a hand, touch the wall to orient herself, and make a slow circuit of her prison. The space was windowless, square-built, and with only one door, smelling of unseasoned timber and straw from the thatched roof. And it was completely empty, save for herself. Not so much as a handful of straw on the earthen floor.

When she'd finished her circuit and reached the bolted door once more, Isolde let out a breath of relief, then gritted her teeth and set herself to wait in the blackness that seemed to press like a solid force against her eyes.

Isolde touched the marks on her face and hands—meant to simulate the oozing sores of pox—then pressed her hands against the stitched bag of goose down that swelled out the belly of her gown. She could do nothing, for now, but wait for the blond guardsman to return. Wait and see whether Octa would be taken in by her story or no. Or whether—

But she wasn't thinking of Marche. When she'd turned away from Piye and Daka and faced towards Octa's camp, she had set aside all acknowledgment—all fear, even—that Marche might be here to recognize her. And now she had to concentrate on putting him out of her mind, every bit as much as—

She caught herself before her mind could again fly back to the abbey. As much as anything else, that might make her lose her courage.

All the same, each moment she stood in the darkness seemed

to stretch on endlessly. The earth floor was muddy, and there was nowhere else for her to sit, so she stood in the center of the room, listening to the sounds of the encampment outside. A pair of dogs yapping and snarling at each other, their barks punctuated by men's drunken shouts. A dog fight, she supposed, with the watchers calling out wagers on the outcome. Occasionally, too, she heard a higher-pitched woman's voice, raised in argument or complaint or sometimes an outraged shriek. One of the inevitable camp followers, she supposed. Or a slave girl.

Isolde shivered. Any other king but Octa of Kent, she thought, would simply have bound prisoners hand and foot and staked them to the ground in a tent. The utter dark and the looming sense of the hut's four solid walls were plainly meant to terrify.

And she was alone here—entirely alone. And, at this moment, very conscious that even if she succeeded tonight, men were going to fight and die. Doubtless fewer than would die if Octa, Cerdic, and Marche united to crush Britain. Maybe even fewer than if Octa broke any treaty he might have made with Cerdic and attacked Wessex after all. But still, the cold truth was that lives would inevitably be lost because of what she was doing now.

When at last she heard the sound of the bar scraping across the door, her every muscle jumped and tensed. It was the same man—the blond guard who'd shut her in—his broad, flat-featured face eerily lit by the flame of the burning brand he carried in one hand. He was tall enough that he had to stoop to see under the lintel of the door, and he blinked, peering blindly into the darkness before his pale eyes fastened on Isolde.

"Come with me," he said again. "Octa orders that you be brought before him."

Again the blond guard led the way through the encampment, this time stopping before a tent that had been set up in a central position and was larger than the rest, though still constructed of the same coarse goat hide. Grunting at Isolde to follow, he ducked under the flap of the tent, a pool of light spilling out through the opening and onto the muddied ground. Isolde's heart was pounding as she followed the guard inside, her stomach clenching in anticipation of what she would find. But save for herself and the guard, the tent was as empty as the prison hut had been.

A single rush light burned on a roughly constructed central table, casting a dim, smoky glow over the space inside. And the rush must, Isolde thought, have been set in tallow, because the reek of the smoke was even worse than the stench of the guardsman's uncured skin cloak or the smell of the encampment outside. A chair covered by another silvery pelt stood to one side of the table, together with a rough three-legged stool. Apart from that, the space was bare. Some filthy rushes had been strewn on the dirt floor, and a heap of skins that might have served as a bed was piled in one corner. No more squalid and dirty a space than the rest of the camp, but no less, either.

The light the burning rush cast, though, was certainly poor, and Isolde felt a faint stirring flicker of hope. She stole a glance down at her hands, clasped tight on a fold of her cloak. The marks she and Mother Berthildis had applied did indeed look like the still oozing pustules of a recovering pox victim. Enough that she herself might have been fooled, at least from a short distance. And the air here was chill enough that she could keep her cloak on without drawing suspicion. The rest—

Isolde broke off in her thoughts abruptly at a sound from outside. A low, rasping voice sounded just outside the door, growling a command, Isolde thought, to some unseen companion. Then the tent flaps parted again, and she was face-to-face with Octa of Kent.

She knew him at once, of course, from the glimpses she'd had of him in the scrying waters. And for one horrible moment, she saw him again, laughing as he rode down the screaming old woman. Saw Emyr, the weeping, shivering man whom he had tortured into madness years ago and whose suffering her grandmother had ended with a draft of nightshade. Heard Cerdic's thin, creaking voice, *You would go alone to seek out Octa the Butcher? Octa of the Bloody Knife?*

Isolde focused on drawing a slow, steadying breath, telling herself that Octa—whatever name he had won for himself, whatever reputation he had carved—was a man like any other. Telling herself that she had spent seven years of pretending witchcraft to survive as Con's high queen—and she'd done it by learning to read faces and eyes. To take a man's measure quickly, almost at a glance. She could do the same with Octa now.

You'll have to, she thought. Your own life—Britain's survival—depends on it.

Octa was growling another order, this time at the blond guardsman who had brought Isolde here. *Remain here*, Isolde guessed he must have said, because the guard took up a position at the tent's doorway, feet planted apart, arms folded on his broad chest. Watching, Isolde saw the big blond guardsman flinch instinctively at Octa's address, saw him drop his gaze to the muddy rushes on the floor, and avoid his king's gaze.

Octa let his gaze rest on the guardsman a moment, then dropped into the single chair and fixed his eyes on Isolde. "Well?" He spoke in a thickly accented version of the British tongue. "You come here to see me—why?"

Isolde heard an echo of Madoc's words. *Some say he's mad. I don't know.* She wouldn't have called the man before her anything but sane. But all the same, as he watched her, something moved behind his eyes. Something that made Isolde think of a wild caged beast.

The crooked scar on his jaw stood out like a livid, writhing snake, the ends of his long silver-blond braids were matted together with what looked like black pine pitch, and beneath a heavy fur-lined cloak he wore about his neck a circlet of what Isolde realized with a jolt were the joints of human finger bones.

The sight, though, was oddly steadying. Because in that moment, Isolde saw her way.

Octa of the Bloody Knife was a man accustomed to being feared. A man whose every movement, whose every word, whose every choice of dress was built around inspiring terror in those he faced. Like Fidach, Isolde thought, with his many-skinned robe and room of grinning skulls. But unlike Fidach, she didn't think Octa would respect anyone who stood up to him and refused to be afraid.

If she had any chance at all—not just of persuading Octa to believe her story, but of ensuring he made the choice she wanted—that chance lay not in simply rejecting fear but in appearing completely oblivious that Octa expected her to be afraid at all.

Isolde drew another breath, ruthlessly pushing everything she knew about the man before her—every vile story she'd ever heard about him—aside. She tried to fix in her mind a memory of Garwen, of her round, slightly foolish face and honking voice. Then, with scarcely a perceptible pause after Octa's question, she opened her mouth.

"My lord, have you ever been sick at your stomach? I mean really sick—so sick that you just heave up every bit of food you try to take—and just the smell of something like roasting meat or soured ale is enough to set you retching for an hour and put you off your meals for days?"

Octa's silver-blond brows drew together. "What in the name of all the—"

Isolde broke in before he could finish, talking over him, clasping her hands over the pillow that swelled out the belly of her gown, the words flooding from her mouth in her best imitation of Garwen's breathless prattle. Outside, one of the quarreling dogs gave a sharp bark that changed midway into a yelp of pain. A roar—of approval, Isolde supposed—went up from the men who must be watching the fight.

"Because that's what this breeding has been like for me. Just sick enough to die, the whole way through. And my ankles always swollen, and the pains in my back—" Isolde rubbed the base of her spine and thought of every crabbed and crusty old warrior she'd ever nursed, and there had been many of them. The old men whose sole remaining pleasures were in describing their ailments to all who came near. "It's like being stabbed with a red-hot sword. Not to mention the—"

Octa's brows were still drawn together in a fierce frown, and he broke in, his voice dangerously calm, "I assume, woman, that there is a point to all this. Do you think that you could come to it before I lose all patience?"

Isolde ignored the quickening of her pulse, the chill that danced across her skin. The point, she told herself fiercely again, was to appear completely unaware that he expected her to be quaking in terror. And already she thought she'd managed to unbalance him, if only a bit. Beneath the obvious impatience on the Saxon king's face, she could see a kind of startled puzzlement, too, as though he were unsure quite what to make of her.

If nothing else, she thought, you have to be the first petitioner who's ever come before him and made him listen to a catalog of the trials of pregnancy.

"Just as you like, lord." Isolde summoned up a wide, tolerantly forgiving smile to direct at the Saxon king. "Not as though I'd expect a man to understand, anyway. But if you think it's easy smiling and nodding at an old goat like Cerdic's maundering stories about his youth when you're wanting nothing but to lie down somewhere quiet until your insides stop tying themselves in knots, then I'm here to tell you you're wrong. And—" She let an aggrieved note creep into her tone. "What's more, it's all my lord Cerdic's fault in the first place. He's the one that got me in this state."

Octa was eyeing her, one hand fingering the knife at his belt. The hilt was of worked gold and as thick as Isolde's wrist. At Isolde's final words, though, his brows shot upwards in a look of skepticism. "You're saying that's King Cerdic's child?"

Isolde nodded with exaggerated patience and gave him a look such as one might give a small, backward child. "Well, of course. Haven't I just been saying so?"

Octa studied her with narrowed eyes. Then, abruptly, he threw back his head and gave a shout of laughter that sounded like the scraping of knives and ran like ice up Isolde's spine. And then, when he'd stopped laughing, he fixed Isolde with a hard, cold stare and said, "You lie."

Isolde again ignored the thud of her heart against her ribs—though she wondered suddenly what Trystan had felt, all those years ago, walking into the enemy camp with his face and arms bruised by his own hands. But that thought led her back to wondering what was happening at the abbey. Wondering whether Trystan was still lying in Mother Berthildis's rooms, drawing slow, shallow breaths. *Or*—

Isolde clenched her hands, digging her nails into her palms, and made herself look at Octa blankly. "Lie? Why would I want to lie about it? It's not as though I'd choose to be bearing King Cerdic's child. Old wretch." She screwed up her mouth and then spat on the ground by their feet. "Near nine moons I spend carrying the bastard's brat—and then he casts me out. Just because I've caught the pox." She gestured to the marks on her face. "Which as I'm sure you'll agree, my lord, was hardly my fault. But no—out he tosses me like so much rubbish. So if you think I'm happy to be still carrying his child—"

Octa looked at her narrowly, his hand on the hilt of his knife. And then he smiled, a slow, unpleasant smile, his fingers tightening around the blade as though about to draw it from its sheath. "Then perhaps you'd like me to get rid of the child for you. I've done as much for many women of your kind."

Isolde swallowed the bile that had risen in her throat and smiled back at Octa, a smile wide enough to crack the painted pox marks on her cheeks. *No. No. You are not going to be sick. Let fear in now—let yourself think about what he's saying and you'll be just one more woman quaking in terror at Octa's feet.*

She said brightly, still in her best imitation of Garwen's voice, "Well, now. I knew you were a kind one the moment I laid eyes on you. I've an eye for faces, you know. And as soon as I saw yours, I said to myself, that man has a good heart." She tilted her head to one side. "I'd some doubts about coming here, I'll admit.

Because if you'll pardon me for mentioning it, my lord, there's a terrible number of nasty stories told about you. And the way Cerdic talks about you—well, it would fair scorch wood. But I thought, well, no man can be as black as he's painted. And it's not as if I'd take Cerdic's word if he told me the sky was blue. So I—oh!"

Isolde broke off with a sharp cry, bending over double and clutching at her middle. She breathed heavily for a moment, then straightened and looked up at Octa again. "Just a stray pain, lord. They come now and again towards the end. I doubt the child will actually be born tonight."

The mixture of disbelief, anger, and something like horrified distaste on Octa's face might have been funny at any other time. But any amusement Isolde might have felt was canceled by the cold weight of knowing that if the story she told was a lie, there were countless, countless numbers of women in the land who could tell it and speak nothing but truth. And by the grim certainty that she might well become one of those women herself if she failed.

As it was, she watched Octa's hand slowly relax its grip on the knife and felt nothing but a queasy wash of relief and a wish that she could wipe away the trickle of cold perspiration that was sliding down the back of her neck.

Outside, someone had started a drinking song; Isolde could hear a dozen or more upraised voices, hear the men pounding their shields with the butts of spears or swords in time to the words. Octa drew in his breath, and she could almost see him recalling the presence of the guardsman still posted at the tent's entrance, watch him taking a grip on himself, struggling to regain control of the situation, to keep firm hold on his dignity.

He gave her a wary look, as though half expecting a screaming infant to drop from her where she stood. "Very well," he said at last. His fingers moved over the necklace of finger bones, so that they rattled together on his breast. "You came. Why?"

He'd settled, Isolde judged, on the conclusion that pregnancy—

or the pox—had turned her brain. And she judged, too, that she
had this one moment—no more—to convince him that listening
to her any further was worth his while. So she drew in her breath,
met his gaze, and said, "Because I want you to kill Cerdic for me.
That's what I'm offering you, lord. Cerdic and all the rest of his
army—all trussed up like winter geese and ready for the chopping
block."

Octa shifted position, kicking absently at the rushes on the
floor, still eyeing Isolde narrowly. Weighing what she'd just said
against her patent insanity. Finally he said, "How?"

ISOLDE STOOD IN THE PITCH DARKNESS of the log-built prisoner's
cell, trying to stop shivering. She'd given Octa the story she'd
worked out with Cerdic: that Cerdic had been planning a surprise attack on Octa's camp, and that his armies were massed in
the bowl of the next valley but one. That sickness, the constant
bane of armies on the move, had struck Cerdic's troops, and that
they were now pinned down in their encampment, made all but
helpless by the same pox that had afflicted Isolde herself.

Octa had been an impatient audience. Several times he'd interrupted Isolde's story with a sharp question or an accusation
that she lied—that she couldn't possibly know as much as she
claimed. It had taken every shred of Isolde's resolve to keep staring at him in blank-eyed wonderment or smiling like a woman
deranged.

And then in the end, when she'd finished speaking and stood
with the cold prickles of sweat drying on her skin, Octa had said
nothing at all. He'd simply sat, staring at her, the crooked scar on
his jaw livid in the dim light, his eyes flicking over her from head
to foot. Isolde had been wondering whether she was going to
have to manufacture another pretended birth pang to make him
let her go, when he'd turned to the greasy-haired guard.

"Take her back to the holding cell. Then return here to me."

And so now Isolde stood in the resin-scented darkness again, with no idea whether Octa had believed her or no—much less whether he was going to rise to the bait she'd twitched before his face. And still less idea how she was ever going to get out of this place, this prison hut and the Saxon encampment, alive.

At least she'd neither seen nor heard anything to suggest Marche was part of the encampment or even close by. But maybe that was as far as luck could take her tonight.

The air felt close and stuffy. Isolde had already taken off her cloak, and now she wished that she could take the pillow from under her gown as well. She and Mother Berthildis had stitched it in place so that it wouldn't slip and give her away—and so it hadn't. But now it felt hot and uncomfortable against her skin. Though certainly far less cumbersome than the actual weight of a child would have been.

Despite everything, Isolde found herself smiling a little at the recollection of the look on Octa's face when he'd thought there was a chance of her birthing a squalling baby in his own private war tent. She rested her hands lightly on her middle. Maybe he'd be right, at that, if he assumed that breeding unhinged a woman's mind. Because the list of uncomfortable symptoms she'd described for Octa was true. She remembered them all vividly—every one.

And yet, she thought, you'd never, never wish a single one of those miseries away if it meant giving up the joy of having your babe inside you all that while.

Isolde smiled faintly into the dark again. And then she came to with a start, as realization struck. Just now, and for the first time—the very first time, since her stillborn baby girl had been born—she'd thought of the months of carrying her without any underlying shadow of pain.

That ought to mean something, Isolde thought. But before she could catch hold of the wisp of realization and think what that something was, a sound from outside the hut made her freeze in place. She'd grown accustomed to the shouts and raucous laughter from the surrounding camp, so that she'd not been paying much mind. But now she became suddenly aware that the laughter and drunken bursts of song had stopped and that the shouts were coming from only two or three voices, no more. She heard, too, the steady thud of booted feet, the clash of weaponry being assembled and drawn on.

Isolde felt suddenly faint, and, heedless of the muddied ground she sank down, resting her forehead on her upraised knees. Octa had risen to the bait after all. The army encamped around her was preparing to march out.

IF HE WASN'T ALREADY IN HELL, he must be dying, then. He thought one of the loose, slithering memories that kept sliding through his grasp was of knowing he wasn't likely to survive the night.

He felt a flicker of irritation, even in the midst of crushing pain. Adding insult to injury that dying should—Satan's hairy black ass—hurt this bloody much. So much that he couldn't get hold of what he would have wanted his last thoughts to be. Something—

And then like a jolt of lightning, like another stab with a red-hot sword, remembrance tore through him, and he thought, *Isolde*—

But it was too late. The cold was closing in around him, muffling him, making even the monotonous chanting sound impossibly distant and far off. The weight was pressing, pressing against his chest. Just for one blessed moment, he had a clear sight of Isolde's face: heart-stoppingly beautiful, with its delicate features, dark-lashed gray eyes, and curling night-dark hair.

Then a wave of blackness reared up, swallowed him.

And everything was gone.

ISOLDE WOKE WITH A GASP TO the sound of men's shouts, the clash of metal on metal—and blackness. Utter blackness, so that for a moment she blinked, disoriented, unable to remember where she was, or, for a panicked, thudding beat of her heart, think whether she could have gone blind.

Then remembrance flooded back in a rush. The journey from the abbey. Her audience with Octa. His order to take her back to this place, the prison hut.

She'd heard Octa's army march out, towards the trap she and Cerdic had laid. Towards the valley where Cerdic's armies were not pinned down by disease, but readied and waiting for Octa's attack.

She'd established almost at once that there was no way of getting out of this place. The walls were built of uncut logs, the door a solid plank of heavy oak. She'd been trapped inside, in the midst of an empty camp. She remembered the fear that had washed through her at the realization. But she'd also gone two nights running without rest. And, with nothing else to do but sit and wait for what would come, she must have fallen asleep.

To wake, now, to the discovery that the camp around her was no longer empty.

Fear arrowed into her again. Because the shouts and screams and clash of battle outside could mean only one thing: that the fighting between Cerdic's and Octa's armies had been carried back here. Which might, she thought, have been a reason to hope for rescue. Save that Cerdic's forces could have no way of knowing where she was. Nor, unless Cerdic himself was among them, could she imagine any of his men caring one way or the other whether she lived through this night or not. And—

Another realization struck her like the bolt of an arrow. The acrid scent of smoke was beginning to filter in from outside, catching in the back of Isolde's throat. Cerdic's men must be firing the camp.

Isolde reacted instantly. Groping in the darkness, she found her cloak and stuffed it into the chink between the ground and the bottom of the door. Then, drawing Piye's knife from where she'd secreted it in her boot, she sliced the pillow neatly from the inside of her gown and rammed that under the door as well.

Not that it would save her. She could keep the smoke out a short while longer this way. But blocking off the door would be useless if the logs or thatch of the hut took fire. And despite the cloak and pillow, the smoke was growing thicker. Isolde coughed and wiped at her stinging eyes, imagining the crackling flames spreading from tent to tent outside, drawing slowly closer to run fiery tongues up the hut's outer walls.

She tried kicking at the door, but it was still blocked solid. And the roof was well out of her reach. So she stood in the center of the room, arms locked about her, shivering and straining to hear the sounds from outside. Flinching involuntarily at every fresh ring and clash of axe or sword. Cursing the blanketing darkness that left her blind.

And then her throat closed off so that she choked and coughed and dashed at her streaming eyes again. Because the darkness had lightened. A yellow-orange glow was seeping into the hut. And then, with a hiss and a sharp crackle, one corner of the thatched roof over her head kindled and took flame.

Isolde jumped back, flattening herself against the opposite wall just in time to avoid being hit by falling, burning thatch. The dry straw caught almost immediately. The fire was spreading. Another moment and the whole roof would be ablaze.

Isolde could feel the heat of the fire on her face. Already the smoke was making it nearly impossible to breathe. Her vision darkened and her head spun as she coughed, lungs burning for air. Outside the hut she could hear a war dog barking and yelping, a mad, frantic sound that cut through even the ringing confusion of battle and the hiss and pop of the flames.

She was going to die. For a moment Isolde thought of all those who—perhaps—waited for her beyond the veil to the Otherworld. Her grandmother. Her father and mother. Her baby girl. Con. There had been times—many of them—when she would have felt nothing but sweet relief to think of leaving this world, of joining them in the one beyond. But now, all at once, she knew absolutely that she didn't want to die.

She kicked again at the door, as hard as she could. At the very least, she refused to simply stand here and wait for the flames and the smoke to claim her. She could keep fighting to the last.

She kicked the door again, felt it give, if only slightly. And then she stopped, frozen in place as a crash sounded from outside, making the panel before her shake and shudder. Another crash. Someone outside was delivering what must be a series of smashing axe blows to the bar across the door.

Isolde didn't even have time to be afraid or wonder who it was about to break down her prison door. Another blow—and another—and the door burst open. Outside was a sea of fire and smoke, but through the haze a lean, powerfully muscled form bounded at Isolde, nearly knocking her to the ground.

Isolde blinked, sure for a moment that she was still blinded and imagining sights where there were none. Then Cabal thrust his nose hard against her neck, and she knew that he was real. Real, alive, and in the midst of Octa's burning army camp.

Isolde caught hold of the big dog, but before she could move, hands were reaching at her from the smoky darkness, grabbing her, hauling her outside the burning hut. Cabal was still barking frantically, pushing at her with his head, baying as bits of burning straw showered them from above. Then they were outside, in the comparatively clearer air, and as the roof of the prison hut collapsed altogether in a fiery crash, Isolde saw the man who had pulled her clear of the flames: thin, sharp features, leaf-brown eyes, and swirling blue patterns tattooed across his cheeks.

Fidach.

Isolde knew, in a distant way, that she ought to be surprised. But she seemed to have passed beyond a point where she was capable of feeling shock. If Cabal had proved to be the one wielding the axe, she would have given him the same blank stare she was giving Fidach now.

Fidach's furred coat was gone; he wore breeches and a shirt open at the throat and plastered by sweat to his skin, so that every line of his emaciated chest was plain. He was coughing, fighting for breath, but he dragged Isolde farther away from the wreckage of the hut before he turned to her.

All about them the camp was burning, patches of dry grass underfoot going up in flames, tents collapsing in bursts of glowing sparks. Fidach had to shout to be heard over the roar. "Are you hurt? Can you walk?"

Isolde shook her head. "No. I mean, I'm not hurt. I can walk."

"Good." Fidach wiped sweat from his eyes with the back of his wrist. "Then get behind me and keep close. Let's get out of this."

The stumbling journey through the camp was a nightmare of roiling clouds of smoke and heat and leaping flames. Isolde kept a fold of her cloak over her mouth and nose, and in front of her Fidach had slashed a strip of fabric from the hem of his shirt and tied it across his face. But even still, Isolde felt dizzy, her eyes watering and her lungs stinging and burning, and again and again a stray spark would land on Cabal's fur, forcing her to stop to beat it out. The big dog kept close, pressed tight against her side, muscles bunched beneath his coat, teeth drawn back in a snarl.

The camp seemed all but empty, though. Two or three times Isolde caught sight of men locked in swaying combat, their bodies backlit by fire and obscured by smoke so that they seemed like warring gods at the end of the world. No one challenged their progress. Though whether Octa's forces had been defeated and scattered, or whether Cerdic's attacking army had been defeated and driven off, Isolde had no idea.

Only once as they came to the edge of the camp, finally leaving the scorching heat and smoke of the fire behind did Isolde stop and ask Fidach, "King Cerdic—"

"Will do very well without your help or mine. Come on."

Fidach had tethered a horse—a big, raw-boned gray—in the shelter of trees surrounding Octa's camp. Isolde looked back once over her shoulder at the blaze of fiery red behind them, standing out against the night sky. Then she let Fidach help her up to sit behind him on the horse's back and simply hung on mindlessly as Fidach turned the gray's head away from the burning encampment and urged her onward into the stretch of woods.

Under the canopy of trees, it was still dark enough that Fidach kept to a walking gait, watchful of tree roots and rocks that might make the horse stumble or fall. Cabal, trotting along at their heels, had no trouble keeping pace. They didn't speak at all as they made their way through the forest. Isolde was too exhausted to rouse herself to speak, though now that she could breathe again without choking on smoke and ash, she had begun to wonder in a vague, distant way. Where had Fidach gotten the horse—and how had he come to find her? And, for that matter, why he should have troubled to save her life at all?

Finally, Fidach pulled on the gray's reins and drew up at the edge of a small, bubbling stream. The sky had begun to turn gray with the coming dawn, so that there was light enough to see his face. His features were streaked black with soot and ash, his hair matted with ash and sweat. Isolde could guess that she must look about the same: every part of her exposed skin felt itchy and gritty.

Still without speaking, they both waded ankle deep into the stream and washed, scooping the water up in their cupped hands. Cabal lay on the bank, lapping the water up with his tongue. Fidach pulled off his shirt, and Isolde wished she could be rid of her filthy, crumpled, sweat- and water-soaked gown as well. She settled for pushing her sleeves back, scrubbing at her hands, her arms, her neck and face. The water was shockingly cold and left her skin tingling, but it was blessedly cool on Isolde's parched throat when she raised her cupped hands to her mouth and drank.

When she had finished washing and drunk several handfuls, Isolde started to feel the return of something like coherent thought. She wrung the water out of the hem of her gown, then turned to Fidach, noticing for the first time that he had a long, bleeding cut on one arm. She wondered for a moment whether he'd won it fighting a way inside Octa's camp, and for a moment she could picture him—fighting an unknown foe, delivering slashing sword blows with the same lightning speed he'd shown in fighting Trystan. Though he must have been slow at least once, if he'd come away marked from the fight.

She cleared her throat, then breaking the silence between them that had lasted since leaving the encampment behind, said, "Do you want me to tie that up for you?"

Fidach glanced at the cut as though he, too, were seeing it for the first time. Then he shook his head, pulling his shirt back on, and thrusting his arms into the sleeves. "Don't bother. It's not deep."

There was another silence in which the bubbling splash of the stream and the early morning trill of birdcalls from the surrounding trees seemed very loud. Then: "How did you find me?" Isolde asked.

Fidach turned to her. The petty tyrant who lived for power, whose every word, every look was planned with calculated effect seemed entirely gone—though what remained in that man's place, Isolde couldn't quite tell. His face looked gaunt, the skin tightly stretched over his cheekbones, and as exhausted as Isolde felt. He rubbed at his face with his wet sleeve, then nodded towards Cabal.

"You can thank your war hound for that. He led me straight to the hut. Set up such a clamor I knew you had to be inside."

Even his voice sounded different. Pleasant and deeper pitched. There were an almost countless number of questions that Isolde might have asked. How Fidach had come to find Cabal or to be looking for her at all, to start. But fatigue was closing over her like a muffling gray cloud, and she found she couldn't make herself ask any of them.

Fidach was swinging himself up onto the horse. "Are you ready to go on?"

And so instead of asking any of the other questions, Isolde pushed a stray curl of damp hair back from her face and said, "Where are we going?"

Fidach looked mildly surprised. "Back to the abbey. Is that not where you'd want to go?" A flood of remembrance swept through Isolde like a chilling tide. Trystan. Back at the abbey, she'd see whether he'd survived the night or was . . . already gone. As a rule, she despised the practice of dressing up life's end in a gentler name. *Passing away. Passing on. Leaving the world.* But even in thought she couldn't bring herself to use the word *died* there.

She nodded wordlessly, and Fidach put out a hand to help her up onto the saddle. "Let's be off, then."

FIDACH REINED UP JUST BEFORE THEY reached the abbey gates, slid down off the gray's back, then helped Isolde down. Isolde had fallen into a strange kind of mindless gray trance, half exhaustion, half dread of what she would find at journey's end. And now that they were here, just outside the abbey walls, her every muscle tensed with the almost overwhelming urge to go straight in to Trystan, to know once and for all whether he still lived or whether—

She made herself turn to Fidach, though, and ask, "Do you want to come inside? I could stitch up that cut for you." She gestured to the patch of blood that was seeping through Fidach's sleeve.

Fidach glanced up at the abbey walls, then gave Isolde a wry half smile. "I think the walls of any house of holy women would likely cave in around my ears if I stepped inside. I'll do well enough."

Cabal had pressed himself close against her side, and Isolde absently rubbed his head, frowning. "Be sure to keep the cut clean, then."

Fidach coughed, then tilted his head, the smile broadening into almost the mocking grin she remembered from before. "Afraid I'll die before my time?"

In the harsh dawn light, he looked like a walking corpse, his head like one of the grinning skulls hung on his own walls. Isolde shook her head. "If you'd died before last night, I'd be dead now as well."

Fidach must have understood the unspoken question, because he looked away, up at the abbey walls once again, drew in a breath, then let it out again. When he looked back at Isolde, his face was sober, all trace of posturing gone. As though, she thought again, he'd abandoned the face he wore before his men— in the same way he might have thrown off his many-furred cloak. His eyes now looked puckered with fatigue, and Isolde could see a black smear of ash still on his neck and places where his hair had been singed.

"I command a band of masterless men," he said. "Men whose only law is that of their own hunger, their own ambition and greed. Such men understand only one kind of leader—one who rules through fear. And a man without honor—without conscience—is more to be feared. That is simple truth."

He paused, seeming to expect some kind of response, so Isolde said, "I suppose that's true."

Fidach jerked his head in agreement and coughed again, covering his mouth with his hand. "But just because I cultivate the reputation of a man without honor, it does not follow that I have none." Another of those wry half smiles played about the corners of his mouth. "A man whose death hovers so clearly at his shoulder begins to be cautious what risks he takes with his soul. And whatever a man's soul is—and as to that, who can say?—it is contained in his word. Like water in a jar. Shatter the jar—break a sworn oath—and a man's whole self leaks uselessly away onto the muddy ground."

Another explosion of coughing interrupted him, making him hunch his shoulders and bend forward until the racking fit had stopped. When he straightened and took his hand from his mouth, Isolde saw once again the smear of blood on his palm.

Isolde had a sudden picture of a younger Fidach, the warrior's tattoos on his cheeks bright and new, his body vigorous, healthy, and whole. Oath-sworn, maybe, to one of the chiefs of the Pritani country, the wild lands beyond the Romans' great northern wall. Learning the warrior's arts—skill with a sword, how to fight on horseback—and then suffering some disgrace, outliving his chief in battle, maybe. Or maybe simply the discovery that he was a lover of men. Something, at any rate, that made him all at once outlaw, untouchable. And so he'd created this identity, this public self he wore like a cloak: a man who knew all, who fed off other men's fears, and so was feared himself. A man to whom appeals of conscience were useless, because he had none. And yet all the while that young warrior lived behind the other man's eyes.

It might, Isolde thought, be like that. Though she supposed she would never know for certain. The force of will that was keeping Fidach on his feet and upright now was surely strong enough to guard whatever secrets lay in his past.

As though again reading her thoughts, Fidach shook his head. "I doubt the smoke did me any good. But then didn't I tell you a dying man may fear everything or nothing at all?" He paused, the faint smile fading, his eyes on Isolde's. "I undertook to keep you safe. I gave Trystan my word that I would see you safe from harm. A man in my position gathers all the information he can. Knowledge is power—I told you that also. And there are many in these parts—Cerdic of Wessex, to name but one— who pay handsomely for such intelligence as I can provide. So I might—would—have been willing to negotiate with King Octa of Kent. To pretend that I had something—or someone—of value that he sought. To pretend that I was willing to trade that someone for a price in gold. But in the end, Octa would have been left without his prize. And Cerdic of Wessex—or whichever of Octa's other enemies offered the highest price for the intelligence—would have been the richer by whatever I had learned of Octa's movements and plans."

Fidach paused, throat contracting as he fought off another fit of coughing. "So as you must realize now, after you and Trystan left the camp, I set my men to combing the countryside for your tracks. And eventually ran across Piye and Daka last night—who, after a good deal of persuasion on my part and oath-swearing that I meant you no harm—told me where you'd gone and why. They had gone to round up any of the other men they could find. Our plan was to break into the camp and take you back by force. But then I saw Cerdic's men set the place on fire, and knew I had to get you out myself, without waiting for any of the others to come."

Isolde looked at him, still feeling dazed with weariness—and with the effort of trying to fit the man before her inside Fidach the mercenary leader's skin. She tried to call up some kind of reply to what he'd just said. *Thank you*, seemed absurdly inadequate, but it was all she could think of.

"Thank you."

Fidach waved that away. He cast one final look up at the abbey walls. "I understand Trystan was wounded?"

She'd been seeing Trystan's still, bloodlessly pale face since the moment she'd left him the night before. Even so, Fidach's words sounded in Isolde's ears like cracks in breaking ice. Isolde nodded, unable to trust her voice enough to speak, and Fidach's leaf-brown eyes met hers in a long, sober look. "Then I wish him good luck."

And then he turned away, back to the horse, taking hold of the reins. Isolde saw his mouth tighten further with the effort of dragging himself up into the saddle, but then he was astride the gray, turning the animal's head away from the abbey, back along the forest path they'd just traveled. He looked back at her, though, and made Isolde an odd little half bow. "And I wish you luck as well. Lady Isolde of Camelerd."

He spoke her name in a way that made Isolde wonder whether he'd known who she was all along. But then he urged the horse forward and was gone, vanishing into the early dawn shadows of the surrounding trees.

Chapter Eighteen

I SOLDE SAT BACK FROM BENDING over Trystan's bedside, letting out a hiss of frustration through her teeth. He'd been moved overnight from Mother Berthildis's lodgings to a room in the guest hall, and Isolde had gone to him as soon as she'd entered the abbey gates. She'd felt as though she was escaping the burning, smoke-filled hut in Octa's camp all over again when she'd seen that his chest still rose and fell with each indrawn breath, felt the light but perceptible beat of his pulse.

Piye and Daka had not yet returned, but she'd found Eurig and Mother Berthildis both with Trystan: Eurig asleep sitting up on the hard wooden settle by the hearth, Mother Berthildis kneeling at Trystan's bedside and chanting a prayer in a voice that was cracked with age but surprisingly sweet. She'd heard from Mother Berthildis as much as the abbess knew of the last night's battle. That Octa's armies had been ambushed and routed by Cerdic's men, and that Cerdic himself had ridden out to chase down the fleeing, tattered remains of Octa's forces.

Isolde had felt a distant kind of relief at hearing that her proposed plan hadn't led Cerdic into defeat after all. But she'd not been able to manage anything else.

She'd bathed—more thoroughly than in the forest stream—washed the lingering reek of smoke from her skin and hair, and changed her filthy, ash-streaked clothes. And she'd slept a few hours, too, because she'd been so tired that bright sparks were flashing across the field of her vision and she'd known she'd be no good to Trystan or anyone else that way. And then she'd come back here, to find that Daka and Piye had at last come back. Though of Fidach, they had no word at all.

She'd been wholly and completely thankful to see the two brothers safely returned. And she'd felt a flicker of worry for Fidach, alone and with the unstitched cut in his arm. But now that the four men—Piye, Daka, Eurig, and Hereric—had left the room to seek rest or food, she'd no thoughts, no attention at all save for the long, broken body before her. For trying, again and again, to reach Trystan as she had Hereric—as she had Piye. Because there was absolutely nothing else she could do for him now.

She'd checked the wound in his side and found it angry and blackened from being cauterized, but with no trace of the poison she'd feared. She'd tried—again and again—to get him to take water from a spoon, but he never swallowed. The liquid just ran uselessly onto the pillow. So she'd taken his hand and tried using the Sight to speak with him.

Except that that effort was equally useless. Again and again, she met with blank darkness that was like running up against a solid stone wall.

She knew, too, that despite her failure to see Marche in the scrying waters before, the Sight was still there, still a live pulse inside her, a small, growing seedling in her chest. Mother Berthildis had remained and now sat in the corner, still chanting a soft, sweet prayer that contrasted oddly with her hunched form and age-yellowed face. And if Isolde concentrated, she could feel the hot twinges of rheumatism in the prioress's knees, feel the dull ache that settled in the joints of her hands.

If she concentrated—Isolde's fingers twitched with the urge to smash something—she could probably feel every stray ache and pain in every man, woman, and child in the entire goddess-blessed abbey.

But nothing at all from Trystan.

"What are you trying to do?"

Mother Berthildis's voice broke in on Isolde's thoughts, making her look up from Trystan's still face. "What do you mean?"

The abbess waved one clawlike hand impatiently. "You've been sitting there without moving for the last four hours, at least. And it's not just fear for that young man's life—fear that he'll slip away and die if you move. I've seen that often enough before to know what it looks like. Plainly, you've some purpose in being here. The look in your eyes alone would scorch leather. So what is it you're hoping you can do for him?"

Isolde hadn't been going to tell the older woman. She couldn't think of a single thing to be gained by giving the abbess a true answer to what she'd asked. And if she did tell the truth, Mother Berthildis would probably think her leagued with the devil. Or mad.

But Isolde couldn't find the energy to care. Against all odds, against even her own expectations, she had somehow survived to return from Octa's camp. And she was left now standing exactly where she'd been before: looking down at Trystan's unconscious body, his certain death staring her in the face.

She rubbed her temples. "I'm trying to speak to him. To bring him back from wherever he is now."

Mother Berthildis tilted her head to one side, her wide, flat mouth pursing in thought. "You can do that?"

Isolde nodded. "Yes." Although a voice in the back of her mind sneered that maybe she truly was mad. Maybe nothing of the Sight was real. Maybe it was all just her own imagination and fancy.

Mother Berthildis studied her a moment, the small black eyes shrewd. Then she nodded thoughtfully. "Yes. I've met with skills of that kind before. A wondrous gift, it seems to me."

"A gift?" Isolde's eyes strayed again to Trystan's face. "I suppose it could be, if it weren't that it vanishes whenever I've need of it most."

Still eyeing Isolde, Mother Berthildis tapped her fingers lightly against her upper lip. "Vanishes? What do you mean?"

Isolde rubbed at her temples again. Her efforts with Trystan—combined with the lingering effects of breathing so much smoke the night before—had left her with a fierce headache. She tried, though, to think clearly, to look without prejudice or bias at the small old woman before her, hunched in her chair, the white nun's veil framing her shriveled face. She tried, too, to think of a courteous way of phrasing her next question. But in the end she couldn't summon the energy for that, either, and it came out more bluntly than she'd intended. "Why should you want to hear this?"

But Mother Berthildis seemed to take no offense. A smile as surprisingly sweet as her singing voice touched her mouth and the corners of her tiny dark eyes. "No reason. Save that it seems to me that you are a young woman who carries her burdens alone, without sharing them, without drawing on anyone else for aid. Admirable, no doubt. But even the best of us come to the end of our strength at times. And even speaking of a trouble can at times be good for the soul."

Isolde closed her eyes a moment. And then, almost before she knew she'd made a decision to speak, she heard the words start to pour from her in a flood. Sitting there at Trystan's bedside, she told Mother Berthildis everything. Even with Trystan, the night he'd woken her from the dream, she'd not let herself speak so freely. She kept her eyes closed and simply told Mother Berthildis the whole: everything about herself, about the return of the Sight, about Marche and the dream and being able to summon him in the scrying waters to enter his mind.

The abbess listened in silence that was utterly undemanding—and yet somehow as audible as words might have been. And when Isolde had at last finished, Mother Berthildis sat without speaking a moment more, her eyes on Isolde, her head tilted to one side. Isolde waited in silence.

At last the abbess cleared her throat. "And you're sure, are you, that the reason you were granted these glimpses—these visions of

Lord Marche—is because you were meant to learn from them what his movements were? Learn where and how he pitched his attacks so that you might warn your king's council of his plans?"

Isolde locked her hands tightly together in her lap, and instead of answering asked, "You called the Sight a gift. A gift from God, did you mean?"

Mother Berthildis inclined her head. "I would deem it so, yes."

"Well, then," Isolde said. "I'm not sure whether I agree. I'm not even sure whether I believe in God—your God—or not. But I would rather believe that the Sight was granted me for some purpose. That the dreams, the visions of Marche were sent me for a reason—a way to bring good out of harm. Not just—" Her voice cracked slightly. "Some kind of cruel trick. A way to keep me living that night over and over again."

"Oh, that they were sent for a purpose, I've no doubt. None at all." The abbess dismissed that with a wave of her hand. "It's what that purpose may be that I'm unclear on."

Isolde shook her head. "I'm not sure what you mean."

Mother Berthildis again fixed her bright, glittering black gaze on Isolde's face and was silent another moment before she spoke. Then: "I would say myself that you've at last forgiven yourself for wedding Lord Marche. But what about Marche himself?"

Isolde thought of the night she'd told all this to Trystan. Remembered that afterwards she'd felt lighter, somehow. As though a bleeding wound inside her had been cauterized, burned free of poison, and could now heal. Now—now she wasn't sure what she felt. Though it had hurt somewhat less, this time, to tell the story. She'd not had to work as hard at not choking on Marche's name.

It made it easier to ask, now, "What do you mean, 'What about Lord Marche himself?'"

Mother Berthildis's penetrating black gaze rested on hers. "How do you feel about Lord Marche?"

"How do I—" Isolde stopped. The abbess fixed her with a look that was as searing, in a way, as last night's flames. The look she'd said once could make strong men crack and confess their crimes. "I—" Isolde stopped again. She thought of the man she'd glimpsed in the scrying waters, who woke weeping for all he'd lost, who filled himself with rage to drive away a constant, cold, deadly fear. She drew in a shaky breath and then said, in barely a whisper, "I . . . don't hate him anymore."

Speaking the words brought a rush of feeling that was almost loss or grief. Because she wanted to hate him. She'd hated him since he'd killed her grandmother. Walled them both up in the plague-ridden garrison to die. Since he'd killed Con and forced her to wed him and stood her before the king's council to be tried for a witch and burned. Had murdered Myrddin and—

The list went on. But though Isolde told over the list of Marche's crimes in her mind, touching each one as Octa had touched the necklace of human finger bones, she couldn't find any of the old hatred. Nothing but a strange, hollow space where anger and hatred had been.

Mother Berthildis was watching her, still with that look that made Isolde feel as though the older woman knew every part of her thoughts. "Christians," the abbess said at last, "believe in forgiving our enemies. Up to seventy times seven."

Isolde felt again that hollow, blossoming loss inside her. She raised a hand and brushed at her cheek. Then she said, quietly, "That's very hard."

Mother Berthildis snorted. "Hard? Of course, it's hard. What virtue is there in loving only those who talk to us sweetly and do us no harm?" The abbess paused, then added, in a gentler tone but with the same fierce intensity in her eyes, "And if what God has granted you no longer comes, then maybe it's because you no longer have need of the powers He saw fit to bestow."

Mother Berthildis reminded her of her grandmother, Isolde realized abruptly. The two women could hardly have been less alike. Morgan had been slender, dark, and graceful, even in age bearing the traces of very great beauty, while Mother Berthildis's toadlike face never could have been anything but

ugly, even when young. But something about the look in the old
nun's eyes made Isolde think of the grandmother who'd raised
her and then died in the plague seven years before. A kind of
fearlessness—a willingness to face the truth without flinching,
to act with decision without care for consequence or future pain.
That, Isolde thought, Morgan and Mother Berthildis might
have shared.

And all at once she was caught by a wave of longing for the
past as strong as any she'd ever felt before. Because what did it
honestly matter whether she hated or didn't hate Marche? She
still couldn't reach Trystan. Without water, he had another day—
or at the very most two—before he would die. And just now,
Isolde wished with every part of her being that her grandmother
could be here with her now. That Morgan could tell her what to
do for Trystan and take the overwhelming weight of responsibil-
ity off her hands.

But Morgan was dead, and there was no one else—no one but
Isolde. She drew in her breath and turned back to Mother Berthildis, noting with a stab of compunction how tired the old woman
looked. She'd likely gone entirely without sleep the night before.

"Thank you," Isolde said. "And now—please, you should go
and rest. I'm sure you've many duties to see to—many others in
the abbey who need your care."

Mother Berthildis nodded and heaved herself to her feet. "A
place of this kind doesn't run itself, that's certain." But instead
of turning to the door, she went to Trystan's bedside, her fingers
sketching a cross in the air above his head. "I will be praying for
him, though. And for you, also."

"Mother?" Isolde hesitated, then asked, "You truly believe,
then, that praying for a man can save his life?"

A look of remoteness, almost of sadness, passed across the abbess's face and she shook her head. "No. If it's God's will that this
young man die, nothing you or I or anyone else can do will alter
that. But if we can't ask God to change His will, we can pray that
He will help us alter our own."

Isolde looked at her. "So that's your solution? I should pray for your God to help me be glad Trystan is about to die?"

Mother Berthildis seemed to take no offense at the bitterness of Isolde's tone. Instead, she reached out and lightly framed Isolde's face between her parchment-dry hands. "No. But you can pray—as I will—that God will be with you both. That you will never forget His love for you. And that if He chooses to speak to you, He will also grant you ears to hear."

WHEN MOTHER BERTHILDIS HAD GONE, ISOLDE sat without moving a long time, staring down at Trystan until she felt she'd memorized every line of his lean features. Until she could still see every thread of the gold-brown hair slipping free of the leather thong, every faint scrape or trace of a bruise that darkened his skin, even when she closed her eyes.

She felt a twist of disgust with herself. Had she actually thought that Mother Berthildis and her God would have anything to offer her now? The god who ordered his followers to forgive their enemies—which might be virtuous but was undeniably stupid as well. Unless you wanted your enemies to keep hurting you until you were dead.

This was the god, too, who ordered women to keep silent and submit to men like Marche of Cornwall. Or shut them up in walled abbeys like this one, dressed them in long black robes and tight, uncomfortable veils, and set them to chanting dull-voiced prayers.

And how strange, she thought, to believe in a God, and yet believe that fleeing the world He'd created, locking yourself away behind thick stone walls, was the best life you could live.

Isolde thought with another of those quick aching stabs of her grandmother, raising her brows at one of the black-robed priests who'd come to try to save her soul from the fires of hell. Morgan had eyed the man coolly and then said that if he was fool enough to follow a god who'd no more power than to get himself nailed to a wooden cross, she, Morgan, had better sense. And yet—

Isolde thought of her own answer to Madoc, weeks ago, after their return from Ynys Mon. Sometimes, she'd said, I've felt as though everything stops, as though the whole world pauses between indrawn breaths. So maybe that's a god—or someone else beyond the Otherworld's veil—thinking about me?

Isolde closed her eyes. *Let Trystan die, and I will never believe in you for as long as I live,* likely wasn't what Mother Berthildis had meant by asking God for help. Besides, if anything listening to her now needed her belief to be a god, he wasn't worth praying to at all.

She sat in silence a moment, the image of Trystan's face still imprinted on the blackness of her lids. Then she whispered into the silent room, "Everything that I may have to bear, I can. I ask nothing for myself. But please, please show me how to help Trystan."

Before she could decide whether she heard or felt anything, though, beyond the stillness of the room and the blackness of her own closed lids, a sound at the door made her start, her eyes flying open. The men had returned: Eurig, Piye and Daka, and Hereric, with Cabal padding along at their heels. They moved silently into the room, darting quick, tension-filled looks at the still, blanket-shrouded figure on the bed. Eurig was the first to speak.

"Is he—"

"Still alive," Isolde said. "No change."

Eurig nodded, and he and the others filed to take up the places they'd held before: Hereric on the settle by the hearth, Eurig on the room's single chair, Piye and Daka against the far wall. Night must be falling, Isolde realized. The room was growing dark. Sitting and watching Trystan's face, she'd not noticed the fading light and lengthening shadows, but now she could scarcely see the other four men.

She pulled herself to her feet and lit the room's single oil lamp, blinking as the sudden flare of light hurt her eyes. Then she sat down again by Trystan. Her stomach clenched as she saw how pale and lifeless his face looked. Like an effigy carved in stone. Eurig's voice made her look up.

"Can he hear us?" He nodded at Trystan. "Does he know we're here?"

Isolde shook her head, feeling frustration twitch at her fingertips once again. "I've no idea. Maybe. Why do you ask?"

"I just—" Eurig stopped and cleared his throat. The tips of his ears reddened, but he pressed on. "I just wanted to . . . talk to him, like."

"Go ahead." Isolde moved to make space for Eurig at Trystan's bedside. She rubbed tiredly at her eyes. "Maybe you can do him more good than I can just now."

Eurig stood by the bed, feet planted squarely apart, hands clasped behind his back. He cleared his throat again, then began, eyes bright in his round, homely face as he looked down at Trystan. "I just wanted to say . . . to tell you thanks," he began. "That doesn't exactly cover saving a man's life. But I just wanted to tell you that I've never forgotten what you did. Getting me out of the mines."

Piye interrupted with a burst of rapid speech in his own tongue, and Eurig nodded heavily. "Daka and Piye say the same. We'd none of us have lived through that battle between Goram and Cynlas of Rhos if it hadn't been for you. So . . . thanks. From all of us."

Eurig swallowed convulsively, then took a step back from the bed. Isolde's vision had blurred, and she blinked, feeling drearily that she had done almost nothing else on this journey but cry or try to stop herself from crying. And then she stopped and sat up, as the sense of Eurig's words slowly worked its way through the muffling gray fog.

"What do you mean?" She turned to Eurig. "What fight between Goram and Cynlas of Rhos?"

Eurig blinked at her, surprised at the question, but he said after a moment's hesitation, "This would be three years ago, or as near as makes no difference. King Cynlas and his son took a raiding party across to Goram's lands in Ireland. Wanted to take the fight onto Goram's own ground instead of theirs. And they were willing to pay anyone willing to come and swell their ranks."

"Can you . . ." Isolde swallowed, her eyes straying to Trystan's face. "Can you tell me what happened?"

At the moment she didn't particularly care whether Trystan had betrayed Cynlas and his son three years ago. But it was something of a shock to find that she might learn the truth of it now, of all places and times.

She looked back at Eurig, though, at his wearily slumped shoulders and reddened eyes, and added quickly, "I'm sorry—never mind. You can't have slept at all last night. You look as though you need rest more than anything else."

Eurig smiled at that, his face lightening for a moment as he shook his head. "Not half as much as you do, I'll wager. I'll do well enough. As long as you want us here, we stay." His words were echoed by nods and murmurs from the other three men, and Eurig went on. "And as far as telling you what happened goes, I don't mind. That is—" He cast a doubtful look at Isolde. "If you're sure you want to hear. It's an ugly story. And not one to sound any sweeter for being retold."

Isolde shook her head. "Please. I'd like to hear."

Eurig dropped once more onto his chair. For all he'd said he'd not mind telling the story, Isolde thought he braced himself before speaking, as though in expectation of pain, and a spasm passed across his face. "I told you once," he said at last, "that years ago I was a different man, living a different life from what I have now. A man with a future. A home. A wife and son." He stared straight ahead, and Isolde knew that whatever he saw, it was not the unadorned plaster of the opposite wall. "I was oath sworn to Gethin, son of King Cynlas of Rhos. Gethin commanded his own army, and I was one of his fighting men." Eurig's face worked again, as though he tasted something bitter. "Not that Gethin deserved the oaths I or his other men swore. He was ambitious. Greedy for power and wealth. It weren't enough for him to be just a king's son."

Eurig paused, looking down at his own blunt-fingered hands. "This was five—no, nearer six years ago now. Not so long after the fighting at Camlann. Things were peaceful, or mostly so. So Gethin, he ordered the body of his troops to guard the western border of his lands. The rest of us he left guarding the eastern shore—the coast. Just as skeleton force of fifty or so, we were. And not expecting any trouble."

Eurig stopped and was silent a long moment, his brown eyes looking back across the years. "We were hit—hard. A raid from Goram of Ireland's forces. Tore through us like wolves through a flock of lambs. Bad enough, you may say, but it happens. But it weren't just chance that Goram's men had struck just then. Not just chance, either, that left just a handful of us to face him when he and his men came. Gethin had planned it all. Paid Goram a price in gold to attack. The idea was to give Cynlas a defeat so that he'd have to retaliate against Goram. Not too big a defeat." Eurig's mouth worked again. "Just the fifty or so of us, after all. But enough that Cynlas would take up the insult. With luck—luck for Gethin, anyway—his father would be killed. Especially if he, Gethin, could play snake in the grass amidst his father's camp."

Eurig stopped speaking, still looking down at the hands planted squarely on his knees. After a moment's pause, Isolde said, "You sound very sure."

Eurig glanced up. "Sure? Oh, aye. I'm sure. Goram thought it was a right good joke. I can still hear him laughing while he was watching his men clap us in leg irons—those of us that had survived the fighting, anyway—and drag us off like so many head of cattle to be sold as slaves. Gave us each the brand of murder, too." Eurig pulled back the sleeve of his tunic to show the mark on his inner arm, his mouth twisting. "On account of the men of his we'd killed, defending our own lives."

The knuckles of Eurig's hands had whitened beneath the skin, but he drew breath and went on, after only a moment's pause. "I ended up a slave worker in the tin mines. But I told you about that already. And how I got free." His eyes went to Trystan, and he reached up reflexively to touch the scar on his neck, the mirror of Trystan's own. "That's when we met up with Hereric here." He jerked his head in Hereric's direction, and Hereric, who had been following the story with a slight frown, gave a brief nod of confirmation.

Eurig went on. "I've no idea what happened between Gethin, Cynlas, and Goram. I was too busy crawling on my belly through some filthy tunnel, choking on air you could cut with a knife it was so hot and filled with dust. Cynlas survived, so Gethin's great plans couldn't have worked out after all."

"But why—" Isolde checked herself before she could finish what she'd been about to ask.

Eurig's eyes lifted once again, and she saw in his gaze the same shadow of pain as when she'd told the story of the fisherman and his selkie wife back at the crannog. "Why didn't I go back to my wife and son, you were going to say?" Eurig let out his breath. "I meant to. Got as far back as the next valley over to where our settlement had been. Night was falling when I got there. So I stopped and begged shelter off an old man and woman with a holding up in the hills—just a cow and a goat and a patch of rocky soil. They'd no idea of who I was. But they were friendly folk, willing to offer a stranger a bed and a hot meal. And while I was sitting at their table and eating their bread and stew, they talked over the news of those parts. And they let fall that my wife had married again—a farmer with a settlement not so far from this old couple whose bread I was sharing for the night. She'd thought I was dead, of course."

Eurig's hands tightened on his knees again, then he looked up and said, as though answering a question, "Oh, aye, I could have gone and claimed her back. She'd wedded me first, after all. And I would have, if I'd thought she was fretting for me—or if this new man had been mistreating her. But he wasn't. And she wasn't. The next morning, I went down to their holding and spied a bit—kept to the trees so that I wouldn't be seen. I saw Carys, my wife, sitting outside on the front stoop of the house, churning butter with her sleeves rolled up. And she was happy—every bit of her fair shouted it. She'd always been a pretty woman." Eurig gave a small, sad twist of a smile. "Too pretty by half for the likes of me. But now she was . . . like a rose. Just blooming. I saw this new husband of hers come back from the fields, and her run to greet him and put her arms about his neck and him swing her off her feet and plant a kiss square on her mouth. Saw my son—he'd been just a baby the last I'd seen him—go running out, too, and have his new da' hoist him up and give him a ride on his shoulders all the way back to the house."

Eurig stopped and shook his head, shoulders hunching. "What did I have to offer 'em in exchange if I turned up, back from the grave? Make my wife trade a husband with land and property for one with none? And it wasn't only that. I wasn't the man who'd gone away anymore. Was I going to give my son that kind of father—a broken man who'd scare him at nights, waking up screaming with nightmares of time spent as a slave in the mines?"

Eurig shook his head again, big hands clenching so that the muscles in his forearms bunched under the skin. "No. They deserved better than that. Better than what I'd become." He stopped. He closed his eyes a moment, then opened them and cleared his throat. "I'd loved them both well enough to think of nothing but making my way back to them when I was free of the mines. But I loved them too well to make them live with me as I was."

He stopped speaking, bowing his head. Isolde's throat ached, and she touched his arm. "I'm sorry," she said softly.

"Aye, well." Eurig looked up and gave her a painful twist of a smile. "At least I can think of them still and know that they're happy." He paused, then began again. "I watched them a bit that day, my wife and her new man and my son. And then I turned around and started walking. Met up with Trystan again—he'd told me where he'd be. Him and Hereric both."

Eurig cast another glance at the big Saxon man still sitting on the settle by the hearth, and Hereric nodded again. Eurig shrugged. "We joined up with Fidach's band after a time. Not a bad life, all in all. But all the same, when Gethin himself approached Fidach to ask for help in another raid on Goram, it seemed like some god somewhere had heard every prayer I'd uttered in the mining camp after all." Eurig shook his head. "I'd spent those years praying for the chance to get back at Gethin for betraying us. For killing off his own oath-sworn men as easy as you might wring a litter of stray kittens. And all for nothing, too. Because Cynlas still lived. He was still king of Rhos. But the thing was, Gethin had a mind to try again—that's why he'd come to Fidach."

Isolde looked up, surprised, and Eurig nodded. "Aye, we knew that from the first. The idea was that Cynlas would be ambushed and killed by Goram's forces—but it would look to be on account of the mercenaries he'd hired had betrayed him for more gold in the end. What can you expect of a lot of outlaw, broken men after all? Cynlas would be dead, and Gethin would be left without a stain on his hands. Well—" Eurig's gaze strayed to the bed once again. "Trystan knew the whole of what Gethin had done years before. He'd heard it all from me. So when Gethin comes to Fidach, offering gold in exchange for this job he has in mind, Trystan stands up, cool as you please, and offers to be leader of the group Fidach sent. Piye and Daka went, too." He nodded at the brothers. "And I was one of the band, as well. Took care to keep my beard long and my face dirty, in case Gethin should recognize me. But the truth was, I needn't have bothered." Eurig's face worked as though he tasted something bitter. "He'd likely forgotten what I and all the rest of the men he betrayed looked like as soon as I was out of his sight years before—if he'd ever known."

Eurig stopped, looking down at Trystan again, and rubbed a

hand across his fatigue-reddened eyes. "Well, I don't know the whole of what went on. But Trystan went to Goram—alone, I know that, because we all thought he was as good as dead—and somehow got Goram to believe Gethin was fixing to double-cross him." Eurig's features tightened. "It was still a fight. Goram wasn't exactly going to pack up his armies and go home without striking a blow at Cynlas's forces. But at the end of it, Gethin was dead, and Cynlas was alive. And Trystan had got the three of us"—he nodded at Daka and Piye again—"and himself out of the fighting and on our way out of reach of both Cynlas and Goram."

Eurig stopped speaking. While he'd been talking, the night had closed in, the room utterly dark save for the light of the burning oil lamp. Outside in the passage, Isolde heard the now familiar shuffle of footsteps that meant the abbey sisters were making their way to the chapel for prayers. She hesitated, then asked, even though she already knew what the answer would be, "And Cynlas never found out the truth about his son?"

Eurig shook his head. "Not from us, he didn't. I asked Trystan in the beginning whether we shouldn't just tell Cynlas what Gethin planned. But Trystan said no. If Cynlas had managed to get through twenty-odd years of Gethin's life without knowing his son's character, he wasn't going to take the word of men like us about it. Besides, well . . ." Eurig stopped again. "Cynlas may be a hard man, and have a devil of a temper on him, too. But he's a good leader. You'd go a long way and find many a worse king before you found a better one. Trystan said he deserved *not* to know that his own son had been plotting his death. Especially since the knowing wouldn't do him any good."

Isolde nodded. She was still sitting beside Trystan's bed, and now she looked down at him again. At the angry, purpling bruises showing above the blankets she'd drawn across his chest. The stubble of beard on his cheeks, gold in the lamplight. She wasn't, she realized, even surprised by what Eurig had just told her. At some point on this journey, unknown even to her, any doubts she might have had of Trystan had simply and silently dried up and blown away.

Now, hearing the truth of Gethin's death at King Goram's hands, she felt no shock, only the sense that she'd known this all along. She looked down at Trystan's face and traced in its lines both the boy she'd grown up with and the man he was now. And she thought that somehow, somewhere along the way, she'd come to know them both equally well.

Still, the wave of guilt that crashed over her for ever having had doubts of him—and for everything that had happened to him on this journey because of her—was almost unbearable. Isolde pressed her eyes tightly closed, willing back that sobbing wail that started again in the back of her mind. A cry against the unfairness of it, that she'd broken her own heart in trying to keep Trystan safe. Only to have him brought before her again to die.

A hand fell on Isolde's shoulder, making her look up. She'd been expecting Eurig, but it was Hereric who had come to stand beside her. Hereric, with his flaxen-colored beard and pale blue eyes, who touched her on the shoulder and looked down into her face, and with his one hand made a series of signs.

Isolde tell a story. Like for Hereric. Hereric's eyes were still shadowed by his illness, but their gaze was clear, unafraid, and absolutely sure. *Isolde tell a story. Like for Hereric. And Trystan will live.*

Isolde choked on something midway between a laugh and a sob. Because she could just see herself telling her little children's story about the two stupid giants and their stupid fight over the hammer, and having Trystan get up from his sickbed, his wounds miraculously healed. But she had to say something. Hereric was looking down at her, still with that look of utter confidence in his eyes. And maybe a tale wasn't such a bad idea after all. At the least, it might keep them—all of them—from talking anymore. Stop anyone's asking how much longer she thought Trystan might last, and her having to say, *Unless he drinks something, maybe just one more day.*

It might stop all of them thinking about how hideously fragile a man's life was, how easily it could slip away. Which was, after all, Isolde remembered, the reason she'd walked the ramparts back at Dinas Emrys and wished with every part of her strength that she could never have to love anyone again.

And then she stopped, her whole body going suddenly still. She thought of Taliesin singing her his tale as payment for intruding on her peace. And herself, as she'd listened, having one of those moments where time seemed to stop and stand still. Feeling afterwards as though the sound of the harper's voice had somehow lifted her up and then set her back down in a different place from where she'd been.

The memory rose before her mind's eye, and yet—strangely—seemed to come from outside herself. She closed her eyes again. Was that an answer to what she'd asked of the silence all around her before the men had come in? She didn't know. But for the first time in all the time she'd spent at Trystan's bedside, she felt a tiny, faint flickering, not of hope, exactly, but of feeling that at least she was where she was meant to be, doing what she was meant to do. She drew in a shaky breath, lifted her gaze to Hereric's, and said, "All right. I'll tell a story. For Trystan."

THE MEN WERE QUIET AS ISOLDE drew in her breath to begin the story she'd listened to on the ramparts of Dinas Emrys weeks ago. The night that Trystan had first come back. She could still hear, from the chapel outside, the low rhythmic chant of prayers. She could hear the soft sounds of movement as her companions settled more comfortably in place, and Cabal's softly snoring breaths from the corner where he slept.

One by one, Isolde blocked them out, kept her eyes locked on Trystan's face as she started to speak. "In a time that once was, is now gone forever, and will be again soon, a young woman's lover

was stolen away from her by the Fair Folk to pay the seven years'
tiend to the gods of the earth."

All the time watching Trystan, counting his every slowly
drawn breath, Isolde told the story of the maid's search for her
lost love amidst the cold and winter snows. Of how she'd found
him again, blanched and thin and terribly altered from the man
she'd loved. And of how he'd told her that to win him free of the
Fair Folk, she must pull him down from his fairy mount on the
night of the sacrifice and hold to him tight, no matter how he
changed in her arms.

*"And so she held the serpent fast. And again felt the form in her
arms begin to change, until she held a great, snarling bear in her arms.
The beast struck at her with its claws and roared with rage, and she
could smell the blood of a kill on its mouth and fur. But again she held
fast, and the bear's body began to shift and change.*

*"And then the maid held in her arms a glowing, red-hot iron rod
that burned her arms and hands until she almost screamed aloud with
the pain. But she held in her heart the memory of her love's own face,
the boy she'd grown up with—"*

The men had been listening in silence as Isolde spoke, but
at that Eurig stirred in his place beside her. "Had they grown up
together? You didn't mention that bit."

"Oh, yes." Isolde nodded, not letting herself look up from
Trystan's face. "She'd known him all her life. Since they'd spat
apple seeds at each other across a garden wall. Since she'd cried
to see him taken away to train with the other boys who were to
train for fighting men. Since he'd taught her to throw a knife and
fish for river trout, even though she could never keep quiet and
kept scaring the fish away." Her voice wavered slightly and she
swallowed hard. "Since she'd mended his hurts for him, because
when he went into a fight he hadn't the smallest care for keeping
himself—"

She broke off, drawing in her breath with a sharp gasp, wondering whether she'd only imagined what she'd just felt because
she'd wanted it so desperately. No . . . not just imagining. She

could feel a faint, a very faint prickle of awareness. Of . . . *cold.*
Bone-deep cold that ached like a tooth gone bad.

Isolde drew another shaky breath and turned to Eurig. "Do
you think . . . could you leave me alone with Trystan for a while?"

Eurig looked a bit startled, but he nodded. "If that's what you
want, of course we can. But—" His eyes strayed to the still form
on the bench, a furrow appearing between his brows.

Isolde's every nerve was quivering with a wish to concentrate,
to turn back to Trystan and continue with what she'd been about
to do. But she made herself tear her thoughts away, focus on the
men long enough to say, "Nothing's wrong. And I promise I'll
send for you if . . . if there's any change. It's only that I think I've
a chance of reaching him if we're alone."

She was peripherally aware of Hereric, signing something to
the other three. Of Eurig, Piye, and Daka getting to their feet,
bidding her good night and good luck. Of herself thanking them
and asking them to take Cabal with them as well. Her attention,
though, was already focused on Trystan. And on the stomach-
twisting fear that what she'd felt had only been chance, an ac-
cident of some kind, and that she'd not be able to find that tiny
thread of awareness again.

When the door had closed behind the men, though, she
closed her eyes and reached out towards Trystan in her mind.
When Kian had asked her to see Trystan back at Dinas Emrys,
she'd had a brief indistinct glimpse of him. She ought to—had
to—be able to break through to him again now.

At first she met with only the familiar blackness, and her
heart lurched sickeningly against her ribs. But then she felt again
that faint, featherlight brush of awareness, growing into . . . *cold.*
She was cold to the bone, and locked somewhere in the—

The thread of awareness broke and snapped off.

Isolde drew in her breath and began again. Slowly, carefully . . . reaching . . . stretching out a hand to—

Unable to think. Unable even to move. Cold. Trapped somewhere
where there was nothing but the dark and the—

But before she could try to speak to Trystan, in whatever place he now lay, before she could try to reach him in the midst of the cold prison that held him fast, the connection snapped again, leaving her bone weary and utterly alone.

Isolde closed her eyes, and this time she didn't even have to conjure Morgan's image from the darkness. Her grandmother's face was simply there, bright against the blackness of her closed lids.

Please. Isolde wasn't even sure whether she actually believed this might do good. Only that she was desperate enough to try. *If you've ever helped me before, help me now. Show me what I'm not thinking of. Please, show me what I haven't yet tried.*

But she hardly needed to ask. Even as the words formed in her mind, the answer was there: a faint, distant echo of a nearly forgotten day that went through her like water rising from the rain-soaked ground and spreading from the roots to the leaves of a tree.

He almost never smiles, she had said.

Then her grandmother's voice, unaccustomedly soft, *It's because he's no one in his life to love him.*

And her own child-self's answer: *I do. I will.*

Whether this was Morgan's answer or an answer to prayer— or both—Isolde didn't know. Or for now, especially care. She didn't let herself hesitate or even stop to think. Her hands were shaking, making her fingers clumsy, but she slipped off her boots, her stockings, untied the laces of her gown, and pulled it over her head. Finally, she stood in only her thin linen shift, shivering a little, the chill night air raising goose flesh along her bare arms. She drew back Trystan's blankets and then, moving slowly and very carefully so that she wouldn't jar his broken ribs, eased herself down to lie at his side.

He stirred just a little at her touch, and Isolde held herself very still. Then, slowly, slowly, she inched closer on the narrow wooden sleeping bench, fitting herself next to him so that she lay curled against his side, her arms about him and her head resting on his shoulder. His skin felt frighteningly chill against hers, and

Isolde suppressed another shiver as she drew the blankets back up, covering them both.

She closed her eyes, and at first met with only the solid blackness again. But then she felt it. A faint, faint glimmer of connection in her mind. A sense of cold that seemed to leech into her very bones.

Isolde held her breath, afraid that this fragile thread of awareness would snap and leave her as helpless as before. She could feel the beat of Trystan's heart under her cheek, the shallow rise and fall of his breath. She closed her eyes, trying to slow her own heartbeat, to match her breathing to his, all the while holding tight to the tiny, pinprick channel of awareness that had opened between them. His chest felt smooth and cool as polished stone against her cheek and the palm of her hand.

Isolde fitted herself as closely to him as she could, still mindful of the broken ribs and the bandaged wound in his side. She imagined the warmth flowing out of her own body and into his, like a hundred tiny hands, pulling him back from the place where he was locked in the cold and the dark. Pulling him back to her, back towards life.

Then she began, her voice just a whisper in the dark, silent room. "In a time that once was, is now gone forever, and will be again soon, there was a girl who had lost everyone she'd ever loved. She'd grieved so many times that she even made herself forget her whole past, because it hurt too much to remember everyone who was gone. But even that didn't help, because she never really stopped looking back. And by the time she was grown, she never wanted to love anyone, ever again, because it hurt too much to think of losing anyone more. And then, by a wonder, one of those she'd thought lost forever came back to her. A boy she'd known when she was young, now grown into a man. And they set out on a journey together across lands she'd never been.

"And for most of the journey she was frightened and hungry and cold and exhausted, because they met with dangers she'd not even imagined. But at the same time she was . . . in a way, she was happier than she'd ever been. Just because she was with him. Because he made her laugh, and he took care of her when she was hurt and held her when she cried, and because he knew her better than anyone else had, ever in her life. And—"

Isolde's whisper cracked, and she squeezed her eyes more tightly shut before going on. "And he kept her safe, even if it meant getting hurt himself. And when she was with him, she started to look forward instead of back into the past. She stopped missing herself the way she'd been years ago, and started to be glad of where she was now. But all the time, she kept telling herself, *No, no, you can't love him again. You'll only break your heart.*

"And so she left him, because she didn't want him to be hurt any more than he already had been. And because . . . because she was afraid as well." Despite her best efforts, Isolde could feel hot tears spilling out from under her closed lids and onto Trystan's chest, but she went on, her voice barely a breath of sound now in the dark room. "But then he was hurt again—almost killed. And she realized that trying to push him out of her life would be like ripping the warp threads from a weaving on the loom. And that a part of her would die if she never got the chance to tell him what she felt."

Isolde stopped, trying again to imagine warmth flowing from her to Trystan, trying with every part of her will, with every fiber in her body, to speak to him through the tiny channel that had opened between them before, to where she could still feel him lying, prisoned in the cold and the dark. And then she whispered, "I love you, Trys. Please, please don't die."

Chapter Nineteen

ISOLDE DRIFTED UP FROM A wonderful dream towards the surface of waking. Then remembrance tore through her and her eyes flew open. It wasn't a dream. She'd somehow fallen asleep the night before and was still lying at Trystan's side, her body fitted close against his. She felt a moment's heart-stopping panic as she realized that she could no longer feel the beat of his heart under her cheek. And then she realized that that was because he'd shifted, drawing slightly away—likely that was what had wakened her—and that his eyes were open, staring at her as though he'd never seen her before.

Isolde stared at him with the same blank astonishment, for a moment unable to trust her own eyes, unable to let herself think that this was anything but part of the dream. And then remembrance of another kind ripped through her as she realized that she was lying in Trystan's bed with her arms about him, dressed in nothing but her thin linen undershift.

She slid from under the blankets, jumped up, snatched up her gown, and yanked it over her head, pulling it on with such haste that she felt one of the seams give.

When she looked back at Trystan, her breathing gradually slowing, she saw that his eyes had drifted closed. For a moment, she wondered whether she'd imagined his ever having woken at all. Then his lids flickered open again, his brow furrowing as though the pale dawn light filtering in through the window hurt his eyes.

"Isa?"

Isolde had to swallow twice before she could make her voice work. Before she even knew she'd moved, she was kneeling by the bed. She couldn't help reaching out to make sure he was actually there, alive and speaking to her. She touched the back of his hand lightly, smoothed the hair away from his brow. "Yes. I'm here."

Trystan blinked again and turned his head on the pillow just a bit to look at her. His voice sounded hoarse. "I'm not dead, am I?"

Isolde shook her head. "No."

Trystan closed his eyes against the light once again, and then he said, his voice still raspy and faint, "Good. Even in hell death shouldn't feel this bad."

Isolde gave a choked-up laugh, and before she could stop herself she'd again reached to smooth the hair back from his brow. "Next time keep to drinking yourself to death. I can almost guarantee it would hurt less."

One side of Trystan's mouth lifted in a half smile. "I'll keep it in mind." He drew a labored breath, wincing a bit, then: "Isolde?"

"Yes?"

The furrow appeared between his brows again. "What happened? Where—"

"Shhh." Isolde stopped him, lightly squeezing his hand, and spoke above the lump in her throat. "I'll tell you. But later. Now you need to drink something." She reached for the cup on the table beside the bed. "Can you take some water, do you think?"

·   ·   ·

ISOLDE PUSHED OPEN THE DOOR TO Trystan's room in the guest hall. She'd helped Trystan to drink a cupful or two of water, had sat with him even after he'd fallen asleep again because she'd found she couldn't stop watching the steady rise and fall of his breath, the healthy color slowly ebbing back into his face. But when he'd waked again towards afternoon, drunk a cup of broth sent up from the abbey kitchens, and then slept again, Isolde had at last torn herself away and gone to the kitchens herself to join Eurig, Piye, Daka, and Hereric for the evening meal.

She'd sent to them at once, that morning, to let them know Trystan was conscious. But she'd been ravenously hungry— and more than that, she'd wanted to share her brimming thankfulness with someone else, see the certain knowledge that Trystan would live reflected back at her in the eyes of the other four men. The abbey had been quiet, deserted save for the sisters and the travelers come to beg aid. Of Cerdic's army there was no sign—which must mean that the forces of Wessex were still riding in triumph over the scattering remnants of Octa's troops.

Now, returning from the kitchens, Isolde was expecting to find Trystan still asleep. But when she entered his room, she found he was awake—awake and propped up a bit against the pillows on the wooden sleeping bench, supporting his weight on his elbows.

"You shouldn't be sitting up," Isolde said.

Trystan grimaced. "Tell me." He was still bare to the waist, and the bruises on his chest and ribs stood out like angry purple blossoms against his skin. He shifted a bit, the muscles of broad shoulders pulling taut, swore under his breath, and grimaced again. "I woke up a bit ago and you weren't here. I was just trying to decide whether I was losing my mind or if you'd actually ever been here at all when you came in."

He smiled a bit, and Isolde turned away to light the lamp, feeling the blood rise in her cheeks. She had no idea what—if anything—Trystan remembered of the night before. But still, now that the crushing weight of anxiety was lifted from her, she felt unexpectedly shy.

It took her three tries to get a flame started, but at last the lamp was burning, casting its pale yellow glow into the deepening shadows of the room. Isolde looked up to find Trystan watching her, his face unreadable in the dim light, his eyes startlingly blue.

"Isa—what happened?"

"You were hurt. Eurig and the others brought you here." Isolde poured more water into the cup on the bedside table and handed it to Trystan, then settled herself on the low stool at his side. "It's a house of Christian holy women. The abbey of Saint Eucherius."

Trystan took the pottery cup from her absently, but he didn't drink. Instead, his head lifted quickly and he asked, "Eurig? And Hereric? They're all right?"

Isolde nodded. "Safe. All of them. Piye and Daka, as well." She stopped, wondering how she was going to even begin to tell him the rest. Before she could even make a start, though, he let out a breath and said, "I'm glad. But that wasn't what I meant. I meant—" He stopped, drew in his breath, and went he went on, his voice was tight with control. "What in God's name were you thinking of, going off on your own like that? At night—with Fidach and his men out hunting you. And Octa and Cerdic's patrols roaming the area as well? Christ, Isa, you could have been—"

"I know." Isolde stopped him before he could finish. "I know." She pressed her eyes briefly closed. She'd been expecting this—bracing herself for it—ever since Trystan had first woken that morning. And she had sworn to herself that she wasn't going to flinch from telling Trystan the whole. But before she could begin, he said, still in that dangerously calm tone, "Just tell me—did you drug me on purpose so that you could get away? Convince me to take a heavy draft of poppy just so you could get free?"

"Did I—" Isolde's head jerked up and she looked at him, appalled. "Of course not. I know that maybe doesn't make much difference. Since I left anyway. But I would never have done that. Never. It was just that I . . ." She took a steadying breath and made herself meet Trystan's gaze. "I'm sorry, Trys. Truly. You had fallen asleep. And I was sure—almost sure—I could get to this place, and Cerdic, on my own. I knew you'd argue, though, if I told you what I wanted. I knew you'd have kept your word to see me safely the whole way. But this journey had already cost you enough—more than enough. I wanted you to be free to turn around and go back to Hereric and go somewhere—the two of you—where you could be safe."

Trystan had neither spoken nor moved while she spoke. He sat there, looking at her, the untasted water cup still in his hand. Isolde swallowed and went on, determined this time to give him the whole unvarnished truth, regardless of whether or not he ever wanted to speak to her again when she had. Regardless of whether she was inviting him to break her heart all over again.

"And if I'm being completely honest, I wanted . . . I wanted to leave before you could. Because sooner or later you were going to—not that night, I don't mean, but after you'd seen me safely to Cerdic and back. And I . . ." Isolde's chest was starting to ache and her eyes stung, but she ordered herself to go on. "You were the best—the only—true friend I've ever had, Trys. I didn't want to watch you walk away, out of my life for good."

There. Isolde let out her breath. She'd finished. She'd told him the whole. Trystan was still watching her, his face all but expressionless. Then he said, in the same level tone, "That's what you thought I'd do? Walk away and never look back?"

For all his still-muscled calm, there was something in his voice Isolde didn't understand. She shook her head, looking up to meet his eyes, and said, "You did once before, remember?"

"Gods and demons and serpents of hell!" With one sudden, violent movement, Trystan hurled the cup he'd been holding against the opposite wall, where it smashed into fragments, water dripping to pool on the floor. Isolde stared at him in shock, a distant part of her mind registering that she'd known him to lose his temper this way maybe only twice before in all the years she'd known him.

"What would you have had me do? Tell you the truth? Tell you that I'd loved you ever since I could remember? That you were the only good thing that's ever happened to me in my life? Maybe start making up godawful rhymes about love and the angels above? Tell you what it did to me to find you and then have to leave you again? By all that's holy, Isa, you'd just seen your husband killed and his throne taken by his murderer. Do you think I'd have burdened you with what I felt for you as well?"

Trystan drew in a breath and then went on, with only slightly less violence than before, "I'd sooner have crawled naked across a bed of swords than leave you. But I knew Marche would want to settle the score between us—that I'd only be a danger to you if I stayed. And I knew that if I let myself spend another day—Christ, another hour, even—near you, I'd be throwing myself on the ground at your feet, asking—begging—you to let me stay. Even if it meant risking your life."

He stopped, passing a hand across his face. Isolde sat frozen in place, unable to speak, unable even to move. She felt as though a giant hand was wrapped around her chest, wringing the breath from her lungs. Trystan looked at her, his voice softening a bit at the expression on her face. "Look, I know that even the thought of the two of us together is . . . impossible. Unimaginable. A woman in your place and someone like me. And even apart from that—God, I'm like a walking curse. Look at Kian. Look at Hereric. Even if things were different—if I hadn't—"

He stopped. "Even if I weren't an outlaw and a mercenary and a Saxon spy, I'd not ask you to come anywhere near me. But all the same—" Trystan shook his head, his blue eyes on hers. "Christ's bleeding wounds, Isa, if anything had happened to you that night when you left me behind in the forest, if you'd been killed, I'd have—"

He was silent so long that Isolde asked, in a voice barely above a whisper, "You'd have what?"

"I don't know." One side of Trystan's mouth tightened in a humorless smile, and he let out a breath, shaking his head again. "I don't know. I was going to say *I'd have put a knife through my chest,* or *kept walking until I got to the sea and thrown myself in.*" He pushed a hand through his hair and made a sound, half disgusted, half angry. "I suppose I couldn't have left Hereric on his own like that. But still—" His hand lifted as though about to touch her cheek, but then he seemed to check himself, his fingers tightening and his arm falling back to his side. He shifted, wincing at the movement. "I'd have wanted to—powers of hell, I'd have wanted to."

Isolde sat motionless, still frozen in place. She tried to make her mind work, to think of something to say, but the effort was like trying to catch hold of fog in both hands. Before she even knew what she'd done, she was on her feet and out of the door, and then she was almost running blindly down the passage.

She'd no idea where she was going—she'd no coherent thoughts at all. She felt as though she'd been plunged abruptly from darkness into painfully dazzling light. Or maybe from light into dark. She passed through another door and found herself outside, in the abbey courtyard, where she stood, her whole body shaking as she drew in gulps of the cool, grass-scented spring air. Then, when she no longer felt as though she were trying to breathe underwater, she closed her eyes and played out every part of the journey from Dinas Emrys in her mind. Every moment, every day.

She thought about herself, frightened all the time of letting herself care anything for Trystan. Afraid of loving him, afraid of breaking her own heart. And yet never so much as wondering what he felt about her. Not even once. And then she thought about Madoc, whose proposal she'd promised to answer if and when she returned. And about Camelerd, the land hers by birth, the land she was bound by duty to protect. She thought about King Goram of Ireland.

She thought about Con, lying cold in his grave in Cornwall.

And about her tiny stillborn girl. And about waking that morning in Trystan's bed, with her head on his shoulder and her arms around him and his body warm and solid against hers. About the dream she'd had the night before, and feeling absolutely safe, as though she'd finally come home.

I know that even the thought of the two of us together is . . . impossible.

Plainly, Trystan didn't remember what had happened the night before, or anything about what she'd told him. That made everything at once easier and harder still.

She stood in the dark, silent courtyard listening to the abbey sisters singing the evening prayers in the chapel for a long, long time. She wondered for a moment whether all those prayers were ever answered. Whether she would get an answer, if she closed her eyes now and asked for another sign from whatever had sent her the story she'd told for Trystan the night before.

She didn't ask, though. Maybe some part of her knew that her choice had already been made, her way ahead fixed and immovable as the ending of Taliesin's tale. Maybe that was an answer in itself.

Instead, she found herself closing her eyes and whispering into the surrounding dark, as passionately as she'd ever asked anything in her life, "Please, let me be brave enough for this."

Then she drew in her breath, opened her eyes, and turned back towards the guest hall.

TRYSTAN LAY ON HIS BACK, STARING up at the ceiling and trying not to think. Which was more or less a laughably futile effort. He felt as though Isolde's words were being pounded into his ears like wooden tent stakes. *You were the best—the only—true friend I've ever had.*

Yes, right. She'd saved his life as well. As hazy as his memories of the last days were—and he wasn't even sure how long he'd been in this place—he knew he'd not be alive at all if not for Isolde. And in payment he'd thrown all that at her.

Trystan let out a disgusted breath, seeing again the stricken look in her gray eyes, the way the blood had drained from her already pale face, leaving her white to the lips.

Well done. Making her cry had been an especially good touch.

It didn't help, either, that every time he closed his eyes he saw Isolde as she'd looked that morning, sound asleep beside him, her black hair tumbling all around her face and her body warm and soft against his. Or that every time that happened, every single smallest twinge of desire he'd suppressed over the last weeks—or years—jumped out and hit him collectively with the force of another couple of broken ribs.

The whole goddamn bed still smelled like her, too—sweet and fresh, a compound of whatever it was she used to wash her hair and something unique to her.

Gritting his teeth, he curled himself forward and into a sitting position, swearing as every muscle in his body seemed to scream in protest. But for all that, it wasn't as bad as last time. The stiffening bruises had started to relax their hold. When he'd managed to drag himself upright, he was breathing hard, but that was all. A day or two more and he might actually be able to walk.

Trystan closed his eyes. Breath of the saints. If he'd any shred of decency left, he'd haul himself out of this bed, here and now, and be gone before Isolde could return. Whatever she'd said before, she'd hardly want him anywhere near her now. Trystan shifted again and then froze as the door of the room swung open again.

Isolde stood very still in the doorway, then stepped inside.

Chapter Twenty

ISOLDE STOOD IN THE DOORWAY, looking across at Trystan. While he'd lain unconscious, she'd watched him, memorized every lean, chiseled line of his face until she'd have said she knew it as well as her own. Now, though, with Trystan looking back at her, she felt as though she were seeing him for the first time. She'd planned what she was going to say—practiced saying it over and over again in her mind on her way here. But as her eyes met Trystan's, the words completely deserted her, leaving her standing in silence, as frozen as before.

Finally, Trystan cleared his throat. "I'm sorry."

Whatever Isolde had been expecting him to say, it wasn't that, and astonishment broke her moment's paralysis. "You're sorry?" she repeated. "Trys, I was just standing here wondering how you can possibly not hate me after all that's happened to you because of me. And you say *you're* sorry?"

"Yes, well." Trystan gave her a faint, crooked smile. "It takes a lot to change my mind." Then he stopped, sobering. "Come over here."

Isolde felt her heart lurch and then quicken. "Why?"

Trystan let out a breath, part exasperated, part a short laugh. "Because if someone put a knife to my throat right now, I might—possibly—manage to drag myself out of bed and walk across the room to where you're standing. But I doubt I'd have breath enough to speak when I got there. And I'd rather have you closer than a room's length away to say this."

Slowly, Isolde crossed the room, sat down on the wooden stool at the bedside. Trystan had pulled himself upright enough that she had to tilt her head back slightly to look up at him. He was silent a long moment before he spoke, just looking at her, and then he shook his head and said, softly, "God, Isa." He pushed a hand through his hair. "I thought I'd gotten over thinking about you all the time, you know that? Locked you away with the part of my past that was over and done. But then, when I saw you again, six months ago, standing in the doorway of that filthy prison cell, it was as though—" He stopped, shook his head again, and let out a breath. "It's too late for me. I can't imagine not loving you. Nothing you say now is going to alter that. So just tell me what you need from me. If you want me to stay with you, I will, and I swear on my life I'll never mention this night—never so much as speak the word *love* to you again. If you want me to go, I'll leave. Whatever happens next, the choice is yours."

Isolde looked into Trystan's eyes, the startlingly clear blue eyes of the boy she'd grown up with. The eyes of a mercenary, an outlaw, a former slave. A Saxon spy and the grandson of a Saxon king. She drew in her breath and said, "Marry me."

For a half heartbeat, Trystan's face was absolutely blank. Then he passed a hand across the back of his neck and stared at her. "*What* did you say?"

Isolde took another unsteady breath. "I said marry me." She smiled a bit, one sided, looked down at her own hands and then back up at Trystan again. "Though I should probably have added a 'please.'"

Her smile faded, though, and she went on, part, at least,

of the speech she'd practiced all the way from the courtyard out-side coming back to her. "You said that the two of us togeth-er was impossible—a woman in my place, and someone like you. But that's not true. Or if it is, it's the other way round from what you meant. You've never told me what happened after Camlann, but I don't have to know. I don't have to know what else you've done these last seven years. I know you. And I know you're—" Her voice wavered, but she made herself go on, the words com-ing in a tumbled rush. "You're the best man I've ever known. And I don't think I deserve to have you love me that way—the way you said you do. But if you do, I love you the same. I always have—I must have been in love with you from the time I was six years old. Part of me didn't want to, because . . . because everyone I've ever loved has died." She swallowed. "And the thought of loving you still scares me to death, because I do know you. And I know you'll never just sit back and stay out of danger and keep yourself safe. But at the same time—" She stopped, feeling tears pricking behind her eyes. She shook her head. "I do know you, Trys. And I know you're the only man I would have for my husband. If you still want me."

"If I still—" Trystan shook his head helplessly. "God, Isa," he said again. "But you don't—you can't—"

Isolde reached out, stopping him, putting her fingers across his lips. Her heart was still beating quickly, but she felt as though she'd crossed a fast-moving river to safety on the opposite shore. All doubts behind her now. "I can. I do."

"I—" Trystan took her hand, wrapping his fingers around hers. He looked down a long moment, at their joined hands, resting on the blankets between them, and then he gave a shaky laugh and said, "I keep thinking I'm going to wake up and find I'm dreaming this." He looked up at her. "Did you really just ask me if I'd marry you?"

Isolde smiled, and the movement made one single tear escape her brimming eyes. She wiped it away, though, with the back of her hand and nodded.

Trystan looked at her a long moment, and then, very lightly, he raised his free hand and very lightly brushed it across her cheek. His eyes were the color of a clear morning sky. He said, very quietly, "I would love that."

There are three fountains
In the mountain of roses,
Each, I pledge to you.
One of love, to drink deeply together,
The second of desire, to trail our hands in its heated flow,
The third of fidelity, that quenches our thirst
When all other waters fail.

We are young; we are old.
In heaven, in earth, at the end,
In straits, in expanse, in form,
In body, in blood, in soul,
In the valleys and mountains, under the stars

"Thou art always, husband."
"Thou art always, wife."

WIFE. TRYSTAN HEARD HIMSELF SPEAK THE word. He looked down at their hands, bound together with the thread of ribbon Isolde had taken from the girdle of her gown. He could feel the sweet sting of the knife mark on his palm, fitted against Isolde's own cut hand. *In body, in blood, in soul.* He held himself utterly still, afraid to move. Knowing he should. Knowing he shouldn't be ignoring the voice in the back of his head that said he couldn't—shouldn't—be here. Knowing that there was no possible way he was going to be able to keep this.

I said marry me. Though I should probably have added a please.
She'd said it with a smile and a look in her eyes that made
her so beautiful it actually hurt. And he'd wanted to say yes to
her—Jesus God, he'd wanted to—with a force that still made
his chest ache. The wave of longing had almost choked him.
Maybe making her happy now would make up for whatever
happened after tonight.

She did look happy. There were tears sparkling in the lashes
of her wide gray eyes, but she looked up at him and smiled. The
sheer shining gladness in her smile made him feel like he'd been
kicked in the chest.

And it terrified the hell out of him.

Trystan cleared his throat. "You can't be this happy just to be
marrying me."

Isolde shook her head. She smiled again, the tears still brimming in her eyes. "Trys, I would be this happy just to know that
you're still here with me, still *alive*. Marrying you is—"

She stopped, shook her head again. Then she leaned forward,
their joined hands still between them, and pressed her mouth
against his. Her lips were warm and soft and impossibly sweet,
but he made himself draw back, before the last lingering remnants of his self-control could entirely shatter apart. His heart
was hammering, and he had to hold still a moment while he tried
to remember how to breathe. "I'm not sure . . . I'm in the best of
shape for a wedding night."

Isolde turned away to cup her hands about the single lamp's
flame. But before she blew it out, she turned and gave him another smile over her shoulder. The kind of smile she'd given him
in every impossible fantasy he'd ever had, waking or asleep. Except that this time it was—merciful God—real.

And then she blew out the lamp, darkness falling across the
room like a sword stroke, and he heard her whisper, the smile still
in her voice, "I'm sure we'll manage somehow."

•   •   •

HE KISSED HER AS SHE SLIPPED into the bed beside him. Kissed her as though she were both the only light on a dark path and the only warmth on a cold night, his hands sliding lightly across her throat to tangle in her hair. It was the softest, sweetest kiss. The pressure of his mouth was dizzyingly gentle and tender. But before Isolde could move towards him, he drew away again, holding her at arm's length. She heard him draw an unsteady breath.

"Isa, I can't—" Maybe it was the utter darkness that made his voice sound so different, low and shaky. "You know I love you. And I want you so much I can't breathe. But if I start kissing you again I won't be able to stop. And I'm afraid—" He stopped. "I'm afraid I'm going to hurt you—do something that will remind you of—"

"You won't." Isolde reached for his hand, found it in the darkness and threaded her fingers through his. She didn't know whether she had—or would ever—forgive Marche, as Mother Berthildis had said. And just for a moment, at the thought of his name, she felt his presence move into the room—shadowy and indistinct, as though reflected in rippling water. But the hate—both for him, and for herself—was gone, the bleeding wound inside her still healed and finally clean. The abbess had been right about that.

And, with Trystan's hand still warm on her bare skin, the fingers of his other hand twined with her own, she pushed all thought of Marche, all memory away—easily, this time, and without any struggle. Pushed it away to the place where she could bear to hold it, closed and locked the door. "You won't," she said again.

ISOLDE WOKE TO THE ROSY GLOW of dawn filtering through the room's single narrow window. Her head was on Trystan's shoulder, and her curled hand rested on his chest. For a moment, she lay absolutely still, unwilling to let go of the moment, unwilling to let anything dislodge the memory of the night before. The memory of another of those moments when time had seemed to stop, the whole world balancing on in indrawn breath before it shattered into a hundred fragments, swirled, and then slowly drifted back together, leaving her whole, the same and yet also forever—and miraculously—changed.

Trystan's breathing now was even and slow, but as soon as she stirred, his arms tightened around her.

"Awake?"

Isolde nodded, then drew away a little, propping herself up on one elbow so that she could look down at him. She thought his eyes looked tired and a little shadowed in the pale gray light, and she put her hand on his cheek, a prick of concern piercing the rosy glow of her own happiness.

"Didn't you sleep?"

He shrugged. Smiled up into her eyes. "A bit. But I've done nothing but sleep for the past—God, I don't even know how long."

"Three days."

"There you are, then." He raised a hand to smooth a tangle of hair back from her face and smiled again, a slow, one-sided smile that stopped her heart. "I don't mind watching you sleep, though."

Isolde reached out and, very lightly, as she had once before, traced a line with her fingertips from his brow to cheek to jaw. Trystan let out a breath and caught her hand. Then he said, his eyes still on hers, "What are you thinking?"

"I was thinking—" Isolde stopped. When she went on, her voice was a whisper. "I was thinking that sometimes I've wished I could go back—back to the time before Camlann, and to being myself, the way I was then. But now I wouldn't—not for anything. Because this—right now—is the most perfect thing that's ever happened to me."

For a long moment, Trystan was silent, simply looking at her.

The way he'd looked at her the day before, when he'd told her he loved her ever since he could remember. As though his whole heart was there, in his intensely blue eyes. He started to speak, stopped, and then wordlessly pulled her down to him, into his arms, and when he finally spoke his voice was low and muffled by her hair. "Warn me when you're going to say something like that, all right?"

Chapter Twenty-one

ISOLDE GLANCED UP FROM THE wound she was stitching—a nasty sword cut in the arm of the big, blond-haired man before her—and caught Trystan watching her. He was sitting a little distance away on a makeshift seat fashioned from a fallen log, with Cabal lying at his feet amidst a group of Cerdic's fighting men who were watching a game of dice, trading news and friendly challenges and insults.

The day was warm, the air smelling of freshly turned earth and the wild meadow sweet flowers that were blooming on the hill. Isolde had already taken off her cloak, and still the noonday sun above felt hot on her skin, making her halfway wish she'd chosen to work inside one of the tents instead of out here, in the open air of the encampment's practice yard.

More than a week had passed since the battle between Cerdic and Octa, and some of the men wounded in the fighting had begun to trickle back to Cerdic's encampment on the hills surrounding the abbey. Cerdic himself had still not returned, but one of his chiefs had sent a message through Mother Berthildis to Isolde, asking for her skills as a healer among the wounded and sick.

Isolde had agreed readily, thankful for the chance of hearing word of the fighting that was still going on—ever more distantly, now, as Octa and his army fled back towards Kent. And the news she'd had was good; Octa had lost nearly a third of his fighting men in the trap Cerdic had sprung on him the week before, and the remains of his forces were continuing to scatter in the face of Cerdic's advance.

Isolde knew she couldn't yet count that her own undertaking had succeeded in full. Cerdic had made her no promises about making alliance with Britain. But at the very least, the threat Octa posed to Britain had been considerably reduced. And she was thankful, in a way, that she could do nothing—go nowhere—until Cerdic himself returned to say whether he would agree to talks of peace with Madoc and the king's council.

Her eyes found Trystan again, leaning back in his place among the other men, booted feet stretched out in front of him, arms crossed on his chest, ostensibly joining in the conversation going on around him. Isolde knew he was giving the men's talk only half his attention, though.

As though feeling her gaze on him, Trystan looked up and smiled at her in a way that made Isolde's heart squeeze tight in her chest and carried her back to the night before. Back to Trystan drawing her mouth to his and kissing her so tenderly, slowly, and almost reverently, in the way that never, ever failed to make her pulse skip a beat and her very bones seem to melt. As though she'd just given him a gift indescribably precious and sweet.

Now, meeting Trystan's eyes, Isolde felt a blush of color rise to her cheeks, but she gave him an answering smile, again grateful that for now, at least, they didn't even have to speak of what would happen when—eventually—they had to leave this place.

"Thank you, lady." The voice of the man whose wound she was stitching made her jerk her attention back to him and the cut in his arm.

"You're welcome."

Isolde hadn't expected Cerdic to speak of their bargain, or of the role she'd played in the battle. One thing to rely on a woman to gain the upper hand over Octa and the Kentish forces—another to admit it to his men. But plainly a rumor at least of Isolde's own part had spread even down to Cerdic's infantrymen. There were more than two dozen wounded here, and all of them crowding round her, anxious for Isolde to see to their hurts. Even the ones whose wounds were already healing well wanted her to touch the bandages for luck.

Fortunate, in a way, that she'd passed beyond the point where she could be surprised by anything—anything at all that happened now. If she'd seen in the scrying waters that she'd end this journey surrounded by a group of Saxon foot soldiers begging her reverently to salve their wounds and touch their bandaged legs and arms, she'd have thought it another completely fantastical joke on the part of whatever controlled the Sight.

The sun was sinking in the horizon when at last she'd finished and turned away from the last man. She and Trystan left the camp, walking back towards the abbey through the deepening twilight. Cabal raced ahead of them through the tall grass, came bounding back, and then swerved to race ahead again. Trystan still winced a bit when a movement jarred his healing ribs or stretched the wound in his side. But his long strides kept pace with hers easily, and he climbed the hills without any change in his breathing, one arm resting across Isolde's shoulders.

In the purple shadows of the hills, with the rays of the setting sun casting a last, lingering glow over the valley floor, the stolidly built abbey walls were transformed to something almost otherworldly. Like one of the fairy dwellings that appeared at the hour of change only once in a hundred years. Or a shrine to the old gods of the rocks and streams and hills, instead of the new God of the Christ.

When they'd come nearly to the halfway mark between the abbey and Cerdic's camp, Trystan broke the silence between them to ask, "What did that man mean—the one with the broken leg—who said they'd never have broken Octa's shield wall and set him on the run if not for you?"

Isolde knew at once which man Trystan meant, though at the question she realized abruptly that if Cerdic's armies knew the truth of what she'd done, Trystan still knew nothing at all. She'd not told him before—not because she'd wanted to keep anything from him. More because she'd not wanted to live over that endless night she'd spent in Octa's camp again, even in thought. The whole of it felt like a nightmare, so far separate from the rest of the past days as to seem scarcely real.

Now, turning to look up at Trystan, Isolde hesitated a long moment. Trystan's eyes moved over her face, reading her expression, and he cocked an eyebrow at her.

"I'm going to like it that much, am I?"

Isolde laughed shakily despite herself. "Something like that. But I suppose I'd better tell you the whole."

So, standing with him in the flower-scented darkness beyond the abbey, Isolde told Trystan everything. About drugging Cerdic's guards to gain admittance to his rooms. About the bargain she'd struck with him, about the nighttime walk across the countryside to Octa's camp, about persuading the guard to let her inside to speak with Octa himself. Her voice wobbled a little, but she went on, told him about meeting with Octa. About the fire and the smoke and being trapped in the prisoner's hut, and about Fidach's unbelievable appearance in time to save her life.

She told him everything. And when she'd finished, Trystan stood in silence, just looking at her, for a long time. Then, finally, he shook his head, and said, "You . . . Holy mother of Christ, Isa. And you tell me I take insane chances with my life."

Isolde smiled just a little. "And so you do."

"You actually walked into Octa of Kent's war tent and—" Even in the rapidly fading light, Isolde saw the unwilling smile beginning to tug at the corners of his mouth. "And convinced him you were Cerdic's cast-off slave girl and about to bear Cerdic's child?"

Isolde nodded, and Trystan shook his head helplessly and started to laugh. And then he stopped, cupped her cheek with one hand, and said, his voice turning suddenly husky and low, "God, I love you."

And then, all at once, Isolde found herself turning to him, clinging to him, hiding her face against the breast of his linen shirt. "I was so frightened, Trys. More terrified than I've ever been." She swallowed hard. "I thought you were as good as dead—that even if I lived through the night, I'd get back to the abbey and find you were gone."

She felt his arms come around her, warm and solid and strong, and he held her tightly while her whole body shook with the memory. And then, when the fit of shivering had passed, he said, his arm still around her shoulders, "I . . . heard you. That sounds crazy, I know. But I had—I was in this place where everything had just . . . stopped. And then I heard your voice. I couldn't tell what you were saying. I just knew I . . . had to come back, that's all." Trystan shook his head. "And then the next I remember is waking and finding you there in the bed with me, sound asleep." From somewhere nearby came the soft call of a night bird, and Trystan smiled a bit. "I thought I really must have died."

Isolde tipped her head back to look up at him through the gathering dusk. "You don't remember what I said?"

Trystan shook his head.

So Isolde told him that, too, standing with her arms about him as she had that night, feeling again the beat of his heart under her cheek. Though the beat was strong and steady now, and his arms came up to hold her. When she'd finally finished, he was silent a long time, and then he held her off at arm's length, looking down at her. It was too dark by now to see his face clearly, but his hand came up, lightly touching her brow, her temple, her hair, as though he were still unsure whether he was awake or dreaming, and half afraid she'd vanish at the touch. Finally he said, "I don't deserve you."

Isolde captured his hand. It was his left hand; she could feel the disfigured fingers, the rough edges of the scars. She turned the hand, raised it, and pressed her lips lightly against his palm. Then she smiled up at him. "I think you do."

And then an odd jolt of fear struck her seemingly from nowhere—struck with a force that was almost a physical pain—and she had a sudden flash of the vision she'd glimpsed before leaving for Octa's camp. Trystan and Marche, locked in a desperate battle with swords.

She blinked to clear the memory from her eyes. Whether the Sight had shown her *will be* or only *may be*, she couldn't know. She'd made peace with that, at least, about the workings of the Sight.

But she drew Trystan's head down, kissed him almost fiercely, and said, "Just remember it and keep yourself safe, that's all."

IT HAD TO BE NEAR MIDNIGHT. Trystan could hear the call of a nightingale in the orchard outside the guest hall. He lay on his back, with Isolde curled close beside him, the slender shape of her a now familiar warmth. Even if he'd dared let himself fall asleep more often than he did, he wasn't sure he'd have wanted to. He wouldn't have wanted to miss a moment, a single heartbeat, of these nights.

Tonight, though, he knew by Isolde's breathing she wasn't asleep either.

"Isa?"

She stirred, turning her head, the soft cloud of her hair whispering against his shoulder. "Yes?"

"Are you . . ." He stopped, hesitating, knowing she deserved to have him ask this, but unable to find the right words. "Are you sure this—the two of us, like this—is what you want? Are you sure you're all right?"

She didn't even hesitate. God help him. Just lifted her head and pressed her mouth lightly to his, one hand reaching to touch his face. The warm sweetness of her lips was almost enough to make him forget where he was, the cool touch of her fingertips on his skin—Christ, it was almost enough to make him forget his own name. Then she pulled away just enough to whisper, "Of course I'm sure."

She held back, though, when he started to draw her towards him again.

"Are you sure *you're* really all right, Trys? I don't want to hurt you, and—don't laugh. I'm a healer and it's not that long ago that you had two broken ribs and—"

She broke off as Trystan pulled her head down, stopping her mouth with his. He felt her melt against him, like sweet living fire in his arms, but he made himself draw back and say, "I wasn't laughing at you. I was laughing because you may be a healer—but right now you're a healer without any clothes on, sharing my bed. And you expect me to have wits enough to put two coherent words together and answer questions about broken ribs?"

They were both laughing as he kissed her again, but then he stopped and drew back, one hand trailing lightly from her cheek to her neck to her bare shoulder and down, tracing her body's perfect, delicate curve. Her skin was impossibly smooth and soft. Holy gods, he didn't want this ever to end. Or if this was a dream, he didn't ever want to wake.

"What's that line in the old stories about the Land of Youth?"

"An earthly paradise is the land, delightful beyond all dreams. Fairer than aught thine eyes have ever seen." Her voice was low and sweet and sounded a little breathless in the dark.

Trystan drew her mouth back to his, and then said, his own voice cracking on a husky whisper, "If this isn't paradise, I think it's the closest I'm ever likely to come."

ISOLDE WOKE WITH A START AND automatically put out a hand to reach for Trystan. In the days following the worst of the fighting between Octa and Cerdic, the abbey guest hall had been crowded with those seeking refuge within the abbey walls. Isolde had offered to give up her own room so that it might be put to use by some of those taking flight, and Mother Berthildis had accepted, though she'd then fixed her keen black gaze on Isolde's face.

"I thank you for it," the abbess said, "for it's quite true we can do with the extra space. Every time I visit the abbey kitchens I expect to see an entire family taken up residence in the soup tureen. But if you're intending to share a bed with that young man whom you've pulled back from death, you'd assuage my conscience considerably if you'd tell me that I may add prayers for your marriage to my list of supplications tonight."

Isolde thought of the night she'd stood in the courtyard outside the chapel, listening to the nuns chanting their evening prayers, and asked for courage to face the choice she'd in her heart already made. Then she'd smiled at Mother Berthildis and answered, "I told you before that your God may not mean to me what He does to you. But you've promised me your prayers all the time I've sheltered here. And I've had more escapes from danger and death than should be possible in anyone's life. And I've seen Trystan healed as well. So I do thank you. Truly. I would welcome either your Christian God's blessing or yours."

The abbess nodded and then smiled, wrinkles fanning out across her yellowed face. "Well, I'm glad to hear you're properly wedded. Though truth be told, I'd not have blamed you too harshly either way. He's handsome, your young man." She shook her head. "Ah, well. I knew long before I was your age that I'd best devote my life to Christ, because for certain no living man would want to wake and find me in his bed."

Her voice had been dryly amused, but Isolde thought she saw a faintly wistful look in the old woman's small black eyes. As though picking up the thought, though, Mother Berthildis had straightened her round shoulders and said with her usual briskness, "Of course, marriage to Christ doesn't leave you with a man's muddy boot prints all over your clean floor. Or with another babe in your belly year after year until you're worn out before you're thirty. I'm well content with my lot." She'd firmed up her mouth, but then softened slightly as she looked at Isolde. "I will keep the both of you in my prayers, though."

In the nearly three weeks, now, that she'd slept beside Trystan, Isolde had grown used to waking when he moved. She always knew when he was dreaming because he would mutter or twist in sleep. She could hardly ever distinguish the words of what he said. The words were too low and indistinct, and usually in the Saxon tongue. He almost never woke, but he usually quieted at her touch. She would put her arms about him and curl up close against his side until his ragged breathing steadied and she no longer felt the frantic hammer of his heart against her breast. She wasn't sure, either, whether he remembered the dreams the next morning. If he did, he never spoke of them.

Now, though, her fingers met only empty space on Trystan's side of the bed, and she sat up quickly, pushing her hair out of her eyes. This, too, had happened once before. She'd come awake sometime in the darkest watches of the night to find Trystan standing absolutely still, back against the opposite wall, his every muscle rigid as stone and his breathing quick and hard. She wasn't sure whether he'd been dreaming still, or half awake, but he'd let her draw him back to bed, and as soon as she'd lain down beside him he'd fallen into a deep—dreamless—sleep.

Now, turning to search the darkened room, Isolde found him standing in the shadows under the room's single narrow window. He was standing absolutely motionless, and yet his whole body looked braced, the broad muscles of his back and shoulders tensed in the faint, pale threads of moonbeams that were the only light.

Isolde swung her legs out of bed, shivering a bit as her bare feet touched the cold flagstone floor. She crossed to touch Trystan's arm lightly, as she had before, and said softly, "Trys?"

Before, she'd only had to touch him, speak his name to have him relax enough that she could bring him back to the bed. This time, though, he jerked violently away as soon as her fingers brushed his skin, whirling to seize her arm in an iron hard grip, dragging her forward and then spinning, pinning her between him and the wall. The movement caught Isolde off balance, knocking the breath out of her as her back struck the wall with bruising force. Not that it would have made a difference if she'd been prepared. At any time, Trystan would be able to overpower her easily if he tried.

The room was too dark for her to see his face, but she could hear his harsh, ragged breathing, smell the faint salt tang that told her he was covered in cold sweat. His fingers dug painfully into her shoulders and she thought for a moment that he was going to slam her into the wall again. For a moment, she thought of what she'd been thinking to tell him in the morning, and her heart started to hammer because she knew there was absolutely nothing she could do to stop him breaking her skull open against the wall if he didn't wake in time.

Instead, though, he flung her halfway across the room, so that the frame of the hard wooden bed caught her in the ribs, making her gasp aloud. She was out of his reach, though. She had a choice. She could sit here, not go near him again, and wait for him to wake on his own. Or she could leave the room entirely, seek a bed in one of the novices' cells or another room of the guest lodgings—several of them empty, now, as the fighting grew distant and the refugees began to gather their belongings and return to their homes.

Isolde could leave—and a part of her acknowledged that that would likely be the wisest thing to do. But she didn't hesitate, even as from across the room she caught a word or two—intelligible, this time—of what Trystan was whispering in a voice flat with rage. Isolde drew in her breath, steadied herself against the bed, and then crossed back towards Trystan, this time keeping up a soft, soothing murmur, a string of comforting nonsense words as she moved to lightly touch his wrist again.

"It's all right. I'm here. You're safe. Completely safe."

She felt his muscles bunch and tighten under her hand as before, and braced herself, expecting him to seize her or throw her off again. But then she heard his breath catch and he relaxed, if only a bit. Cautiously, and still murmuring her string of soothing words, Isolde slipped her hand up his arm, eased herself closer until she could put her arms around him. He was damp with sweat, his skin almost as chill as it had been when Eurig and the others had first carried him to the abbey. Isolde felt a convulsive shiver shake him, though he hadn't woken yet.

Still moving carefully and very slowly, Isolde started to draw him back towards the bed. "You must be cold. Come with me, now. Come and get warm."

She managed to get Trystan back to the bed, managed to coax him into lying down under the blankets, and all still without having woken. And when she lay down beside him, he turned to her, gathering her against his chest in his sleep. Isolde didn't sleep again, though, but lay with her eyes wide open, staring unseeingly into the darkened room and wondering how she could possibly have been so stupidly, utterly blind.

She could see Kian, muddied and with lines of weariness about his mouth, sitting beside her in the woods after the ambush on the journey from Ynys Mon. The echo of Kian's voice was overlaid with a memory of Trystan, drinking himself on board the ship, night after night. *You get yourself stinking drunk if you can before battle,* Kian had said. *And if you can stay drunk enough after the battle's over, you've a chance of keeping the nightmares away.*

DAWN WAS BREAKING WHEN ISOLDE FELT Trystan come awake with a jolt. He lay still without speaking, though, without even moving. Then he turned towards her, raising himself so that he could look down at her. His eyes looked shadowed and faintly bruised, and his face was stubbled with a day's growth of beard.

Wordlessly, he took Isolde's wrist, lifted her arm up to the light. She heard the breath hiss between his teeth, but then, still without speaking, he collapsed back onto the bed, throwing an arm up across his eyes.

Looking down, Isolde realized that darkening bruises had appeared on both her arms, marks of Trystan's grip on her the night before. She silently castigated herself for not thinking of that and putting on something that would have covered them. She likely had bruises on her back and ribs, too, but at least her shift made them invisible for now.

"Trys—" she began. But he cut her off, one arm still across his face.

"Please tell me I didn't hurt you any worse than that."

"You didn't—"

Trystan sat up in a sudden explosion of movement, not even wincing at pain the movement must have caused his still healing ribs. "Powers of hell, Isa, tell me the truth." His voice was almost angry, but then he drew a breath and said, more quietly, "Please. Just tell me. What did I do to you? I remember—"

Isolde put a hand on his arm. "You really didn't, Trys. You . . ." She stopped, searching for the mildest possible way she could describe it. "You were dreaming. I touched your arm, and you took hold of me and pinned me against the wall, that's all."

"That's all?" Trystan pushed a hand through his hair. "Jesus God, Isa, that's all? I could have killed you. I could have woken up and found you dead at my feet. I—" He stopped, dropping his head into his hands. "I told you I didn't deserve you. I should never have—"

"Stop it." Isolde pulled on his arm, trying to make him look up at her, but she might as well have tried to shift stone. Instead, she slipped out of bed, dropping to kneel in front of him so that he was forced to look down into her face. "Don't ever, ever say that."

"Isa—" Trystan reached out as though about to touch her cheek, but then clenched his hand so hard she saw the muscles quiver as he seemed to force his arm back to his side. He closed his eyes as though he couldn't bear to look at her anymore. When he spoke, his voice was rough, almost desperate, though still low with the effort of control. "Please. I . . . couldn't stand it if I ever hurt you again." He looked down at his right hand, held palm up, so that the mark of the handfasting cut—healed now to only a thin pink line—showed plain. "And it's not as though we could ever have—"

Before he could finish, though, an urgent knock sounded on the door. In an instant, Trystan had sprung up, dragging on his breeches and, by force of long practice, reaching automatically for the knife that lay on the room's single wooden table. When Trystan opened the door, though, it was to find Eurig standing on the threshold outside.

Eurig, Piye, and Daka had left the abbey some weeks ago but remained camped in the area, together with the rest of Fidach's band. After hearing Isolde's story of Fidach's saving her on the night of the great battle, first Eurig, Piye, and Daka, and then the rest of the band had combed the area, searching for sign of their chief. They'd searched with a single-minded devotion that made Isolde understand that Fidach could not, after all, owe the allegiance of his men to fear alone. Trystan, as he recovered enough, had joined in the searching as well. But all their efforts had come up empty. After Fidach had parted from Isolde outside the abbey gates, he might truly have vanished among the surrounding forest for all the traces found of him.

Now, despite the nightmare, despite all Trystan had just said to her, Isolde saw him come instantly alert, at the ready for whatever might have brought Eurig here at this hour.

Trystan slipped the knife into his belt and asked, "Something wrong?"

Eurig looked past Trystan and caught sight of Isolde, perched on the edge of the bed and dressed only in her shift and the shawl she'd quickly tugged round her bruised shoulders before Trystan opened the door. Eurig's eyes widened a bit and he gave a start of surprise at sight of her, then quickly turned back to Trystan. Isolde could see his ears reddening, and he cleared his throat twice before answering Trystan's question. "There's a trader out-side—come from the east. Daka stopped him on the road yester-day. Thought you'd maybe want to hear what he has to say."

Isolde could almost feel Trystan deliberately setting all thoughts of the night before aside, summoning the resolve to cast one quick, questioning glance at her. She nodded. "Of course. Go. I'll be fine."

Eurig cleared his throat again and drew out a roll of parch-ment, glancing briefly back at Isolde and then just as quickly away. "Got a message for you, too. Left with the porter at the abbey gates this morning. I said I'd take it, seeing as how I might be seeing you, though I didn't expect—" Eurig stopped, the flush spreading over his face. "Well, anyway, here you are."

Another time Isolde might have smiled at the way he thrust the rolled parchment into her hands without ever actu-ally looking at her again. This morning she only thanked him and drew the shawl a little more closely around her shoulders.

She waited until Eurig and Trystan had gone before breaking the seal on the message and unrolling the parchment. The mes-sage was brief, and in Latin of so fine a hand that she knew it must have been written by a paid scribe.

> To the Lady Isolde of Camelerd:
> Octa has gone to ground among his network of shore forts and sent for reinforcements. Marche's troops are on the move. Send to your king Madoc of Gwynedd to bring every man he can rally, and we may crush the pair of them once and for all.

And it was signed *GEVVISSÆ CYNING*. King Cerdic of Wessex.

Isolde sat looking down at the message for some time. Then she got up, washed her face and hands in cold water from the basin, dressed in her old gown—travel worn but clean now, thanks to the washerwomen of the abbey. She combed and smoothed and braided her hair.

When she went out into the abbey courtyard, she saw Trystan and the others standing grouped about a man she didn't recognize: an immensely fat man with bushy eyebrows and a small, pursed-up red mouth like a baby's. Trystan seemed to be asking the stranger questions, Eurig interjecting a word from time to time as Piye and Daka looked on, dark faces impassive and grave. Hereric was there as well. The big Saxon man had nearly regained the flesh the fever had stripped from him; save for the empty sleeve pinned up over the stump of his arm, he looked almost his old self.

Isolde saw Trystan's head lift as she came into the courtyard, saw his glance move briefly in her direction before turning back to the stranger, so she knew he'd seen her. She knew, too, that he would have motioned her over if she could have done any of them any good, so she sat down on a hard wooden bench that stood against the courtyard's outer wall.

Though many of the refugees had departed by now, the abbey was still bustling and busy. Groups of the black-robed sisters moved this way and that, carrying water, baskets of clean linen, and platters of bread, and in one corner of the court a mother was keeping watch over two black-haired little girls, setting them to spin course woolen thread on drop spindles. The younger of the two kept breaking her thread and getting loudly taunted for it by her sister before their mother stepped in to settle the quarrel.

Isolde watched them until she realized with a start that Trystan had left the group and come to stand beside her. She tipped her head back and looked up at him, shading her eyes against the rising sun at his back. He was outwardly calm, but his face was as grim as ever Isolde had seen it, his eyes distant and hard.

"What is it?" she asked.

"It's about Fidach," Trystan said. "He's a prisoner. Captured by Octa's men."

Isolde nodded. She felt cold begin to spread through her like ripples on a pond—but no surprise—so she supposed a part of her must have expected something of the kind. She sat still and listened while Trystan repeated for her what the trader—the man she'd seen him questioning—had said. That he'd traveled along the old Roman road network into Kent and had heard of a band of Octa's men who traveled with a man bound in chains. A gaunt-bodied man with swirling blue tattoos over his cheekbones.

When Trystan had finished, Isolde closed her eyes and saw Fidach coughing from the smoke of the fire, his face streaked with ashes and his hair singed. *Just because I cultivate the reputation of a man without honor,* he'd said, *it does not follow that I have none.* And she saw again the pitiful, broken man who'd escaped Octa's torture all those years before, only to die at Morgan's hand because she'd deemed that kinder than letting him live.

Even still, there were at least a dozen things Isolde could have said: *You don't know this trader—he may be lying. Fidach is dying in any case. Trys, you're barely recovered yourself.*

She never for a moment actually considered saying any of them, but a horrible, cowardly part of her wished she might have. She did think, though, of what she'd planned to tell Trystan this morning.

Isolde opened her hand and looked down at the cleanly healed scar of the handfasting across her palm. Three weeks since she and Trystan had exchanged that vow. Just time enough for her to be almost entirely sure that the past days' glimmer of a guess was now certainty. And she felt something twist in her chest, tight to the point of breaking at the thought of sending him off to fight—maybe to die—without ever knowing.

"I think I'm—" She actually started to speak the words, but then she clamped her jaw tight shut before she could finish, forcing herself not to go on. If she could finally say *I love you,* to Trystan, she now had something else she couldn't tell him. Or at least not here, today.

She opened her eyes, looked up at Trystan, and saw his

shadowed blue gaze, the small twitch of a muscle at the corner of his mouth. She remembered his ragged whisper in the depths of the nightmare the night before. And she knew she absolutely couldn't burden him any further. Or make it any harder for him to leave.

So instead she drew a shaky breath, looked up into his face, and said steadily, "I know. I know you have to go."

HE WAS PACKED IN SCARCELY ANY time at all. Sword belt. Knife. Pack with a meal and a change of clothes. That was all. Isolde had followed him to their room and sat on the edge of the bed while he made ready to leave. The bruises on her arms were covered now, but still Trystan flinched inwardly every time he looked at her. And yet he couldn't stop himself from watching her, sitting there, beautiful and delicate, like a princess in one of the tales she told.

Trystan turned away and told himself for the—Jesus, what was it now?—hundredth time that it was better this way. Better. Right. Like having a nice clean cut throat instead of bleeding to death drop by drop. But better for her, anyway.

Only when he'd hoisted the traveling pack onto one shoulder did Isolde break the silence.

"Did you know about Fidach—what he was really like, I mean—when you first went to ask him for aid?"

"You mean did I know he was more or less a decent man when he stopped being a posturing fool?" Trystan nodded. "I thought we'd better not take a chance on my judgment of him—when Piye said he'd plans to sell us to Octa. That's why I said we'd better leave. That and I didn't trust that another of the band wouldn't deal with Octa for our capture, even if Fidach refused. But I fought with Fidach for a whole season. And you can't fight with a man without coming to know his character as well as your own. Or better, sometimes. I knew I could trust Fidach to honor a bargain." He'd sworn to himself he wasn't going to touch her, but somehow he couldn't keep himself from reaching out, touching her cheek. "If I hadn't, I'd never have let you within a day's journey of him."

And then—he didn't know how it happened—she was somehow up, off the bed, and in his arms. He didn't kiss her, because that would have shattered the last remaining fragments of his self-control. Just held her tight against him, burying his face in the softness of her hair, trying to imprint this feeling on every nerve in his body. Every single separate sensation of holding her this way.

Finally, he said, "The message Eurig brought you—it was from Cerdic?"

He felt Isolde nod against his shoulder. "He says that if Madoc will send troops to join in fighting Octa, Cerdic will agree to a treaty with Britain."

"And you still don't know if there's a traitor on the king's council. If one of the council sent the men who attacked us on the boat."

Isolde shook her head. "No."

Trystan silently ticked off every possible danger on an overland journey back to Gwynedd. A series of imagined outcomes flashed across his mind, each hitting like a punch in the gut. He closed his eyes. "Isa, I know you'll want to go to Madoc yourself, but—" He stopped, trying to think of something to say that would persuade her. Telling her it would be dangerous would be about as useful as telling her she might get wet in the rain. God knew, she'd never lacked courage or flinched away from facing danger before. Finally, he gave up and said, "Please. Don't go. The abbey must have riders to carry messages. Send one of them. Just stay here."

He'd braced himself for her to argue, to ask him what right he had to make a request like that. But instead he felt her nod again, and she said, without looking up, "No. I won't try to go myself. I'll stay here."

STAY HERE, AND I'LL COME BACK *for you.* Isolde willed him to say it. She wished it so hard she could almost believe Trystan actually had spoken the words aloud. She could feel his surprise that she'd agreed so readily not to make the journey to Gwynedd herself, but he said nothing. Instead, he just held her. His arms about her were so warm and solid and strong, and she wondered how she was going to bear it when inevitably he let her go. When she had to come back to this small, plain furnished room and sleep on the hard wooden bed alone.

They stood together a long time, and then finally Trystan spoke. "Every time my heart beats," he said, "every breath I take, I'll be thinking of you."

And then he stepped back, letting his arms drop back to his sides.

Isolde didn't let herself cry. She walked with Trystan in silence back to the courtyard where the other four men were waiting, and she managed still to keep from crying as she bid them all good-bye. She kissed Eurig's cheek, which made him blush again. She took Daka's hand and smiled when Piye said something in his own tongue that his brother translated for him.

"He says thank you again for the ring," Daka told her. "He had another fit last night, but this time he not be afraid. He know your magic would keep him from coming to harm."

She watched Trystan speak a few words to Hereric in Saxon, watched Hereric sign a reply, and then clasp wrists with Trystan. And then they were turning to leave, going out through the abbey's main gate. Though Hereric turned away from the others and came back to stand beside Isolde.

Trystan say Hereric stay with you, he signed. *Keep safe. Guard.*

Isolde nodded. She looked up at Hereric and tried to smile. "Thank you, Hereric. I'm glad to have you stay with me."

The attempt at a smile must have been even more miserable than she'd thought, because Hereric's broad face furrowed in concern and he touched her arm. *Trystan come back,* he signed.

Hereric's light-blue gaze held the same utter, unshakable confidence as when he'd bidden them good-bye at Fidach's camp. As when he'd told Isolde to tell a story so that Trystan would get well. Isolde shut her eyes. Tried to remember, *Every breath I take,*

I'll be thinking of you instead of the half-finished *it's not as though we could ever have—*

She thought about Piye, holding up Garwen's crudely made curse ring and smiling at her in farewell. Maybe that was the sum total of faith. Transforming an iron ring and a handful of Latin nonsense into a charm against the powers of night. A sanctuary for old women too ugly to wed any but the Christ, as Mother Berthildis had said. Still, though, Isolde opened her eyes, looked through the abbey gates to where she could still see Trystan and the other three walking down the road towards the surrounding forest, the rising sun slanting down on their backs. And she thought, *Please, please, I don't even ask that he come back to me. Just keep him—keep them all—safe.*

Hereric's touch on her arm made her look up again. *Isolde finish story?* he signed. At first Isolde had no idea what he meant, and she looked at him blankly. *Story about girl?* Hereric frowned, seeming to grope for the right signs. *Lover stolen away?*

Isolde let out a shaky breath, scrubbed a hand across her eyes. "You mean the story I told for Trystan? About the maiden who saved her love from the Fair Folk?"

Hereric nodded. *Girl. Man. What happened?* he asked in gestures. *Isolde never told story end.*

Isolde didn't answer at once. Cabal had padded out from his bed in the abbey stables, and across the courtyard she could hear the two little girls laughing, their quarrel forgotten as they tossed an empty wooden spool for him to fetch. She turned slowly from Hereric to look out to where four men were just about to vanish amongst the trees: one bald and homely, two with skin black as coal, and one broad shouldered and tall, with a scarred left hand, gold-brown hair laced back with a leather thong.

Without looking away, Isolde raised a hand to rest her palm lightly over the girdle of her gown. "The end of the story," she said, "is that the maiden bore her love a son."

Author's Note

A S WITH *TWILIGHT OF AVALON*, *Dark Moon of Avalon* is a blend of historical truth and Arthurian myth. King Cerdic of Wessex and King Octa of Kent are both taken from the Anglo-Saxon king lists for the time. Little is known about them but their names, however, so I have freely (some might say shamelessly) invented lives and personalities for both. The British King Cynlas of Rhos is mentioned in the sixth-century historian Gildas's *De Excidio et Conquestu Britanniae* or *On the Ruin and Conquest of Britain*. Madoc of Gwynedd is loosely based on the historical sixth-century King Maelgwn Gwynedd, who was indeed a leading king of the age and whom Gildas identifies as "Dragon of the Isle." Dywel of Logres, though, is entirely fictional. Indeed, the kingdom of Logres is really confined to Arthurian legend; Geoffrey of Monmouth uses the name "Loegria" to describe the territory containing most of England before it was taken by the Saxons. Isolde's kingdom of Camelerd, too, appears in Arthurian legend but not in the historical record.

Oddly enough, the facet of *Dark Moon of Avalon* that readers may find hardest to believe—the relatively high degree of autonomy and political clout Isolde wields—is actually one of those most grounded in historical fact. The sixth century was

a time of change, during which the growing influence of the
Christian church was beginning to limit and restrict female freedom. However, dark age Celtic women, particularly among the
nobility, had far more power than their later medieval counter-
parts. Early Welsh and Irish law gave women significant rights
concerning property, divorce, protection from rape, and the
raising of children. The Celts had many powerful goddesses, as
well, and a history of warrior queens (such as Queen Boudicca)
who took to the field of battle and fought both against and
alongside the men. Female druids served as diplomatic envoys
in negotiations between rival kings.

The one true anachronism in *Dark Moon of Avalon* is the
Christian abbey in which Trystan and Isolde take refuge toward
the end of the book. That kind of monastic establishment really
belongs to an era two or three hundred years later than that of
Dark Moon. But religious houses are so much an important part
of the Arthurian world and the Arthurian tales that I allowed
one to creep into my story, as well.

When looking for a (reasonably) credible explanation for
why a Christian convent would have been established in the
midst of a dark-age Saxon king's lands, I came upon the story
of King Aethelbert of Kent, who married Bertha, the Christian daughter of Charibert, king of the Franks. Bertha was
a Christian, and her influence may have led to the decision
by Pope Gregory I to send Augustine as a missionary from
Rome in A.D. 597 an event which is seen as the beginning
of the relatively swift conversion to Christianity of the Anglo-
Saxon world. Although my story takes place a full generation
earlier, I freely (or shamelessly) grafted a bit of King Aethelbert's story onto my Cerdic's and gave Cerdic of Wessex
a Frankish wife of the Christian faith. In fact, nothing at
all is known of Cerdic's wife (or, possibly, wives), though
many historians have theorized that Cerdic himself may have
been of mixed Saxon-Celtic heritage, as I have made him in
Dark Moon.

For more on the book's historical background and a partial bibliography, please visit my website, www.annaelliotttbooks.com. I was fortunate to find many wonderful resources while writing *Dark Moon of Avalon*; any errors in the book are entirely mine.

Acknowledgments

I WOULD LIKE TO THANK THE following:
My daughter, Isabella, for continuing as a toddler to be an incredibly good sleeper and all-around great kid. Nathan, my husband and webmaster and full-time peerless helpmate. My mom and dad, warm and great and supportive as always. My lovely in-laws, for countless hours of babysitting. My superb agent, Jacques de Spoelberch, and my wonderful editor, Danielle Friedman.

And special thanks this time around to my fabulous writing partner, Sarah, who was a sounding board and an invaluable help throughout the entire writing process; who checked my historical facts and dug up countless new research resources; and who, when it came time to write the wedding scene and I was drawing an utter, complete blank on credible dark-age Celtic marriage vows, responded to my plea for suggestions within the hour with the beautiful lines that appear in the final version of this book. You are a gift.

Thank you all.

Dark Moon of Avalon

For Discussion

1. "She'd been called Witch Queen for all the seven years she'd been wedded to Con . . . [a]nd in all that time, she'd had not a flicker of true Sight, what her grandmother had once called the space inside where one might hear the voice of all living things . . ." (page 11). How would you characterize Isolde's experience of the Sight? Why was her gift of the Sight absent during her first marriage? To what extent do Isolde's visionary abilities differ from those of her grandmother, Morgan? Why might some people compare her abilities to witchcraft?

2. What does Isolde's recurring dream of Lord Marche and their wedding night suggest about the nature of their connection? How does the fact that Marche is Trystan's father complicate Isolde's feelings about her brief marriage to Marche? In what respects do Isolde's memories of that night hint at the post-traumatic stress of a victim of sexual assault?

3. "Camelerd was hers, her own domain by right of her birth, however little her place as Con's High Queen had allowed

her to attend herself to its rule" (page 24). In what respects does the political intrigue of the region shape the plot of *Dark Moon of Avalon*? How would you characterize Isolde's relationship with Madoc, Britain's High King? Why does she trust him, and he, her? How much of Isolde's decision making is based on what is best for Camelerd and its inhabitants?

4. Why is Trystan's identity as Marche's son a threat to his safety? What does Kian's willingness to conceal Trystan's true parentage suggest about his loyalty? Why does Isolde feel the need to protect Trystan from Madoc, Cynlas of Rhos, and other leaders?

5. What is the significance of the ballad that the court musician Taliesen plays to Isolde—the tale of a maid whose lover is held captive by the Fair Folk and turned into a series of savage beasts (page 113)? How does the tale relate to Isolde's own struggles to reconcile her true feelings for Trystan? What role do stories and legends play in the course of the novel?

6. "And you want me to take you—you alone, without a guard—across the Saxon war lands? Get you inside Cerdic's court so that you can propose an alliance to him?" (page 128). Why does Trystan agree to journey with Isolde through dangerous country to help her meet Cerdic? How would you describe their experience as fellow travelers? Who is more vigilant against their anonymous pursuers, and why?

7. How does Hereric's injury hinder Trystan and Isolde's progress on their travels? How would you characterize Trystan's allegiance to Hereric? What is unique about Hereric's method of communication? How does Isolde attempt to soothe Hereric in her healing efforts, and to what extent is she successful?

8. "That's the trouble with growing up with someone. They know too much about you" (page 288). What do Trystan and Isolde know about each other that other people don't know, and to what extent do you agree with Trystan that he and Isolde know "too much" about each other? How does their childhood together enable them to read each other's thoughts? What accounts for their mutual concealment of their true feelings for each other?

9. "This whole journey, she thought . . . has been running away of a kind. Running from Madoc's proposal. From the men who attacked the boat. From Fidach. Even, in a way, running from Trystan" (page 323). What explains Isolde's compulsive need to run away? What might she be running toward? What is Trystan running away from, if anything?

10. How did you feel about Isolde's revelation to Hereric in the closing scene of the novel? What does Isolde's decision not to delay Trystan's departure reveal about her strength of character? How is her decision informed by her views of fate?

A Conversation with Anna Elliott

What do you think accounts for our culture's ongoing fascination with Arthurian legend?

There are legions of answers, of course—all different, and all valid. But for me, the unique enchantment of the Arthurian legends lies in their blend of fantasy and history. The world of the King Arthur legends is a recognizably historical one, part of our own past. Many scholars have explored the possibility of a real, historic Arthur—who, if he existed, was most likely a Celtic warlord of the mid-sixth century, a warrior who led a triumphant stand against the incursions of Saxons onto British shores. Trystan, whose existence as a real historic figure is suggested by a memorial stone in Cornwall, was likely a roughly contemporary warrior, possibly the son of a Cornish petty king, whose cycle of tales were eventually absorbed into the legends growing up around Arthur and his war band.

And yet the world of the Arthur tales is one steeped in magic as well. It's a world filled with the voices of prophecy, with enchanted swords and otherworldly maidens and the magical Isle of Avalon, where Arthur lies in eternal sleep, healing of his wounds, waiting to ride once more in Britain's greatest hour of need.

That combination of historical truth with the wonderful potential for magic was what most of all drew me to the Arthur stories when I first studied them in college. And it was what delighted me about living in my own version of the Arthurian world while writing the *Twilight of Avalon* trilogy.

In writing your fictional version of the famous legend of Trystan and Isolde, what new elements did you want to incorporate in the retelling?

I intended the *Twilight of Avalon* trilogy to be a blend of legend and historical truth. The fifth century, when scholars agree a historic Arthur might have lived, was a brutal, chaotic time in Britain. Roman Britain had crumbled; Rome's legions had been withdrawn from this far-flung outpost of the empire, leaving the country prey to invading Pictish and Irish tribes from the west and north and to Saxon invasions from the east. It was in many ways also a crucible in which the British identity and sense of place was forged. And it is against this backdrop that Arthur appears, a war hero who led—or at least may have led—a victorious campaign against the invaders, driving them back for perhaps the space of a man's lifetime and so inspiring the roots of a legend that still captures our imaginations today.

I was fascinated by this possibility of a real King Arthur,

and fascinated by the world in which he might have lived. So I decided to set my story there, to make my particular Arthurian world grounded in what scraps of historical fact we know of Dark Age Britain. And yet I wanted, too, to honor the original stories and their magical, legendary world—a world that after centuries of telling and retelling, is as real in its own way as historical fact.

It was a bit of a balancing act, I discovered. My Isolde is the granddaughter of Morgan (sometimes known as Morgan le Fey in the original Arthur stories; a healer and enchantress of great renown). Isolde is gifted through Morgan with both the knowledge of a healer and with the Sight, which enables her to receive visions and hear voices from the Otherworld. All of which fitted in with what I'd read of both the legends and historic accounts of Celtic spirituality, pre-Christian Celtic belief, with its emphasis on the powers of herbs, on trances and dreams that transcend physical boundaries and touch an Otherworld that is separated from our own by only the thinnest of veils.

And yet, too, there were those elements of the original Trystan and Isolde tale that were harder to fit in with any degree of historical verisimilitude. Like the famous love potion, which in the original legend causes Trystan and Isolde to fall helplessly in love. So in those cases I took a more symbolic approach, which I've always felt is a way—though certainly not the only way—of reading the fantastical elements of the Arthurian tales. Dragons, for example, can be literal scaly monsters. But they can also be seen as a metaphor for the evil that exists outside the bounds of organized society. And a love potion like the one Trystan and Isolde accidentally imbibe can be viewed as a metaphor for the overwhelming, all-consuming nature of passionate romantic love.

So in *Dark Moon of Avalon*, Trystan and Isolde do journey together by boat, as in the original tale, and it is over the course of the journey that they deepen and develop their relationship, which again is true to the original legend. But the purpose of their journey is based on what scraps of historical fact we can gather about the shaky political situation of sixth-century Britain. And they don't need a literal draft of a magical potion to fall in love—only the magic of their own powerful emotional bond.

I did take a fair number of liberties with the legend—liberties that are, I hope, justified. After all, after so many centuries of retellings, adding yet another version of the story seemed silly unless I could add something new to the age-old tale.

Can you describe the challenges you experienced in narrating the book from the perspectives of *both* Trystan and Isolde?

I actually loved—and found it very easy—to write from both Trystan and Isolde's perspectives and have them share the narration of this story. I think, especially when there's romance involved, that it adds so much to be able to see what both protagonists are thinking, for the reader to see exactly what's in each character's mind, to know how they see each other, what they reveal to each other and what they're each holding back. I did try to always make Trystan and Isolde's narrative voices very distinct from each other—but that wasn't really a challenge. Each of them talked to me from the first in a very individual way, which I hope comes across on the page.

What kind of medical research did you do to establish Isolde's role as a healer?

Very little concrete information about Dark Age medicine has survived, but I used a variety of period herbals (books of herbal cures) as resources to find remedies that Isolde might credibly have used. And then another of my favorite resources was a wonderful book called *Medicinal Plants in Folk Tradition: An Ethnobotany of Britain and Ireland* by David E. Allen and Gabrielle Hatfield, which catalogs the various medicinal uses of most plants native to Britain and Ireland in traditional herbal healing and details the geographic areas where each folk remedy was most commonly found.

I also read a lot of firsthand accounts from army doctors and combat nurses—from men and women who served in WWII through Vietnam and the war in Iraq—to get a sense of what their experience was like, what the challenges and hardest moments were that they faced. Obviously the technology and medicines available to treat battle wounds have changed immeasurably since Isolde's time. But I think the emotions of caring for wounded men are still very much the same.

You chose to portray the villainous Marche through flashbacks and allusions rather than actual scenes in the novel. Why?
One of the major themes that emerged in the writing of this book was the internal journey that Isolde makes to heal from the trauma in her past (which of course in some ways mirrors the literal journey she makes from Gwynedd to Wessex with Trystan). Marche is in many ways both part of and representative of the past trauma she needs to heal from in order to move on towards her future. So in this book Marche was more important as a part of Isolde's internal journey—as a presence filtered through her own mind, in a way—than he was as an active character in the political or military aspects of the plot.

The dog, Cabal, is as compelling as the human characters in your novel. Did you base the relationship between Isolde and Cabal on any connection you've experienced with an animal in real life?
We did always have cats and dogs when I was growing up—and since my only brother was thirteen years older than I am, the pets were quite often my playmates. Though Cabal is really more of a composite of dogs I've known and what I knew from research about dogs trained for fighting and military use. My dogs were some bouncy, ridiculously friendly golden retrievers and a miniature poodle—pretty much as far from war hounds as you can get!

Why is Isolde so openly antagonistic toward Christianity? To what extent would her position be considered dangerous or provocative in her milieu?

Hmmm . . . That's kind of an interesting reading, since I didn't at all intend for Isolde to be seen as antagonistic to Christianity per se. The sixth century in Britain was a time of change, in which the old pagan religion was rapidly being replaced by Christianity. Isolde has been raised by her grandmother Morgan, who did follow the old pagan ways—and who certainly felt a great deal of antagonism for the new Christian faith. Isolde herself sees the differences between the old religion and the new—sees, in particular, the difference in women's positions and power within the two faiths. But I don't think I'd say that she feels the same hostility as Morgan for the Christian God. She's simply seen so much tragedy and lost so much in her life that she's suspicious of *any* faith, Christian or otherwise, that promises all the answers to life's hardest questions. But she is searching for answers, since she believes that some higher power must govern her own gift of the Sight, as unpredictable and unreliable as it sometimes seems. And she respects those Christians that she meets—like Mother Berthildis—and even wishes a bit that she could have that kind of perfect faith at times.

Why does the figure of Morgan, Isolde's grandmother, loom so large for so many characters in the novel?

I could say that thematically Morgan represents the legendary Arthurian world that forms the backdrop for the world of the *Twilight of Avalon* trilogy—and that would be true in many ways. But, honestly, the real reason that Morgan is such a force in the books is that from the moment I heard her voice narrating the prologues that frame the action of all three books in the series, she's simply been one of the most vivid characters in my mind— and one of my favorites as well. She's a very strong woman—very determined to make sure her influence is felt.

You end the novel with a bombshell of sorts—why does Isolde

decide to keep Trystan in the dark about their changing future as husband and wife?

That was very tough to write! I've been pregnant twice now, so I do know exactly how much Isolde would want to tell Trystan and how heartbreakingly hard it would be for her to keep herself from giving him the news, especially when he's going into danger and she's not certain she'll see him again. She's very strong, though—probably far stronger than I would be—and she doesn't want him burdened with worry for her and a baby while on a dangerous mission. And even more than that, she knows Trystan is still carrying the scars from his past and from his relationship with his own father. He's not in a place yet to hear the news that he's going to be a father himself. Isolde feels passionately that both Trystan and their baby deserve the pregnancy to be happy news—and she's willing to wait to tell Trystan until that can be true. Of course, this is one of the key elements of the emotional journey they make individually and together in Book 3, *Sunrise of Avalon*.

What did you discover in the course of writing *Dark Moon of Avalon* that surprised you?

One of my favorite parts of writing *Dark Moon of Avalon* was the character of Fidach, because he was such a complete surprise. I'd penciled him in as more or less of a straight villain when I was outlining the book. But then I got to the point when Isolde was trapped in a burning building in Octa's army camp and I needed a way for her to get free. I was pondering ideas when Fidach suddenly raised his hand and informed me that a) he was homosexual, which I'd not even considered before, and b) he was in fact a man of a rather high degree of honor who was going to risk his own life to save Isolde's. Who am I to argue? I absolutely loved writing him after he'd taken charge like that.

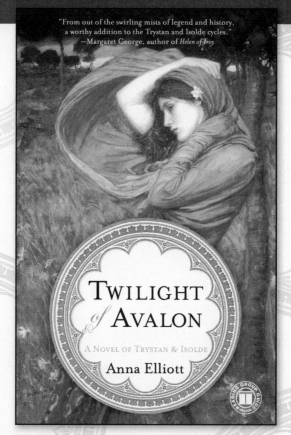